MW01133393

OPERATION
GHOST
FLIGHT

Stephen Yoham

Copyright © 2017 Stephen Yoham
All rights reserved
Second Edition

PAGE PUBLISHING, INC.
New York, NY

First originally published by Page Publishing, Inc. 2017

ISBN 978-1-68409-713-5 (Paperback)
ISBN 978-1-68409-714-2 (Digital)

Printed in the United States of America

To my lovely wife Judy, who has worked at least as hard as I have to bring this novel together. Also, to my parents and siblings, for all that they have instilled in me over the years.

PROLOGUE

The wiper blades scraped at the accumulating sleet as Connecticut State Trooper Pete Mitchell surveyed the wreck through his windshield. A barely recognizable late-model Lexus had struck the center support of an overpass. The impact split the vehicle completely in two. The front end melded with the concrete, while the remainder, twisted and shredded, rested in the southbound lanes 150 yards away.

No one could have survived this crash, Mitchell thought grimly. He glanced around. Fortunately at that hour, and in those conditions, no other cars were on the road.

The trooper stepped out of his vehicle, and his stomach lurched. Remains of the sole occupant, a white male, were scattered on the highway and in both sections of the mangled vehicle. It was about as bad an accident as he had ever seen.

After securing the area, he climbed back into his patrol car and ran the Washington DC license plate. The information that was transmitted back warranted an urgent call to his superior, Lieutenant Bruce Donaldson.

"Sir, I'm sorry to disturb you at this hour, but I have a situation that demands your immediate attention."

"What time is it?" Donaldson asked sleepily.

"Three a.m., sir. I'm at the scene of a fatal accident on Interstate 95, just north of Bridgeport. And according to the DMV, the vehicle is registered to Senator Sean Buchanan."

There was a long pause before Donaldson asked, "How many occupants and how many fatalities?"

"One, sir. Owing to the condition of the body, positive identification will have to be determined at the morgue, but the personal effects I found in the wreckage are Senator Buchanan's. Looks like a DWI. An empty bottle of Scotch is wedged against the floorboard."

"In your opinion, Pete, is the senator the victim?"

"Yes, Lieutenant, I believe he is."

"OK, I'm on my way. Listen, Pete, guard the victim's identity. If it is Senator Buchanan, I'll take the bad news to Washington DC personally, and I don't want anyone to know until after I've made that trip. The last thing we need is a media circus up here broadcasting this tragedy all over national television before I can tell the vice president that he's lost his son. For now, it's just between you and me, Pete. Understand?"

"Yes, sir."

CHAPTER

1

H. Hunter Mahoy slapped a blank tape into his microcassette recorder, leaned back in his cushy black leather executive chair, then found a space on his desk for his size 11 shoes. Through the large window, tantalizing shafts of brilliant sunlight streamed in from the cloudless blue Miami sky. The palm trees in the parking lot swayed ever so gently. *It's the tenth of October, and the weather's absolutely perfect for flying,* he thought. *And here I am stuck in this damn office again.* He longed to be up in that wild blue in his high-performance sailplane, soaring like a bird. Up there he'd be free of all commitments, of all demands on his time—for a while, at least.

He pulled his focus back inside. Eyeing the paperwork on his desk, he sneered. *Man, would I love to blow off this crap!* He hated his job. Hell, he hated his profession: tax consulting. What a joke! All he did was help wealthy clients and corporations wriggle out of their tax obligations. He'd had it up to his eyeballs with the levels of corruption that passed for business. And the hand-holding between business and politics was making him sick. His stomach churned at the thought of it. What a life! He should've stayed in the air force—at least he'd be flying. Hell, he was only thirty-seven—years of flight time left. Maybe he should consider reenlisting.

He glanced out the window one last time then swiveled his chair to face the door. He couldn't afford any more distractions. He had way too much to do this week before he could even consider starting his vacation.

He sighed heavily then pressed the record button. "Therefore, I recommend that the Gomez Brothers Corporation take most of the funds from their operating accounts and place them in jumbo CDs. The corporation could then borrow against those CDs, loan the money back to itself, and place all the funds into an interest-bearing sweep account. I further recommend—"

"Excuse me, Hunter. I'm sorry to interrupt."

"Not at all, Amanda. What's up?"

Thirty-four and drop-dead gorgeous, Amanda Taylor had it all. The sight of her long silky blonde hair, cornflower-blue eyes, gorgeous curves, and shapely legs always stopped him midstream. Her appearance today had the usual effect.

"Enrique Gomez's secretary just called. The brothers are on their way. They'll be arriving early."

"Lucky me! Why do Mondays always start this way?"

"I knew you'd be thrilled."

"It's just as well. I can—oh, damn this thing!" He shook the microcassette and mashed the stop button several times.

She laughed. "It's stuck in record again, isn't it? One of these days you'll have to break down and actually buy a new one."

"Me? Spend some money?"

She crossed her arms and glared at him. "H. Hunter Mahoy, you're not cheap, and you and I both know it. Your house, your fancy sailplane, your expensive suits all attest to that. Your thoroughly average car puzzles me though."

"Hey, my Accord LX is a nice car." He smiled inwardly at the thought of the cherry-red Ferrari 328 sitting in his garage. He'd bought it as an investment, but rarely drove it because he wanted to keep the mileage low. No one at work knew about the pricey sports car, even though he'd owned it for almost two years now.

"Yes, your Honda's nice, Hunter, but you should have a Mercedes or a Lexus or a BMW like mine."

"And the only way you can afford that Beemer is because I pay you too much."

Smiling slyly, she countered, "You do, but I'm worth it."

She certainly was. His job would be unbearable without her. He studied her figure as she strolled out the door. "Amanda?"

She poked her head back into the office, one hand on the doorjamb. "Yes?"

"I love it when you address me by my full name."

"I'll do it more often if you tell me what the *H* stands for."

"It stands for *Hopeful*. When are you going to dump that lawyer boyfriend of yours? I'm not getting any younger, you know."

She smiled. Perfect white teeth. "I really do wish I'd met you first, Hunter," she said, then disappeared down the hallway.

"So do I," he mumbled. "So do I."

With a sigh, he got back to his dictation. He'd been at it for another twenty minutes and had just flipped the tape over when Amanda buzzed him on the intercom.

"The Gomez brothers are here."

"Thanks. Send them in."

He hurriedly dictated one last thought, pressed the stop button, then tossed the player into the top drawer of his desk as he stood to greet his clients. "Hello, Enrique. It's good to see you again." They shook hands. "Pedro, you're looking fit. Ah, Juan Carlos, haven't seen you for a while."

He hated the brownnosing bullshit. It was demoralizing. He wished he never had to speak to these ungrateful bastards again. They were, by far, his most repulsive clients.

"Please gentlemen, have a seat. Unfortunately the conference room is occupied, so we'll have to tough it out here."

"*Buenos dias*, Hunter. We passed by to see what you could do for us," Enrique said in a thick Cuban accent. "We do not want the government to take all our money."

"Of course not, Enrique. That's why you hired this firm."

Hunter surreptitiously studied the three men. In his midforties, with a stocky build, black hair, and brown eyes, Enrique was the best dressed of the trio. The cuffs on his crisp white Egyptian cotton shirt fell perfectly below the sleeves of his expensive dark-blue double-breasted suit. The diamond-studded cufflinks matched his tie clasp. A Rolex, no doubt platinum, graced his left wrist.

Pedro was so similar in age, physique, and appearance to Enrique that they could almost pass as twins. He was dressed equally professionally but without all the expensive accouterments. Even so, his navy-blue pinstriped suit, burgundy silk shirt, and solid burgundy tie had clearly set him back a bundle.

Juan Carlos was a cousin; he bore little family resemblance. In his late twenties, he was cocky and arrogant. He didn't usually say much, but when he did speak, he was often vulgar and unrefined. His long black hair begged for a comb. His close-set, beady brown eyes seemed lifeless half the time, menacing the other half, like those of a shark constantly on the prowl, waiting to attack. His pockmarked complexion evidenced a past case of bad acne, and a five o'clock shadow always plagued his face. Unlike his cousins, he was casually dressed in gray slacks and a light-blue polo. The bulky diver's watch clinging to his left wrist seemed out of place, as if it didn't really belong to him. *Had something recently happened to a diver somewhere?* Hunter wondered. *Had the shark attacked?*

Hunter didn't like or trust any of the Gomezes. At best, they had a reputation for shady business dealings. Though he had no proof, he was sure that the sale of cocaine helped to finance some of their many investments. *No telling what else these guys are into: money laundering, racketeering, prostitution. The list is probably endless.* If Hunter had any choice, he wouldn't be talking to them now. But seeing dollar signs, his bosses had refused to pass on having the Gomez Brothers Corporation as a client.

"Gentlemen, I have good news. I've devised a plan that will save you a great deal of money. You'll still have to pay some tax, of course, but the number will be much more palatable."

"No, no! We do not want to pay any tax," Pedro said. "The stinking *Tío* Sam has not worked for it."

Hunter faced the window and clenched his teeth. The ungrateful son of a bitch! He'd come into this free country, started a business, operated on the fringes of, or outside of, the law, and made a fortune. Now the man didn't want to pay any taxes.

"Well, if you don't like the laws of the United States, Pedro, you can always move back to Havana." He planted a smile on his face then turned around to see the reaction.

Juan Carlos, already on his feet, rushed at Hunter. He stopped just inches away. His ugly face filled Hunter's vision. "*Carajo!* We would be there right now except for that damned senator who was to make a law that would let our business go into Cuba. After we spent millions, that bastard Buchanan cheated us by making a law against it."

Enrique popped to his feet. "Damn it, Juan! *Basta!* Shut up and sit down!"

Juan Carlos spun on his heels and faced him. Enrique's menacing glare sent chills up Hunter's spine. Pedro stood and stepped between the two. "*Silencio!* Sit down, Juan."

Hunter cleared his throat. "Gentlemen, please. I was trying to make a point. The United States has strict tax laws. The penalty for not obeying those laws can be quite severe. My job as your tax consultant is to do everything I can to save you as much money as possible without breaking those laws. Would you like to hear what I have to say?"

A smile returned to Enrique's face the instant his focus shifted away from Juan Carlos. "Yes, we would. And please excuse Juan. Sometimes his temper gets away from him."

The three men took their seats, and Hunter nodded. "I understand." But his curiosity got the better of him. "Buchanan…would that have been Senator Sean Buchanan who died in a car accident a few years ago? Up north somewhere—Connecticut, I believe."

"The squeaky *puerco* got what he deserved," Juan Carlos snarled.

Enrique's face instantly darkened, and in Spanish he ordered his cousin, "I told you to shut up!"

Secretly fluent in Spanish, Hunter smiled inwardly. In Miami, he carried his knowledge of Spanish like a concealed weapon: he never used it without good reason. And if he did, he made sure to hit the target.

Juan Carlos jumped to his feet. He shouted at Enrique in Spanish, "Do not tell me when to talk! I know what I am doing!"

Enrique also stood and shouted back in Spanish, "The only thing bigger than your opinion of yourself is your mouth! No one needs to be reminded about that senator!"

The two men squared off, arguing loudly in Spanish, until Enrique slapped Juan—a loud, hard slap, a slap that he would feel for hours.

The stunned silence was interrupted when the door swung open. "I'm sorry for the interruption, gentlemen," Amanda said. "I knocked, but it went unnoticed."

Hunter eyed her. "What is it?"

"I need you out here right away, Mr. Mahoy. It's important."

He marveled at her professionalism. She never slipped up by addressing him as Hunter when clients were present. He turned to the Gomezes. "If you gentlemen will excuse me, I'm sure I'll only be a minute."

He followed Amanda out, closing the door behind him. "What do you need?"

She smiled. "Nothing. I just thought you'd like to get out of there for a while."

The argument in his office started up again. He chuckled. "Have I given you a raise lately?"

"Yes. Last month."

"Well, you've just earned another."

She gestured at the door. "What's going on in there, Hunter? You have them screaming at each other."

He grinned wickedly. "Maybe they'll kill each other so I won't have to deal with them anymore. I'll tell you about it later."

She brushed a piece of lint from his shoulder. "Are you really going to give me a raise, Hunter?"

"Absolutely."

"How much?"

"That depends on you." He studied her face. Supermodels didn't have anything on her. "Will you be my date for Matthew Perlis's retirement party Friday night?"

She frowned. "I can't. I'm going with Simon."

"That's too bad. If you'd ditched the boyfriend, you could've been a rich woman!" He sighed. "Now the *H* stands for *Heartbroken*." He patted his chest for emphasis.

"Hunter!"

"Yep. Heartbroken Hunter," he said then smiled ruefully. "I guess I'd better get back in there. It sounds like it's quieted down. Thanks for the break, Amanda."

He reentered his office to find all three men sitting quietly. "Sorry, gentlemen, couldn't be helped." He moved around behind his desk. "I'll get right to it."

As he settled into his chair, he spied the cassette player, its wheels still turning, in the partially open top drawer. He left the device alone. He sure didn't need the Gomezes knowing that he'd recorded their entire conversation, even if it had been by accident. He sat down and shifted some paperwork then laced his fingers on the desktop and explained the tax plan he had in mind.

When he had finished, they all left smiling.

Amanda waited a few moments after the Gomezes had departed, then knocked and entered Hunter's office. He smiled that devastatingly sexy smile of his, and her heart fluttered.

"Are they gone?" he asked.

"Yes, thankfully. Those guys give me the creeps, especially Juan Carlos. He makes my skin crawl. I can't stand the way that scumbag looks at me."

Hunter approached, his baby blues consuming her. "Juan Carlos is the whistle-and-catcall type, that's for sure. And I'm not defending him in the least, Amanda, but you're a gorgeous woman. Men are going to look at you. I'm guilty of that myself."

"I realize that, Hunter, but it's how it's done. Juan Carlos looks at me the way a hungry animal looks at a piece of meat, salivating and licking its lips, ready to pounce at any second. It unnerves me, and at the same time makes me feel trashy and cheap."

"Cheap? I didn't think you knew the meaning of that word, Amanda."

He flashed that devastating smile again. She couldn't help staring at him. *Man, he was attractive.* She especially loved the character lines on his deeply tanned face, which betrayed his passion for the outdoors, a passion that she secretly wanted to share with him. Calm and cool under pressure, he'd never once lost his temper with her. He'd never even raised his voice to her. She couldn't imagine working for anyone else.

Though she'd often asked, he refused to say why he'd become a tax consultant instead of remaining an air force pilot. At first she speculated that he'd left because of money, but she came to realize that money didn't seem terribly important to him. Lord knows he paid her plenty. Maybe he didn't like taking orders. Whatever the reason, it wasn't because of the flying. He loved to fly. She envisioned him standing next to a fighter jet: lean and muscular, one hand lovingly touching the aircraft, the other clutching a helmet, his longish brown hair rustling in the breeze, while a pair of mirrored sunglasses selfishly hid a portion of his ruggedly handsome face. His alluring smile beckoned to her. *Maybe I should break it off with Simon—for good this time.*

She sighed. "When you look at me that way, Hunter, I feel—well, desirable, attractive, and appreciated."

"What're you talking about, Amanda? You've never caught me looking at you *that way.*"

His words surprised her, and she laughed shortly. "You're discreet, Hunter, but you're not that discreet."

He shifted his weight. His eyes left then came back to her. "Are you implying that I—"

"I'm not implying anything," she said, grinning. "I'm saying flat out that you've undressed me with your eyes at least a thousand times. You know it, and I know it."

He actually blushed. "Amanda, I—I can't believe you said that."

She crossed her arms, challenging him with her stare. "Can you look me in the eye and tell me I'm mistaken?"

He inched closer. Their noses almost touched. She stood perfectly still, waiting, hoping, yet fearing his next move. If he crossed the paper-thin barrier between them, their relationship would never be the same again. *So be it,* she told herself. He brushed back a strand of her hair. As her eyes searched his, he breathed deeply, as though reveling in her scent.

"You're incredibly intoxicating, Amanda, but you're mistaken. It couldn't possibly have been more than seven or eight-hundred times."

She burst out laughing then cupped her hand over her mouth as if to contain what had already escaped. "At least you admit it," she said through her laughter. "H. Hunter Mahoy, you've just restored my faith in men. I fully expected you to lie."

"*Really?*" he asked softly. "I thought you already knew the *H* stands for *Honest.*"

He ran his fingers through her hair. Time stopped. She suddenly thought of Simon. "I—I'd better get back to work now," she whispered.

"Yeah, me too."

As he prepared to back away, she kissed him, short and sweet. "That's for telling the truth, Hunter, and don't stop looking at me. I like the way you do it."

*   *   *

"Good morning, Mr. President." Lamar Hager, the chairman of the Joint Chiefs of Staff, stood in the Oval Office, hat in hand, his dress blues impeccably pressed and creased.

"Good morning, General."

President Nelson Weber studied the officer. A lean six-two, handsome with chiseled features and jet-black hair despite his sixty-four years, Hager looked every inch the ladies' man of his reputation. Never married, he lived up to his nickname around town: Geritol's Most Eligible Bachelor.

Despite numerous previous visits, the general took in the Oval Office. The president was aware of how the room always seemed to impress visitors, no matter how many times they might have been there. Hell, it still impressed Weber, and he spent hours there every day. Whether it was the actual physical beauty, or its palpable sense of history, there was no doubting that it was a special place, all right.

Weber especially liked the fourteen-foot-high walls that embraced the ceiling at its continuously curving dental-crown molding. The navy-blue-and-gold circular carpet, embossed with the presidential seal of the United States, was another favorite of his. Most visitors, however, probably due to where they enter the room, seem to focus on the mahogany desk and the three tall windows at the far end of the oval.

"Thanks for coming over on such short notice, Lamar."

"Don't mention it, sir. You had something you wanted to discuss with me?"

"Yes. Have a seat." Weber gestured toward a chair.

Ever the professional soldier, Hager sat erect and attentive.

"Lamar, I wanted you to be the first to know that I plan to close a number of military bases across the country and scale back operations at many others."

"Again, Mr. President? This is distressing news, a horrible way to start the week. How many this time?"

"Forty-two closings and curtailed operations in at least fifty-five others."

"Forty-two! I don't understand, Mr. President. Why are you doing this? You've cut the military to the bone already."

"For one and only one reason: the budget. It must be brought under control. We can't just keep printing and spending money with no accountability. If we do, there'll be hell to pay."

Rising, Hager countered, "There'll be hell to pay if we close all those bases, sir. We need those bases and their experienced personnel. The United States must maintain a strong and capable military, one that can respond to any situation anywhere in the world on short notice. Look at the Middle East. Or Asia. And what about terrorist attacks within our own borders? We can't afford to cut the military!" He landed a soft fist on the desk. "We just can't."

Nelson Weber rubbed his temples. The general was right. It was a horrible way to start the week. "The fact is, we can't afford not to, Lamar. If we don't get the budget under control, we could lose the entire military, not just the bases that have to be closed. If this country were a private enterprise, it would have been out of business a long time ago. We're several trillion dollars in debt—most of it owed to the Chinese and Japanese—we spend money like water, waste is running rampant, and nobody seems to care."

"Get it from some other place," Hager demanded, his voice elevating, his eyes locked with the president's. "Don't take it from the military!"

It was the president's turn to slam his fist on the desktop. "Damn it, Lamar, I'm taking it from everywhere I can! The military is only one portion."

Nothing broke the silence as they glared at each other. Finally Hager gripped the president's desk and leaned forward. Weber tried not to stare at the obvious missing forefinger of the left hand; an artillery-loading accident many years ago had laid claim to that digit.

"Mr. President, I simply cannot believe that the mightiest military in the world is going to be brought to its knees by *budget*. You served in the air force, Mr. President. You flew in Korea. You of all people should understand how important machinery and manpower are to the military. I beg you to find another way. Please don't cut the military again."

President Weber rose and stepped over to the center window. The general's impassioned plea came from the heart. The military had been Lamar Hagar's home and life since he had doctored his birth certificate at fifteen and enlisted. He rose through the ranks the hard way and saw action in every major theater of battle the United States had been involved in since the Korean War. As a general, he became a logistics and tactics expert. Now he was the highest-ranking serviceman in the military—aside from his commander-in-chief, the president himself.

Weber stared through the glass. The morning sun was setting the autumn leaves aglow, the wind demanding they take flight. A squirrel foraged at the base of an oak. Winter was coming. The trees would soon be bare and the sky a dismal gray. He could feel it already. He sighed and turned back to his guest.

"Lamar, if there was any other way, I'd gladly take it. I don't want to cut the military; I simply have no choice. The best I can do at this juncture is give you the option of choosing which bases to close.

You'll need to compile a list, starting with the least damaging. That way we'll know which ones to keep if we're fortunate enough to not have to close all of them."

"Does that possibility actually exist, Mr. President?"

Weber nodded. "It does. But I make you no promises."

*   *   *

Hunter settled into his office chair and closed his eyes, his encounter with Amanda still dominating his thoughts. He envisioned her face and tasted her kiss again. *What a remarkable creature. Am I in love with her?* he wondered. Perhaps he was.

He opened his eyes and rolled his wrist. "Damn! Twelve-thirty already," he said aloud. "Hey, Amanda!"

Her footfalls sounded in the hallway; then she leaned into the open doorway. "Yes?"

"What time is our flight to Houston tonight?"

"Seven-ten, but we'd better be heading for the airport by five o'clock. You know what the afternoon traffic's like."

Hunter frowned. "Guess I'll have to skip lunch again."

He started sorting paperwork, assembling what he needed to take with him when he spotted the cassette player in the drawer. Curious to know what the Gomez brothers had said while he was out of the office, he rewound the tape then pushed the play button.

He only half paid attention to what was being said until Juan Carlos's voice declared, "The squeaky *puerco* got what he deserved!" Hunter focused on the hatred in the man's tone. He hadn't picked up on that before. He played it again. *"The squeaky puerco got what he deserved!"*

Why would Juan Carlos hate the senator so much that he'd be glad the man was dead? Hunter replayed the statement one more time before allowing the recording to continue. It soon reached the part where Amanda had interrupted. Now came what he was curious to hear. They spoke in rapid-fire Spanish.

"Damn it, Juan, you stupid asshole! If you say one more word about Buchanan in front of Mahoy, I will beat you until you cannot talk! Do you understand?"

"What is the big deal, Enrique? Everyone knew we worked with Buchanan and planned to go into Cuba. The secret is, we really did go into business there. And we did it with the help of the dead senator's father."

"Sometimes you act so young and stupid, Juan. I swear I cannot believe it! We do not want to get people interested in our business. Did you see how Mahoy remembered Buchanan was killed in a car wreck?"

"So what, Enrique? Everybody thinks it was an accident."

Hunter's ears pricked up.

"Come on, Juan, use your head! Believe what I am telling you. We do not need an investigation into that crash. There were hundreds of people at the Kennedy Center in Washington that night; someone might remember that you accompanied the senator's pretty female aide when she went back for the senator's briefcase. Someone might figure out that you put that bottle of Scotch in Buchanan's car."

Hunter raised his eyebrows and turned up the volume.

"So I put it in his car, Enrique. That proves nothing."

"No, but what Bass gave us to put with it would. And even though we did not make Buchanan drink from the bottle, we knew he would. And we knew he liked to drive fast."

Juan Carlos chuckled. "We sure did."

"Do us all a favor, Juan—shut up about it. It is history. Never mention it again. We need Mahoy thinking about our tax problems, not about that accident."

"You worry too much, Enrique. Mahoy is a do-boy. As long as we pay his bosses, he will do what they tell him. He is just another stupid *gringo*. I will say one thing, though. He has one real nice-looking pussy in his office. If she was my secretary, I would fuck her right here on this desk every day. Maybe he is licking her right now while we wait on him. I bet she tastes good! She's got nice tits too, don't you think?"

Hunter's own hackles rose as Enrique, his voice filled with disgust, snapped, "Shut your foul mouth, Juan! I am sick and tired of hearing your voice. Just shut up!"

"Do not talk anymore, Juan," Pedro chimed in anxiously. "Be quiet."

Hearing his own voice on the tape again, Hunter pushed the stop button. "Those filthy, murderous bastards!" he muttered. He sat motionless for a few seconds before energetically pushing back his chair and springing to his feet. He tossed the recorder into his briefcase, grabbed his coat, and left his office.

"Where are you going, Hunter?" Amanda called after him. "You have another client coming in about an hour."

"Cancel it for me, Amanda," he said over his shoulder. "I have an errand to run that can't wait. I'll meet you back here in time to go to the airport."

CHAPTER

2

Forty minutes later, Hunter strode into the FBI office in the federal building in downtown Miami and asked to see the bureau chief.

"Do you have an appointment?" the young receptionist asked, studying him with hazel eyes that were reminiscent of a cat's.

"No, I don't, but it's extremely important that I see him. Is he available?"

"I'll check for you, sir." She picked up the phone, the forefinger of her other hand poised to press a button. "Your name?"

"Hunter Mahoy."

He listened in on the receptionist's half of the conversation while taking in the lobby—high ceiling, brown-tiled floor, commercial art on the walls, a couple of silk plants. Nothing extraordinary.

"Uh-huh. Yes, sir. No, I understand. Yes, sir. I'll tell him." She faced Hunter again, adopting a business smile and showing off her pretty teeth. "I'm sorry, Mr. Mahoy. Chief Espinosa has a very busy calendar. You'll need to make an appointment."

Hunter stepped closer to the desk. "Look, Ms. Suarez," he said, reading her name plate, "I'm leaving town in a few hours, and it's important I see him now. Please call him back." He leaned forward and lowered his voice. "Tell him it's in reference to the death of a US senator."

She raised her eyebrows, nodded, and immediately called her boss a second time. She faced Hunter again as she hung up. "Chief Espinosa will see you after all, Mr. Mahoy." She gave him directions to Espinosa's office before returning her attention to the busy switchboard.

Hunter hurried to the bank of elevators, pressed the button for the eleventh floor, then watched the number lights impatiently as the cab sped upward. He exited the elevator into a spacious lobby and was directed down the hallway by yet another receptionist.

As he entered José Espinosa's office, a secretary with teased black hair and heavily made-up brown eyes looked up from her paperwork. "Mr. Mahoy?"

"Yes, ma' am."

"Chief Espinosa's waiting for you. You can go right in." She pointed toward an open door.

Hunter walked in, briefcase in hand. The middle-aged man behind the desk rose and removed his wire-rimmed glasses, revealing deep-set dark-brown eyes.

"Ah, Mr. Mahoy, I presume."

He stuck out his hand. His colorful Bugs Bunny tie made an interesting contrast to his formal white button-down shirt and navy-blue trousers. He had a firm handshake, which Hunter appreciated.

"Thanks for seeing me, Mr. Espinosa. That's a great tie, by the way."

The chief glanced down at it and grinned. "A birthday present from my eldest daughter. I admit it screams for comment." He gestured toward the chair in front of his desk.

"Have a seat."

Hunter sat down and nodded toward the window. "Killer view of Government Cut. Lots of cruise ships in port today."

"Yes. And it's all much too distracting. That's why my desk faces away from it. Sometimes I have to keep the blinds closed so I can concentrate."

Hunter grinned. "I can relate to that. Had the same problem this morning myself." The grin faded, and Hunter got serious. "I appreciate you seeing me without an appointment. I've just come across some disturbing information that you should know about."

"I'm most curious to hear what you have to say."

Hunter opened his briefcase and removed the tape recorder. "I assume you've heard of the Gomez Brothers Corporation, Mr. Espinosa."

"Of course. Who in Miami hasn't?"

"Good point. Anyway, I have a recording of the three owners discussing the death of Senator Sean Buchanan in that auto accident up in Connecticut a couple of years ago."

Espinosa nodded. "I remember that incident quite well, Mr. Mahoy. It was three years ago. I was in Washington that night at the very function the senator attended just before he died. I even spoke with him that evening. The Gomezes were there too. I remember Enrique and Pedro talking at great length with the senator's father, Vice President Albert Buchanan. The senator's death was tragic news." He shook his head then started cleaning his glasses with a handkerchief. "When I heard about his death the next morning, it really rattled me, Mr. Mahoy. Buchanan was a young man with truly great potential. I can still see his handsome, smiling face. What a senseless accident."

"It wasn't an accident, Mr. Espinosa. Senator Buchanan was murdered."

The chief's eyebrows shot up.

Hunter started the recorder and set it on the desk. As it played, the chief leaned forward, concentrating on the dialogue. At the end of the pertinent information, Hunter stopped the device then placed it back in his briefcase.

After several moments of silence, Espinosa cleared his throat. "That's an interesting recording. When did you get it?"

"Today, sir. During a meeting with the Gomez brothers in my office."

"Do you understand what they said in Spanish? If not, who translated it for you? Who else knows about it?"

Does he think I'd tell him even if there was someone? Hunter thought. "That doesn't really matter now, does it, Mr. Espinosa?"

"I suppose not. The brothers are completely unaware of that recording?"

"Yes, and I'd like to keep it that way. People have disappeared in Miami over far less important matters."

"I have to be honest with you, Mr. Mahoy," Espinosa said, holding his glasses up to the light before wiping away another smudge. "There's really not a lot on that tape for me to act upon."

Hunter couldn't keep the look of surprise off of his face. "You're kidding, right? They practically admitted to killing the senator."

"No, Mr. Mahoy. They admitted to putting a bottle of Scotch in the senator's car."

"What about when Enrique said what was put with the bottle would prove something? Mr. Espinosa, that bottle was tainted!"

"I believe you're reading too much into it. They may simply have been referring to another gift besides the Scotch. It may even have been money. The Gomez Brothers have been known to offer a bribe from time to time."

Hunter sprang to his feet, fists at his sides. *This bastard is blowing me off! The friggin' bureau chief of the Miami branch of the FBI is dismissing incriminating evidence.* "I can't believe this! You're acting as though this is nothing. We're talking about the murder of a US senator. And what about their secret investing into Cuba? They did admit to that."

"Hundreds of companies have invested in Cuba, Mr. Mahoy. Most prefer to keep it as quiet as possible because of the political climate."

Shit! Did the Gomez brothers have this asshole in their pocket? Hunter wondered. *If they did, he'd made one giant mistake coming here.* "So you're not going to do anything?"

They stared at each other.

"What would you have me do?"

"Your job, damn it! Ask some questions. Look into it. Investigate. What harm could that do?"

Espinosa rose, paced the length of his office, then stood at his desk. "Let me tell you a little story. Years ago when I was a field agent, my partner and I opened a file looking into some of the early business practices of the Gomez brothers. No sooner did we get started when orders came down from on high for us to drop the investigation. My wife and I had just bought a house, our first house after years of renting, and our eldest daughter was starting college. I needed my good-paying job. After two unpleasant calls from FBI headquarters in Washington DC, I persuaded my partner to drop it. The next thing I know, I'm promoted to assistant bureau chief. A month later, my boss was forced into early retirement because of another dispute with headquarters about the Gomezes. I went from field agent to bureau chief in a span of just five weeks."

"What you're saying is that you're afraid of the Gomez brothers and what they might do?"

"And you aren't? You just finished telling me you didn't want them to know about the recording."

They stared at each other. The silence screamed. Time crawled. A jetliner tracked through the window on its final approach into Miami International.

Finally Espinosa threw his arms out from his sides. "Look, Mr. Mahoy, there's nowhere to go with it. The accident happened three years ago. The car's long since been scrapped. There's no evidence. There's nothing to trace, nothing to follow up. All we have is your recording, and that's open to interpretation. If I act on that alone, I guarantee you I'll be busted out of the FBI before I even know what happened."

"Awww, *pobrecito*," Hunter mocked, rocking his arms like a cradle. "You going to do your job or just worry about keeping it?"

"Listen to me! The Gomez brothers have serious clout in Washington. They know the vice president personally. I've often speculated that they have an influential friend inside the CIA as well. Your tape bears witness to that. Stanley Bass is the director of the CIA. All I'd accomplish with that recording would be a minor ripple, not even a wave, before I'd be gone, and everything would return to exactly as it is right now. Believe what I am telling you."

Hunter stood and angrily shut his briefcase. The guy was a chicken shit. "So you're going to let them get away with it?"

"I didn't say that. I simply need more to go on." He nodded at the briefcase. "Leave that recording with me. I'll play it for a couple of my associates and see what they think."

Hunter stared in disbelief. *Espinosa didn't really think anyone could be that stupid, did he?* "No, thanks. I'll hold on to the original until I've made some copies." He turned and headed for the door.

"Mr. Mahoy, I really think you should leave that recording with me."

"Sorry," he said over his shoulder. "I'm going to need it to get some action elsewhere on this matter." He slammed the door on his way out.

Hunter angrily strode for the elevator and fumed all the way down to the ground floor. He was still fuming when he hit the front entrance of the building. "FBI must stand for Federal Bureau of Indifference," he muttered as he walked briskly toward his car, parked two blocks away. "If Espinosa thinks I'm going to forget about this, he's sadly mis—"

Slammed savagely to the ground from behind, Hunter skinned his left hand on the sidewalk and split his forehead on a parking meter post. His assailant planted one foot on Hunter's arm and the other squarely in the middle of Hunter's back. He snatched the briefcase then ran down the street before rounding the corner. Hunter didn't get a good look at him, noting only that the thief was white and wore dazzling white Nikes and a loose-fitting black T-shirt.

"Son of a bitch!" He struggled to his feet, blood trickling down his face. His head pounded, and his back ached.

An older man approached, concern etched on his weathered face. "You all right, mister? That fellow really kicked the stuffing out of you. It all happened so fast, I didn't even see it coming." The man pulled a handkerchief from his pocket and offered it.

"Thanks," Hunter said, accepting the hankie. "I didn't see him coming either. I didn't even hear him coming. That's probably why he wore sneakers."

"You want me to call the cops, mister? They'll probably get here pretty quick."

Hunter examined his reflection in the passenger-side mirror of the nearest car. He winced as he wiped the blood from his face. "No. The guy's long gone. They couldn't do anything."

"I guess you're right. Can I help you get somewhere?"

Hunter faced him and smiled ruefully. "I'll be fine. My car's on the next block, but thanks for asking. And thanks for stopping, sir. Can I pay you for the handkerchief?"

"Keep it. It's the least I can do. I hope the bastard didn't get anything valuable."

Hunter patted his pants pocket. As a precaution, while riding down in the elevator, he'd removed the recorder from his briefcase. "No, he didn't. He probably thinks he did, but he didn't."

*   *   *

Amanda double-checked the files she'd compiled on Hunter's desk then glanced at her silver-and-gold Seiko. "Damn, Hunter! Where are you?" Just then keys jingled at the outer door. "It's about time! I thought maybe—oh, my god! Hunter, what happened? You're bleeding!"

He rushed past her into his office. "I know. I got mugged. Then I got stuck in traffic. Now I have a headache you wouldn't believe. Get me a shirt from my suitcase, would you, Amanda? This bloody one won't do." He looked at the now uniformly pink-tinged hand-kerchief in his hand. "I'll be in the bathroom. There's a first-aid kit in there somewhere."

Amanda joined him a minute later and handed him a couple of aspirin. "Take these and sit down, Hunter. Let me do that." She leaned over and took up the task of cleaning his wound. She caught him studying her eyes, her face, and then her breasts.

Smirking, she said, "Like I said before, Hunter, you're discreet, but not that discreet."

He blushed. "You know what the *H* stands for, Amanda? *Helpless.* I just can't help myself. You're eye candy for these peepers."

She ignored his flirting and winced as she worked close to the gash in his forehead, which oozed fresh blood. "I don't know, Hunter. This looks like it could use a few stitches."

"I found two butterfly bandages," he said, offering them in his outstretched hand. "They'll have to do for now."

As she pulled the wound together with the first bandage, he moaned softly.

"Sorry. Did they get anything?"

"My briefcase. Wasn't much in it, though. I'm glad I didn't have any of the paperwork for tomorrow's meeting in there. That would've been a disaster. We'll have to find another carrying case for those."

"Your old satchel's in the file room. I'll get it in a minute. There. I'm finished." She stepped back to survey her work. "That doesn't look too bad."

He studied her shapely figure. "No, not bad at all."

Amanda cracked a smile before she left to find the old satchel. While she was gone, Hunter opened his floor safe then placed the recorder inside. Next, he typed a short letter, plus an address on an envelope. He sealed the letter and stuck it with the other paperwork for their trip. Then he returned to the bathroom for another look in the mirror. He fingered the wound on his forehead and winced. Getting away on routine business suddenly seemed like a very good idea.

CHAPTER

3

Morgan Lindsey's alarm clock screamed away on her nightstand at four in the morning. "No!" she groaned. "It cannot be Friday already. I just went to bed." Her hand groped around in the darkness until the horrible racket was finally silenced. "Get up," she told herself. "You have to get up. Don't go back to sleep."

She willed her body into an upright position, feeling older than her thirty-eight years at the moment, then sat on the edge of the bed with her eyes closed, wondering if it was all worth it. But then she always wondered that whenever she got up at such a ridiculous hour, something she seemed to be doing more and more lately. This time she had to finish a lengthy article before the weekend press run at the *Washington Herald.* The piece, spotlighting corruption within the mayor's office, absolutely had to be in print before the special mayoral election in five days. She'd finished the rough draft the previous day. Now she needed her big break, the one that would let her name the wrongdoers in a recent multimillion-dollar real estate deal that might benefit certain prominent DC politicians.

Morgan hauled herself off the bed then shuffled to the bathroom, bumping into the doorjamb on the way. "Sure hope that guy calls again today," she mumbled aloud as she stepped into the shower. She'd missed three calls the day before from a mysterious source who'd promised to deliver to her, and only her, irrefutable proof of those involved. Though worried about meeting this person alone in what would no doubt be some isolated place, she'd already decided to do so if the person called again. She was determined to stay by the phone today since her source had left a message saying he'd call again. If she had to, she'd close the piece as it was. It would still cause a stir. But if she could get proof, it would likely instigate a criminal investigation, maybe even alter the outcome of the election. On a personal note, the article might also elevate her journalistic status and boost her income as well.

Morgan emerged from the life-restorative hot water fully awake and ready to start her day. She did her hair and makeup then started the coffeemaker. The pot gurgled reassuringly in the background as she shifted clothes in her closet and picked out an outfit that would be suitable for both the chilly weather and the meeting with her source. She dressed quickly. After casting an appraising glance in the full-length mirror at what even she had to admit was a dynamite figure, she headed to the kitchen for her morning dose of caffeine.

A half hour later, Morgan wheeled into the parking lot of the *Washington Herald*, whipped into the nearest space, and bounced her red Pontiac Grand Am hard against the bumper. "Damn! Misjudged that one," she muttered to herself.

As she hustled toward the building, the biting wind sent fallen leaves racing past her feet and her camel-colored overcoat flying like a flag in a tempest. She turned her back against the blast, fought to tie the belt, then pulled the hood over her head, thereby effectively ruining her earlier efforts on her shoulder-length strawberry-blonde hair. She ran the remaining distance holding the hood with one hand and clutching her bulky brown leather purse with the other.

"Good morning, Morgan," the security guard greeted her. "Looks brutal out there."

She laughed, crinkling up her brown eyes. "It's a woman's worst nightmare, Nick, the ultimate bad hair day." She doffed the hood and ran all ten fingers through her disheveled mane.

He smiled. "You're early this morning. Almost caught me sleeping at my post."

"I seriously doubt that. Hey, Nick, you see that game last night?" Unlike many of the other *Herald* employees who tended to treat the service personnel in the building as if they were invisible, Morgan was always courteous to the guard and considered him as much a peer as her coworkers.

"No. I was tired. Turned in early."

"Too bad. You missed a good one," she said over her shoulder as she headed for the elevator. "See you later."

*   *   *

Hunter strolled the hallway toward his office Friday morning and reflected on the three-day trip to Houston that he and Amanda had just completed. Only her presence had made the seemingly endless client meetings bearable. He wondered just what he'd do if she ever left his employ, then quickly answered himself, *I know what I'd do. I'd just quit this line of work. I'm sick of it anyway. The bosses, the meetings, the long hours—especially at tax time—the ungrateful clients, the traveling. Shit, I don't need the money that badly.*

As his office door came into view, his right hand habitually slid into his pocket for the key. It took him a moment to realize that the door was slightly ajar. "What the…"

He pushed the door fully open and stood there, staring. The outer office, Amanda's office, had been ransacked. Stepping inside, Hunter looked around. Amanda's empty desk was like an island in the middle of a maelstrom. Everything that usually cluttered the desktop was now on the floor. To one side lay her computer monitor, the keyboard, her desk calendar, and what seemed like several reams' worth of papers. On the opposite side the raiders had flung the telephone and her Rolodex, its file cards scattered everywhere like fifty-two pickup. Paper clips, pencils, and pens littered the forest-green carpet. Two tropical landscape watercolors that had previously hung on the walls were also lying on the carpet, their protective glass shattered. Cushions had been flung from the sofa, chairs thrown clear across the room. A pile of magazines lay beneath the smashed thick glass top of the overturned coffee table.

Hunter stepped behind Amanda's desk. All the drawers were open and rifled through, some of the contents strewn on the floor. The file cabinets had similarly been trashed. He walked to the door of his own office and glanced in at an identical scene.

He was still standing there when Amanda arrived.

"Good heavens!"

He faced her. "Had a visitor."

"That's obvious," she said, her hand pressed against the side of her face. "But who? And what in the world were they looking for?" She maneuvered across the room slowly, surveying as she went, then set her purse on her bare desktop.

Hunter picked up the phone and put the receiver back on the base. "I don't know," he said, setting the instrument on her desk. "Maybe they got mad because we weren't here."

"Any idea what's been stolen?"

"Haven't had a chance to sort that out yet. Just arrived myself." He scanned the room. "But I have a suspicion nothing's missing."

"*Nothing!* Then why all this?" Her outstretched arms took in the room.

"They were looking for something."

"What?"

"I'll tell you in a minute." He stepped around and over the destruction in his office, then peeled back the carpet to expose the floor safe. It didn't appear to have been tampered with. He opened it anyway. The tape recorder was intact. Relieved, he relocked the safe.

Hunter then checked the alarm box in the closet before working his way back through the maze to the front door where he studied the alarm keypad. Finally, he knelt and inspected the outside doorknob.

"I don't see any signs of tampering. And I know I turned on the alarm before we left for Houston."

"You did," Amanda confirmed as she collected her Rolodex cards. "You went back and double-checked, remember?"

He rubbed his chin. "The intruders were real professionals. So either they wanted to give the appearance of amateurs, or they got really pissed when they couldn't find what they were looking for and wrecked the place."

"So just what were they looking for, Hunter?"

He crossed the room, righted two chairs to face each other, then sat in one and patted the seat opposite. Amanda obliged him.

"I haven't told you before now because I was concerned for your safety." He reached over and caressed her face. "The last thing I want is to have any harm come to you."

"I know that," she said softly, a puzzled look in her eyes.

He sighed heavily, then leaned back, and cupped his hands behind his head. "Now that things have escalated, I'm really concerned for your safety. You need to know what's happened."

He described in detail the conversation on the accidental recording, followed by his meeting at the FBI office, and the mugging immediately afterward.

Amanda held up her hand. "Wait a minute, Hunter. Are you telling me the FBI mugged you?"

"Yes. It had to be. Don't you see? That's the only place I went. The bureau chief, José Espinosa, tried to get me to leave the tape. I told him to forget it. He watched me put it in my briefcase, and the next thing I know, some guy slams me to the sidewalk. He didn't try to steal my watch or wallet—he wanted that briefcase."

Leaning forward, Amanda slowly shook her head in amazement. "It makes sense," she agreed, "and whoever wrecked this office knew how to bypass a lock and an alarm. The FBI would know how to do that."

"True, but so would associates of the Gomez brothers. I can almost guarantee it."

"So…what do we do now?"

"I don't know, Amanda, but I'll tell you what we're not going to do. We're not going to waste a lot of time by calling the police in on this. The point's moot." He placed the cushions back on the couch and picked up one of the paintings. "Let's clean up this mess. We'll figure out the rest over the weekend."

*　　*　　*

"Darn Friday-afternoon wild-goose chase," Morgan Lindsey grumbled as she stomped into her tastefully decorated corner office on the eighth floor of the *Washington Herald* building. Despite her intention to stay by her phone to catch the call from her mysterious source, she'd gone out to pursue what turned out to be a dead-end on the mayoral scandal. Time was growing short. *I hope I haven't missed my mystery man while I was out wasting time chasing down that farcical lead.*

She plopped her purse onto the antique mahogany desk, tossed her coat over the back of a tapestried Victorian chair, then punched a button on her answering machine. No messages.

"Crap," she said as she rooted in her purse for an extra-strength Tylenol. She pulled out the bottle of Evian that she kept in a drawer, downed the tablet, then scooped up her mail and sorted through it. About half flew into the trash unopened. An envelope with a question mark for a return address, however, caught her attention. She flipped it over then back to the front again. It was postmarked "Houston, Texas."

She didn't know anyone in Houston.

*   *   *

United States Air Force Captain David Cunningham banked his stealth fighter into a tight turn high over Cuba and thought about the missions he'd recently flown to locations all over the island. His targets had been mostly hotels and resorts in tourist areas along the coast, but he'd also destroyed a few communications facilities, including a skyscraping radio antenna. Cloaked in secrecy, his flights always occurred at night, but his targets were easy to hit with the use of laser-guided munitions. He considered the missions milk runs because of his aircraft's invisibility to radar; no one even knew he was there.

He smiled. The brass had it all figured out. The US media had taken the bait, blaming the explosions on civil unrest. They ran frequent stories describing how the Cuban people were completely frustrated with the Castro regime, the island ripe for another revolution.

Cunningham rolled out of his steep diving turn to align with that evening's objective. *Just a few more seconds.* He waited, his thumb hovering over the red button. Piece of cake. He pressed the release fast and hard, using more effort than necessary, then kept the cross-hairs centered. Impact. He smiled again. Another direct hit, his target in flames. Time to go home. He initiated an aggressive climbing turn when suddenly the compressor stall warning sounded. "Damn it! You know better than that, you idiot!" he shouted at himself.

He shallowed the climb and babied the throttles. Too late. Both engines stalled, leaving him at low altitude. "*Shit!* Now I've done it."

He'd been ordered to maintain the secrecy of the operation at any cost. In the event of a problem, he was to fly out to sea and eject. But nothing was wrong with his aircraft; he simply needed time to restart the engines. He sure wouldn't have it from this altitude.

He switched on the infrared imaging. Visible now were several narrow roads that intersected a plateau of agricultural fields just ahead. It was a no-brainer. He'd go for solid ground rather than eject into shark-infested waters at night. He lowered the landing gear, aligned with the nearest roadway, and prepared for contact.

The instant the wheels touched down, the hard-packed, unpaved surface, littered with deep potholes, brutally attacked the unsuspecting aircraft.

"Damn! What rotten luck!" he muttered, gritting his teeth.

When the dust settled, the plane rested at the edge of the road with its right wing jutting into a sugarcane field. Cunningham's lower back hurt. He wanted to restart the engines and depart immediately but figured he'd better check the undercarriage first. He popped the canopy and climbed down. Everything appeared to be intact as he approached the front landing gear. Then he heard a hissing sound.

*   *   *

Leaning back in her chair, her feet propped on the desktop, Morgan Lindsey pondered the question-mark return address for probably the hundredth time. In the hour that had elapsed since finding the letter, Friday afternoon had slipped into Friday evening, and still the question mark stared at her. The symbol had obviously been typed there to compel her to open the envelope. *What arrogance*, she thought. For that reason she'd resisted the temptation for as long as she had. She'd even tossed it into the wastebasket, twice, before retrieving it again. *Maybe I'll just trash it for good and be done with it.* Instead, she rolled her eyes then ripped it open.

The moment she started reading, she sprang forward. Her feet slapped the floor, and her mouth opened as if it had a mind of its own.

> Morgan,
>
> The death of Senator Sean Buchanan three years ago was not an accident. He was murdered. The three owners of the Gomez Brothers Corporation in Miami tainted a bottle of Scotch then placed it in the senator's car, knowing full well he'd drink from it during the long drive ahead of him that night. They had an accomplice in the CIA who supplied them with the substance in question.
>
> I know their motive, opportunity, and method. What's needed is proof if these bastards are ever to be charged and convicted.
>
> I'll contact you soon about this. Whatever you do, be extremely careful whom you tell. And stay away from the FBI and the CIA. The Gomez brothers have people in their pockets. I can attest to that personally.
>
> Watch your back on this one, darling.

Letter in hand, Morgan rose and stood by the window that overlooked the White House. With night falling, the landmark magically illuminated before her eyes. Where on earth would she begin? And whom should she trust? She reread the letter, focusing heavily on the last word: *darling*. Was it from someone who knew her or a complete stranger? Would she ever really find out?

She returned to her desk, flopped into the chair again, then propped her face in her hands.

The door suddenly opened. "Dinner for your thoughts," Jack Burton said as he entered.

Morgan looked up. The newspaper's forty-something managing editor, decked out in a gray Armani pinstriped suit, exuded confidence. She noticed that his black shoes and belt were a perfect match for his thick, wavy hair—other than the gray-flecked sideburns. He sauntered over to her desk and looked down at her, his brown eyes twinkling.

"Hello, Jack. I'd take you up on that offer except that right at this moment my mind's a total blank."

"Yeah. I have that effect on women everywhere I go." He flashed his pearly whites as he sat on the corner of her desk.

She couldn't help but smile. "How'd you get to be so conceited, Jack?"

He shrugged. "Comes with the territory, I guess. You know, always telling everyone what to do, how to do it, and when to do it. That's just one of the many pitfalls of being the boss. So, what's up, Morgan?"

Pretending to make more room for him, she rearranged the paperwork on her desk to hide the letter.

"Is your mayoral election piece in shape?" he asked. "It'll have to go to press by Sunday afternoon at the latest."

"I know. I'm still hoping my informant will contact me again." She rubbed her temples with her thumbs.

"So am I," he said. "If your guy comes through, we're really going to make some headlines." He smiled sympathetically. "You're sure putting the hours in on this one. Tell you what, since you're stuck in this office, a prisoner to the phone, I'll have dinner brought in to you. Why don't you call that Thai restaurant you like so much? Order whatever you want. If they can't deliver it, I'll go pick it up myself."

"Now see, that's why I let you be my boss, Jack. At times you can be quite thoughtful and charming."

"Really? And here I thought it was because I let you talk me into things, like giving you this coveted corner office with a much better view than my own."

She smiled. "It'll always be that way, Jack. You don't stand a chance against me."

Smirking, he strolled for the door. "Gloating doesn't become you," he said over his shoulder.

She chuckled then got serious. "Say, Jack. If a really alarming incident came to my attention, and I found it impossible to get any proof, would the paper run a story on it in hopes of stirring up some evidence?"

He thought for a moment. "We might let you write a piece on the Op-Ed page, but it'd have to be incredibly important. And be written in a way that wouldn't specifically implicate anyone. We'd also have to state before the story that it's strictly your opinion. You might not want to stick your pretty little neck out on a piece like that, Morgan." He walked back to her desk and looked her in the eye. "Why? Do you have something I should know about?"

She hesitated, looked away, then back again. "I might in the near future."

*   *   *

Captain Cunningham walked about a quarter mile in each direction, horrified at the condition of the roadway, and wondering how he hadn't seriously damaged his aircraft. Killing his flashlight, he scratched his head in thought. He could still get airborne by compensating for the flat tire on the nose gear; the takeoff roll would be rough, but as he gained speed, he'd lighten the load on that wheel with the flight controls. The real problem was the archaic road.

Cunningham spent the next few hours moving medium and large-sized rocks to the section he'd use as a runway, filling in many of the worst potholes with his bare hands. At about half past nine, it began to rain. "Damn! What else can go wrong?" he grumbled as he brushed off his hands and ran for the aircraft, barely discernible in the darkness.

By the time he'd reached the stealth, drizzle had become a deluge. Exhausted, soaked, and frustrated, he climbed into the cockpit to rest. With visibility practically nil during the downpour, he couldn't possibly take off from the narrow, makeshift runway, especially in the dark. The heavy raindrops drummed a steady rhythm on the skin of the aircraft, a soothing rhythm that lulled him right to sleep.

CHAPTER

 4

Hunter wheeled up in front of the historic Biltmore Hotel in Coral Gables Friday evening and tossed his keys to the valet, a handsome kid still in his teens who didn't seem terribly impressed with the white Honda Accord; hell, it didn't even have leather interior. *Maybe I should've dusted off the Ferrari,* Hunter thought as he sprinted up the front steps. He was running an hour late for the retirement party being thrown for Matthew Pearlis, a senior partner at the firm, but Hunter wasn't sweating it. The extravaganza was sure to last into the wee hours. He stepped into the ballroom where he immediately maneuvered toward the bar, greeting coworkers and clients along the way.

"Hunter! Over here," senior partner Aaron Masterson called, waving one arm high over his head.

Great! Just my luck, Hunter thought. *Here I am in a target-rich environment with every secretary in the firm all dolled up, and I'll probably get stuck with one boss or another the whole friggin' night.* He tipped the bartender then strolled toward Aaron's table, fabricating a smile on the way.

Though only fifty-eight, the frail and thin Aaron looked more like seventy. His bald pate glistened in the reflected light of the chandelier that hung directly above the round linen-covered table where he was seated.

"Hello, Aaron. Good to see you. You look like a million bucks in that tux." Hunter schmoozed. "Where's your lovely wife?"

"Pamela's around here somewhere," he said with a wave of his hand. "Probably on the dance floor. You know, it's interesting that you mentioned money just now, Hunter. That's what I want to talk to you about. Have a seat."

Hunter reluctantly claimed the empty chair next to his boss.

"The other partners and I have decided it's time we rewarded you for your hard work and perseverance."

"I earn a fine salary now. There's really no need to—"

"Nonsense," Aaron cut in. "We're offering you a full partnership in the firm, complete with your choice of any new car you desire, an expense account for you and your personal secretary up to five-thousand dollars a month, a larger and fully furnished office, and membership in the exclusive Palladium Club."

"I-I don't know what to say, Aaron." Hunter tried to sound enthused. "I'm overwhelmed." A year ago, he would've been. "I hadn't expected this at all." *It's about time. I've busted my ass for them.* He pulled a handkerchief and pretended to need it. "A full partnership. Wow! What a surprise! I—" He wiped at his eyes. "Will you excuse me, Aaron? I need a few minutes by myself."

"Of course. Take all the time you need."

As Hunter moseyed away, he looked back once. Aaron was still smiling. At the bar Hunter ordered another white Russian and thought about the offer. It was a great one—no, an *exceptional* one. To become a full partner within a decade was unheard of. The offer wouldn't have been made if Pearlis hadn't been retiring, but that didn't matter now. He took a hit off his drink. What was he going to do? He'd be crazy to decline—and probably go crazy if he accepted. How could he possibly explain that he so loathed his job he was willing to walk away with absolutely no idea of what he'd do to earn a living?

If he had any sense at all he'd—the sight of Amanda, wearing a low-cut little black dress, stopped him in midthought. Her golden hair was pulled up into a chignon, and the sparkle in her eyes rivaled that of her diamond pendant and earrings. Just looking at her, his heart skipped a beat. Her long, slender legs carried his focus up to that short dress. He couldn't take his eyes off her. It wasn't fair that one woman could be so mesmerizing, so desirable. If he accepted the partnership offer, it'd only be because of her. She positively took his breath away.

He frowned. Her ever-present boyfriend, Simon Levine, a full-of-himself prosecuting attorney for the State Department, accompanied her. But just then Simon grabbed her arm and tried to pull her from the crowded dance floor. She yanked herself free and turned away from him. Without warning, he jerked her around and then shoved her; she stumbled backward into another couple.

"What the hell's the matter with you?" Simon shouted. "You think I'm going to wait forever for you to make up your damned mind?"

Heart pounding, Hunter started toward them, his right hand already curling into a fist.

"Simon, you've had too much to drink. You're making a scene," Amanda said in a calm but elevated tone.

"I'm sick and tired of you telling me I've had too much!" he screamed. *"You've had a few yourself, you nagging bitch!"*

Hunter stopped in midstep. The string quartet quit playing. All conversation ceased. The room fell silent. Amanda slapped Simon's face so hard that he actually stumbled to his knees. Amanda stood motionless, one hand on her chest, the other over her mouth, as Simon knelt there dumbfounded. Finally, wordlessly, he got to his feet and stormed out, shoving a few people aside on his way. With remarkable composure, Amanda retreated to a darkened corner of the extravagant hall. The quartet took up again with "As Time Goes By."

Hunter made a quick return to the bar then approached the window where Amanda stood staring out at the city lights, a tear running down her cheek. He handed her the drink he had gotten for her.

"You all right?" he asked softly.

She gulped the alcohol then looked at him. The sparkle had faded from her eyes. It tore him up to see her like that.

"I wish that hadn't happened here tonight," she said sullenly. "It was so humiliating! I know everyone's talking about it."

He handed her his monogrammed handkerchief. "Amanda, most of the people at this party are your friends. We're all proud of how you handled yourself. It's none of my business what prompted the argument, but I know it wouldn't have happened if Simon had been treating you right. People will always talk—that's human nature." He glanced around. "Some are probably talking right now about how I'm moving in on you when you're vulnerable. I don't care what they think. I simply wanted to make sure you're OK. Can I get you anything?"

She wiped at her eyes. "I could sure use another drink."

He handed her his.

She downed it almost as quickly as the first.

"Hey, go easy with that stuff, darlin'. It'll knock you on your keister."

"You've always been sweet to me, Hunter. I have a secret I want to share with you: I've been interested in you for a long time, probably almost as long as you've been interested in me." She gazed into his eyes and traced a character line on his face with her index finger. "I felt like a leper after that argument, but you came to my rescue, my hero!" Her eyes twinkled. "Did anyone ever tell you that you look like the Marlboro man? All you need is a horse."

He pretended to tip his hat. "Ah, shucks, ma'am. I get that all the time."

She laughed softly. "So what do you say, cowboy? Will you twirl with me a spell?"

"I'd love to, darlin'."

Taking her by the arm, he escorted her to the center of the nearly empty dance floor. She stepped into his outstretched arms and whispered, "Hunter, I'm a little tipsy. Hold me close so I won't fall."

He grinned. "I intend to, because you're lovely and I want to, not because you're tipsy."

As he pressed her body against his, he became acutely aware of her breathing, her every heartbeat. Her perfume further intoxicated him.

She rested her head on his shoulder and whispered, "I'm glad you're here, Hunter."

"So am I," he said softly.

"Hunter?"

"Yes, Amanda?"

"What does the *H* in your name really stand for?"

He chuckled. "It stands for *Happy*."

She looked into his eyes. "Hunter, I've known you for three years now. Are you ever going to tell me what your full name is?"

"Maybe someday—if you play your cards right."

She pulled back abruptly. "I want to see your driver's license right now."

He shrugged then reached into his coat pocket and handed her his wallet. "Suit yourself."

She opened it eagerly. On his license was printed H. HUNTER MAHOY. She checked his voter's registration, his pilot's license, and the credit cards as well. They all read the same way.

He smirked then drew her close to him again, and resumed dancing. "The mystery remains, darlin'. But like I said, if you play your cards right…"

When the music stopped, everyone clapped.

Hunter looked around at all the spectators to their dance. "See? I told you they're your friends."

She scanned the room herself then wiped away fresh tears. As they left the dance floor, she stumbled. He caught her.

"I'm really dizzy, Hunter. Maybe I'd better go home now. Will you take me?"

"Of course."

He supported her as she collected her purse and evening mantle.

"You're more than just a little tipsy, Amanda," he whispered as they headed toward the lobby. "You're smashed."

"I know." She giggled. "But it feels good."

As he helped her into the passenger seat of his four-door Accord, he admired the way her short dress didn't quite cover the essentials. Reluctantly, he placed her mantle in her lap to cover her then connected her seat belt.

"This car's really spinning," she slurred as he climbed into the driver's seat.

"Can't be," he teased, fastening his own belt. "I haven't even started driving yet. You might feel better if you recline the seat." Realizing she'd have trouble finding the release, he reached across to do it for her, his face just inches from her breasts.

"You like what you see?" she asked, sounding almost sober.

"Lie back and relax now, Amanda. We're on the way to your address."

"What's wrong with my dress?" she asked, pushing the wrap aside. It fell to the floor.

The movement largely exposed her black lace panties. Hunter decided he'd better get moving. "Never mind," he said hoarsely, placing the car in gear.

"Whoa, I'm glad you're driving, Hunter, 'cause I couldn't!" Those were her last words. In a few minutes the motion of the vehicle lulled her to sleep.

As if he wasn't already having enough trouble concentrating on his driving, Amanda unknowingly made matters worse when she snuggled farther into the seat, spreading her legs a bit. He chided himself for stealing long looks but continued to do so. For the first time in his life, he actually looked forward to catching red lights.

He entered her housing development from Southwest 137th Avenue then followed the curvy drive lined with sidewalks, white-rail fencing, and berms of lush landscaping. Underground utilities and attractive lamppost streetlights added to the upscale appearance of the place. He turned left onto Fox Trot Lane then, three houses down, pulled into the driveway of Amanda's spacious two-story residence. Its creamy plaster exterior gleamed in the moonlight.

He plucked Amanda's keys from her purse, got out and unlocked the front door, then came back and carried her inside and up the stairs to her bedroom. As he gently placed her on the queen-sized four-poster bed, she stirred.

"We home?" she asked.

"Yes, and I'm going to leave now. You get some sleep."

Supporting herself with one of the bedposts, she pulled herself off the bed and stood. "Wait. I can't sleep in my dress. Would you unzip me?"

He'd wanted to do just that for months, but now he was almost afraid to. He wasn't sure he could trust himself.

She slipped the spaghetti straps from her shoulders.

"Amanda, I really should be going..."

"Please, Hunter."

Giving in, he felt himself growing hard as he unzipped her. *No bra,* he thought. The instant he released the zipper, her dress slipped to the floor.

She turned slowly and faced him, wearing only the skimpy panties and a kittenish smile. "Stay with me, Hunter."

Fixating on her voluptuous breasts, his arousal complete, he fought to maintain control of his desire. He groaned. "You're gorgeous, and I want to, more than you know, but I can't. Not tonight, not like th—"

Abruptly, she pulled him into her arms and kissed him passionately.

He lost it. His tongue instantly responded to hers. He slid his hands excitedly over her breasts, then down her body and into her panties, which soon fell to the floor. As the passion intensified, his morals wrestled with his emotions for every scrap of decency still within him. Mustering every ounce of strength he had, he pulled away, the vision standing before him etched in his brain forever.

"Amanda, I have to go," he pleaded. "I'll call you in the morning. Your purse is on the dresser with your keys."

"My spare key, it's by the side door, under a potted plant," she mumbled.

Smiling, he helped her back into bed, stealing one last titillating look before pulling the covers over her. He left the house, locking the door behind him, then drove home as fast as it was safe to, to take the coldest shower of his life.

*　　*　　*

Hunter's alarm sounded to bright sunshine and a clear, blue sky. He grinned. Perfect soaring weather—it would be the first time he'd go in more than a year. The sun was already warming the ground. The heat would rise in thermal columns, creating lift for the sailplane.

He showered, wondering as he soaped his body if he had dreamed the entire episode with Amanda. He dressed and ate breakfast. Feeling the excitement he always felt as he anticipated a flight, he eagerly loaded his equipment into his car. Homestead and the gliderport lay some thirty minutes away. As he drove past the endless farm fields of the Redlands, he flipped off the climate controls and rolled down his windows. The crisp, dew-laden Saturday morning air embraced the scent of recently plowed dirt. The earth smelled fresh and alive, invigorating. He breathed deeply. From high above, he recalled, the whole area resembled a giant patchwork quilt, blanketing what he considered to be the best part of South Florida.

He soon entered the rough gravel road that led to the airport hangar and the narrow grass runway, the west end of which jutted out into the watery Everglades. He parked next to a long and narrow white fiberglass trailer sitting on the edge of the runway. The trailer housed his disassembled sailplane.

He stepped from his Honda into a soft breeze that rustled the saw grass ever so gently. The quiet seemed surreal. A great blue heron alit from across the runway and sailed right past him. He watched it until it glided behind a thicket. Then he switched on his cell phone and punched in Amanda's number. No answer. *Probably still asleep,* he thought. He'd try again later.

Hunter plucked a credit card from his wallet to pay for the glider tow then stuck the wallet under the seat before grabbing his camera. It swung from his neck like a pendulum when he reached into the glove compartment for an extra roll of film. Now he was ready for the stroll to the aging hangar.

The concrete-block structure, built in the early sixties, had never been repainted or refurbished. Vines clung to its mildew-laden walls, which were largely hidden behind old aircraft parts, oil drums, a rusting yellow hulk that once was a school bus, and a few junked cars. The inside of the hangar, relatively clean, housed three sailplanes, the tail-dragger towplane, a tractor for mowing the runway, and the office—a spartan ten-by-ten area in one corner with a desk, a file cabinet, a telephone, and a trash can.

"Well, well. Look who we have here," tow pilot Brandon Thorpe said as Hunter entered the hangar. "*Haphazard* Hunter Mahoy. Man, I thought maybe you fell off the face of the earth, it's been so long."

"Yes, much too long," Hunter agreed, shaking hands. "Good to see you, Brandon. And don't start with that *Haphazard* business. It wasn't my fault I had to land off site that day. You're the one who had the runway all tied up with gliders and airplanes and people. I had to land somewhere."

Brandon laughed. "Yeah. But did you have to choose that freshly tilled, rain-soaked field? I have to admit, though, you did a skillful job of slipping into that mudhole with the strong crosswind. *Slipping*—get it?"

"Very funny," Hunter said, hiding a smile. "I've been trying hard to forget that incident."

"I'll bet. First, you got your sailplane stuck. Then you got your car and trailer stuck. And then the tow truck got stuck. What a friggin' mess! Half the people who came to fly that day ended up out there in that mush trying to help—hell, three of 'em sank their cars up to the axles too. We slopped around in that mud for hours, disassembling your bird and sticking it into the trailer. The event was more like a mud-wrestling match than the recovery of a glider." He laughed. "*Then* the whole conglomeration of vehicles had to sit out there for two weeks until the field dried up enough to get them out of there. What a fiasco! But hey, look on the bright side, you're a legend out here now. They even named the field after you."

Hunter propped his left hand on his hip. "What are you talking about?"

"Yeah, didn't you know? It's called *Hogpen* Hunter's field."

Hunter threw the box of film at him. "Get out of here!"

Brandon ducked, but the box beaned him on the top of the head. "I'm serious, Hunter—I mean, *Haphazard*," he said, laughing and tossing the film back. "Everyone around here now calls it *Hogpen* Hunter's field. Ask anybody."

Hunter held up his hands in surrender. "OK, uncle already. You happy now?"

Brandon good-naturedly slapped Hunter on the back.

"Seriously, Hunter, what happened with you? You used to come out every weekend. Did you reenlist in the air force so you could finally fly the stealth?"

"I almost wish I had, Brandon. No, the closest I got to that was sitting in the cockpit with a buddy standing on a stepladder explaining the systems to me."

"You move out of Miami?"

"Nope. Been buried in work is all. The more I do, the more the big shots want me to do. The money's great, but the load's taking its toll."

"That's not good, buddy. Life's too short."

"I know. And now I have a bigger problem. They want to make me one of the big shots. Last night they offered me a full partnership. It'd mean a lot more money if I accept, but it may be years before I see the light of day again. I'd be able to retire in about ten years, though, before my fiftieth birthday."

Brandon shrugged. "Money isn't everything. The key to happiness is landing precisely where you intend without complications." He chuckled. "I don't envy you having to make that decision."

"Man, you got that right." Hunter sighed. "So, my sailplane is ready to go?"

"Yep. Your bird's definitely in good shape. Your friend Fernando takes excellent care of it. He had the annual inspection done about a month ago. You planning to fly today?"

"You bet I am!"

"Good day for it. Staying local or flying cross-country?"

Hunter raised his hand to block the sun and studied a flock of buzzards circling high overhead. "Haven't decided yet. Depends on what I find once I'm airborne. The wind's favorable for cross-country, though, and so's the high cloud base. I may just fly northwest and see how far I can go."

Brandon nodded. "Sounds like a plan. When you're ready, roll your bird onto the runway. I'll bring the towplane around in a few minutes."

Hunter assembled his gloss-white fiberglass sailplane in record time. He did his preflight inspection and a final check of the controls then slipped into the harness of his thin-pack parachute before climbing into the one-seater engineless craft. It was a snug fit in the cockpit, but wearing the chute was a necessary evil.

Brandon taxied down in the towplane, hopped out to connect the towline, then climbed back into the tail-dragger. Hunter double-checked that the altimeter was set at zero. His pulse quickened. He wagged the rudder from side to side, indicating that he was ready for takeoff, and Brandon advanced the towplane's throttle. Both aircraft started rolling.

Fifteen seconds later they had cleared the grassy runway, climbing in unison. As the earth fell away beneath him, Hunter wondered how he had let a full year go by since he'd last gone soaring. He vowed not to let that happen again. From now on, work would simply have to wait.

His altimeter was coming up on three-thousand feet. He leaned forward and yanked the release. Instantly freed of its burden, the towline shot forward of the sailplane, coiled in midair, then stretched out again as the towplane banked left, initiating its return to the gliderport. Hunter banked to the right. The horizon rotated in the Plexiglas canopy as the compass swung around to a westerly heading.

Silence ruled. Except for the occasional whirring of a control cable, the wind slipping past the airframe created the only sound. Now he had to be skillful with his maneuvers to remain aloft without the use of power. He searched the sky for the white, puffy clouds that would provide the needed lift and spotted several farther west. Fast approaching the nearest one, he prepared for the bump of rising air. The strong thermal updraft kicked him in the butt as he passed underneath the giant cotton ball. He began circling upward immediately. Ten minutes later, at sixty-six-hundred feet, he reached the base of the cloud.

It was just after 1:00 p.m., and Hunter had soared more than twenty miles northwest of the gliderport. Looking down at the swampy Everglades, he could barely make out the closest road to the north, US Highway 41, the Tamiami Trail, which bisected the 1.5-million-acre national park. About twenty-five miles to the east was US Highway 27. To the west, roads were nonexistent; the Everglades extended all the way to the Gulf of Mexico. *I sure would hate to have to land down there*, Hunter thought idly. *That kind of terrain gobbles up aircraft.*

He picked up his autofocus camera and snapped a few pictures to record cloud formations, visibility, and the terrain he'd flown over. He also captured a few images of the instrument panel—showing the altimeter, variometer, compass headings, and so forth—and a couple more looking out over the nose as well. He'd later use the photos to help him remember the flight for his log. When he was done, he placed the camera back in his lap then tried calling Amanda again. No luck. He tossed the cellphone on the dash.

Countless thermals later, he checked his digital flight clock. Four hours and fifteen minutes since takeoff. He smiled. A new personal record. *Not bad for a guy who's a little rusty at the controls,* he told himself. Working the last few thermals pointed out that the conditions were deteriorating. His altimeter indicated 5,200 feet. Hunter decided to stay in that thermal, even though it was weak, obtain all the altitude he could, then head for the gliderport. It'd take him about thirty minutes to get back against the wind. He was already mentally adding the half hour to the time he'd been aloft. Within his grasp lay the elusive five-hour endurance time that most sailplane pilots strive to attain. To guarantee himself the coveted badge, he might have to loiter over the airport for a few minutes.

*   *   *

"Holy shit!" Captain David Cunningham shouted. "I've slept past sunrise!" He checked his watch. "Son of a bitch! It's Saturday afternoon!" He could scarcely believe that he'd slept all that time with his stealth fighter just sitting there in broad daylight. *Colonel Blake's*

going to have my rank for this! What a fucking blunder! I've got to get out of here!

As he prepared to start the engines, he glanced at the muddy road. Another section of his makeshift runway had washed away in the downpour. "*Fuck!*" he snarled as he climbed down from the cockpit and promptly slipped in a patch of mud. He hurriedly camouflaged the aircraft with sugarcane then started filling the trench with whatever he could find.

An hour and a half later, Cunningham finished repairing that and two other areas. He stared down the roadway then shook his head. *I hope this bird ends up in the air instead of a ditch.*

He climbed back into the plane, latched the canopy, fired up the engines, advanced the throttles, then held back pressure on the stick. The rough takeoff roll rattled his eyeballs. "Come on, baby. Climb for me!" he pleaded. The ride improved greatly once the nose wheel left the ground. "That's it. Reach for the sky, sweetheart."

Cunningham breathed a sigh of relief the instant the craft became airborne. Retracting the undercarriage, he turned due south to get offshore as quickly as possible. As Cuba slipped behind him, he thought about what he'd tell Colonel Blake. Nothing worthwhile came to mind. He banked the stealth fighter to the right and accelerated to maximum speed, remaining well out over open water as he flew around the western tip of the island. A northeast heading from there would point him straight for the Everglades on the southern tip of Florida.

*   *   *

"Ah, finally," Hunter said aloud. "Thought I'd never make it back to cloud base. I'll complete this revolution then head back." The gliderport was just barely visible off in the distance when he rolled out of his turn and punched into the late afternoon sunshine. He checked the altimeter again: 6,300 feet. "Good. More than enough altitude to reach the port, even against the wind." He checked the air speed: fifty miles per hour. The compass heading: southeast. The variometer showed only a slight amount of sink.

Suddenly a black flash darted before his eyes, coupled an instant later with an explosive ka-boom! The sailplane shuddered and careened to the right. *"What the—?"* Hunter instinctively edged the control stick slightly to the left to counteract the roll. Nothing. He thrust the stick as far to the left as it would travel, but the sailplane continued to flounder. "Son of a bitch!" he said. "Why can't I—?"

He looked frantically to the left then to the right. He pressed his face against the canopy and froze. His stomach lurched into his throat. A third of the right wing had been completely sheared away. *My god!* he thought. *I'm going down!*

He forced himself to breathe evenly, though his mind whirled. The sailplane had already rotated past forty-five degrees; it had an air speed of seventy-five miles per hour at an altitude of 5,800 feet. *I've got about fifteen seconds to bail out!* Fumbling to unbuckle his seat belt, he grasped the camera in his lap. Impulsively, he snapped a picture of the damaged wing then released the belt just as the nose of the sailplane dropped below the horizon. Airspeed increased drastically. The wind shrieked against the Plexiglas, a heart-stopping shriek that grew louder and louder. In a few seconds the craft would angle farther nose down and enter a spin. He had to get out now!

He reached for the canopy release and glanced at the instrument panel for the last time. Air speed: 120. Altimeter: 4,900…4,800…4,700. Variometer: pegged in descent. The aircraft, now completely on its side, pointed sixty degrees nose down, the sky no longer visible. *Shit! This thing's going into an inverted spin!* Hunter tucked his head and jerked the handle. The Plexiglas canopy flew off into the slipstream and disappeared.

He snatched his camera, released the controls, and half climbed, half rolled out of the cockpit. Drawing on years of skydiving experience, he turned with the pressure of the wind, moved away from the sailplane, then turned back again to watch it rapidly accelerate away from him. Camera in hand, he captured a few pictures as it death-spiraled toward the ground.

With the sailplane safely below him, he yanked the ripcord and watched the parachute trail out over his head. It fluttered like a giant white ribbon before the thin nylon canopy blossomed abruptly, jolting him as it arrested his descent. *Man, that's a beautiful sight!* He pulled down on the left steering toggle and held it there. A complete revolution allowed him to study the terrain in every direction. The sailplane's fuselage had slammed into the ground; apparently, though, its wings had sheared off when the craft had gained excessive speed. One wing, a good distance away, resembled a slender white pencil nestled in the saw grass. It would likely remain there for a long time. A turkey vulture cruised in close to him then began spiraling upward in a weak thermal, almost as if mocking the folly of man.

Unlike the vulture, Hunter had to accept the grim reality that when he landed, he'd be stranded in the middle of the Everglades, miles from anywhere, with just a few hours until nightfall. His best chance of rescue would be to stay with the wreckage, which remained quite visible from the air: brilliant white against a dark background. He doubted that he could stay out of the water by sleeping inside the fuselage. It was a possibility, but not a likely one. He searched for something else, *anything* else, that would provide more protection from the elements.

A hammock of trees stood off to the south, and another stood farther to the west. He couldn't see much to the north. The east didn't look promising, either, so he steered toward the wreckage, slightly northeast of him. Even though this would take him farther from the hammocks, it remained his best choice. He could hike back to the hammocks if he had to.

He soon floated directly over one of the wings, but the main wreckage still lay ahead. The other wing clung to the saw grass just east of the fuselage. He snapped pictures then scanned farther northward. He squinted. Almost due north, a small structure blended well with the swampy terrain. He couldn't be sure of its size or condition. He squinted harder. It looked like a cabin.

Eight-hundred feet below his sneakers, the saw grass waited to consume him. He'd land about half a mile short of the wreckage. He estimated that the cabin was three miles north of that and made a mental note of the sun's position to his left. On the ground, he'd be unable to see the structure; his only reference for guidance would be the sun—and that, of course, would only be until dark.

He snapped another picture of the wreckage, let the camera hang from his neck, and prepared for impact. The swamp hit harder than he'd expected and instantly soaked him to the waist. Also, the water was much colder than he'd imagined. His parachute canopy settled atop the rustling saw grass, a white flag surrendering to gravity.

Hunter unbuckled the straps and shed the harness, swatted a couple of mosquitoes, then started sloshing northeast toward the wreckage and, with any luck, a quick rescue.

CHAPTER

5

That Saturday afternoon, Morgan Lindsey had just made arrangements to meet with Lieutenant Bruce Donaldson of the Connecticut Highway Patrol when her phone rang.

"Morgan Lindsey speaking."

"Hello, Ms. Lindsey," a male voice responded. "I believe you've been expecting my call. I have something for you that I'm sure you'll find quite valuable."

Her heart skipped a beat. "Yes, I'm so glad you called again. Can we meet somewhere?" She grabbed a pencil off her desk.

"I have a restaurant in mind," the man said. "It's private, and the food is excellent. I can be there in an hour. Would that be all right with you?"

"Of course," she said. "What's the name?"

"If you're Morgan Lindsey, you'll know the restaurant because we dined there together when you interviewed me about a year ago. Shortly after that, we met again in California at a political rally."

Morgan's jaw dropped. Her mysterious source was Senator Joel Greenley, which meant that the information he'd provide would be solid and verifiable!

"Ms. Lindsey, are you there? Ms. Lindsey?"

"Ah...yes, sir. I remember the place, and I look forward to seeing you again."

"And I you," he said.

Morgan hung up and jumped to her feet, then hurriedly shuffled through the clutter on her desktop. *Crap! Where'd I leave my cell phone? Oh, here it is. Now, where's my purse? Ah, good.*

She grabbed her coat and flew out of her office. She wouldn't be late for *this* meeting. Greenley was a walking encyclopedia when it came to Washington politics. He was precisely the catapult she needed, and an honest and respected one at that.

Morgan arrived at Stefano's ten minutes early. Sandwiched between a travel agency and a used-book store, the tiny Italian eatery wasn't well known, but its regulars returned often. The instant she opened the squeaky, weather-beaten door, the delectable aroma of garlic and oregano started her salivating. She made her way along the six-foot-wide strip of green-and-white tiles that divided two rows of semiprivate booths. Virtually all the booths were empty, the crisp white-linen tablecloths, fresh daisies, and lit candle lanterns that adorned each table going unappreciated. *Saturday must be their slowest day*, she thought, *though it is a little early for dinner.*

She perked up at the sight of the senator sitting in the more secluded alcove dining area toward the rear, her sixty-three-year-old white knight, waiting to come to her rescue. He was diligently studying the menu, his reading glasses tilted so steeply on his huge head that the stems were pressed into his gray hair way above his ears.

She smiled. "Hello, Senator Greenley. It's nice to see you again."

He stood and shook her hand. "Ms. Lindsey, you're early. How nice. We'll have more time to enjoy each other's company."

They sat facing each other. He focused his brown eyes on hers. "Would you care for some wine, Ms. Lindsey?"

"I'd love some, Senator. And please, call me Morgan."

"Very well, Morgan. I'm Joel." He filled their glasses from a bottle of Robert Mondavi Cabernet Sauvignon that he'd already ordered then touched his glass to hers, toasting, "To honesty and informality."

The waiter appeared, and Morgan ordered a Caesar salad and a bowl of pasta e fagioli. The senator ordered lasagna. They both went for the garlic rolls.

For the next hour and forty-five minutes, both her appetite and her reporter's instincts were sated. She got the crucial information she needed for the article on the mayoral election and more. The guillotine would see some action. So would that catapult.

"Morgan, it's been a pleasure," the senator finally said, standing. "Unfortunately, I have a five-thirty meeting at my office, so I'd best be on my way."

"Before you go, Joel, I have one question about a totally unrelated subject. It won't take but a minute."

He glanced at his watch then eased back into his seat. "Fire away."

"I'm sure you recall when Senator Sean Buchanan died in an automobile crash about three years ago."

"Yes, I remember it well. What a tragic story. His father, the vice president, took the news hard. Hasn't been the same person since."

"Well, that leads into what I want to ask." Morgan leaned forward and lowered her voice. "I received an anonymous letter stating that Buchanan's death was a murder made to look like an accident. Poisoning, in fact."

The senator's eyebrows shot up. "That's quite an allegation."

Suddenly the front door swung open, and two men wearing dark overcoats and sunglasses entered. Morgan made a quick assessment: *midthirties, conservative suits. Could be Feds.*

Then, laughing, the men removed their overcoats and sunglasses, and sat at a booth near the front of the restaurant. *Casual business meeting*, she concluded. No concern to her.

She drew in a deep breath then exhaled slowly. "If Sean Buchanan's body needed to be exhumed for tissue samples, do you think Al Buchanan would consent?"

Joel Greenley rubbed his chin. "Al might—if he thought the results would conclusively prove or disprove such a claim."

"That's what I figured. If you don't mind, I'd like to keep the letter a secret for now. At least until I can substantiate the information in some way."

"I understand. Let me know if I can be of any help."

"I will, Joel, and thank you."

* * *

The vegetation and knee-high water slowed Hunter's progress considerably. Now he knew why Marjory Stoneman Douglas referred to the Everglades as the River of Grass. This terrain could hide the tracks of an army, much less one man. With every step, the spongy underwater vegetation rebounded, and the saw grass swayed back into place. Besides being tall enough to restrict his view, the razor-sharp saw grass repeatedly cut his hands and bare arms as he tried to protect his face. It also threatened to slice through his short-sleeved jumpsuit. A few annoying mosquitoes buzzed around, but fortunately they weren't as bad as they could be, or likely would be, come nightfall.

As he trudged along, he analyzed what had happened. Something had obviously collided with his aircraft. The explosion alone indicated that because his sailplane carried nothing explosive. It had no engine, no tanks for gasoline, no electrical connections of any sort, no battery, nothing that could cause that kind of damage, or make that sound, for that matter. The dark streak perplexed him the most; it had to be a jet fighter that was really cooking, he reasoned. That would explain why he couldn't determine its size, color, shape, or anything else about it. And since he didn't see any aircraft in the area prior to or after the impact, a fast-moving fighter made the most sense. Also, military aircraft heading up the West Coast from Homestead Air Force Base would likely cross over the Everglades in the general vicinity.

He spotted something white just ahead and sloshed toward it. It was part of the sailplane, though not the part he'd hoped. The broken wing that he'd seen just before landing the parachute lay before him. He inspected it closely. The shear began at the leading edge of the wing and progressed to the trailing edge, with most of the damaged area tainted by black scrapes. Whatever had collided with him was obviously painted black. Now the dark flash made even more sense.

The damaged wing had landed slightly east of the fuselage, he recalled, so he splashed due west until the main wreckage came into view. The fuselage lay crumpled on its side, more damaged than it had appeared from the air, the cockpit half submerged, its seat and instrument panel soaked. He wouldn't be sleeping in there; that was for damn sure. A swarm of mosquitoes had already made it their new home. A snake would likely take up residence there too. He searched the cockpit for his cell phone to no avail. If only he'd remembered it before he bailed out. It's probably underwater somewhere now. The compass had survived the impact, but he had no way of removing it from the instrument panel. He tried out the idea of sleeping on top of the fuselage, but at his slightest move, he slipped back into the water.

Eager to spot the structure he'd seen from the air, Hunter stood on the fuselage as best he could, balancing like a tightrope walker. He studied the terrain to the north, craning his neck to see over the saw grass. Wobbling about didn't help. He slipped off the fuselage, splashing himself in the face when he hit the frigid water. He climbed up again and slipped off again. He did better on his next try. He finally located the elusive structure just to the left of a small hammock.

The structure wasn't huge by any means; it did, however, appear large enough to escape the elements, so at least he could sleep for the night. He estimated it would take two hours to trudge the distance, providing he stayed on course and didn't miss the cabin altogether. If he was lucky, he'd arrive by nightfall.

*   *   *

Captain David Cunningham parked his stealth fighter and shut down the engines. He'd just popped the jet's canopy when his commanding officer, Colonel Randolph Blake, screeched to a stop in a Jeep and hopped out. He looked pissed.

"Captain Cunningham! Where in hell have you been?" he shouted. "And why did you return to this base in broad daylight?"

Cunningham exhaled deeply before climbing down from the cockpit. He saluted. "Sir! I developed engine trouble at the end of my bomb run, sir. With the altitude I had at the time, I couldn't fly out to sea, so I made an emergency landing in a remote area and camouflaged my aircraft." He hoped Blake would buy it.

The colonel stood fast and crossed his arms. "What do you mean you couldn't fly out to sea? Wasn't your target on the coast?"

"No, sir. My target was inland." Cunningham maintained his ramrod-straight posture, focusing on a spot on the wall just above Blake's head.

"What happened to your engines?"

"They stalled, sir. Both of them."

"Pilot-induced compressor stall?" Blake squawked angrily.

"No, sir," Cunningham lied, keeping his face expressionless. "The engines sputtered some before they quit. It seemed more like a fuel-flow problem, but I'm not sure. I sat for hours before I could get them to restart. My nose wheel went flat in the meantime."

Blake stepped closer and peered into Cunningham's eyes. "Captain, are you saying you took off with a flat tire on the nose gear?"

"Yes, sir, just as soon as I could. The engines sputtered a couple of times during my return flight as well, sir." Another lie. A necessary one, he reasoned. Hard to disprove anyway.

"Did anyone see you or your aircraft while you were in Cuba?"

"No one saw me in Cuba, sir. I'm certain of that. But an incident occurred just a short time ago over the Everglades, and it's possible my aircraft was seen then."

Blake's expression hardened even more. "I'm all ears, Captain. What happened?"

"Actually, I'm not completely sure," Cunningham admitted. "I may have suffered a midair with another aircraft. I saw a white flash and felt a slight bump. That was it. I haven't had a chance to check my aircraft for damage yet, sir. For all I know, it may've just been a large bird. I was traveling at high speed at the time."

They checked the fighter together and discovered a dent and white paint scrapes on the right wing.

"It was a large bird all right!" Blake screamed. "A man-made one! Damn! Now I'll have to call Washington, and we'll have to conduct a search immediately." He leaned into Cunningham's face, forcing the junior officer to pitch backward. "Maybe you'll be lucky, Captain. Maybe we'll learn that the other pilot didn't survive."

*   *   *

Hunter snapped two pictures of the fuselage, swatted a few more mosquitoes, then set out at an ambitious pace toward the structure. The faster he moved, the more cuts and scratches he got from the saw grass. He tried not to dwell on the painful aspects of his trek, concentrating instead on keeping the sun over his left shoulder as he remembered from the parachute ride. Though he turned his ankles several times on the hidden limestone surface, he slogged on, soaked, tired, and frustrated.

He wondered what Amanda was doing right at that moment. *Probably lying around with an ice pack on her forehead. Poor thing.* He was glad he'd left his cat with his next-door neighbor instead of asking Amanda to watch it. She needed a vacation as bad as he did, and she sure didn't need him asking favors of her while he was gone. He recalled the first time she'd met his cat; she'd misheard his name as Mistletoe. Cuddling it, she'd asked if he'd named it Mistletoe because he'd gotten it at Christmastime. He'd clarified that the cat's name was Missile Toes because when it got wound up, it raced through the house like it had rockets on its feet.

Hunter froze. A water moccasin lay in a clump of saw grass not an arm's length ahead. Damn big one too. Four-footer or more. Served him right for not paying attention. He hated snakes. He didn't wish them any harm; he just didn't want them around him. Ever so slowly, without once taking his eyes off the slithering beast, he backed away, then circled right, giving the snake a wide berth.

He had to keep moving. With the sun chasing the horizon, he had about forty-five minutes of good light left. Since the structure rose above the saw grass, once he neared it, it would likely be easier to see than the sailplane had been. Even so, he worried about not reaching the shelter by nightfall. Finding it in the dark might prove impossible unless he bumped right into it.

He dreaded the possibility of having to spend the night in the watery saw grass. Because the body loses temperature thirty times faster in water than it does in air, he would definitely risk hypothermia. Wildlife also worried him; so far, he'd seen one small alligator and three snakes, including the water moccasin. Avoiding them in the daylight wasn't difficult, but after dark would be another matter. He could easily walk right up on one without being aware of its presence until too late.

He increased his pace and second-guessed his decision to leave the wreckage. Though spending the night there wouldn't have been any picnic either.

Coming upon a cluster of limestone jutting from the water, he spooked a flock of cattle egrets. He clambered onto their abandoned perch to see over the saw grass. The sight of the structure about a half mile to the north raised his spirits; the sun disappearing below the horizon did not.

As twilight set in, one of his fears was realized: the mosquitoes came out in force. Their persistent buzzing around his face compelled him to vigorously flail his arms about his head. He stumbled and tripped often in the fading light, straining with every step to see the structure.

Hunter stopped for a moment and was dumbfounded to find that he still had his mini-Mag flashlight in his pocket. He'd used it to check the connection of the controls in the wings when he assembled the sailplane. He hurried on with even more determination, his light slicing away at the approaching darkness.

Finally, looming across a saw grass–free lagoon, he saw the shelter, a rustic hunting cabin with decorative lattice attached to its support pilings and a dock just above water level. Then Hunter heard it: the unmistakable heavy croaking–grunt of a large alligator. An old gator. One that had lived for many years because it knew how to survive, how to hunt its prey. A gator that was very close by.

He shone his light all around but didn't see it. It grunted again. *Shit! It's somewhere between the cabin and me.*

He stood perfectly still, training his flashlight beam out in front of him. The mosquitoes buzzing around his head sounded like a bunch of tiny chainsaws, all eagerly carving into him. They could've just about picked him up and carried him the rest of the way; there were so many. He did his best to ignore them.

"Where are you, Old Surprise? Come on, now. Show yourself," Hunter said aloud.

A noisy splash directly ahead practically wrenched the flashlight's beam to it; the beam caught the last few displaced silvery water droplets that fell back into a ring of ripples in the swamp water. The gator had been on the dock. Now it was in its own element, its silent, watery hunting ground not fifteen yards away. Hunter wondered if his uncontrollable shaking was the first stages of hypothermia or sheer fear. Or both. Certainly it was fear that drove him forward; he couldn't stay where he was.

"OK, Old Surprise," he said softly, more to calm himself than anything, "I know this is your home. I just dropped in for a short visit. I hope you've already had dinner."

The mini-Mag beam whipped around like the rotating beacon of a lighthouse. One trembling step after another brought Hunter painstakingly closer to the dock. He swallowed hard as he drew within ten feet of where he'd seen the splash. The rusty nail heads in the dock's planking were visible now.

"Just a few more steps, Old Surprise, and you won't have to worry about me anymore."

He envisioned the prehistoric beast chomping down on his shaky legs at any second. His pulse ran fast, like an overwound cheap clock; his heart pounded as though it would explode. After what seemed a lifetime, he finally placed one hand on the dock. At that same instant he spotted the gator under the surface, swimming straight for him. He clambered out of the dark water so fast his own splashing scared the hell out of him.

Weary and half eaten alive—by the mosquitoes, he studied his salvation. A narrow wooden stairway led up to a screened porch, a welcome refuge from hungry bloodsuckers. He had bites on top of bites.

It took Hunter mere seconds to make his way up the stairs and into the sheltering porch. He shone his flashlight onto the cabin itself.

The front wall had one window and a door. He jiggled the knob, but the door was locked. He didn't really expect otherwise. He peered through the window. Although small, the cabin appeared cozy. A single bed hugged the wall to the right, while a kitchen cabinet with a sink claimed the wall to the left. A round unfinished wooden table and a couple of chairs occupied the middle of the room. A folded newspaper and a cardboard box sat on the tabletop, while a throw rug underneath the table decorated the otherwise bare plywood floor. A short hallway led to two other rooms that he couldn't see into.

He tried the knob again with more energy. It wouldn't budge. The window, sealed tight, had bars on the inside; he wouldn't get in that way. He shone his flashlight around the porch and back to the front door. A doormat. Could it be that easy? he wondered. He flipped the mat over eagerly. No key. That would've been too much to ask. But a key had to be hidden somewhere.

He climbed onto a weather-beaten rocking chair and trained his flashlight along everything he could see from that level. He reached for the far side of a rafter and lost his balance. A few choice words flew into the night. As he righted the chair, his flashlight reflected off something small and shiny. The key! It must have been hidden in the chair, the last place he would've thought to look.

*　　*　　*

Enrique Gomez stepped wearily through the open door of his brother's office on Saturday evening. He closed the door behind him then flopped down on the imported Italian leather sofa and rubbed his eyes with both hands.

Pedro leaned back in his chair, puffed on a Cohiba, and blew smoke rings toward the ceiling. "A long day, huh, Enrique? What is up?"

"We have a problem, Pedro. Your damn cousin, Juan Carlos, did not follow the instructions we gave him."

Pedro frowned. "He's your cousin too."

"I know. And believe me, I wish he was not. Then I could have the great pleasure of getting rid of him."

"Did he look for the tape?"

"Yes, he sure did." Enrique stood, straightened an oil painting on the wall, then began to pace. "When Juan could not find the recording, he became angry."

Pedro groaned. "Not again. What did he do this time?" He stubbed out the cigar and braced himself.

"Not much. Just destroyed Mahoy's office and his secretary's as well."

"How do you know?"

"Juan bragged about it!" Enrique slammed his fist down on Pedro's massive oak desk. "Can you believe that? The fucking asshole bragged about it to my face!"

Pedro locked eyes with his brother. "Shit! We should have known. Juan cannot control his temper."

Enrique resumed his pacing. "Do you not see? He did it because we told him not to. He is becoming more difficult to control. And he has made matters worse. Mahoy will know we learned about the recording from José Espinosa."

"Good. Then the *gringo* will not go to the FBI anymore."

Enrique spun around and faced Pedro. "It is not good. It is very bad. Now we do not know what Mahoy will do with that tape."

Pedro shrugged. "Maybe we can buy it. Everyone has a price," he said, cracking his knuckles.

"I thought of that. I tried to call him at his office. His service says he is on vacation. His home number is not listed. He could be anywhere." Enrique sat down. "This whole mess is Juan Carlos's fault."

"Are you forgetting the *gringo* made the recording?"

"That is not the point, Pedro. Juan did not have to open his big mouth in Mahoy's office. We should let Juan hang with what is on that tape. He is the one who put the tainted bottle in the senator's car. The problem is, he would finger us as accomplices and reveal things we do not want anyone to know. No. We have no choice. We have to protect him to protect us. I swear, Pedro, if I had not promised *Tía Olivia* on her deathbed in Cuba to look after her precious son, I might have done him in myself by now. Damn him!"

*   *   *

Hunter let himself into the cabin, shivering uncontrollably, even though he was out of the water and the wind. He hadn't realized just how cold he'd become. He walked down the short hallway and found a bathroom complete with a toilet, a sink, and a bucket with a rope tied to the handle for dipping water from the swamp. Turning, he stood in the doorway of the tiny room opposite the bathroom: an eight-by-eight bedroom furnished with a single bed and a well-used chest of drawers. Nothing more could have fit in the room. A search of the drawers made his day. He found a pair of blue jeans, shorts, T-shirts, even socks.

He set his flashlight and camera on top of the chest and undressed, checking his pockets out of habit. The credit card he'd used at the gliderport was still with him. He placed it next to his camera then wriggled into a snug pair of Levi's that were a couple of inches too short. He managed to zip them but didn't bother with the button. On the other hand, an extra-large T-shirt fit just fine. He gave only a brief moment's thought to the incongruity of the sizes.

He walked back to the kitchen and found a kerosene lantern and a box of matches keeping company on the kitchen counter. Lifting the lantern's chimney, he ignited the wick and adjusted its burn, then killed his flashlight and warmed his hands above the globe. He finally stopped shivering.

He did some further investigating. The lower cabinets, about six feet long, had a double-basin sink without water hookups, though the drains were connected; they were attached to a pipe that penetrated the floor. An overhead cabinet hung on each side of a small window. He eagerly checked the cabinet on the right. It contained only dishes. But the cabinet to the left housed an assortment of canned goods. Choosing a can of tuna, he searched the only two drawers for an opener. One drawer held silverware, the other junk. Neither had a can opener, so he used a knife.

He inventoried the lower cabinets while dining and found pots and pans, several bottles of Pepsi, three gallons of drinking water, a half-full large jar of Maxwell House instant coffee, paper towels, and a can of insect repellent. *Sure could've used this earlier,* he thought, handling it. The last cabinet on the right stored a propane camping stove but no propane. He polished off the tuna and a couple of glasses of Pepsi, then stepped out onto the front porch.

Reveling in their domain, hundreds of frogs—maybe even thousands—sang almost in unison, yet each was separately distinct. Meanwhile, Old Surprise grunted down below as if welcoming him to the neighborhood. Flashlight in hand, he descended to the dock to look for the lingering dinosaur. Two eerie greenish-yellow eyes stared at him from about twenty feet away. Damn. He was a big one, maybe twelve feet, the largest Hunter had ever seen.

The mosquitoes weren't too bad for the moment, so he studied the terrain in the darkness. The glow on the eastern horizon betrayed the location of a city he couldn't see, Miami. To the south-southeast glowed the lights of Homestead. Miles and miles from anywhere, he wondered how long he'd be stranded out there. Amanda came to mind. Why hadn't he stayed with her? If he had, he probably wouldn't have gone soaring, and he might even be in bed with her right now. But then again, things could be worse; he could have been injured or killed in that midair, or stuck in the cold swamp water with the mosquitoes all night. So even though he might have a difficult time returning to civilization, Hunter felt truly grateful to be at that cabin. Looking up, he said a short prayer.

Millions of tiny lights beckoned from the clear, moonless night sky. He hadn't seen the stars that brilliant in years and was able to pinpoint several constellations. Far to the north, cloud cover was moving in. He recalled the weather report for the next couple of days: another front would pass through, bringing more rain and colder temperatures. But standing in dry clothes at a shelter with a soft bed, he wasn't terribly concerned about the weather.

He went back inside. Since the small bedroom would be warmer, he chose to sleep there, grabbing the blanket from the bed in the kitchen. He lay down, listening to the frogs' enchanting serenade and trying to think about the future. But his thoughts quickly faded as he drifted into sleep.

CHAPTER

"Good morning, gentlemen," Colonel Randolph Blake began. "Sorry to drag you out on a Sunday, and a cold and wet one at that. The search you're about to conduct is for a light aircraft that went down yesterday. Only eight of you were selected because I've been ordered to keep a lid on this thing." He leaned against the podium. "I don't want anyone else to know what we're doing. I don't even want them to know we're here. Understood?"

He scanned the briefing room, making eye contact with each of the assembled search personnel. These men, four of his best pilots and four trackers, wouldn't let him down. "You'll operate as two-man teams. Two teams will search from the air, the other two from air-boats in the swamp itself. Major Dennis Kruzinski will be in charge of the air search. Captain Marco Garelli, you'll control the ground operation."

"Colonel Blake, sir," Major Kruzinski said, "in light of today's weather, wouldn't it be more practical to begin the search tomorrow?"

Blake nodded curtly. "It would, but time is of the essence, so we must begin immediately. I realize visibility will be extremely limited, and we have a large area to cover, but we might get lucky. Besides, today's bad weather has two advantages. No one else will be out there, plus it'll cloak our activity nicely."

Captain Garelli stepped forward. "Sir. Do we know how many people were aboard the downed aircraft?"

"As yet, no downed aircraft report has been made to any agency," Blake said. "That's to our advantage. All we do know is that one of our stealth fighters collided with it. Judging from the damage to the stealth, the civilian aircraft has likely been rendered unflyable. It's possible that the person or persons aboard perished, but we have no way of knowing their status until we locate the wreckage."

"If we find anyone alive, should we follow standard procedure of requesting a Medivac helicopter?" Garelli asked.

Blake hesitated. "No. Contact me directly. I'll handle that." He scanned the men. "If there are no other questions, let's get started. And remember, exercise radio silence unless you spot something."

*   *   *

Hunter woke to the sound of rain pounding the cabin roof. He lay there for a while, listening to the pleasant rhythm of the heavy downpour as he tried to go back to sleep, but his mind had already engaged in thought. Every muscle in his body ached when he stood. He stretched his stiff, sore frame then ran in place for a minute to get his circulation going. He hadn't planned a course of action, but considering the weather and how he felt, he would simply stay put and hope for a search plane.

He hobbled to the bathroom where he studied his saw grass–scarred, mosquito-bitten reflection. As bad as his face looked, his arms and hands fared much worse. Using fresh water, he washed away the dried blood and dirt. The lacerations soon became less obvious, and his appearance greatly improved.

Outside, the deluge consumed all visibility beyond a quarter mile. He wouldn't see any search planes until the weather improved. Standing on the cold, damp porch, he considered the condition he'd likely be in if he had stayed with the sailplane wreckage. He shivered. Again he gave thanks for his good fortune.

Back inside, he made a more diligent search for propane, finally checking the box on the table. More good fortune: it contained one new bottle of propane, along with a few old newspapers and more canned goods—mostly soups, a can of bug spray, a roll of paper towels, a bottle of dish detergent, and a can opener. Obviously the supplies had been brought to restock the cabin, but why were they on the table in a box? He examined the newspapers. They were dated August 21 and August 22, 1992. Just two days before Hurricane Andrew blew into town. So that was it. Someone must've come out in a rush to secure the cabin for the storm and didn't bother to put away the new supplies. But that was almost two years ago. Why hadn't they returned?

Hunter connected the propane canister to the stove, and the welcome aroma of coffee soon filled the air. He rummaged through the junk drawer and found batteries, a deck of cards, a short length of rope, a notepad, pencils, a pocketknife, a few single-edged razor blades, a key, and a butane cigarette lighter that sparked but wouldn't flame.

Cradling the hot coffee cup between his hands, Hunter stared out the window. Because of the cold, he'd be foolish to try to walk out of there. If he didn't make it to civilization by nightfall, he'd be in real trouble. Besides, he didn't relish the idea of trudging through the water and saw grass and mosquitoes and snakes and alligators again. To get to a road, he'd have to deal with all that for at least twenty miles. The three miles he'd trekked the day before were quite enough, thank you very much. No, he'd stay at the cabin until a plane or an airboat found him. He had a warm, safe shelter with enough supplies to last for several days. He shook his head wryly. True, it would be peaceful and relaxing out there in that solitude, but he sure hadn't planned to spend his time off this way. Some vacation!

The remainder of the day passed uneventfully. He played solitaire for a while, but soon after twilight faded into total darkness, he turned in. Old Surprise bid him good night from close by the dock.

Waking early the following morning, Hunter shambled into the kitchen. With little else to do, and the rain continuing, heavy at times, he sat at the table thumbing through the old newspapers. One headline in particular caught his attention: HURRICANE ANDREW

Approaching South Florida. The article described the storm's westerly course and predicted it would slam into the South Florida coastline within the next twenty-four to forty-eight hours. It advised readers to stay tuned to weather reports and prepare for evacuation from any low-lying areas because Andrew was expected to strengthen as it approached land.

And strengthen it did, Hunter recalled, dropping the newspaper into his lap. Hurricane Andrew had literally destroyed most of South Dade County and the Homestead area, including Homestead Air Force Base, which supposedly had hurricane-proof hangars. The official reports months later claimed that Hurricane Andrew had had maximum sustained winds of 140 miles per hour, with gusts to 180. Rumor and speculation persisted that the storm had been much stronger, however, because reports had been made of instruments recording winds of slightly more than two-hundred miles per hour in some locations.

Hunter remembered the whole area looking like a bombed-out war zone. A great deal of damage had occurred to structures that were supposed to have been hurricane-proof. Concrete telephone poles lay broken and shattered, their reinforcing steel twisted like pretzels. Concrete tie beams had sheared away, concrete roof structures had failed, and so on. Relief workers flooded in by the thousands. Then the military arrived, its helicopters flying back and forth transporting who knows what, its armed personnel assigned the task of controlling traffic and preventing looting. Most people in South Florida had become complacent about hurricanes, but not anymore. Not after Andrew.

Hunter read the newspapers from cover to cover. While studying the obituaries for August 22, he heard the sound of an engine in the distance. Dropping the paper, he bolted through the door then hobbled down the steps to the dock. He searched the drizzling gray sky before realizing that the sound emanated from low on the horizon. An airboat. The noise grew louder but then began to fade.

Straining his eyes and ears, Hunter stood staring off into the distance for a long time, hoping the craft would return. It didn't.

*　　*　　*

Sergeant Amos Ferguson shoved the throttle to idle and the airboat slid to a stop. He removed his glasses then wiped the rain from his face with his bare hand. "Hey, Captain, how much farther to the next cabin we're supposed to check?"

Garelli dropped his map and binoculars into his lap and peeled off his sopping-wet gloves. He blew warm breath into his cupped hands. "If I knew for sure where we were, I could tell you," he shouted over the unmuffled engine, "but the visibility in this rain makes navigating nearly impossible. I can't see far enough ahead to recognize *anything*!"

Ferguson studied the amount of rainwater that had collected in the bottom of the boat; he'd have to turn on the bilge pump again soon. "I know. This is really stupid. The only way we'll find anything out here today is if we crash right into it. Why don't we return to the cabin we just left and sit this one out? No one will ever know."

"Sounds like a great idea to me," Garelli said. "I'm so cold my fingers are numb, and I'm getting the shakes. If the brass is in such a hurry to find that damned wreckage, why don't they come out here and look for it themselves?"

"Because they can order peons like us to do it," Ferguson said. He advanced the throttle again to retrace their path.

*　　*　　*

"Morgan Lindsey?" the towering highway patrol officer asked, his eyes hidden behind dark sunglasses.

Morgan sized him up. His toned body, muscular in all the right places, fit perfectly into his crisp light-brown uniform and nicely complemented his chiseled features. The wide gloss-black accessory belt—complete with pepper spray, handcuffs, and holstered gun—flashed brightly in the sunlight, as did his silver nametag. She couldn't read it.

"Yes. Good morning. You must be Lieutenant Donaldson."

"No, Ma'am. Pete Mitchell." His vise-grip handshake consumed hers. "Welcome to Connecticut, Ms. Lindsey. Lieutenant Donaldson asked me to apologize for him. He got called out on an emergency. He'll join us later if he can."

"I see."

He tipped his sunglasses and peered over the lenses. His pale-blue eyes made direct contact with hers. "Now don't be disappointed. I can be quite charming. It's a beautiful autumn Monday. We can have lunch, get to know each other, get married, whatever." He beamed a smile that would've made a blind person squint.

She laughed. "Are you always this forward?"

"No. Usually I hide in the shadows and shiver."

"Yeah, right," she said. "I've got a big picture of that."

His face abruptly sobered. "On a more serious note, Ms. Lindsey, I was the first one on the scene of Senator Buchanan's horrific accident that night. Lieutenant Donaldson felt that I could answer many of your questions in his absence. I thought we might visit the accident site if you'd like."

"Yes, that'd be great. And, please, call me Morgan."

A few minutes later they roared out of the state police parking lot in his patrol car, heading toward Bridgeport on Interstate 95. They passed a fully loaded logging truck, then a blue and white motor home with Georgia plates; a tabby cat was watching from the back window.

Morgan opened the conversation. "I researched the *Washington Herald* articles about the incident, so I know it sleeted that night. But just how bad was the weather, Pete?"

He gave her a quick glance. "Well, I've been out in worse conditions, but not often. In fact, I parked under an overpass to keep the sleet from coating my windshield, and because it was far safer than driving. I got the call at two-forty-seven in the morning." He adjusted his sunglasses. "Traffic is always light on the interstate at that hour, but that night it was virtually nonexistent, and for good reason. Even though I'd just sprayed some deicer on my windshield, I could barely see out by the time I arrived at the accident scene fifteen minutes later."

She turned to face him. "So the road was slippery."

He nodded. "The salt spreaders and plows had done a good job of keeping the interstate open, but yes, slippery would be an accurate description."

"Do you think it's possible that Buchanan simply lost control of his car because of the weather and not necessarily because of the alcohol?"

He turned down the volume on the police radio, which had suddenly sprung to life. "No, I don't. Buchanan's vehicle had been traveling in excess of one-hundred miles per hour when it struck that bridge support. No one with a clear head would've been going that fast in such bad weather. And the autopsy proved he'd been driving under the influence."

Mitchell slowed his patrol car near an overpass, steered into the median, then killed the engine. He leaned back, stretched his long arm across the back of the seat, and stared out the windshield in silence. Half a minute later, the Georgia motor home passed them by, the tabby still watching.

"You're not going to try to convince me we've run out of gas, are you, Pete?"

He smiled sadly and studied her with his bottomless blue eyes. "No, Morgan. Though I wouldn't mind pulling that on you some-time, I'd never do it here." He swallowed hard and got out of the vehicle.

Kicking herself, she followed. "I'm sorry, Pete. That was incredibly insensitive of me. I didn't—"

"It's all right. Really." His shadow eclipsed her. "Come on now. Let's take care of business."

He choked up describing the many locations in which he'd found Sean Buchanan's mutilated body. Morgan started to cry. She'd never before considered just how awful that part of a highway patrol-man's job could be. And she now better understood why, according to Senator Greenley, Albert Buchanan was still having a difficult time dealing with his only son's death.

They returned to the patrol car. As they traveled south through Bridgeport on their way back to the station, she asked, "Did the Scotch bottle survive the impact, Pete?"

"Yes, almost unscathed. Isn't that ironic as hell? I found it wedged neck down without a cap. The cap was never located. The investigation had concluded that a certain amount of the liquor had flowed from the bottle while it was stuck in that position, but just how much couldn't be determined."

"So it could've been nearly full at the time of the crash?"

"Or nearly empty."

Morgan mulled over something he had said. "What did you mean that the bottle was almost unscathed? Was it cracked?"

He glanced in the rearview mirror before changing lanes. "Cracked? No. But a portion of the label was torn away."

"What became of the bottle?"

"I don't know. Because the accident involved the death of a senator, the FBI handled the investigation. I suppose the FBI has the bottle, if it still exists."

She rested her head on the seat back for a while, the soothing hum of the powerful horses under the hood the only sound.

Mitchell interrupted her reverie. "I know this is going to sound like a pickup line, Morgan, but I know this great little restaurant on the water. Can I treat you to lunch?"

*　　*　　*

Hunter turned to climb the stairs from the dock when he noticed the many telephone-type wooden poles supporting the cabin. Was something heavy, perhaps the roof, weighing on the unusually large support in the center? He hadn't noticed it before because of the lattice and extensive X bracing attached from post to post, but now that he studied it, the large support seemed out of place. At least three-and-a-half feet in diameter, it dwarfed the other supports, all less than a third its size.

He was still pondering the puzzle when the drizzle suddenly intensified, so he hurried upstairs to the porch, where he watched the rain come down in sheets. Wave after wave skimmed across the swampy landscape, the saw grass swaying in unison with each torrent. When Hunter went back inside, he yawned at the gloomy interior. Giving in to his sleepiness, he lay down on the bed in the main room and soon fell asleep.

Hunter woke several hours later and ventured back onto the porch. A startled great blue heron lumbered from the dock and landed a short distance out in the swamp. The rain had let up, but the sky was still overcast. He stared into the expansive view and wondered when he might be rescued. His car was at the gliderport, so surely someone must be looking for him by now. Then he remembered telling the tow pilot, Brandon, that if conditions allowed, he might fly cross-country. *Shit*. Brandon probably assumed he'd flown upstate and put down somewhere. Hunter rubbed his chin. Days could pass before anyone became concerned. And since glider pilots weren't required to file flight plans, they wouldn't know where to look anyway. Plus, he hadn't told anybody at work what he planned to do on his vacation, not even Amanda. He'd purposely been vague because he didn't want anyone to find him. He wanted some peace, to be left by himself for a while. He looked around and laughed. It might just work out that way.

His best hope involved the midair collision. The other pilot would certainly report the accident and the crash of an aircraft, unless the other aircraft had also crashed. But he hadn't seen any smoke while suspended from the parachute, so the other plane had probably made it to a base or an airport somewhere. There would be a search, he concluded. Aircraft would take to the sky as soon as the weather improved.

Another nightfall was approaching. Time for dinner. Hunter sat at the table and dined on chicken soup, canned peas, and Pepsi. Several peas rolled off his fork and fell onto the floor. Reaching for them, he glanced at the throw rug under the table and recalled the support columns. The table was directly above the largest member. Scrutinizing the rafters, the walls, and even the kitchen cabinets, he couldn't understand why a support was needed in the middle of the cabin, especially such a large one.

He didn't dwell on it long; the frogs were warming up for their nightly gig, a well-rehearsed repertoire. Hauling himself out to the porch, he settled into the weathered rocking chair to listen for a while. Old Surprise was quiet that evening. Probably out looking for dinner. Already Hunter longed for company and conversation. Way off to the north, the flashing wingtip lights of a jetliner making its final approach into Miami International Airport caught his eye, too far away to do him any good.

He loved flying. The view of the earth's surface from thirty-thousand feet always captivated him. And the concept of cruising along at five-hundred-fifty miles per hour in total comfort while eating dinner, watching a movie, or sleeping still fascinated him. He yearned for passage on that jetliner right now. In a matter of minutes, even a small plane would travel the distance he was stranded from the city.

He thought of the most recent trip he'd taken for work, to Houston. What a pain! He'd been on tight deadlines to meet clients who barely had time to see him. Even so, every one of them wanted him to find more ways to beat their taxes. He understood that desire. He had it too. Everyone did. But they were never satisfied. Never.

He decided right then and there to leave the firm rather than become a partner. But what would he do? Reenlist in the air force? It was a possibility, he supposed. Maybe he'd take a job flying charters down to the islands. That'd be fun for a while.

He considered the myriad places he'd flown to. His favorite trips had been with Morgan Lindsey. They'd known each other since college and had planned to marry but for an insurmountable argument. Morgan had moved to Washington DC to take a job as a reporter for the *Washington Herald*. He hadn't spoken with her for nearly three years now but had made a habit of picking up a copy of the *Herald* from a bookstore near his house. He monitored her career through the articles she wrote.

They'd met the beginning of their freshman year at Florida State University in Tallahassee. He'd arrived with his belongings a few days before the start of the fall semester and was having difficulty locating a place to live; everything seemed to be taken. Then he answered a newspaper ad for a roommate to share expenses in an apartment. To this day he remembered the exact wording of the ad: STUDENT DESPERATELY NEEDS MALE ROOMMATE TO SPLIT EXPENSES OF LARGE FURNISHED TWO-BEDROOM APARTMENT AT THE OAKS, ONLY THREE

Blocks From Campus. Must Be Neat, Quiet, and Responsible. Serious Inquiries Only. $400 Per Month.

He'd stood poised to ring the bell when Morgan opened the door, startling both of them. She'd taken his breath away. She was so beautiful. He told her that he was responding to the ad, but she interrupted to inform him the newspaper had made a mistake. The ad was supposed to request a *female* roommate. Excusing herself, she pushed past him, explaining that she was running late to catch a bus. He hustled down the stairs with her and doggedly explained his problem. He swore he could easily afford the high monthly payments.

His pleading and delaying tactics caused her to miss the bus, to her obvious frustration. He offered to drive her to her destination, but she refused. He insisted, saying it was his fault that she'd missed the bus, and he wouldn't take no for an answer. Finally she relented, and on the way, he persuaded her to give him a try.

Hunter smiled at the memory. He'd bribed her with an offer to pay the entire rent and lend her his car whenever she needed it.

After their freshman year, he received an appointment to the Air Force Academy in Colorado Springs and finished out his college there. On their mutual graduations, he remained in the air force while she accepted a job in Miami. Their relationship endured the distance for several years, with him flying into Homestead Air Force Base as often as possible to see her. Soon after flying in Operation Desert Storm, he left the service. He interviewed for a job as a tax consultant in Miami and got hired on the spot. He moved in with her again, and they stayed together until she accepted the job in DC, leaving him involved up to his eyeballs at the firm in Miami.

Hunter missed Morgan terribly and had nearly called her on numerous occasions, but always resisted.

He smiled as he imagined her investigating Sean Buchanan's murder like a bloodhound on the scent. He wondered if she'd made any progress. He could see her now: making calls, writing notes, chasing leads. She was neck deep in it already. He had no doubt of that. From the moment she read his letter, she'd be on a collision course with the facts. It was her nature; she was powerless to stop it. He knew that better than she did. And she would have read the letter. He had no doubt of that either. The question mark for a return address would've gotten under her skin. He grinned. She would have resisted opening the envelope until she couldn't stand it any longer. He figured it sat on her desk for an hour and a half tops.

Hunter was awakened Tuesday morning by the sound of a plane close by. He bolted upright then leaped to his feet. Hurrying to get outside, he ran smack into the table in the main room, bounced off, and flew out the front door. He was down on the dock in an instant. Blocking the sun with his hand, he searched the clear, blue sky. Then he spotted it: a single-engine Cessna directly overhead at about a thousand feet, traveling northwest.

"Hey, look down here! Come on!" he shouted, waving his arms wildly. "Look back! Come on! Come on!"

But the plane continued traveling northwest, not deviating from its heading.

Hunter stared after it wistfully. If only he'd heard it sooner, he might have been outside in time to attract the pilot's attention. He watched the plane shrink to a tiny dot then disappear completely. He consoled himself that it was still early. The clear weather and excellent visibility suggested there'd be others.

As he climbed the stairs, his aching thigh reminded him that he'd slammed into the table. No doubt he'd soon sport a colorful bruise in that spot. He entered the cabin expecting to see the table knocked out of place. To his surprise, it hadn't moved at all. It remained perfectly centered on the throw rug.

Perplexed, he shoved it. It didn't move. Then he tried to lift it. No dice. Kneeling, he peeled the rug back to the table legs, exposing a joint in the flooring. He moved to the other side and lifted the rug. Same thing. A third side revealed another seam in the floor, along with a small hole about one inch in diameter. What the—?

Hunter suddenly realized that the massive support underneath the structure had to be a hollow tube for storage, with the table mounted to the access hatch. He stuck his index finger in the hole and tried to lift the floorboard, but it was latched. He wiggled his finger around the underside of the hole until he found and triggered the release mechanism.

He tried again to raise the hatch using the finger hole. It was too heavy. He stood and paused for a second, then reached out and placed both hands beneath the lip of the table. As he lifted, the hatch opened. The empty mug he'd left on the table the previous day crashed to the floor, shattering noisily; the newspaper fell on top of it. The table tilted back as the hatch opened to expose, of all things, an inner hatch. It resembled the type Hunter had seen in submarine movies: a round metal hatch with a wheel that rotated to unlatch the mechanism, after which the hatch would swing open on a single hinge point. He scratched his scruffy face and stared at the anomaly, but only briefly.

Kneeling again, he placed his hands on the wheel and strained to turn it to the right. It wouldn't budge. He then tried to the left. Though stiff, it moved. He continued turning until it stopped. Releasing the wheel, he stared at the hatch, assuming that when he opened it, he would find a cache of guns or food stores or maybe even money. He was apprehensive about opening it. He didn't know why, really, just a feeling—maybe because the idea seemed so unlikely for a rustic hunting cabin out in the middle of the Everglades. Finally he reached over, placed his hands on the cool steel wheel again, and lifted.

CHAPTER

Colonel Randolph Blake snapped to attention. It was half-past eight Tuesday morning, and the chairman of the Joint Chiefs, General Lamar Hager, had just entered the briefing room.

"Good morning, sir," Blake said, saluting crisply.

Hager reciprocated. "At ease, Colonel. This had better be important. My schedule was jammed enough before this morning's jaunt here to Homestead Air Force Base. You want to bring me up to speed?"

Blake explained in detail then held his breath. Why in hell had Hager made the trip anyway? He could have stayed in Washington and been updated by phone.

Hager paced silently toward the map wall at the end of the room, his hands clasped behind his back. Turning, he said, "You've exercised good judgment, Colonel. And we're most fortunate not to have lost the stealth fighter. But we must find the civilian aircraft and its pilot. Check with your search teams to see if they have anything to report."

"General Hager, sir, they have orders to contact me the instant they have a sighting. I don't see—"

"Do it anyway."

"Yes, sir." Blake pivoted and headed for the communications room where his operator reported that there'd been no word as yet. Sighing inwardly, the colonel went back to the briefing room. "Nothing, sir," he reported.

This happened twice more within the hour, with Hager constantly reminding Blake that they had to find that damned plane fast.

When Hager had paced to the far end of the room yet again, Blake cleared his throat. "If I may make a suggestion, sir, why don't you ride with one of my pilots? You'll be right up there where the action is, plus be another pair of eyes searching for the wreckage. That way when something's spotted, you'll be the first to know."

Hager instantly spun around and pointed his left index finger at Blake. He seemed about to say something then apparently changed his mind. He stood frozen like an ice sculpture, emotionless as a stone. But then he smiled. "If I were in your shoes, Colonel, I'd want me out of here too. I accept your offer."

Relieved, though taking pains not to show it, Blake had his aide escort the general to the tarmac.

Blake sighed heavily and eased into a chair the moment Hager left the room. He leaned forward, elbows propped on his knees, and buried his face in his hands. Finding the pilot of the downed aircraft was important. Any idiot could see that. But why was Hager so damned uptight about it? Hell, these things took time. The general knew that. Obviously there was more to the operation than what Blake knew, and he'd just as soon keep it that way. For now his only concern involved finding that damned wreckage and the pilot. He dreaded the possibility of coming up empty-handed again on this third day of the search, especially with Hager on his back.

Blake rose then crossed over to the wall map. The search grids, marked with red highlighter, practically jumped off the paper at him. He rubbed his chin with one hand and traced a line on the chart with the other. The flight crews thought they were searching too far north. They could be right. Maybe they should look farther south. He hustled over to the communications room and gave the revised order. Now all he could do was wait and hope.

*　　*　　*

Morgan Lindsey was strolling down the corridor to her office Tuesday morning when she heard the phone on her desk ringing. She broke into a run, digging in her purse for her keys at the same time. "Crap! Where are they?" she said aloud. She fished them out just as she reached her door. As she hurriedly turned the key in the lock, she heard her answering machine pick up. Dr. Harrison Shafer was leaving her a message. She flung the door open and scrambled for the receiver. "Dr. Schafer? Hello. Thank you for…returning my call." She reached for a pencil and tried to catch her breath.

"No problem. What can I do for you, Ms. Lindsey?"

"I understand you performed the autopsy on Senator Sean Buchanan three years ago. If you don't mind, I'd like to ask you a few questions."

"Not at all. What would you like to know?"

"Did you find anything unusual during the examination, Doctor?"

"No. From what I remember, everything was consistent with the means of death. Nothing out of the ordinary showed up on the toxicology tests either other than the elevated level of alcohol."

Morgan tapped the eraser end of the pencil on her desk as she spoke. "Given the—how shall I put this?—condition of the body, would the autopsy have been done differently than, say, with a completely intact subject?"

"No, not really. While I'd have to admit that Buchanan's autopsy was more difficult to perform, essentially the same procedure was followed. And the same tests were conducted." He paused. "You're tiptoeing your way to a specific question, aren't you, Ms. Lindsey?"

She had written the word *poison* on her desktop calendar and was doodling around it. "You're most perceptive, Dr. Schafer. Yes, I am. But I don't want to offend you."

"Hit me with it. I can take it."

"OK, brace yourself: could Senator Buchanan have been poisoned?" She cringed then waited. A pigeon flew past her window. A horn sounded on the busy street below. Somewhere far off in the distance, a siren wailed mournfully. All the while, she repeatedly slid her fingers down the pencil, flipped it to the opposite end, then slid her fingers again. "Dr. Schafer?"

He paused a few beats longer. "The answer is yes, Ms. Lindsey. Why? Do you have any indication that he was?"

"At the moment I'm drafting a scenario to that effect. I have no actual proof. But you say it's possible?"

"Yes. I'm sure you realize that hundreds of poisons exist in the world. Plant derivatives, chemicals, fungi, insects, snakes, medicines, and synthetic drugs are all examples of where poisons originate. A great many would be evident in a standard autopsy, but some can only be detected by knowing what poison, or poisons, to look for."

She slid her fingers to the pointed end of the pencil and started scribbling some notes. "In my story, exhuming the body is suggested," she said. "If the type of poison was known, would it still be detectable three years later?"

"It's possible, but there'd be no guarantee." Shafer paused again then asked, "Tell me, in your scenario, has the body been cremated?"

"Oh, my gosh! I hadn't thought of that. Was he, Dr. Schafer?"

"I've no idea, Ms. Lindsey," he said through his laughter. "Just thought I'd throw you a curve. I'd appreciate you letting me know what you find out. And if there's anything I can do to help, don't hesitate to give me another call."

*   *   *

Hunter stared into the open hatch. My god! *What in hell have I stumbled on?* Slack-jawed, he sat on the floor and gaped. "I don't believe this," he said aloud. "If I wasn't seeing it with my own…this wasn't meant to be found."

Should he close the hatch and latch it again? Place the table back upright and pretend he'd never found it? He couldn't. His curiosity would never allow that. He'd have to investigate further.

He leaned forward until he could see straight down into a round concrete shaft that descended deep into the ground. A metal ladder was bolted to one side of the solid concrete wall. Was he dreaming? He shook his head, blinking a few times. Single-bulb light fixtures, spaced about ten feet apart, burned on the wall directly behind the ladder. There must be a generator, he reasoned, but where? And why was the shaft there in the first place? He grabbed a spoon, held it over the center of the opening, then released it. It fell for a long time, making a tinny sound when it finally hit bottom.

"This shaft is dry?" *Maybe I am dreaming. Maybe this really isn't Tuesday, and I'm not really stuck way out here in the Everglades in this tiny cabin. Yeah, right. I wish.* He had a vivid imagination but doubted whether even his subconscious could dream this. Part of him didn't really want to explore any further—Pandora's box and all that. But nothing would stop him from going down for a look.

He snatched his flashlight off the counter, stuck it in his pocket, and started descending. There wasn't a lot of room in the shaft. Damn humid too. Every so often his shoulders rubbed against the damp walls. The shaft was suffused with a slightly musty odor that grew stronger the farther down he traveled. *How far does this thing go?* he wondered. The heat from each light seemed to increase the sweat accumulation on his brow. Even there, deep beneath the Everglades, the bulb covers entombed hundreds of tiny insects. He glanced up; the hatch was just a mere dot of light at this point. Soon he detected another aroma quite different from, but mixing with, the musty odor. He sniffed a couple of times, concentrating on it. *Man, that's familiar, really familiar.*

Suddenly the shaft emerged into a huge chamber, but the ladder continued down the wall of the chamber to the floor. Hunter stepped off the bottom rung wide-eyed and openmouthed. It wasn't a chamber at all. It was a tunnel. A massive dome-shaped tunnel. And it was cool, like a cave. "Pandora's box, all right," he mumbled, pirouetting slowly until he'd made a complete revolution. The distance from the floor to the highest point of the ceiling exceeded thirty feet. The floor stretched at least seventy feet from one wall to the other. And the tunnel itself extended in each direction for as far as he could see.

Aided by the perspiration on his face, he detected a slight draft, which suggested that fresh air somehow entered the passageway. Kerosene! That's what that smell was! Which got Hunter wondering, *Why does the tunnel smell like kerosene when it has electric lighting?*

Lights mounted several feet apart at the apex of the ceiling cast their patterns on the floor below, leaving dark shadows in between. Though minimal, the fixtures adequately illuminated the tunnel's basic shape, size, and direction. All surfaces were solid concrete. The floor was pitched to center drainage grates placed at regular intervals. Hunter reasoned that they collected the water that leaked in periodically. The grates probably connected to a pipe for pumping the water back to the surface.

Two painted white lines on the floor ran parallel to the walls. One on each side of the center grate, they were spaced halfway between the grate and the side walls. Tire tracks marred the floor.

On the wall opposite the ladder, several conduits clung to the concrete at about eye level. Hunter crossed the tunnel to study them more closely. One had a diameter of at least ten inches. Three others measured about four inches across, mounted with a couple of smaller ones. Attached according to size, the conduits graduated from larger to smaller, the largest one being the closest to the floor. All the lines were electrical except for the largest one, which was constructed differently and clearly had a special purpose.

Though he could only guess at the destination of the massive tunnel, Hunter certainly knew who built it: the military. Only the military could secure enough funds for something like that and keep it a secret both during and after construction. Someone had once told him of a fuel pipeline running from Miami International Airport to Homestead Air Force Base. He'd always thought that even if it existed, it'd be just a pipeline buried underground, not a huge tunnel with room to drive vehicles in each direction. He studied the large conduit. It had to be a fuel pipeline, a jet fuel pipeline. That explained the kerosene smell. And mounting it at the bottom made sense in case of leakage.

He returned to the ladder, picked up the spoon that he'd dropped earlier, and looked up. He remembered that the hatch hinged on the west side of the shaft. That meant that the tunnel traveled approximately northwest and southeast. It might be his best option to return to civilization, but how far would he have to walk? He knew of nothing to the northwest, so southeast, toward Homestead, would be the direction he'd take. But for now, he'd return to the cabin to eat and check for search aircraft.

Hunter counted the ladder rungs as he ascended. The exhausting climb forced him to stop a few times to catch his breath. He suddenly wished that he'd worked out at the gym more often. Heavily winded when he finally reached the top, he rested for a while.

The sound of an engine pulled him to the lower dock. The roar, low on the horizon and to the south, was the roar of a military fighter: music to his ears. It grew louder and faded twice before the sound died completely. He sighed. A fighter jock from Homestead just out on a training run, he decided, though he never saw the craft. Discouraged, he now believed that no one was searching for him, nor would they for quite some time. Three weeks could pass before anyone at work would miss him. He'd be out of food and water by then.

To hell with waiting for a rescue that might never happen. I'm taking the tunnel. It has to come out somewhere. Walking on level concrete, he could easily cover twenty-five miles in a day. He might even get home in time to take Amanda out for a midweek dinner. The military might not like him knowing about their little secret, but so what. They wouldn't kill him over it.

*   *   *

Major Dennis Kruzinski banked his F-15 fighter sharply and concentrated on the area where he thought he'd seen a flash. He smiled when the longshot paid off. The shiny surface of the wreckage reflected the sun's brilliance at precisely the right moment. Kruzinski eagerly radioed Colonel Blake. "Eagle one to Big Dog. Do you copy?"

"This is Big Dog, Eagle One. Say your message."

"Big Dog, I have objective in sight. Repeat, objective in sight."

"Roger, Eagle One. What quadrant?"

"It's outside the assigned area, Big Dog. I'd estimate it twenty miles due south of Quadrant Four."

"Twenty miles south…roger, Eagle One. Any activity?"

"Wait one. I'm making a pass right now…ah, negative. No activity at this time."

"Roger, Eagle One."

Kruzinski spotted the discarded parachute. "Big Dog, Eagle One. I have a cotton flower a half mile southwest of the objective. Repeat, a cotton flower a half mile southwest. I see no activity there either."

"Roger, Eagle One. Excellent work. Return to base."

"We copy, Big Dog. Returning to base. Eagle One out."

*   *   *

Colonel Blake hated that Eagle One had spotted a parachute. That meant the pilot of the downed aircraft hadn't died in the crash as Blake had secretly hoped.

He waited for over an hour for the airboat crews to arrive at the site. Once they did, they confirmed Eagle One's report. Blake ordered them to load the sailplane wreckage on the two boats, retrieve the parachute, and return to base.

*   *   *

Hunter rifled through the junk drawer for a notepad and a pencil, then sat and sketched the two main roads that he'd seen from the air: the Tamiami Trail running east-west and US Highway 27 running north-south. Next he drew a small circle about where the city of Homestead should be and placed a dot for the approximate location of the cabin. He then drew a line from the northwest to the southeast, passing through the dot that represented the cabin. The southeast line crossed directly over where he'd established Homestead. The line to the northwest crossed the Tamiami Trail and would not lead to any notable landmark until it reached Naples on the Gulf Coast.

He wished for a real map. The longer he stared at his sketch, however, the surer he became that the line to the southeast would take him to Homestead. It made perfect sense. The military would have built the tunnel to one of its facilities: Homestead Air Force Base. And where else would a jet-fuel pipeline end? He'd have to walk more than twenty-five miles to get there, though. If he maintained the average person's walking speed of three miles per hour, it'd take him at least eight hours. He was glad his sneakers had finally dried out. Even so, he'd probably have blisters on his feet before it was over. Unsure exactly where the tunnel would end—never mind how he'd return to his car or house—he decided to stay in the cabin for the rest of the day and begin his journey early Wednesday morning after a good night's sleep.

He planned his trek. He'd need to carry food and water. Opening the junk drawer again, he pulled out the length of rope and tied it into a loop. When draped over his shoulder, it hung down to his waist. He removed a gallon jug of water from the lower cabinet, attached the rope to the handle, and slung the homemade canteen strap around his neck. Damn, it was heavy. The rope was already biting into his shoulder. Then he had an idea. Wrapping one of the socks around the rope cushioned it enough to make it tolerable. And, of course, he'd be drinking as he went, so the weight would constantly diminish. It seemed tolerable. As for food, he'd have to make do with a can of tuna and a can of soup.

The rest of the day passed slowly. The expanse and isolation of the Everglades made him feel as though he was the only person on the planet. He felt small and insignificant, a drop of water in a vast ocean.

Soon millions of stars danced in the tranquil night sky, harmonizing perfectly with the frogs' recital. Old Surprise returned and chimed in as well. Hunter truly enjoyed his final evening at the cabin, though he soon retired so he'd wake early and get a good start.

*   *   *

Bleary-eyed, Morgan Lindsey lingered in front of her kitchen window at dawn Wednesday morning, a steaming cup of espresso in hand. She barely noticed the fiery-red maple tree in her front yard as she mulled over what she had learned.

The Scotch bottle from Sean Buchanan's wreck is my only lead. If it's not in the FBI evidence room, I'll wrap up my article and have it on Jack's desk by noontime. Though concerned with her decision to go to the FBI after being warned not to in the anonymous letter, she reasoned that she had no other choice.

She drained the cup and clanked it into the sink with the other dirty dishes that she'd planned to wash two days ago, grabbed her purse, then strode for the garage. The interior of her Pontiac was really cold, especially the driver's seat. Shivering, she vowed to have a contractor come out to add heating vents to her garage. *Crap! Where'd I leave my keys this time?* Cursing, she dumped the contents of her purse onto the passenger seat. No luck. She sighed and hopped out to retrace her steps from the night before. The keys were sitting on the bathroom vanity, along with a reminder note to pick up her dry cleaning. Finally she set out again on her latest crusade.

Her story on the mayoral election and real estate scandal had already catapulted her higher than the lid she'd blown off that corrupt political contest. As a result, the election had been postponed indefinitely, pending the outcome of a congressional investigation. Jack was so thrilled he'd given her a sizeable raise. But if she could prove that Senator Buchanan's death had been murder, it would make the election scandal pale by comparison.

Morgan arrived at FBI headquarters in the J. Edgar Hoover Building where she spent nearly an hour being handed off from agent to agent. She now stepped into the office of agent number six, a man in his late fifties, with thinning graying red hair, who wore his bifocals low on the bridge of his nose. He was diligently reading a report on his desk when she knocked on his doorframe to announce herself.

"Excuse me, are you Francis O'Donovan?" she asked.

"I am. Top O' the morning ta ya." His ruddy complexion and friendly smile meshed well with his lovely Gaelic accent.

She smiled in return. "Good morning. I'm Morgan Lindsey from the *Washington Herald. Please* tell me you're the agent who handled the inquiry into Senator Sean Buchanan's fatal accident a couple of years ago. I've been shuffled around here so much I'm beginning to feel like the joker in a loaded deck of cards."

He laughed. "It gets like that sometimes. Don't despair. Ya are indeed in the presence of the person ya seek." He cocked his head.

"It's been a while since anyone has shown an interest in that old case. It was a real corker. Please sit down."

She eased into the chair in front of his desk. "Thank you. What I'm most curious about, Mr. O'Donovan, is the Scotch bottle found at the scene. Do you know if it was tested for foreign substances?"

"Absolutely. We were fortunate that the bottle retained almost a third of its original volume. Our lab was able ta test it for everything imaginable. It contained only Scotch. No contaminates were found."

Morgan perked up. "Really. That's interesting." She leaned forward, focusing on his face. "Does that bottle still exist?"

"Sure. It's in our evidence room in the basement, along with other items from the wreck."

"If it wouldn't be too much of an imposition, could I see them?" she asked, trying not to appear too eager.

He shrugged. "I don't see why not. I need a break from this paperwork anyway."

"I'm sorry. I didn't mean to—"

"Don't trouble yourself, darlin'. I'd much rather go for a stroll with a pretty lass than read borin' statistics." His lopsided grin preempted her smile.

Morgan picked up on the word *darlin'*. Was it possible that *he* had sent her that letter? "Have you heard of the Gomez brothers, Mr. O'Donovan?" She studied his face for a reaction.

He knitted his brow and scratched the back of his head. "No, I can't say that I have. Why?"

Well, it had been a long shot. "Oh, no reason really. It's not important."

O'Donovan led her downstairs to the gigantic FBI basement warehouse which housed thousands of boxes alphabetized on racks of shelves labeled by year and month. They wandered the aisles until he abruptly stopped, a look of triumph on his face.

"Ah, there it 'tis," he said, pointing to a box on an upper-level shelf. "I knew it was here somewhere." He rolled a ladder over, brought the box down, and opened it for her. "The bottle has long since been fingerprinted, Ms. Lindsey, so ya can handle it however ya wish."

She removed the bottle and studied it. This couldn't possibly be the same bottle that Trooper Pete Mitchell had described to her. For one thing, it had a cap; for another, the label was perfectly intact, not torn at all. And it still had liquid in it. That meant that someone had switched bottles somewhere between the scene of the accident and the FBI forensic lab.

Her excitement was rising, though she kept her voice calm as she asked, "Did Sean Buchanan's fingerprints show up on the bottle, Mr. O'Donovan?"

"A couple o' smudges appeared, but no readable prints were found, darlin'. It was winter, ya see, and the senator wore gloves that night."

Sealed in plastic, the gloves and the shredded clothing that Buchanan had worn that night were also in the box, stained forever with his dried blood.

O'Donovan must've noticed her expression because he said, "The senator's personal effects have been returned ta the family. These items, after all, were not appropriate ta send with them." He closed the box, returned it to the upper shelf, then accompanied her back upstairs to the building's front entrance.

"Thank you for your time, Mr. O'Donovan," Morgan said, shaking his hand.

"T'was my pleasure, darlin'."

She drove straight to her office where, motivated to near obsession, she honed her article for maximum effect before placing it in Jack's hands just after 2:00 p.m. He read it eagerly while clicking the top of a pen with his left thumb. Funny, Morgan thought, watching him. She'd forgotten he was a southpaw.

When he finally looked up, he gaped at her wide-eyed. "How much of this can you prove?"

"Very little, I'm afraid. But here's what got me interested in the first place." She handed Jack the anonymous letter and waited for his comment about the last word. It was coming, sure as she was standing there.

"*Darling?*" He looked up at her. "Who sent you this? An old boyfriend?"

She crossed her arms and tapped her foot. "I don't know, Jack. It's anonymous. For all I know, it could've been you. Will you run it?"

He read the letter again. "Damn! It's a hell of a story. I'll say that...*darling.*"

She rolled her eyes at him. "But will you run it?"

"With your track record, Morgan, hell, yeah, I'll run it!" He turned his wrist until his Boliva stared at him then jumped to his feet. "I'll have to take it to the legal department first, but with any luck, I should have it to the presses in time for the evening edition."

*   *   *

Hunter stood on the porch in awe as Wednesday dawned before him. The Everglades and the sun warmed in unison with color and light. The fiery hues seemed more vibrant, more alive, than he'd ever noticed before. Herons and ibises took flight. A breeze tickled the saw grass. The water glowed orange with the sky. He couldn't recall a more perfect display of nature in harmony with itself.

Eager to start his trek, he tore himself away from the canvas of colors and placed water on the stove for coffee, then heated two cans of soup. He ate on the porch, finishing the sunrise, then returned the key to its hiding place in the rocking chair on the deck, and went back into the cabin.

He locked the door from the inside before opening the hatches. The shaft's musty smell crept silently into the cabin like smoke through a keyhole. The pocket knife, his flashlight, the cans of tuna and soup, and a couple of paper towels went into the pockets of his jumpsuit. Then he slung his camera and the makeshift canteen over his shoulder and entered the shaft. Assisted by the weight of the table, he lowered the hatches. When the wooden hatch had closed completely, he latched it, then closed and secured the inner hatch as well. *Now the military's secret will remain just that,* he thought.

Descending, he remembered his count of eighty-four rungs. At about fourteen inches apart, he calculated that the distance to the tunnel floor was ninety-five to one-hundred feet, a long way in the confining shaft.

At last he hit bottom and checked his watch. Half-past seven.

Hunter started walking southeast. Every section of the tunnel looked exactly the same, and his journey quickly became tedious without any visual references to measure progress. He began to hum every Beatles tune he could remember then graduated to the Rolling Stones.

He had been singing for a couple of hours when another tunnel entered his. Its northeast direction suggested Miami as its destination. Hunter briefly thought about taking it, but the distance to Miami would be greater than to Homestead. Besides, he needed to retrieve his car.

A few minutes later, he came upon another ladder leading up into a shaft like the one he'd descended. Because he was still well out in the Everglades, he assumed it led up to another cabin. He suddenly realized that the structures, cleverly disguised as hunting cabins, were actually observation posts for the tunnel system. No point in climbing up for a look. Everglades were Everglades. He passed it by.

Some five hours into the trek, his stomach started growling, so he sat on the concrete floor, resting his back against the wall. The high-protein tuna chased the chicken soup. A long drink of water afterward not only quenched his thirst but also lessened the tug on his shoulder from the crude canteen. He smashed the cans and dropped them through a slot in the center drainage grate before setting out again.

About four hours, and every song Hunter knew, later, he finally arrived underneath Homestead Air Force Base. He was certain of that because the tunnel opened into a huge underground hangar with monumental columns supporting the roof structure. Hunter could scarcely believe what lay before him. Wide-eyed and gaping, he counted over two dozen top-secret F-117-A Nighthawk stealth fighters, the black wedge-shaped airplanes nicknamed *Black Ghosts* because of their color and their invisibility to radar.

Hunter stepped woodenly into the center of the hangar. *The size of this place is incredible! And what in the world are all these stealths doing here? The Nighthawk squadrons are supposed to operate out of Holloman Air Force Base in southern New Mexico. Something tells me I'm not in Kansas anymore.*

CHAPTER

8

The underground complex Hunter had stumbled on was vast, both in size and scope. The flat concrete ceiling of the colossal hangar was the same height as the tunnel. A series of fluorescent light fixtures ran in rows between the columns, though only a few were currently lit. The remaining fixtures would obviously be used when the hangar became active. For now, the only movement was his own. He crossed to the nearest fighter, reached up, and ran his hand along the leading edge of the wing. A special radar-absorbing material applied to the skin of the aircraft gave the exterior a matte-black finish. This material, along with the odd batlike shape and unique engine exhaust ports, rendered the Nighthawk invisible to radar detection. The stealths were extremely successful at clearing the way for major air strikes by destroying radar installations and tracking facilities in advance.

What a beauty. Sure wish I could take you out for a spin. To fly one, he'd have to reenlist in the air force, something he was unwilling to do after Desert Storm.

Engrossed in his study of the craft, Hunter hadn't noticed the sound of an approaching vehicle until it was almost upon him. Stirred into action, he instinctively hid behind the aircraft. Certainly anyone authorized to be in this complex would have top-secret clearance. He wasn't sure he wanted to be discovered here, even though his presence had come through extenuating circumstances.

A World War II vintage Wileys Jeep approached, stopping a short distance to his left. Two men stepped from the vehicle, one wearing a military uniform and the other, a civilian in a suit. Hunter quietly set his canteen and camera down then crept behind the row of dormant aircraft to a better vantage point.

The men chatted next to a stealth fighter with a stepladder placed near its right wing. The civilian had his back toward Hunter, but the military officer, a man in his late fifties or early sixties, faced him. The five stars on his shoulder ranked him a general. His uniform also carried the medals and ribbons of a highly decorated soldier, one who'd fought many a battle—one who's face was familiar to Hunter. Where had he seen the man before? On an air force base? During Desert Storm? Maybe at the academy in Colorado Springs? He couldn't remember. The gray-suited civilian seemed relaxed; his hands were in his pockets. The general adjusted the stepladder then steadied it as the civilian climbed up for a look at the wing. Hunter watched closely, hoping to see the man's face, but his view was blocked by a concrete column.

"Do you know what it was, Lamar?" the civilian asked as he started back down.

"We do now, sir. A high-performance sailplane. A glider. Took longer than we expected to find the wreckage."

"And the pilot?"

"He apparently survived the collision. We found a parachute not far from the wreckage," the general said. "The fuselage remained basically intact, with no blood inside, so we assume the pilot reached the ground uninjured."

"Where is he now?"

"We don't know yet, sir. It's been five days since the incident, and we've searched the entire time. We didn't realize we were concentrating our efforts in the wrong place until we located the wreckage. Today we checked the observation cabins in the area. They're locked and unoccupied."

"Damn it, Lamar! We need to find that pilot!" the civilian said, kicking the bottom rung of the ladder. "We need to know what he saw, and we need to know now!"

Holy shit! Hunter thought. *They're looking for me!* Now he definitely didn't want to be found in that complex. If he could leave the facility undetected, he'd stick to a story of what he'd seen from the sailplane, which was basically nothing: just a flash and a sound. Then it occurred to him. *Why is the general addressing the civilian as "sir"? Who is this guy?*

"What's being done now to find the pilot?" the suit asked.

"We checked the serial numbers on the wreckage. The sailplane is registered to an H. Hunter Mahoy in Miami. Don't know yet what the *H* stands for—probably *Haggard* about now." The general smiled at his own little joke. "We have personnel staked out at his home and office addresses, and all the logical phone lines have been tapped. We thought we'd find him by GPS tracking his cell phone, but we've had no luck with that. We also have boats and airplanes searching the Everglades." He cleared his throat before continuing. "The man may have hiked to a highway and caught a ride back to town. Or he may still be out there, in a hammock or wandering where we just haven't spotted him. Or a gator could've had him for lunch. The search is ongoing."

"Don't give me that 'search is ongoing' crap, Lamar! This is no press conference!" the civilian snapped. "We need to find that man. It's imperative we maintain total secrecy of this operation, you know that!"

The general's rigid stance mimicked the column Hunter was hiding behind.

"No one can ever know what we've done with these aircraft or what we plan to do. Your pilot shouldn't have been flying this stealth fighter in daylight anyway. Wasn't he briefed on the necessity of night flights only?"

"Yes, he was, but he had little choice given his situation. I credit him with being resourceful in dealing with an emergency after he'd dropped his munitions. In my opinion, he did an excellent job of maintaining secrecy. The collision with the sailplane was a fluke." The general paused. "Don't worry, Al. I'll find the missing pilot."

Al? Hunter thought. *Al who? Damn! Who in hell is he?*

"All right, Lamar. And when you do, contact me immediately. I'll be leaving for California in the morning and will return to DC by noon the following day. I want a positive report about that damned pilot when I get back to my office on Friday. If he knows too much, we'll have to silence him."

Hunter's jaw dropped like a lead weight.

The civilian gestured expansively. "I've had enough of this place. Let's go to your office to discuss the other details."

Watching eagerly as the men turned to leave, Hunter clearly saw the civilian's profile. *My god! It's Al Buchanan, vice president of the United States!*

The men climbed into the Jeep and rode down the hangar for a short distance. They stopped in front of a door, exited the vehicle, and waited briefly. The door opened and they stepped inside an elevator.

Hunter immediately decided he had to find out what they were up to. He raced through the hangar to the elevator door and almost pushed the button, pulling back his finger at the last second. A door to his left was marked stairs. He yanked it open. The stairway only ascended. Taking the steps two at a time, he reached the next level. A small window in the door allowed visual access into a dimly lit hallway. Light spilled from an office several doors down on the right.

Hunter cracked the stairwell door slightly; muffled voices filtered down the corridor to him. *Bingo!* he said to himself.

He left the safety of the stairwell cautiously, checking the inside knob to ensure that the door wouldn't lock him out of a quick exit. He inched along the hallway. The voices grew louder with each step he chanced. He peeled off his sneakers and carried them, afraid they'd squeak on the shiny vinyl-tile surface. Now he was just two offices away from the one the men occupied, but he still found it difficult to understand their conversation. He crept forward with agonizingly slow progress, his pulse racing like a stock-car engine. He was committed now. Retreating wasn't an option. Neither was breathing, it seemed.

When he finally reached the office next to theirs, he tried the doorknob. It was unlocked. He slipped inside the darkened room ever so carefully and left the door slightly ajar. The clarity of the men's voices carried remarkably. Now if he could just quiet his heartbeat.

"Changed to November first? Why?"

Hunter recognized the general's voice.

"At Castro's request," the vice president said. "I couldn't tell you over the telephone. Couldn't take the chance."

"Damn! Another delay!" the general griped. "This operation would've been completed a year ago if Hurricane Andrew hadn't wrecked the base and drawn so much attention to the area!"

"True, but we have better control over the operation's secrecy now. With the fate of this base in limbo, largely due to my complaints about the cost to rebuild, I've managed to keep it absent of active-duty personnel other than a bare minimum Defense Department police force."

"I know you're right, but I hate the delay. I'll have to make some adjustments. What time is Air Force One scheduled to touch down in Guantanamo?"

"It's set for 5:30 p.m.," the vice president said, "and I've already spoken to Stan about it."

"Five-thirty! That's not late enough! You know we can't send the stealth over in daylight. It's impervious to radar, but someone might spot it visually. We can't take that chance! It has to be after nightfall so no one will know where the device came from."

"Relax, Lamar, I know the plan. Don't worry. I'll have Weber's complete itinerary. If it's not dark enough to get them when the plane lands, we'll get them somewhere else. We'll know where they'll be."

"But the airport's the best location," the general complained. "It's an open area. They'll have no protection. After that they might be inside a building or be separated; we might not get them both."

"Yes, I know the airport's the best location. I'll do what I can to have the time changed, but I can't guarantee anything. I have to say, I don't know what you have on Stan, but he's sure being cooperative as hell. He said he'd document any story we claim, so even if we don't get Castro, we can still blame the assassination on him." Buchanan chuckled. "We'll have the military cart him off to prison and try him for the murder of the president. Meanwhile, the stealths will resume their attacks on the designated targets. We'll continue with the plan as designed."

"I guess you're right."

"Of course, I'm right," the vice president said. "The only thing that matters is that we get Weber in Cuba. He'll finally pay for the death of my only son. Sean died on the cusp of greatness."

Hunter sank to the floor of the dark office, trembling. His stomach was tied in knots. *Holy shit! They're planning to kill the president of the United States!* Suddenly the general's identity came to mind. That's why the guy was so familiar! Hunter had seen him on television broadcasts and in newspaper photos: General Lamar Hager, chairman of the Joint Chiefs of Staff. *But who was Stan? Oh, god! Stanley Bass, director of the CIA! It had to be.*

"Sean was the youngest senator in US history. Did you know that, Lamar?"

"Yes, I did. But, Al, your son died in a terrible car accident. Weber had nothing to do with that."

"*Yes, he did!*" Buchanan said, emphasizing each word. "Sean and Weber's daughter, Kate, were dating. Weber didn't approve. He knew damn well that Sean's career would keep him in DC, so he persuaded Kate to go to graduate school in Boston. Sean wouldn't have been on the Connecticut interstate that night if it hadn't been for Weber!"

"Sean had a drinking problem," the general said gently. "The autopsy proved he'd been driving under the influence. His blood alcohol level was more than double the legal limit."

"That was Weber's fault too!" the vice president shouted. "He asked Sean to be at the Kennedy Center that evening. You know how those functions are, Lamar. The liquor flows like water! Sean's accident was Weber's fault, just as sure as I am standing here!"

The general's voice was sharp when he replied, "I didn't realize you're in this for vengeance, Al. I simply thought you're ambitious— and recognize what's best for this country, of course."

The voices fell silent. Hunter wished he could see through the wall.

Finally the vice president spoke again. "I grant you that my motives are complex, Lamar. What's important is that we're on the same side, and we understand one another, you and I. Let's get back to business."

"Agreed. So, how long before the corporations move in and start building new structures where our stealths have destroyed existing ones?" One of the men began to pace. The footfalls echoed into the hallway.

"Let's not bother about that now," the vice president said. "The basic time frames are laid out here in the operations manual, excluding the part about Fidel Castro and Nelson Weber, of course. For now, we need to concentrate on the initial part of the plan."

"Where will you be when the bomb hits?"

"Most likely in DC, but I can't say for sure," Buchanan said. He paused. "Damn, it's already twenty past six. I have a meeting in Miami with a Cuban exile organization at seven-thirty." He sighed. "I wish I'd never learned to speak Spanish, then someone else would get sent to listen to their bullshit about how the administration isn't doing enough to help free Cuba. The exiles say they want to return to their homeland. Won't they be surprised when we declare Cuba a nuclear disaster area because of radiation fallout?"

The general laughed. "It won't be true, of course, but they'll believe it just the same. We'll have the US military evacuate the entire island and send the rest of the Cubans to Miami to join the exiles! The press and local authorities will be so overloaded with the exodus that no one will have time to think about what we're doing in Cuba after that."

"Right. By the time anyone is allowed back onto the island, most of the prime land will be in the hands of US corporations, particularly hotel chains and sugarcane growers. Hell, I might even declare it the fifty-first state!"

Both men chuckled.

"Secure this operations manual, and let's go," the vice president said. "We'll meet here again two days before Weber's trip to Cuba."

"Why come all the way down here, Al? Why don't we just meet in DC?"

"Because it's not safe to meet anywhere else to discuss this. Have you heard about that new eavesdropping system that the government has? It's called Eschelon, and it can listen in on all communications worldwide—and I mean everything: cell phones, computers, taxi cabs, radio, television, satellites, video phones, you name it. The signals are snatched right out of the air. Nothing's safe. I think the NSA runs it, but it's so secret, even I'm not sure. We have to be absolutely certain that no one is listening in on our conversations about *Ghost Flight*. I can schedule another meeting with the Cuban exiles as an excuse to get down here again. The Gomez brothers can arrange that for me on short notice if need be."

"All right, Al. You're the boss. We'll meet here."

A drawer slammed and Hunter heard the jingling of keys.

"All set," Hager said.

Hunter eased the door closed then sat motionless in the dark office as the men strolled past. *The traitorous bastards! President Weber has to be warned!*

Hunter was eager to enter the office where the men had conversed, but he first crept back down the stairs and checked the hangar to ensure they were gone. No Jeep. He hurried back upstairs. To his surprise, the general's office was unlocked. He closed the door and switched on the lights.

The small, tidy office, about fifteen-feet square, was furnished with a bulky wooden desk near the center of the room, a couple of chairs, and a few metal file cabinets in the corner opposite the door. The operations manual was likely in the desk, at least if Hunter had accurately deduced that the slamming drawer he'd heard was made of wood.

He checked the desk. Only the upper right-hand drawer was locked. He jiggled it and applied pressure to the lock, but it wouldn't yield. Stooping, he looked at the underside of the desktop. It was fastened with Phillips-head screws. He patted the pockets of his jumpsuit for the pocketknife and seconds later managed to snap the blade at the tip while still working on the first fastener. "Shit!" he mumbled. "I need a screwdriver." He searched the other drawers for a useful implement to remove the screws but found nothing. Damn! *I need that manual. Without it, who'd believe such a fantastic story?* He'd have to come back later with the proper tools.

On his way out, Hunter stopped to study the building floor plan. It showed six levels, with the lowest level, labeled BASEMENT much larger than the others. The basement layout had the support columns in rows from one end to the other. *That has to be the hangar where the fighter jets are stored,* he told himself. An arrow projecting from the bottom of the basement plan was labeled TO MIA AND DCTF. Another arrow pointing from the top corner was labeled TPNF. They had to represent the tunnel system.

Certainly MIA meant "Miami International Airport," the tunnel that he'd seen heading northeast. He'd guessed correctly about that. He didn't know what DCTF referred to, but he knew it went northwest.

The arrow-tagged TPNF had him stymied for a while until he considered the location of the hangar and the direction the arrow pointed. Of course! Turkey Point Nuclear Facility. That was probably why the power plant had gotten built there in the first place. The underground complex would need power for all phases of operation. Where better to acquire it than Turkey Point? And supplying the power underground would help maintain the secrecy of the base as well.

Hunter decided the top floor, noted as AG, stood for "aboveground," while all the other levels, labeled UG, were "underground." He could leave the complex by simply climbing the stairs to the aboveground level. He'd have to retrieve his water jug and camera first, though.

He turned off the light then listened at the door. All quiet. As he headed toward the stairs, he opened each office along the way. The last one he checked, the one closest to the stairway, had a copy machine. *That'll come in handy!* he thought.

The kerosene smell hit him the instant he stepped back into the hangar. *There's that jet fuel again. Wait a minute—why didn't I see it before? These fighters move through the tunnels to other locations! They can probably return to ground level at Miami International Airport and take off or land there if necessary.* The tunnel to the Turkey Point Nuclear facility was most likely for trucks, not fighters. He wondered where the tunnel to the northwest ended.

The hangar was empty, and he quickly retrieved his gear. Hunter then strode over to the fighter that the general and vice president had been examining and climbed up the ladder that was still beside the wing. The only evidence of its collision with his sailplane was a dent and a few scrapes on the leading edge. He removed the lens cap from his camera and took a picture of the damage. He captured a few shots of the other stealths as well from the higher vantage point.

Scurrying back down the ladder, he did a quick search of the hangar for something that he could use to breach the general's desk. He frowned when he came up empty. He was sure he'd find some tools in there somewhere.

The hair on the back of his neck prickled with tension. He didn't know why; he hadn't seen anyone or heard anything, but he suddenly felt he had to get out of there. He slipped back into the stairwell and started climbing the six flights, glancing through the small window at each level. Every hallway appeared the same: dimly lit, no activity. Winded at the top, he rested for a moment. This door didn't have a window. Curious as to what the floor contained, he started turning the knob when he suddenly noticed a two-wire alarm contact attached to the top of the door. He eased the knob back to neutral. The pocket knife would do the trick this time, even with the broken blade. He carefully stripped the insulation from both wires directly above the contact. After he'd exposed enough area on each wire, he twisted them around each other, bypassing the contact and rendering it useless.

He eased the door open and peered into the hall. It was like all the others. He checked the knob on the hall side of the stairway door to see if it would lock when the door closed. It would. He saw no way to unlock it.

He pulled a paper towel from his pocket, tore off a scrap, then stuffed the hole in the jamb where the lock would normally catch. If someone were to try the knob, the door would appear locked, but if they pushed on it, the door would swing open, and they'd know the catch had been blocked deliberately. That was a chance Hunter would have to take to be able to return to the general's office.

He investigated the floor and soon found the front entrance to the building. It faced another building just across a parking lot. He was on Homestead Air Force Base, all right. He'd been on the base many times in the past.

The doors had standard emergency push bars. *There has to be another way out,* he thought as he stared through the glass. Since he'd also have to rig the catch of the door he exited, there'd be less chance of discovery on a rear or side entrance. He prowled the hallways until he discovered a rear door. It, too, had an emergency-exit handle and was also connected to an alarm contact.

He duplicated the procedure to defeat the alarm before opening the door. The catch in this jamb required more paper than the previous one. He verified that it wouldn't latch, then stepped outside, peering around cautiously. He eased the door closed behind him, pleased that he'd made it out of the underground complex without getting caught. Now what would he do?

*   *   *

As General Lamar Hager flew back to Washington DC that evening, he still felt stunned to realize that Al Buchanan's main purpose for instigating this operation was one of vengeance—and misguided vengeance, at that. He wondered what would happen if Buchanan were to learn the truth about his son's death.

Hager mulled over his own reasons for his involvement in the plan. He'd been immediately interested when Buchanan had approached him two years earlier with a brilliant scheme that would eliminate Fidel Castro plus bolster the need for a strong US military—a need that would've forced President Weber to reverse his devastating course of military budget cutting. Buchanan had mentioned nothing about Nelson Weber back then, but he must have planned the whole operation with Weber in mind.

By the time Buchanan had suggested the operation be altered to include Weber's demise, Hager stood ready to listen. The general firmly believed that US military strength was essential to protect the borders of the country from any aggressor and keep peace worldwide.

Since assuming the presidency, Nelson Weber had not only relentlessly reduced the size of the military and closed bases but also cut back or canceled future aircraft and weapons development. Weber had even considered dissolving the CIA! On numerous occasions Hager had asked, even pleaded with, Weber to reverse this dangerous course of action. The president had steadfastly refused.

Something had to be done to stop him. Hager had been hoping that the upcoming election would install a new and more like-minded person in the Oval Office. But with the election barely a year away, Weber's popularity with the American people held firm at an unprecedented 85 percent. Weber would undoubtedly occupy the White House for another four years, unless someone intervened.

Al Buchanan, on the other hand, had always advocated a strong military. He had promised Hager carte blanche on military spending and future development once Nelson Weber was out of the way. Though Hager had wanted to refuse the offer, he couldn't. It seemed the only way to save the military from Weber's indiscriminate ax. And with Stanley Bass firmly in their pocket, they could alter any portion of the plan at will, if they had to.

It had been ridiculously easy to bring Bass into the equation. He'd started by telling Bass about the foolproof plan to get rid of Castro once and for all. Bass had been trying to get Castro for years—hell, there were nine *documented* assassination attempts on Castro by Bass's CIA alone. Hager wondered how many other attempts the CIA had made. Once Hager had Bass salivating on Castro, he'd hit Bass with President Weber's plan to dissolve the CIA. As director for more than two decades, Bass had seen several presidents come and go, yet he remained the supreme ruler of the secret, covert world of black operations. He had more power than any president ever did, and he wasn't about to let Weber singlehandedly destroy his kingdom. But the real clincher had come when Hager told Bass that he'd seen him give the Gomez brothers a syringe of clear liquid the night that Sean Buchanan had died. Hager had figured out its purpose only after returning from an overseas military exercise a few weeks later. He'd kept the information to himself until this situation commanded its use.

CHAPTER

Hunter sat on the back steps of the building he'd just exited and inhaled deeply. Fresh evening air, sweet and invigorating, poured into his chest. *Wednesday evening,* he thought. Nearly a week since his office had been ransacked. He'd check on Amanda later to make sure she was all right. But for now he needed to get the hell out of there then call someone for a ride. Amanda's phone was probably one of the ones they'd tapped, so he couldn't call her, nor could he go home or to the office. *Damn! I can't go anywhere I normally would. My car's probably being watched too.*

He crept around to the front of the facility and memorized its appearance and location for his return. Then he started for the main gate. Fortunately for Hunter, Homestead Air Force Base had remained virtually abandoned since Hurricane Andrew had demolished it. With just a skeleton police crew on watch, he had little trouble moving from building to building undetected.

As he made his way off the base, he wondered who else was involved in the assassination plot and how he'd warn the president. Whom could he trust? No one in the government, that was for damn sure. At least three top officials were certainly involved. How could he speak with President Weber personally? Call the White House and ask for Nelson? Fat friggin' chance! If he told the story to a newspaper, the guilty parties would simply deny involvement and label him a crackpot. Without ironclad proof, for any reputable newspaper to print the story, the president would have to be dead, with the vice president standing over his body holding the proverbial smoking gun.

Hunter stopped in his tracks. Morgan! He could get Morgan to help. She'd written articles about many of the capital's more prominent citizens. With her contacts, she might be able to get a message to the president. And he could trust her. Besides, he liked the idea of having a good excuse to personally get in touch with her.

With that settled, he concentrated on his immediate problem. He'd call a taxi from outside the base and head to an ATM machine. Thank goodness he still had his credit card. The transaction could be traced, but he'd be long gone before the bad guys found out. He'd stay in a hotel, register under an alias, and pay for the room with cash. Then he'd bathe and have dinner: a thick, juicy steak!

As if on cue, his stomach started growling. The hunger pangs intensified until he wished he'd never even thought about food. One visualized image had been all it took.

He avoided a small security patrol several times before finally drawing within sight of the main gate. The building on his left had three public telephones out front. One worked. He called a local cab company, using his calling card number, and requested a taxi be sent to the west side of the main gate of Homestead Air Force Base, where he would flag the driver. The dispatcher promised a cab in about fifteen minutes.

Hunter figured that the night guard in the main-gate kiosk would be watching for cars and headlights, not a person on foot, especially not one leaving the base. A few trees stood just inside the fence to the left of the gate. He headed for them. With surprising ease, he stole from tree to tree closer to the exit then slipped through the gate itself.

The cab appeared right on time.

"Where to, pal?" the driver asked as Hunter slid into the backseat.

"County Bank at 107th Avenue and Sunset Drive in Miami."

"That'll cost a few bucks," the cabbie warned.

"I know," he said, shutting the door. "Let's go."

Thirty minutes later, Hunter withdrew five-hundred dollars, which he made sure the driver saw. "Now I'd like to go to the bus station in Coral Gables."

"You got it."

When they arrived, he tipped the hackie a five then strolled into the bus station. He waited until the cab was gone before he left the bus station for the Landmark Hotel, just a short walk away. After checking in, he visited a clothing shop in the hotel and purchased two changes of clothes, along with a few toiletries. His fourth-floor room had a commanding view of Coral Gables, including the taste-fully illuminated art deco–orange historic Biltmore Hotel where he'd attended the retirement party. *Was that really just five nights ago?* he mused. It seemed like a lifetime. He turned away from the window. At the moment he had more interest in the bathroom than the view.

A half hour later Hunter emerged from the shower. Rejuvenated, clean shaven, and hungry, he dressed and called room service. Voracious, he ordered more than necessary, but consumed every-thing, savoring each bite. He then leisurely strolled through the lobby on his way outside to hail another taxi. In a screech of tires, the cabbie wheeled to the curb. Hunter hopped in and smiled at the Latin driver, directing him to Amanda's development. He then stretched out across the backseat and relaxed for the next twenty minutes, nearly falling asleep.

When they reached the development, Hunter instructed the cabbie to follow the winding road until he told him to stop. Half a minute later, he said, "This is good. Drop me right here. I'll walk the rest of the way." With the door already open, he tossed the man a Hamilton and a Jackson. "Keep the change."

The grinning cabbie made a quick U-turn then stomped the gas. Hunter strode to the next block, slowing as he neared the corner. He peered down the lane toward Amanda's house. *I don't see anyone watching the place,* he thought. *Better play it safe, though, just to be sure.*

He retraced his steps to where the cab had dropped him then tip-toed through a yard, feeling like a prowler. In no time he stood before the six-foot-high wooden fence that separated him from Amanda's property. He had both hands atop the fence when a heart-stopping guttural growl came from across the darkened yard. He froze, hoping the animal wouldn't charge. Then he heard it coming. Clambering over the rickety structure at Olympic speed wasn't fast enough. The glistening fangs of the lunging rottweiler sank into his left leg. He fell into Amanda's yard, squelching a scream that he desperately needed to release, a scream that would've been heard for blocks. He stumbled to the side door of Amanda's garage and waited for the flesh-eating monster to quiet down.

Blood oozed from his aching left calf. *This is just friggin' great! I'd have done better using the damn front door!* The dog finally quit barking as Hunter searched for Amanda's hidden key. She'd said it was under a potted plant. But which one? There had to be at least twenty. It turned up under the second to the last. "Figures," he muttered.

He unlocked the metal-clad side door then eased inside the garage. The streetlamps glared through the decorative glass panels at the top of the garage door, giving a shadowy existence to everything in the room. Yard tools clung to the wall like a gardener's mounted trophies. Amanda's mechanical beast, her BMW, rested facing the exit, patiently awaiting its master's next command. The lit garage door button glowed like a beacon in the distance, showing the way to the main part of the house.

Hunter caught a glint of the revolver at the last second. His neck and shoulder absorbed most of the blow that was meant for his head. He purposely collapsed onto the hard concrete floor, letting his attacker think he'd been knocked out. Then, worried about Amanda and pumping with adrenaline, he sprang to his feet, slamming all of his weight into his unsuspecting attacker.

The revolver hit the floor with a clatter. They both dived for the weapon. It skated across the cement. They wrestled violently, each trying desperately to get away from the other. Finally the intruder kicked Hunter in the face and scrambled to where the gun lay. Hunter snatched a machete off the wall and rushed toward him. Time slowed. The intruder rose, his outstretched arm approaching eye level. Hunter advanced. The gun came up as the machete started down. The blade flashed, and the gun fired. A voice cried out.

*   *   *

Vice President Al Buchanan's motorcade arrived at the Marriott Hotel on Brickell Avenue in Miami where the mayor of Miami–Dade County, Julio Fuentes, rushed to greet him. Flanked by Secret Service personnel, they strode past the rich mahogany panels and crown moldings of the entranceway. Buchanan checked his appearance in the highly polished brass door of the elevator, adjusting his tie and tugging at the cuffs of his jacket. The vice president was meeting with the Cuban exile group on the fourth floor, away from other functions taking place in the hotel that night. The fourteen-foot-high ornate-ceilinged banquet hall was filled with two-hundred paying guests dressed to the nines. Buchanan gave his speech to a packed house.

When the opportunity finally presented itself, he met privately with Enrique and Pedro Gomez in an adjoining room. They closed the eight-foot-tall door behind them, two Secret Service agents waiting just outside as instructed.

Buchanan smiled. "Gentlemen, I have good news. President Weber's poised to sign the legislation that will allow US corporations to invest in Cuba. We won't have to hide our operations there much longer."

"That is good news!" Enrique said, offering Buchanan a Cohiba. "Pedro and I have combined all our resources into one main account. We will buy as much waterfront property as possible when the legislation becomes law."

"Excellent, gentlemen. We've all worked hard for this day. It fulfills a dream that my son, Sean, had envisioned almost four years ago: the opening of free trade with Cuba."

Enrique made the sign of the cross. "Your son was a brilliant young senator, Mr. Vice President. Florida would have fared much better with him."

Pedro raised his glass. "To this day, *Señor* Buchanan."

They clinked glasses and drank.

A knock sounded on the door, and an aide entered. "Please excuse me," he said, making eye contact with each of them. He handed the vice president a note and an envelope, then stepped aside.

After reading the note, Buchanan stuck it in his pocket. "Gentlemen, you'll have to excuse me for a moment." He smiled. "This requires my immediate attention."

The vice president walked across the room and opened the envelope, then read the contents. He was stunned. Trying to keep his expression level, he walked back to the Gomez brothers, holding the sheets of paper in hand.

"I have an important favor to ask of you gentlemen. This is a fax of an article that appeared in this evening's edition of the *Washington Herald*." He handed it to Enrique. "It was written by the same reporter who exposed the fraudulent mayoral election in DC earlier this week, Morgan Lindsey. The article says that Sean may have been murdered by businessmen in South Florida."

Enrique and Pedro stared at each other with incredulous expressions. They said nothing.

"Could you gentlemen check into this to see if there's any truth to it? You have a better knowledge than most of whom Sean worked with here during his first year as a Florida senator. Of course, the *Herald* states that the article is merely the reporter's opinion, but opinion is often based on fact."

Enrique adjusted his tie and cleared his throat. "We will inquire for you, Mr. Vice President. And we hope this is nothing more than an opinion."

"I have every confidence in you both. Thank you."

*   *   *

Hunter's attacker dropped the revolver and bolted out the side door of the garage, moaning in pain, and clutching the bleeding arm that had been struck with the machete. Hunter's forearm was stinging madly where the bullet had grazed him. He snatched up the gun and raced inside to find Amanda.

He stopped short in the doorway. Furniture had been overturned, picture frames smashed, collectables broken and scattered. The place looked as if a hurricane had roared through. *Hager's people didn't do this,* he thought, remembering the sight of his office a few days earlier. *This is the work of the Gomez brothers, looking for the damned recording!* Holding his breath, he inched up the stairway toward the master bedroom, the gun clutched in his sweaty palm. Step by step, his pulse quickened and his pace slowed. The top step squeaked noisily.

"Come on up whoever you are," a familiar voice said. "I have a *pistola* to this bitch's head, and I am going to kill her if you do not get in here right now!"

It was that filthy bastard, Juan Carlos.

"You have ten seconds! What is it going to be?"

Hunter tucked the gun in his belt behind his back. "Don't hurt her, Juan Carlos. It's me, Hunter Mahoy. I'm coming in."

Juan Carlos shielded himself behind Amanda's totally nude and badly bruised body, the barrel of a semiautomatic pistol pressed against her right temple. Amanda could barely stand. Juan Carlos clutched her by her hair and yanked it a couple of times as he spoke. "This is quite a *puta* you have here, Mahoy. She would not tell me where that tape is for anything."

Like a volcano about to blow, rage welled up inside Hunter. He clenched his fists and forced himself not to charge Juan Carlos right then and there. He wanted to kill the bastard with his bare hands, to choke the living shit out of him to the last breath and watch him squirm and suffer to the bitter end.

"She doesn't know where the tape is, you fucking idiot!" Hunter advanced. "Only a piece of shit like you would stoop to beating and raping a woman."

Apparently believing Hunter had no weapon, Juan Carlos shoved Amanda onto the bed. She landed hard then moaned softly. He pointed his pistol at Hunter and sneered, "I have not yet finished raping her because of you, *gringo*, but I will just as soon as I shoot you." He shrugged. "Or maybe I'll only wound you, then make you sit quietly and watch."

"When hell freezes over," Hunter said, diving to the floor. Rolling, he plucked the gun from his belt.

Juan Carlos shot at him three times, striking him once in the same calf that had suffered the dog bite. Hunter fired two rounds. One ripped into Juan Carlos's right shoulder; the other tore into his chest. Still standing and still holding the pistol, Juan Carlos grimaced. He stared blankly at the blood flowing from his wounds. Dazed, he scanned the room before focusing on Amanda. He started to draw down on her.

"Don't do it, Juan!" Hunter shouted. "Don't make me kill you!"

An instant later, three shots rang out in rapid succession, the last striking Juan Carlos right between the eyes. "That's the *tiro de gracia*," Hunter said as smoke wafted from the barrel of his empty revolver. "And you sure as hell didn't deserve a bullet of mercy."

Juan Carlos dropped his weapon and stumbled backward, his eyes rolling wildly in his head. He crashed through a plate-glass window and fell into the cactus garden below.

The odor of gunpowder permeated the air as Hunter scooped Amanda into his arms. "I'm so sorry, Amanda. If only I hadn't kept that damned recording."

Just barely conscious, she struggled to speak.

He snatched up the phone and punched in the number to his personal physician and good friend, Dr. Russell Keller. As the phone rang, warm blood seeped from his calf. *Come on. Answer, damn it!* Finally.

"Russell! Thank God you're home."

"Hello, Hunter. Is something wrong?"

"I have an emergency. I'm taking my secretary to Baptist Hospital right now. She's been badly beaten and possibly raped. Can you meet us there to expedite treatment?"

"I'll be there in twenty minutes. And I'll call ahead so they're expecting you in case you get there first."

"Thanks, Russell. I'll explain when I see you."

He dressed Amanda as gently as possible, found her car keys, then struggled to carry her to the garage. A wildfire raged inside his left leg. He was seeing stars by the time he placed her in the passenger seat of her BMW. *An automatic. That's a break. I don't know if I could work a clutch right now.*

Police cars were racing toward the scene just as he squealed onto Coral Reef Drive. He stomped the accelerator to the floor, passing other vehicles as though they were standing still. During the run to the hospital, he briefly exceeded one-hundred miles per hour. He would've gone even faster if he'd been driving his Ferrari.

Russell Keller was awaiting their arrival as Hunter wheeled up the emergency entrance ramp and skidded to a stop.

Keller examined Amanda before having orderlies place her on a stretcher.

"Will she be all right, Russell?"

"Hard to say just now." He patted Hunter on the shoulder. "You did the right thing driving her here yourself, and calling me. Time is a major factor with internal injuries, which I imagine she has sustained after a beating like that."

A half hour later, with Amanda sedated and transferred to intensive care, Dr. Keller treated Hunter's wounds. "You'll be sore, but you'll be fine, Hunter. That dog only got your calf muscle, right next to that, um, other injury. Your leg will be as good as new in time. No vital damage. And your arm wound's superficial. It'll sting for a while when that medication wears off, though, you can be sure of that." Keller lowered his voice. "Just between you and me, how's it feel to get bit by a dog *and* two bullets in the same evening?"

Hunter looked away at first then faced the good doctor. "I'm sorry I misled you. I just didn't want to get you into any trouble. I really owe you one. When this is over, Russell, I'll explain everything. But right now I've got to get out of here."

He assumed the police were looking for Amanda's car, so he left it at the hospital and took a cab to the Coral Gables bus station again, from where he slowly and painfully limped to his hotel. After going straight up to his room, he immediately collapsed onto one of the double beds.

The following morning Hunter indulged in a long, hot bath, propping his bandaged leg up on the side of the tub to keep it dry.

He emerged with his stiff, sore muscles only slightly more limber. He still had to shuffle back to the bed. He picked up the phone, dialed long-distance information, then called the number he had been given.

"*Washington Herald.* How may I direct your call?"

"Morgan Lindsey, please."

He was about to hang up after several rings when Morgan finally answered.

CHAPTER

"Hello, darlin'. It's been a long time!"

Morgan's heart skipped a beat. *Darling.* Could it be the guy who sent the anonymous letter? He said he'd contact her soon. "Who is this? Do I know you?" She pulled a pencil from a drawer, hoping to need it.

"Yes, you know me. And you're crazy about me too."

The voice was vaguely familiar. Maybe it was just some guy in the office teasing her. If it was, he'd chosen a bad time. Her phone had been ringing all morning, thanks to her piece on Sean Buchanan. "Listen, I'm busy. Is there something I can do for you?"

"Yes, you can drop what you're doing and come visit me. We have a lot to talk about."

"OK, buddy," she snapped, "if you don't tell me who you are right now, I'm hanging up!"

"Wait, Morgan! Don't you want to speak with an old flame—in Miami?"

Her heart skipped another beat. "Hunter?"

"The one and only, darlin'."

It was Hunter. The realization triggered an avalanche of memories. Memories she'd struggled to keep buried. "Hunter, what a surprise! It's been a long time. Too long." She let that slip. Crap! Why was he calling after all this time? She'd finally put him out of her mind—and her heart. Or so she'd thought.

"Yes, it has," he said. "A little under three years now. You sound great, Morgan. And I actually do want you to visit me. I've come across something only you can help me with. It's really important."

She doodled on her desktop calendar. "I…I can't drop everything to come there, Hunter. I have deadlines to meet." She had no intention of going to Miami to see him. She wasn't about to get sucked into that one. Her life was in DC now, and that's where it would stay.

"I figured that, Morgan, but you'll be interested in what I have to say. It's quite a story."

"What's it about?"

"I can't tell you on the phone. Wish I could. If necessary, I can come to you, but it'd be better if you came here."

Better for him, she thought. "Look, Hunter, I've got a lot going on. I'm in the middle of a really big story, and maybe it wouldn't be such a good idea for us to get together right now anyway. I'll have to—"

"Listen, Morgan. I know this is sudden, but it's extremely important. I don't dare tell you on the phone because anyone could be listening. All I can say is this is the biggest story you'll ever come across in your entire career. And without your help, I may not be able to prevent a catastrophe. I need you to come here."

"Damn it, Hunter! You can't just expect me to drop everything on your command and go running down there like a puppy dog. You're not my master—or my boss!"

"All right, fine. You know what? If you're not interested, Morgan, no problem. I'm not going to beg. I tried that before, didn't I? I'll just call the *New York Times* and get them to help me. Just remember, I offered it to you first—to a friend I thought I could count on. To someone who means something to me, not a total stranger. Forget I called. 'Bye."

She hesitated. "Hunter, wait! Hunter?" She slowly set the receiver back in its cradle then stared at it. Great. After more than three years of not hearing from him, she let him hang up on her.

The phone rang again, and she grabbed it immediately. "Hunter, I'm sorry."

"How'd you know it'd be me?"

"I willed it to be. I didn't want you to hang up before. I just—I waited too long to respond."

"Listen, Morgan. I'm going to repeat only three words I said earlier: it's extremely important."

"I realize that now, Hunter. And I'm interested. What I mean is, I want to help."

"You're not saying that because I threatened to go to the *New York Times*, are you? Wait! Erase that. Forget I even said it. When can you come?"

"I'll catch a flight this afternoon." She jotted down some notes: hair appointment, manicure, airline reservation.

"Wonderful! I'll pick you up at the airport. Leave a message with your flight information at the Landmark Hotel for David Bronson in room 413. Oh, and Morgan? Travel under a fictitious name and pay cash for your ticket. I'll explain why when we meet."

Hunter hung up then punched in another number.

"Baptist Hospital?"

"Amanda Taylor's room, please." It rang for a long time, and he almost disconnected. "Amanda? I hoped you'd answer. How do you feel?"

"Like I've been hit by a semi," she said in a soft, raspy voice. "I'm sore everywhere. It even hurts to breathe."

"I'll bet. You took quite a walloping."

"Thank you for saving me, Hunter. I was just lying here thinking the *H* in your name must stand for *Hero*."

"That's flattering, Amanda. I'd have chosen *Hostile*. When I saw what Juan Carlos had done to you, I lost it."

"Juan Carlos would've killed me, Hunter. I just know it."

"I believe you're right. I feel so bad that I put you in such danger. Can you ever forgive me?"

"Of course. It's not your fault. I would've done the same thing with that recording if I'd been in your place. Please don't feel bad. Dr. Keller said I'm out of the woods now. He moved me into this private room an hour ago. I'll be fine, really." Lowering her voice to a near whisper, she said, "I want to thank you for taking me home from the party the other night too, and I have something to ask you that is, well, embarrassing for me. I don't have any recollection of what happened, um, at my house. Did we, um, what I mean is—"

He laughed lightheartedly. "Amanda, are you saying you don't recall our intimate encounter? I thought I'd be more memorable than that." He grinned at the nightstand.

"Hunter, I—when I woke in the morning, I was completely nude. I never sleep completely nude."

"You mean, almost never," he teased.

"Please tell me I undressed after you left."

He lay back on the bed and closed his eyes, recalling the encounter. "I wish I could, but I wouldn't want to lie to you. You tempted my very heart and soul with your gorgeous naked body and those long, passionate kisses. But nothing else happened. Honest. I can't vouch for my future conduct, though. I barely tamed my desire the other night. I would've called before now, Amanda, but I was stuck in a remote location without a phone for the past few days. I thought maybe we could have dinner when you feel up to it."

"I'd really like that. And thank you for being so thoughtful. Not many men would have acted as honorably. How's your vacation— other than last night, that is?"

He played with the curly phone cord. "It's becoming a real… adventure. I'm not sure where I'll be from one day to the next. I'll have quite a story to tell you when it's over. Hey, Amanda, I may be out of touch for a while. Besides the Gomez brothers, I have another situation that may get hairy. Because I can't risk being found just now, I won't be able to visit you, but I'll call when it's safe for me to do so. Did the police talk to you yet?"

"Yes. Two Latin detectives asked me a bunch of questions earlier this morning. I didn't want the Gomez brothers to find out that you were the one who shot Juan Carlos, so I told the detectives that I did it. I said that Juan broke into my home and tried to rape me, and that I got away long enough to shoot him."

"They didn't buy that yarn, did they?"

"No. They asked what kind of gun I used, what caliber it was, how many bullets it held, where I got the weapon in the first place— questions that I just didn't have answers for. I'm not a very good liar, I'm afraid. They know it was you, Hunter. They told me so. Apparently they lifted your fingerprints off the gun then matched them against the ones in your military service records. When I learned that, I told them what really happened. I told them about the tape recording too, Hunter. They asked where the tape was, but I didn't know."

"Good. What was their reaction? Did they believe your second version?"

"It think they did, that it made sense and was the truth, but one of the detectives acted like he was on a personal vendetta against you, Hunter. He said he's Pedro Gomez's brother-in-law, and that he knew Juan Carlos very well. Get this! He said he couldn't see Juan doing something like that, that it wasn't in his character. And he quickly dismissed the recording as a fabrication by you to ruin the Gomezes. Can you believe that garbage?"

"Yeah, I can, Amanda. It sounds like the Gomez brothers have bribed someone within the police department to get a brother-in-law assigned to the case. Now they can manipulate the facts more to their liking."

"Be careful, Hunter. That detective flat-out said that he thinks I'm trying to protect you because you're my boss and that you're guilty of murder since you haven't come forward to tell your side of the story. It's a real mess, isn't it? I'm sorry."

"Don't worry your pretty little head about it, darlin'. I'll get it straightened out. May take some time, though. Listen, don't go home when you're released from the hospital. Stay with a friend. Or better yet, spend a few weeks with your mom. Have her go with you on that trip to Australia you've always wanted to take. I'll pay for everything."

"Really? You sure you want to do that, Hunter?" She sounded as though she was tiring.

"I'm quite sure. I'd take you myself if I could. Unfortunately, these two problems must be dealt with right now. Maybe I can join you down there later. I'd better go, Amanda, but I'll be thinking about you. Get some rest."

He hung up, lay back on the bed with his eyes closed, and rubbed his temples. *A brother-in-law detective investigating the shooting. The Gomez brothers must have half this damn town in their pocket. What a friggin' nightmare.*

*   *   *

"Darn that thing!" Morgan grumbled as she hurried from the window to her desk to answer the persistent telephone. "This is turning into one long, drawn-out morning." She grabbed the receiver. "Hello? Who?" She sat down and leaned back in her chair. "I'm sorry you have the wrong number. No problem."

She gladly hung up, hoping for some quiet time before the mechanical master beckoned again. Since the Associated Press had run her Sean Buchanan piece in scores of newspapers throughout the country, she'd been fielding calls from just about everywhere. Normally she'd just let the calls go to the *Washington Herald*'s service or her voice mail. But she'd written an unusual story this time. With the number of calls coming in, she stood a good chance of picking up some leads if she spoke with the callers themselves. Otherwise, they might not leave a message or call back. She sure hadn't expected to hear from Hunter today. *Did he have information about this story?* she wondered. No. It wasn't a secret anymore. He would've mentioned it if he did. Or would he? *Oh my gosh! The letter!* Just a short while ago she'd wondered if whom she thought was a stranger calling had sent the letter when he referred to her as "darling." But that thought had been crowded out of her head by the flood of memories over Hunter. Now, though, she thought about the coincidences: his favorite term of endearment, he and the Gomez brothers all in Miami, and Hunter calling out of the blue right after her story hit the street. Maybe he…

The phone rang again. She snatched it off the cradle before the second ring.

"Morgan Lindsey?"

"Yes. What can I do for you?"

"Ms. Lindsey, this is Al Buchanan."

She sat bolt upright in her chair.

"Ms. Lindsey?"

"Ye-yes, Mr. Vice President. I'm here."

"If you don't mind, I'd like to ask you a few questions about your story on my son. Frankly, Ms. Lindsey, your story blew me right out of my shoes. By the way, it's very well written. Your sensitivity and compassion are evident throughout, a rare quality in journalists these days."

"Thank you, Mr. Vice President. That's most kind of you. "*Stop gushing*, she told herself. *It's only the vice president of the United States.*

"I'd like to know if there's any truth to your tale."

Morgan raked her free hand through her hair. "To say that there's truth to it, Mr. Vice President, would suggest that I have proof, which I don't."

"Then you're saying that the *Herald* is on a fishing expedition?"

"In essence, that's correct, sir." She stood and walked back to the window where she stared out at the White House. The phone's cord was stretched to its limit.

"What prompted you to write the story in the first place?" Buchanan asked.

"I received an anonymous letter, sir. It...aroused my curiosity."

"Ms. Lindsey, I'm currently en route to San Francisco to meet with Senator Greenley, so I have some other matters I must attend to right now. But I'd like to meet with you to discuss this further and to read the letter. Would you be agreeable to that?"

"Absolutely, sir. I can be reached at this number most of the time, and my home number is listed under Anne—my middle name.

"Fine. I'll contact you upon my return. I expect to arrive back in DC by noon tomorrow."

Awed with the prospect of meeting the vice president, she initially missed the cradle when she tried to hang up the receiver. As she reset it, it rang, startling her. She grabbed it. "Morgan Lindsey speaking."

"I am calling about the story on Senator Buchanan," the man with a slight Spanish accent said. "I can tell you how he was murdered that night. If you are interested, you will have to meet me in Fort Lauderdale, and it must be tonight."

Morgan managed to keep her voice calm. "As luck would have it, I'll be in Miami tonight," she said. "Can we meet somewhere in between?"

"Closer to Miami? *Sí*. There is a club on South Beach, *La Casa Negra*. Look for me at midnight. And come alone, or you will not find me. Tell the tall bartender that you want to speak with Taco."

The caller hung up before Morgan could say another word.

*　　*　　*

Hunter hobbled through the lobby of his hotel, stopping briefly to read Thursday morning's headlines. Crime, corruption, and mayhem—nothing out of the ordinary. The sun shone brightly as he pushed his way outside. *Damn! Where did this wind come from? It must be blowing at twenty miles an hour. B*etween the wind, the cool temperature, and his injuries, the walk to the nearby bus station was not an enjoyable one. He withdrew another five-hundred dollars from an ATM machine then returned to the hotel and the reservation desk. The pretty, shapely brunette was busy with another customer. He got the overweight, gray-haired woman. He paid for his room for another night then asked to see the manager, who turned out to be the pretty brunette. "Hello, Ms...?"

"Vizcaino," she said. "Lisset Vizcaino." She had a lovely smile and a firm handshake.

"My name is Harry Johnson, I'm in room 430, and I have a real problem."

"With your room, sir?" she asked.

He smiled. "That would be easy to fix. No, my problem is that I was robbed yesterday evening soon after I left my bank. The thugs beat me up." He showed his bandages. "They stole by BMW, my wallet with my credit cards, and all my identification, including my driver's license. Fortunately, they didn't realize that a large wad of cash that I'd just withdrawn was in my other pocket. I'm staying here in your hotel because they have my keys. I won't go home until I can get the locks changed. Anyway, the problem is, since I don't have a car, I need to rent one, but most rental companies don't accept cash and they always require a driver's license. Do you know of a company that would work with me?"

He read the manager's expression as she studied the scabbed-over cut on his forehead and the lacerations on his face. "You have been through a terrible ordeal, Mr. Johnson, and I understand your predicament. I can help you, sir. We have a satellite car rental office here at the hotel. If you leave a three-hundred-dollar deposit, you can charge the car to your room. The hotel will vouch for you. I'll call the rental company personally and make the arrangements."

"Thank you so much, Ms. Vizcaino. You can be sure that I'll be writing Landmark's main office to inform them of your kindness"—something he truly intended to do.

He limped to the rental office where he signed the contract and received the key to a white Cadillac Seville. It had power everything and heated seats. The heated seats felt heavenly on his sore muscles. He dropped his film off at a one-hour photo service, purchased a few tools at an Ace Hardware Store, then traveled to Homestead Air Force Base, downing a couple of burgers and a Coke on the way. On the road that led to the base's main entrance, he drove slowly along until he found what he was looking for: a suitable place to make a cut in the fence. He then made a U-turn and headed back to the photo finisher.

*   *   *

Desi LaRoca dragged a comb through his thick, black hair. Checking his look in the mirror, he raked both sides of his mustache with the first two fingers of each hand. As he strapped on his watch, he said out loud, "*Mierda!* I am going to be late!"

He snatched his brown leather jacket off its hanger then raced out of his pricey third-floor apartment in north Fort Lauderdale. The modeling agency he had to get to was way up on the north side of West Palm Beach. He'd try to make up some time on I-95. If the traffic was bad, he'd be screwed.

Because of the prehistoric speed of the elevator, he took the stairs instead, dashing down two steps at a time. He crossed the parking lot at a brisk pace toward his brand-new silver Corvette, a Corvette he might not be able to keep if he didn't get this job. His personalized tag glistened in the afternoon sunlight. He never failed to read it with pride: TACO. He was still a few strides away when he pressed the remote unlock button.

The car exploded spectacularly, scattering fiery debris in every direction. Blasted backward through the air for several feet, Taco crashed hard onto the abrasive pavement.

*   *   *

On Hunter's return to the hotel, he chanced a stop at his bank and made a large cash withdrawal. He couldn't continue using the credit card for cash advances. And it wouldn't be smart to visit his bank anymore either—hell, it wasn't smart to be there then. Eventually the people searching for him would access his account information for clues to his whereabouts. He had no idea where the events of the next several days might lead, but so far, expenses had been high. That trend would likely continue.

Though he had to admit that his next shopping excursion would be purely for personal reasons, he hadn't seen Morgan in ages. He wanted to look sharp, really sharp. He purchased a complete outfit for the occasion: gray slacks, a white dress shirt with navy pinstripes, a blue-and-gray print tie, a navy blazer, a pair of black dress shoes, and a black belt.

When he returned to the hotel, Morgan's message was waiting for David Bronson in room 413, a name and room number he'd made up that was different from the Harry Johnson name and room number under which he was actually registered. She would arrive on Delta Flight 773 at 4:25 p.m. Hunter tried to concentrate on the need to warn President Weber, but his thoughts kept returning to Morgan. He showered, shaved, splashed on some Polo cologne—her favorite—then left for the airport just after four.

Heavy traffic lengthened the ride and tested his patience. Finally, though, he wheeled into the arrival level at the terminal building, making his way to the Delta section.

She was waiting for him.

He practically flew from the car to where she stood then stopped in his tracks and stared. She wore a form-fitting short red dress with matching red heels and carried a contrasting black leather handbag. Her silky strawberry-blonde hair, obviously styled in a salon, glistened under the artificial light. Her gorgeous figure hadn't changed a bit.

"H. Hunter Mahoy as I live and breathe," she said.

He smiled. "You know what the *H* stands for?"

She rolled her eyes. "You still keeping that a secret? Let's see. Tonight I'd have to say *Handsome*."

"That'll do," he said. "It's good to see you, Morgan. Did you travel in that outfit?"

"No," she confessed. "I changed in a bathroom stall as soon as I got off the plane. What are you staring at?"

He had his hands clasped together at his waist. He'd forgotten how lovely she was. "Perfection! You're stunning, more beautiful than ever."

"Why, thank you. Is that a new outfit you're wearing?"

"This old thing?" He grinned and held the jacket open. "I bought it about four hours ago." She laughed becomingly as they embraced.

"I've missed you," he whispered.

"Really?" She eased away to look into his face. "You could've fooled me. Three years and not one phone call! Not one letter!"

"Where do you get off, Morgan? You haven't contacted me, either. And you're the one who up and went to DC. If you—" He looked away because of the hurt in her eyes. The same look she'd had when they'd said good-bye three years ago. "Sorry, darlin'. I don't want to argue. Really I don't. What's past is past. Let's leave it there. What do you say we have dinner and talk about current events?"

He loaded her suitcase into the trunk then held open the passenger door. A minute later, they roared out of the airport, headed for Coral Gables.

On the way, he told her about the midair collision, which led to discovering the tunnel complex and the hangar with the top-secret stealth aircraft. He'd not yet mentioned the plot to assassinate the president or the players involved. "I have some pictures to show you when we reach the hotel," he concluded.

She seemed fascinated by his adventure story. At the restaurant, Christie's on Ponce de Leon Boulevard in Coral Gables, they dined on Caesar salad, Chateaubriand, new potatoes, and red wine.

"Would you believe I was sitting at this very table one night when President Weber was here?" he asked. "I even shook his hand and talked with him for a while." *Too bad he's not here tonight.*

"What a great story! You must've been thrilled," she said. "A once-in-a-lifetime opportunity, don't you think?"

"Gee, I hope not. I'd like to see him again real soon."

They engaged in pleasant conversation and fond memories over dessert and coffee. Hunter couldn't understand how he'd allowed her to slip away from him in the first place.

"I noticed you're not wearing a ring, Morgan. Seeing anyone?"

"No. Since we broke up, I've buried myself in work. Haven't had much time for romance. And you?"

"The same. The harder I work, the more it seems I have to do. It's a vicious cycle."

They left the restaurant and strolled for the car.

"You're limping," she noted. "Did that happen in the midair collision?"

"No. Got bitten by a dog. Not very glamorous, huh?"

The conversation was effortless on the drive back to Hunter's hotel. There, he carried Morgan's suitcase up to his room and set it on one of the beds then handed her the folder of photos he'd had developed. She sat on the other bed and studied his pictures. He studied her.

"These are great, Hunter! I can't believe these shots of the sailplane going down. You had terrific presence of mind to take them."

"Thanks. They came out better than I expected."

"The fighters in the underground hangar are interesting too. What do you need my help with?"

He sat beside her and disclosed the rest of the story.

When he'd finished, she faced him, her expression incredulous. "If anyone else had told me that tale, I wouldn't believe it. Not in a million years. It's just too amazing!"

"I know. But what's even more astonishing is that they'll likely succeed unless we stop them."

"Do you want me to expose their plans in a *Herald* article?"

"No. I don't want them aware that you know anything about this until after we've prevented it. These people are playing for keeps, Morgan. They'll stop at nothing. If they find us, they'll kill us. It's as simple as that. Besides, we don't know who else is involved."

"I see your point. So now what?"

"The only idea I have is to contact President Weber directly and no one else. Beyond that, I'm open to suggestions. And even if we manage to meet with the president, he may not believe us without proof."

"The proof being…"

"The operations manual." He stood to stretch, rolling his head from side to side. "I'm headed to the complex right now to get it."

"You mean we're headed to get it," she said crisply.

"*What!* No way, darlin'! It's too dangerous. You'll wait here."

She jumped to her feet. "Like hell I will! I'm going with you," she said, poking him in the chest with her index finger. "I want to see this for myself."

"I can't let you. I could never—"

"Damn it, Hunter! I can take care of myself." She propped her hands on her hips and glared at him. "Either I go with you, or I go back to DC. You want my help or not?"

He started to move away, but she blocked his retreat, silently demanding an answer. Seconds passed in complete silence. She held her ground, her back rigid with determination, her luscious lips closed tightly.

Finally he said, "Have I ever told you how beautiful you are when you're angry?"

The smile that she was desperately trying to suppress made him laugh, but she'd already won. "We'd better change. Dark colors would be best."

He pulled some clothes from the dresser. "I'll change in the bathroom. Let me know when you're ready." He closed the door behind him.

When she gave him the all-clear, he found that she'd changed into jeans, a black T-shirt, and sneakers. Her T-shirt, not tight but not loose either, didn't hide her braless approach, especially with the chill in the room. Hunter didn't mind at all.

He grabbed his camera, film, and a large manila envelope he'd bought at the photo finisher. "Ready?"

She nodded.

It was sundown when they left the hotel and drove toward Homestead.

*   *   *

Lamar Hager entered his spacious office in the Pentagon, closely followed by Thomas Kelly, the secretary of the air force. "Thanks for meeting me so late, Tom. I know Thursday night is your bridge night. I'll try not to keep you long. Have a seat." As he gestured at the chair opposite his aging oak desk, he thought about the speech he'd rehearsed in his head for the past few days. He was as ready as he'd ever be. Tom was a sensible man. A practical man.

Kelly eased his stocky 220 pounds into the chair and crossed his ankles.

Hager began, "We've known each other for almost thirty years, Tom. We've fought side by side in the trenches, in the mud, and in the blood of our wounded comrades. Our common goal, our life's commitment, has always been to defeat the enemy for the good of our country."

Kelly sat attentive, his hazel eyes focused on Hager, his weathered hands resting comfortably in his lap. "You're leading up to something, Lamar. Out with it."

Hager drew a deep breath. *It's now or never*, he thought. He leaned forward. "Tom, President Weber has become the enemy."

"Tell me about it," Kelly said, rolling his eyes. "Weber's drastically slowed the development of our next generation of aircraft. Aircraft that should've, and would've, already been in the flight-testing stage if he hadn't interfered. His budget cuts are killing us."

Surprised by Kelly's response, Hager seized the moment. "It's worse than you think, Tom. Weber's planning to close another forty-two bases and cut back operations at fifty-five others!"

Kelly lurched to his feet. "You can't be serious! Why?"

"You just said it, his precious budget. Something has to be done. Weber's sure to get reelected. That'll mean another four long years of this. I don't think the military can take it."

Kelly folded his arms across his considerable chest. "I agree, but what can we do? It'd be difficult to discredit Weber before the election next year. He's squeaky clean."

"I know. Even Stanley Bass can't come up with anything on him. And that's saying something. Maybe we can alter Ghost Flight down in Cuba to tarnish his shining armor. By the way, Colonel Blake found and recovered the sailplane wreckage. We no longer have to worry about someone else finding it."

"Ah, finally some good news." Kelly rose and crossed the room to study a picture of an F-15 fighter. "Hmm, altering Ghost Flight. That's an interesting idea, Lamar. But how?"

"I don't know," he lied. "Let's think about it for a couple of days. We're bound to come up with something."

*   *   *

Morgan adjusted her air-conditioning vent. "Hunter, I still don't see how I can help you stop these guys."

"I hate to admit this," he said, staring down the road, "but I've been keeping tabs on your career. You've interviewed some impressive people in Washington. I thought you might know someone who could arrange for us to meet with the president without first disclosing why."

"You know, I've twice seen President Weber up close at press conferences."

"That's great! Do you think he'd remember you?"

"I don't know, he might. He may remember you more since you've actually met and spoken with him."

Hunter looked at her. "I doubt that. I'm not nearly as attractive as you are. And believe me, men remember attractive women." Nearing the area he'd located earlier, he pulled off the road and killed the headlights. "We'll walk from here," he said, tossing her a white handkerchief. "Tie it to the antenna so the car will look disabled." He popped the trunk and hopped out. Two screwdrivers, a small pry bar, and a Swiss army knife had already gone into his pockets by the time Morgan joined him. He handed her a flashlight and a roll of wire. "Put those in your pocket," he instructed, then handed her a medium-sized pair of bolt cutters.

She turned the tool over in her hand and studied it. "What's this for?"

"The fence. We can't chance passing through the front gate the way I did last night. Come on. Let's get away from this car before someone comes."

He tucked the cutters under his shirt, slung his camera over his shoulder, then led her across a concrete bridge that spanned a man-made canal. Soon they came to a fence corner. They turned away from the highway and paralleled the fence for about two-hundred yards until they reached a bushy shrub. The rising crescent moon provided just enough light to see but not enough for them to be spotted easily.

The chain-link fence stood almost seven feet tall with barbed wire on top. Hunter concerned himself with the bottom. With some effort, he made a cut about two feet high and pulled it aside, creating a flap large enough for them to squeeze through. He then cut several pieces of wire about a foot long from the coil and set them on the ground. "Wait here," he said. "I'll be right back."

He grabbed the bolt cutters and the remaining wire, hustled over to the canal, and tossed them into the water, then rejoined her.

"You really have this thought out," she said quietly.

Hunter squeezed through the opening first before holding the fence apart for Morgan. Then he used the short lengths of wire to tie the fence together again so that the opening wouldn't be obvious. He gathered a few rocks and marked the spot to make it easier to find their way out; then they started toward the building that accessed the underground complex and the general's office.

They walked along in silence, their destination slowly creeping up on them. Hunter studied Morgan's profile in the moonlight. Why had he let her bully him into bringing her along? If they were caught, especially on that base…he shuddered at the thought. Truthfully, though, he wanted her to see the tunnel complex for herself. Even though she believed him, actually seeing it with her own eyes would have quite a different impact.

They quickened their pace as they neared the building. He hadn't mentioned how he'd rigged the doors. If for some reason either one had latched, they'd have a difficult time getting in, even with the tools they'd brought.

"Are we going to break in?" she asked as they reached the back entrance.

"No. We'll use magic." He grinned and pushed on the door.

Before it closed, he pulled the paper from the catch and stuck it in his pocket. Now the door would latch, and without a key, no one else could enter.

"Very clever," she said quietly. "That's something I've always admired about you, Hunter. You plan ahead."

She followed him through the maze of corridors to the stairway that accessed the complex below. He repeated his door trick.

"It's six flights," he whispered.

He glanced through the window at each landing. Everything appeared as it had the previous night: dormant. They stopped when they reached the hangar level and listened for a minute. Silence.

As they strode past several stealth aircraft on the way to the one with the ladder under the wing, Hunter smiled at Morgan's wide eyes and gaping mouth.

"Well, darlin', what do you think?"

"It's incredible! How many planes are down here?"

"I'm not sure—over twenty."

He pointed to the white markings on the wing of the damaged aircraft. "That's where it collided with my sailplane." Something behind the stealth caught his eye. Something that hadn't been there before. "Well, what do you know. Here's what's left of my bird. It's been brought in since last night. I wonder why they stuck it here." He snapped a picture of the wreckage then captured two images of the fighter with the wreckage behind it.

He grabbed her elbow. "Come on. I'll show you the tunnel."

They scurried through the hangar until they reached the tunnel entrance.

"It's huge. How far does it go?" she asked.

"A long way. I walked more than twenty-five miles of it. That's enough sightseeing. Let's get what we came for and get out of here."

They hurried back to the stairway, ascended one level, and went straight to Hager's office. Thankfully it was still unlocked, and they ducked inside.

"The operations manual is in this locked drawer," Hunter said as he jiggled it. "We'll have to remove the desktop."

Morgan stood guard near the door, listening for any sounds in the hallway while he extracted the screws on the underside near the drawer. After a few minutes he said, "OK, I'm ready to give it a try. Pull the drawer when I lift up."

Seconds later they were staring down at the operations manual. Its cover flashed the warning TOP SECRET in bold red lettering. They looked at each other then back into the drawer. Hunter hesitated for an instant before turning the cover.

The three words on the next page said it all: *Operation Ghost Flight.*

He snatched the manual from the drawer and scanned the pages rapidly. The first portion of the text pertained to the US military base at Guantanamo, Castro, and stealth fighters. Flipping to other pages, he found references to beachfront property, sugarcane, and details about evacuation of the island.

He signaled her to follow, and they raced out of the general's office toward the room with the copy machine.

"What are we doing?" she asked, hovering close.

"We can't take it with us. We have to make copies."

They slipped into the copy room. Hunter pressed a button on the machine, and it came to life. "OK, help me here."

After removing the three fasteners that held the pages in the binding, they systematically loaded the machine page by page. About halfway through the manual, the copier ran out of paper. The cabinet beneath the machine had only a few sheets left in an opened ream.

"Damn! Just our luck," he said, banging his fist on the wall. "Morgan, use these sheets up while I look for some more in the other offices."

Hunter went from office to office, with no luck. Unable to find any on that floor, he went into the stairwell about to go to up to the next floor when he heard the screech of brakes coming from the hangar level. He rushed downstairs, his leg really talking to him. Several uniformed men were scrambling around two of the aircraft, directed by an officer.

He raced back upstairs to rejoin Morgan, his leg screaming now. "We have...company," he said, gasping for air. A rivulet of sweat tracked down the center of his back.

He quickly reassembled the original manual while Morgan slipped the copy into the manila envelope. They ran to Hager's office, replaced the manual, and reattached the desktop. A bell dinged and the light above the elevator door lit just as they passed it. They bolted into the stairwell. Morgan scrambled up to the top floor two steps at a time; Hunter took more than twice as long to reach her. Stopping briefly to rest and catch his breath, he stuck the manila envelope under his shirt then tucked his shirt into his pants. Nodding to each other, they pushed open the stairwell door and quickly made their way out of the building, failing to rig the exit.

"Stop right there!"

They froze. A security guard on foot some distance away was heading toward them.

"Run!" Hunter shouted at Morgan.

They dashed toward the nearest building, hoping to round the corner safely. At first the guard gave chase. Then he stopped and began shooting. Two rounds struck near Hunter. Another ricocheted off something, stinging his left ear. He ignored the horrible fire in his leg and pumped like mad.

When Morgan reached the old wooden building, Hunter wasn't far behind. Immediately after she rounded the corner, and a fraction of a second before he was about to, a bullet ripped through the corner trim. The wood shattered at eye level, sending splinters flying right behind Morgan and into Hunter's face. The tiny explosion was so close and so surreal that Hunter actually imagined seeing the projectile as it exited the trim on its way to another impact. The scent of pine filled his nostrils. They hoofed it to the next structure then ducked behind it to check the guard's position. He was nowhere in sight.

"You…all right?" Hunter asked, gulping huge breaths of air, his rapid heartbeat amplified exponentially in his throbbing left leg. He looked for the guard again.

"Fine," she gasped, "but that…was too darn…close."

He touched his stinging ear and drew back a bloody fingertip. "I can't argue that, but we're not out of this yet. In a few minutes security will be all around here. The fence is just ahead. We can probably make it if we forget about the guards and run like hell. I'll try to ditch the manual somewhere if we're caught. Let's go!"

His leg on fire, Hunter sprinted as best as he could, the screeching tires of security vehicles and squawking radios providing more than enough impetus. They hit the ground near the cut in the fence, panting desperately. Lying flat in the dew-moistened grass, Hunter untied the wires, and they slipped through to the outside. He hastily tied the fence together again to conceal their exit then ditched the screwdrivers and pry bar when they recrossed the bridge over the canal. The rental car loomed just ahead.

As he started the engine, Morgan yanked the handkerchief from the antenna. She jumped into the passenger seat with the vehicle already moving. A few minutes later, safely away from the area, they drove north on the Florida Turnpike headed for Miami—just another tourist couple in a rented car out for a romantic drive in the moonlight.

CHAPTER

"We made it!" Morgan laughed cheerfully as Hunter shut the door to the hotel room. Her eyes still gleamed with excitement. "What a thrilling experience!"

"Thrilling? You mean chilling. We could've been killed! No more adventure for you."

Falling onto the bed, she hummed as if oblivious to his distress.

He stepped into the bathroom to study his left ear in the mirror. The bullet had just barely nicked him. He dampened a washcloth and cleaned away the dried blood. A tiny piece of flesh was gone, but that was it. It sure did sting, though, like a mad hornet that wouldn't let go. The leg pain had subsided, but he'd certainly aggravated the wounds; fresh blood oozed into the dressings. He'd have to rebandage them soon. He returned to the other room and kicked off his shoes before collapsing onto the bed next to her.

She leaned up on one elbow, her face becoming serious. "What happened to us, Hunter? We were so right for each other, so happy, and then—" She searched his face. "Was it my fault we split up? Do you blame me for running off to DC?"

He took her free hand in his. She pulled it away cautiously. "I did, Morgan. That's for sure, 100 percent. Now I don't know. Maybe deep down I still partially blame you, but I also blame myself. I realize now that I should've supported your move. It was a great opportunity for you. I was being selfish. After all, I took the job in Miami because I wanted us to be together—you know that. I could've hired on anywhere, even stayed in the air force. I guess the whole thing was just bad timing for me. Maybe that's why I was too stubborn to quit my new job."

"But you had such a great position at the firm, Hunter, and it was lucrative too. I should've stayed. I was being just as stubborn."

"It still is lucrative, more so than ever. I've just been offered a full partnership."

"Wow! See? That's why you needed to stay in Miami. You've really moved up the ladder quickly. You obviously made the right decision."

He brushed her hair back with his hand. "Not really. The job sucks, and so do the clients and the hours. I'm thinking about quitting it altogether."

"You're kidding! You'd give up a full partnership? To do what?"

"I don't know. That's the big question."

He dropped his hand to her cheek and turned her face toward him. He searched her eyes.

She abruptly rose, crossed the room to her suitcase, and picked it up. "Did you reserve a room for me?"

He wrinkled his forehead. "No. I didn't think there was any need to. What's wrong with staying in this room with me?"

She glared at him. "Aren't you being a bit presumptuous? Exactly what're you expecting?" She set the suitcase down and stormed over in front of him, hands on her hips. "You think I'm just going to climb into the sack with you like nothing's happened?" Her voice shook with emotion.

He gaped at her. "That'd be nice, but I'm not expecting a damn thing. This room does have two beds, you know."

After a moment of silence, she threw her arms up in surrender then sat down next to him and buried her face in her hands. He pretended to skim through the pages of the operations manual.

"Oh, crap!" she said, jumping to her feet again. "It's five after eleven! I almost forgot! I have to be at a club on the beach by midnight."

He looked up from the manual. "Oh, I get it, Cinderella. And if you don't make it on time, the plush white Cadillac rental will turn into a faded orange Volkswagen bug."

She opened her suitcase and rifled through it. "I'm serious. I have to meet a guy named Taco. He has some information on a story I've been working." She hurried to the bathroom, clothes in hand, and shut the door.

On his feet now, Hunter tossed the manual aside. "Where exactly are you supposed to meet this guy?" he asked through the closed door, his hands clinging to each side of the jamb just above eye level.

"At a nightclub on South Beach called *La Casa Negra*. I can't afford to miss him, either. I'm at a dead end on this story. His information is vital, and he won't be available again after tonight."

"Is this about Sean Buchanan?"

She flung the door open and stared at him, her blue blouse still unbuttoned. "How'd you know that?"

Ignoring the question, he said, "You could be rushing into real danger, Morgan. Meeting a guy named Taco, alone at midnight for crying out loud! I'm going with you."

She reapplied her faded lipstick then pressed her lips together. His favorite color on her: strawberry red. "You can't go with me, Hunter. If you do, he won't show. He specifically said to come alone. Now tell me, how'd you know what this meeting is about?"

He read the suspicion in her eyes. "Come on. Give me some credit. Your article on Buchanan was in today's edition of the *Miami Herald*. Listen, I'll drive you. I know exactly where that club is. I'll drop you off and park out of sight."

"I wish you could, but I can't chance it. If this guy sees me with anybody, he'll bolt. I'll be fine. Really." She scurried around the room twice. "Have you seen my handbag? It's here somewhere."

He pointed to it by the side of the dresser.

She rolled her eyes, then snatched it up, and slung it over her shoulder. "Can I take your rental?"

He sighed and tossed her the keys. "I don't like it. Be careful, darling." He made sure he pronounced the *G* this time.

"Yes, Daddy!" she quipped then stopped short, a question written all over her face.

"What?" he asked, knowing full well what had her perplexed.

"Hunter, you didn't by any chance mail me a—" She shook her head. "Never mind. I'd better get going." She sprinted for the door.

He stared after her with a lopsided grin on his face.

"I can't believe I made it twenty minutes early," Morgan said to herself. She held her watch up to her ear then shook it and looked at the dial again. "Sure hope this thing's right."

Situated in the heart of the art deco district of South Beach, the bustling *La Casa Negra* had patrons spilling out onto glitzy Collins Avenue. Latin music flowed into the night like unchecked water from a broken dam. *This is good*, she thought. *I'll be safe enough with all these people around.* She hadn't expected the place to be so packed on a Thursday night.

She bumped shoulders with, and squeezed between, jubilant revelers on her way to the bar. The cigarette smoke was so thick she almost needed fog lights to navigate. Someone pinched her butt. The tiny, jam–packed dance floor brought a can of sardines to mind. She flashed an alluring smile at the six-foot-five, stick-thin bartender and ordered a Bud Lite in the bottle.

"You here alone?" he asked when he served her.

She shook her head. "Meeting someone. You know where I can find Taco?"

"Yeah. Over there at that table in the corner." The human barometer gestured with a head movement.

A handsome, young mustached Latin sat with his back to the wall, talking across the table to a pretty girl with silky brown hair. When the girl left, taking her drink with her, Morgan crossed the room. A disposable lighter, an open pack of Marlboros, and an ashtray with several dead soldiers in it lay on the table to his right. A few empty glasses and a Heineken bottle cluttered the area in front of him. She hoped he wasn't smashed.

"You Taco?" she asked.

He eyed her up and down then flashed a smile. A practiced smile meant to display his perfect white teeth. He offered her a seat. "Morgan Lindsey, I presume? I had no idea you would be so *atractivo*. I see you have a drink." He picked up the Marlboros. "Want a smoke?"

"No, I'm fine. Thanks." She slipped into the seat opposite him. Figuring to break the ice by starting her conversation on a friendly note, she said, "I'm curious: how'd you get the name Taco?" She sipped her beer.

He grinned and lit a cigarette, then took a long drag before resting the cancer stick in the ashtray. He leaned back, placed his hands on top of his head, and laced his fingers together. "Years ago, my friends and I made a habit of going out to eat a couple of times a week. More times than not, we ended up at our favorite Mexican restaurant where I always ordered tacos. One night as we stepped into the eatery, my buddy slapped me on the back and said, "What are you going to have, Taco?" He smiled again, genuinely this time. "The name stuck, and I have been Taco ever since."

He checked his watch then leaned forward. "I have a plane to catch in two hours, Ms. Lindsey, so I better tell my story. Have you heard of the Gomez Brothers Corporation?"

Morgan leaned forward as well. "Yes, I have. It's owned by Enrique, Pedro, and Juan Carlos Gomez."

"*Sí.* I have known Juan Carlos since we went to Miami High together. He came in here last week and got really tanked up and started telling me about this Senator Buchanan and how the Gomez brothers had been working with him. At first I did not pay much attention because Juan Carlos was always bragging about something, and most often it was a lie. Then he blurted out that the fucking bastard senator had crossed them, so they killed his sorry ass. Excuse the language, I am merely repeating what he said."

Morgan focused on Taco's model-handsome face. "Did you believe him?"

He took a hit off his drink, carefully setting the glass down again in the same ring of condensation that he'd lifted it from. "Not in the least. I told him he was full of crap. The next thing I knew,

Juan Carlos was telling me how they did it." Taco dragged on his cigarette. He blew the smoke toward the ceiling then lowered his head and stared at his drink, slowly turning the glass in place on the table.

"And how did they?" she prompted in as soft a tone as she could with all the noise around them.

He locked eyes with her. "They injected poison through the cap of an unopened bottle of Scotch using a hypodermic needle and syringe, then put the bottle in the senator's car. They knew Senator Buchanan had plans to drive to Boston that night to see his girlfriend. They also knew he liked to drink."

Morgan leaned forward, her arms resting on the table. "This is really important, Taco. Did Juan Carlos say anything about the type of poison they used?"

"*Sí*. He was quite specific." Taco dug out his wallet. He fingered though it for a slip of paper. "I wrote it down when I got home so I would not forget what he told me." Taco unfolded the note then turned it right side up. "Juan said at first they planned to use—" He squinted at the note and drew it closer to his face. "Ah…chloral hydrate, which would make the senator drowsy and then pass out. But because the senator might pull over and stop when he got sleepy, the brothers decided on a different poison."

"Which was…?" Morgan asked, perched on the edge of her seat. She tuned out every sound in the room and focused totally on the young man's next words.

He slid the note across the table without breaking eye contact. "Cyanide, Ms. Lindsey. They used cyanide. And according to Juan Carlos, it was handed to them personally by the director of the CIA."

"*What!* Are you sure about that?"

"I am sure that is what Juan Carlos said. I do not know if it is true."

A cute, tight-skirted petite waitress appeared. "¿Quiere usted algo más beber?"

Taco smiled. "She wants to know if we want something else to drink."

When they both declined, the waitress cleared away the empty glasses and left.

He watched her go, his head turning automatically to follow her shapely progress.

Men just can't help themselves, Morgan thought. *They have to look.* "Why would the CIA director do something like that?" she said, not really expecting a response.

To her surprise, he said, "I asked Juan Carlos that. Apparently the Gomez brothers and the director were working together to rid the world of *el Tyrano.* You know, Fidel Castro, the tyrant. They were going to assassinate him. When Senator Buchanan found out what they were doing, he threatened to expose them."

"Why didn't you go to the authorities, Taco?"

"For one thing, I was still not sure if I believed Juan Carlos. I tell you, he could make up some fantastic stories. But the bigger reason was because he said he would kill me if I ever told anyone. That I did believe. Juan Carlos was capable of just about anything."

Morgan finished her beer and slid the bottle aside. "What prompted you to say anything now?"

"You did, Ms. Lindsey. When I read your article in the *Miami Herald*, I knew it had to be true. And also because Juan Carlos got himself killed last night."

"So, it's safe for you now."

"No! Not in the least. A few hours after I called you, my Corvette blew up right before my eyes! All the Gomez brothers are dangerous, not just Juan Carlos." Taco picked up his smoke and held it close to his mouth. "That's why I am leav—" He suddenly jerked wildly in his seat, his cigarette falling to the table. In a fraction of a second, his left eye exploded grotesquely. Blood and flesh splattered on the wall behind him. His head kicked back uncontrollably. Another bullet ripped into his forehead. It blasted out the top of his skull, bone and hair going with it. He slumped onto the table. Muffled by the loud, pulsating music, the popping continued as Morgan sat paralyzed by fear. Blood poured from the ragged holes in Taco's head as other bullets shredded the table, his body, and the wall. The beer bottle and Taco's drink glass shattered simultaneously, the pieces flying everywhere.

Someone forcefully broadsided Morgan from her chair to the floor. The person sprawled on top of her, moaning softly as more bullets impacted all around them. Chaos and screaming completely suppressed the sound of the last few shots before the firing stopped. The gunman fled the scene.

"Come on, Morgan! We have to get out of here right now!"

"*Hunter?*"

He pulled her along by the arm. She followed mechanically, staring back at the bloody, lifeless form she had briefly known as Taco.

She was hustled out of the nightclub and virtually tossed into the Cadillac. The vehicle raced along McArthur Causeway for the mainland before Morgan fully realized that Hunter had apparently caught a cab and gone to the nightclub to protect her.

"Hunter, you better pull over. I'm going to be sick."

He did so, and she was.

In a few minutes they were moving again. "I don't understand how anyone could've known about that meeting," he said, "unless—Morgan, did you go to the FBI or the CIA when you were investigating that article?"

"I had to, to follow up on the only lead I had at the time: the Scotch bottle."

"Damn it, Morgan!" He banged his hands on the steering wheel. "I specifically instructed you not to. They must've bugged your office phone." He looked over at her. "Do you carry a cell phone?"

"Yes. I hardly go anywhere without it. I did leave it in the room earlier, though, when we went to Homestead."

"Shit! Now we'll have to change rooms." He shook his head. "We probably should change hotels, but…" He jammed on the brakes and swung over to the side of the road, screeching to a stop just a few feet from the water's edge. "Let me have your cell phone."

"Who you going to call?" she asked, digging in her purse before handing it over.

"No one." He reached out the window with his left hand and made a powerful hook shot over the roof of the car, groaning as he did so. Her phone slapped the salt water with a splash before disappearing below the inky surface.

"Hunter! That was an expensive model!"

"I'll buy you a new one. A cellular can be traced when it's on. And I've often speculated that it can also be traced even when it's off. The manufacturers are installing GPS units in them these days—probably at the government's insistence." He peeled back onto the highway.

"You must be mistaken. The FBI couldn't have bugged my phone. The agent I eventually talked with would never have—" Her head snapped up in surprise. "Wait a second! What do you mean you specifically instructed me not to? Shit, I don't believe it! You *snake*! You sent that letter!"

He merely said, "This situation is getting way out of control."

She turned in her seat and glared at him. "Hunter, I want to hear you admit it!"

He took his eyes off the road and looked over at her. "Yes. I sent it."

"Why did you send it anonymously?"

"To protect you."

"Are you sure it wasn't to protect yourself? To keep the heat off you maybe?"

His jaw tightened. "I'm sure. I'd been to the FBI myself before I wrote that letter. That's how the Gomez brothers learned I have a tape recording of them discussing Sean Buchanan's murder. They knew about me before I sent you that letter."

Morgan felt her stomach lurch. "I'm sorry, Hunter. I didn't mean—" She always seemed to say the wrong thing.

"Forget it," he snapped, staring straight ahead.

After an uneasy stretch of silence, she said, "A recording? Oh, my gosh! Hunter, you have a recording of them discussing…? Where is it? Can I have—I mean, can I listen to it?"

He glanced at her. "When it's safe to get it from where I have it hidden, yes. But I don't know when that might be. The Gomez brothers are self-serving, dangerous, and limitless as far as what they might do."

"At least there's one less Gomez to deal with now," she said. "According to Taco, Juan Carlos is dead."

He winced. "I know. I'm the one who killed him."

"*What!*" She faced him and stared.

He sighed heavily then described the incident, which took nearly the entire ride back to Coral Gables.

They arrived at the hotel and Hunter parked then struggled from the car. He put his hand on Morgan's arm. "After we get situated, you'll have to reposition my right shoulder blade. I must've dislocated it when I hit the nightclub floor."

"Maybe it's broken."

"It's not. I did this once in the academy. It's going to hurt like hell to get it back into place, though. I can tell you that."

While Hunter waited by the elevator, Morgan went to the desk to request a new room, explaining that they preferred one in the back of the hotel. She flashed the key card as she rejoined him.

He raised his eyebrows questioningly. "Only one key? Didn't you get two rooms?"

She ignored him and strolled into the elevator. They rode up silently to their floor where she hurried ahead of him down the hallway to the old room. She unlocked it then raced into the bathroom. It had been a long night.

She came out to find Hunter on the far side of one of the beds, arranging the blankets and pillows to give the appearance of two people sleeping beneath the covers.

"What are you doing?" she asked, her anxiety rising.

He looked up. "Playing out a hunch. Come on. Let's get our stuff and get out of here." He limped to the dresser, his back toward Morgan.

"Oh, my gosh, Hunter, you're hurt!" she cried. She hadn't seen his bloodied shirt back until then, having always been in front of him until that moment.

"Yes, I know," he said calmly. "We'll look at it in the new room."

They gathered their things. When they were safely inside the new room on the next floor up, she locked the door then helped him out of his shirt.

She couldn't believe her eyes. Besides the dislocated collarbone, which had to hurt enough on its own, blood oozed from his left side just above the waist. Morgan led him into the bathroom where she soaked a washcloth with warm water. He sat on the bowl while she cleaned the area. She fretted nervously with every move she made.

"Hunter, you've been shot! We have to get you to a hospital. The puncture's large, and that bullet has to come out of there."

He struggled to his feet, wincing as he did. He hobbled back into the bedroom and stood next to the nightstand where he reached for the phone. He stopped abruptly, grimacing in pain.

"What are you doing?" she asked, rushing to his aid.

"Trying to call Russell Keller, but this dislocated collarbone is killing me. You remember Russell, don't you? We had him and his wife over a few times."

"Of course I remember him," she said impatiently, "but we can't call him now. It's one o'clock in the morning."

"We have to, Morgan. Can't go to a hospital—way too risky. Hand me the receiver and dial it for me." He recited the number.

After a few moments, Morgan got to hear Hunter's end of the conversation. "Russell, it's Hunter. I'm really sorry to disturb you at this hour, but I need your help again. What? Oh. Another injury similar to my last one, only this one's worse. I'm sure I'll be fine after you use your bag of tricks on me. But I don't think I should meet you at the hospital this time. I'd better come to your house. Thanks, Russell. I'll be there in about twenty minutes."

As Morgan hung up the receiver for him, he said, "I've got to ease some of this pain. Help me get this collarbone back into place." He stood as straight as he could against the wall next to the bed. "When I say go," he instructed, "shove my right shoulder as hard as you possibly can toward the wall." He smiled weakly. "Pretend you're mad at me."

She rolled her eyes.

"Ready?" She wasn't going to enjoy this.

"Go!"

The pop was almost as loud as his cry. He fainted. She guided his beat-up body onto the closest bed then gently rolled him over onto his stomach. She called Russell Keller back and explained the situation; he would come to them.

She undressed Hunter, seeing for the first time the blood-soaked bandages on his left leg. *My god!* she thought. *He mentioned the dog bite, but how'd he get these other injuries?* She cringed as she inspected them. He must've been in pain even before he picked her up at the airport. Russell could look at those wounds as well.

The doctor arrived about thirty minutes later. After a brief exchange of pleasantries, he went over to examine Hunter. A few moments later, he said, "Fortunately this bullet lost most of its velocity before it struck him. It must have ricocheted off something else first because it was tumbling. Look here." He moved aside slightly so that she could move in closer. "It didn't go in very deep. See it right there?" He manipulated the flesh with his probe. "It's laying broadside. That's why it made a large entry hole."

"I see it now," she said, feeling more than a little squeamish. "Will it be hard to remove?"

"Nah. But I'm glad Hunter's out cold. He won't feel much that way. Well, here goes."

As he dug with the probe and forceps, Morgan looked elsewhere. No way in hell could she ever be a nurse. Hunter twitched and even moaned a couple of times.

"Got it," Keller announced, holding the forceps for her to see, the bloodied projectile barely recognizable as a piece of metal. "Now a little gauze and antiseptic, and he'll be almost as good as new."

Keller applied fresh bandages to all of Hunter's wounds then cleaned his utensils in the bathroom sink.

Morgan watched for a moment. "Aren't you going to ask me how this happened, Russell?"

He faced her. "No. Naturally I'm curious, but I'm not going to ask."

"Well, I'm going to tell you anyway—part of it, at least. See, even though Hunter warned me not to, I went into a situation that I didn't expect to be dangerous. But it was. Bullets started flying, ripping into everything"—she thought of Taco—"everything. It was horrible. All of a sudden, out of nowhere, there's Hunter to the rescue." She fought back sudden tears. "He saved my life, Russell, with no regard for his own."

The doctor comforted her in his arms like a father comforting a daughter. "I guess some people are just that way, Morgan. Hunter has a history of heroics, doesn't he?"

She pulled back and stared at him. "What do you mean?"

Russell cleared his throat. "Let's see. Besides the incident you just described, there's the one involving his secretary, Amanda. You know her, don't you?"

"Yes. She became his secretary before we…she's very attractive."

"I can't argue that point. A wonderful person too. She's lucky to be alive, though. And she is because of Hunter. Then there's the rescue of my eldest son, Jonathan."

"Your son!"

He peered at her. "Didn't Hunter ever tell you about that?"

She shook her head.

Keller glanced over at Hunter's motionless body then walked to the table and chairs on the far side of the room. Morgan joined him.

"Frankly, it doesn't surprise me that he didn't tell you. He didn't tell me, either. I was a client of his as well as his physician for more than four years before I heard the story from Jonathan. Hunter isn't aware that I know." Russell glanced at Hunter again then continued, "Jonathan and Hunter were good buddies in the air force. They'd been assigned to the same squadron and flew sorties together in Desert Storm. Jonathan was Hunter's wingman over there. One day they were out—"

"Wait a minute, Russell." Morgan interrupted. "Hunter always referred to his wingman as *Stick.*"

"Yes, and Jonathan called Hunter *H.H.* Those were the nicknames they gave each other. That's why I didn't realize until recently that Hunter is the person who saved my son. Anyway, one day they were sent out on a mission, and Jonathan's F-16 fighter suffered a direct hit from a missile. He was badly injured but managed to eject. His parachute landed him a short distance from a desert road. All the while, Hunter was circling overhead and talking to him on a handset. Hunter told him to hide quickly because an Iraqi convoy was just a couple of miles up the road, headed in his direction. Apparently they were the ones who'd fired the missile that'd hit Jonathan's plane. Hunter knew if he attacked the convoy, the trucks would scatter out into the desert. Many would survive, and Jonathan would still be killed."

Morgan sat riveted to her seat. She had never heard a word of this story.

"But Jonathan was too hurt to move. He radioed Hunter to get the hell out of there before he also got shot down. Instead, Hunter swooped in and landed his F-16 on the roadway, ran out to where Jonathan was, picked him up, and carried him back to the plane. Somehow he managed to heft Jonathan up into the cockpit, which is about seven feet off the ground. He dumped his own parachute to make more room, then crammed into the single-seat cockpit in front of Jonathan and fired up the engine. The enemy convoy, charging directly at them, was shooting to stop Hunter from taking off. Hunter couldn't make a U-turn on the narrow road, so he shoved the throttle to full power and started shooting back at the Iraqis as the F-16 gained speed. Jonathan was scared to death. Heavy-caliber bullets were shredding the aircraft, the convoy trucks were looming in the windshield, and there wasn't nearly enough room to get airborne before slamming into the lead truck. That didn't matter to Hunter. He just kept on going full speed ahead. At what Jonathan described as the last possible second, Hunter dumped all the ordnance on board and retracted the landing gear at the same time. It was something that Jonathan said he himself never would've thought to do, especially in a crunch situation like that.

"By dumping the heavy ordnance, the aircraft instantly lightened. With the landing gear retracted, drag was eliminated, and the sleek little fighter virtually leaped off the roadway. Hunter immediately banked the jet into a tight nine-G turn right on the deck. Jonathan was sure the wingtip would strike the ground and cartwheel them into a crash, but it didn't. The first truck flipped over when the powerful blast from the engine of the turning fighter caught it broadside. The rest of the Iraqis kept firing until, seconds later, all the ordnance that Hunter had jettisoned slammed into the convoy, which exploded into the largest fireball Jonathan had ever seen.

"They landed safely back at their base in Riyadh, Saudi Arabia, with the fighter virtually running on fumes—the fuel tanks had holes in them. Ground personnel counted 137 hits on the aircraft. One-hundred and thirty-seven! Can you imagine that? The plane had to be taken out of service because it was too heavily damaged to repair. Out of curiosity, two pilot friends of Jonathan's crammed into the cockpit of a similar F-16 fighter to see what it would've been like to fly it that way. Apparently they were completely baffled. Neither pilot could understand how Hunter had done what he did, especially with such a damaged aircraft."

Morgan was stunned by the story. She didn't know whether to be mad at Hunter for not telling her, or proud of him for what he'd done.

"There's a coda to the story. It was later determined that the truck convoy had been transporting scud missiles topped with chemical warheads that were to be launched at Israel. In all likelihood, Hunter not only saved Jonathan's life that day but also the life of hundreds, maybe even thousands, of innocent Israeli civilians. Hunter was promoted to the rank of major and eventually received a medal for his actions during that mission. Jonathan had asked many a time, but Hunter never disclosed just what medal he had been awarded," Russell concluded.

"Maybe it was a Purple Heart?"

"Couldn't have been, Morgan. Those are only awarded to soldiers who're wounded in battle. Hunter didn't even get a scratch." He looked over at his patient. "Hasn't been so lucky lately, though, has he? Or maybe he has. None of his injuries are all that serious. Anyway, it's a great story, isn't it?"

She nodded.

"I'll always be grateful to Hunter for saving my son's life. Hunter's a good man. A rare breed. You should hold on to him, Morgan."

"He should've told me," she said, her voice barely a whisper. "How could he keep something like that a secret? You'd think he'd want to tell everyone about it."

The doctor shrugged. "I can't say for sure, but it could be that, at the time, he simply didn't want you to worry about him flying more missions. For as long as I've known Hunter, he's never once bragged about any of his exploits—dangerous or otherwise. I guess he just doesn't need to call attention to himself in that way." Russell stood. "I'd better be going." He scratched out a prescription for pain medication and handed it to her. "If you need anything, don't hesitate to ask."

"I have one request, Russell. Could you give me Jonathan's phone number? I'm going to see what I can find out about that medal."

He smiled as he gave it to her. "Don't leave me in the dark."

"Don't worry, I won't. Thank you for taking care of Hunter. And thank you for sharing that story with me. Though I may have to beat Hunter for not telling me about it."

He laughed. "You're more than welcome. Take care now."

Morgan locked the door behind him. She showered, slipped into the sheer, lacy nightgown she had brought, then climbed into the empty bed, completely exhausted. Even so, she remained awake for some time, graphically reliving the nightmare at *La Casa Negra* and thinking about her knight in bloodied armor.

CHAPTER

12

Hunter woke Friday morning in a fog then remembered where he was: the Landmark Hotel in Coral Gables. He looked over at the other bed. Morgan was with him. *What a night!* For a long while, he studied her face and half-uncovered body. She still looked barely thirty instead of nearly forty. He sighed. He'd always loved her. Admitting that to her probably wouldn't change anything between them. Their worlds were worlds apart.

He struggled to his feet, gently covered her, then labored to the bathroom, where he splashed hot water on his face. He couldn't recall Russell's arrival at their hotel the night before, but he did recall overhearing the good doctor's tale about his son's rescue. Hunter wondered just how much time would pass before Morgan asked him about that medal.

She was still asleep when he returned to the bedroom, so he eased into a chair then picked up the copy of the operations manual. He read voraciously, amazed at the scope and detail of the well-thought-out plan. The text actually mentioned the willful demolition of a US aircraft at the United States naval base in Guantanamo Bay, Cuba.

The aircraft would be carrying a high-ranking US official to meet Fidel Castro in an effort to improve relations between the two countries. The text specifically stated that the bomb would explode just after the dignitary had safely exited the aircraft, yet soon enough to make it obvious that he was supposed to have been killed. No specific mention was made of the president of the United States or Nelson Weber, but of course, he *was* the intended target. The plan was also designed to end Fidel Castro's rule of tyranny, and brilliantly placed the blame for the detonation on Castro himself. As a result, the US military would invade Cuba with the excuse to capture Castro for his heinous crime.

The key to the operation, the pretense that the explosion was nuclear, would give the military the advantage of claiming radioactive fallout. Because no one would want to endure that, everyone would be willing to leave, especially with the added bogus threat of another nuclear detonation on the island. This threat would be effective because most people would believe that Castro had the device in the first place, a leftover from the Cuban Missile Crisis maybe. And Castro had tried time and again to get the Americans to leave the military base at Guantanamo. Their continued presence on Cuban soil was a constant thorn in his side and a major embarrassment to him. A detonation by the Cuban leader of a low-yield nuclear device was not beyond the realm of possibility. And it would most certainly have done the trick; the base would have remained abandoned for years to come due to the lingering radiation.

According to the manual, the US military would claim that fallout was landing only on the island of Cuba because of the wind conditions and limited size of the explosion. Therefore, the Yucatan Peninsula in Mexico and, more specifically, the state of Florida would be safe destinations for the exodus of the entire Cuban population of eleven million. Exiled relatives in South Florida would likely hire or purchase boats to locate family members fleeing the island. This would cause South Florida, along with the ninety miles of open waters between Florida and Cuba, to be grossly overloaded with news agencies, people, boats, rescue services, coast guard vessels, and search aircraft. Added to the confusion would be the probability of the Cuban people taking to sea on inner tubes, boards, rafts, or anything else that would even marginally float; many had done so in the past to escape the island. The purpose of all this would be to create pandemonium: keep the press occupied, keep all the humanitarian services occupied, and keep everyone off the island.

A genius dreamed up this one, Hunter thought.

The plan even established a scenario that would require the US official to visit the island in the first place: selective nighttime air strikes by stealth aircraft, causing small explosions on specified targets, mostly in tourist areas. Civil unrest in Cuba had been on the rise for some time. The US media would be fed the illusion that these explosions were the result of the Cuban population's dissatisfaction with Castro's regime. For years Castro had been providing tourists with all the amenities of luxury and comfort while the Cuban populace couldn't purchase even the most basic staples. The need for humanitarian aid would be played up in the press to instigate the visit of the US official.

After the exodus from the island, air strikes would continue at night. The stealth fighters, armed with laser-guided weapons, would target and destroy buildings occupying land in prime waterfront locations. They would also destroy structures vital to the sugar industry, television and radio stations, antennae locations, and the like.

To explain these post-exodus explosions, the press would be told that members of the Cuban military who had not yet been captured and evacuated were placing explosive charges and destroying these structures to keep the US military from using them. But in reality the US military, following orders, would unknowingly clear the way for major US corporations to move in and build new facilities. Eventually, Cuba would be declared safe for the general public. By then, new resort hotels and casinos would already occupy premium beachfront property over the entire island, and the American sugar industry would have built new refineries and cultivated all the useful agricultural land for sugarcane.

Shit, this could work! Hunter thought.

The new acting president would, of course, be Al Buchanan. He'd declare the island US military property, citing such reasons as the murder of the US president by the Cuban government, the *phony* nuclear fallout, which had to be dealt with by some capable agency like the US military, and the abandonment of the entire island by the

Cuban people. By declaring the island US military property, the new acting president would introduce legislation to legally declare it US government land. Then the government could lease the prime property to US corporations. Al Buchanan could control this process, nicely lining his pockets along the way. *What a way to steal a country! This is brilliant.*

The operation also provided for the establishment of a few new US military bases there: two for the air force, an additional one for navy submarines, and one for the army. Hunter wondered if the vice president would have gone to such extremes if vengeance had not been such a motivator. Of course, money, big money, would be another factor. But the *piece de resistance* for Al Buchanan was the US presidency. Clearly the man had no limitations to his ambitions. Hunter stared off into space, his chin propped with one hand.

He was roused from his musing by Morgan. "I'm surprised you're up and about," she said, rubbing the sleep from her eyes. "You should be really sore."

"Oh, I am. You can be sure of that."

"What were you thinking about?"

"The operations manual." He eased back in the chair with a grunt. "I just finished reading what we have of it."

"And?"

"It's unbelievable! You'd better read it for yourself. You need to know everything that's in there, in case something happens to me." He stood slowly. "I'll be back in a minute. I'm going to the lobby for a newspaper. The exercise will probably help me loosen up. By the way, thanks for getting Russell to come here to treat my wounds."

"It was the least I could do after what you did for me at that nightclub, Hunter. You probably saved my life. Hey! What else happened to your leg besides the dog bite you told me about? The other injury almost looks like a gunshot wound."

"It is." He placed his hand on the doorknob. "And that's just part of the price I had to pay to take Juan Carlos out of the picture."

Hunter returned ten minutes later, sat on the bed, and began to peruse the front page. An article about Juan Carlos was prominent below the fold. "Oh, man, would you look at this crap?" he groused, his voice elevating. "I'm so tired of the political corruption in this town. This place is becoming a third-world toilet."

"What are you talking about, Hunter?"

"The Gomez brothers. Somehow they manipulated the *Herald* into lauding Juan Carlos as a businessman who was a pillar of the community, whitewashing his ignoble end." He looked up from the paper. "I can just see it now. The Cubans will trump this into another cause to rally around! It'll be on the front page for weeks. You just wait and see." He kept reading. "Those bastards! I can't believe this shit!"

"Take it easy, Hunter."

He tossed the paper aside. "Taking it easy isn't an option at the moment," he snapped. "I'm the prime suspect for Juan Carlos's murder. The police have an APB out on me! Isn't that just great?" He rose and stared out the window. "This is bad, Morgan. Really bad. It's going to make it much more difficult for us to warn President Weber."

Morgan came up behind him and gently put her hands on his shoulders. "We'll find a way."

Sighing deeply, he returned to the bed and picked up the paper again, next reading an article that described more explosions and unrest in Cuba. They occurred on the northern coast in Matanzas, on the outskirts of Havana, and in a town on the southeastern coast named Santiago de Cuba. The press had taken the bait by requesting humanitarian aid for the Cuban people. In fact, the article concluded with "The United States must do something."

The explosions had been caused by stealth fighters, not human turmoil—Hunter knew that. And even though the article didn't mention a visit by a US official, President Weber was already scheduled to meet Castro on November first.

The next headline got his blood boiling again. "Damn it, we just can't catch a break!"

"What now?"

"Weber's scheduled to fly to Europe and then Japan for economic summits. He leaves Washington this afternoon!"

"How long will he be gone?"

"Let's see…ah—the article says he'll visit several cities in the next eight days."

"What're we going to do?"

"Follow him to Europe, I guess." He grimaced as he lifted Morgan's suitcase to the bed then began assembling their belongings.

Meanwhile, Morgan finished reading the manual and slipped it back into the manila envelope. "Hunter, this is just too incredible! How can they get away with it?"

"A better question would be, how can we stop them? Listen, while I finish packing, book us a flight to Washington DC. It's almost ten. See if one's available for just after noon. We have to make a copy of the manual and stop at the bank where I have a safe deposit box before we go to the airport."

"Won't it be risky going to your bank?" she asked, coming over to him. "Someone may be watching."

He shook his head. "It's not my regular bank. No one knows about the box except me, and now you. We should be safe there."

"That's good. We don't need a repeat of last night." She shuddered.

"Have you ever been shot at before, Morgan?"

She grimaced. "No, can't say that I have."

"Before the other night, neither had I, except when I flew in Desert Storm. It's a scary experience, to say the least."

"You've never told me much about your experiences in Desert Storm, Hunter. Why is that?"

He held her at the waist and fondled her breasts through her lacy nightgown with his eyes. "Oh, I don't know. I guess I didn't want you making a fuss."

She shrugged. "No time like the present."

"We don't have time now." He eyeballed her again. "I really hate to say this, but you'd better get dressed. We need to get cracking."

She turned away obviously disappointed. He grinned to himself. She and Russell would both have a fit if they knew he'd heard their whole conversation last night.

She chose an outfit and changed in the bathroom. "Do you want me to charge the plane tickets on my credit card?" she asked through the door.

"No. We'll pay cash. And, of course, don't use our real names. Nor the name I'm registered under at this hotel either. Make up some new ones. I'm going to put my stuff in your case too, if you don't mind."

She opened the door and tossed him the nightgown to pack. A minute later, she was calling the airlines.

He finished and closed her suitcase just as she hung up the phone.

"We're all set. We're on Delta at twelve-forty-five."

"Good. Let's go." Hunter left the room then limped down one floor and stopped at his previous room. His key card still worked. Morgan followed with the suitcase and stood next to him.

"What're you doing?"

"I'm curious about something." He swung the door open. "Son of a bitch!" he said. "I knew it!"

"What?" she asked, peering around him.

"The covers I rigged last night are full of holes."

"Holes? What kind of holes?"

"Bullet holes. Someone slipped in here last night to kill us."

She blanched. "I didn't hear a thing!"

"You wouldn't have if a small caliber weapon with a silencer was used—that's the weapon of choice for professional hit men. And look here." He picked up a shredded pillow by the opposite bed. "The shots were further muffled by this. I'll bet the assassin was royally pissed when he realized the bed was empty."

"But how could anyone have possibly known we were here?"

"Your cell phone, Morgan. They tracked your damned cell phone." He quickly pulled her from the room and shut the door. "We gotta get out of here right now!"

They hurried down the stairs and out to the rental car. In no time they were across town at a Kinko's, copying the manual.

At the bank, they raided his safe deposit box, pulling out his six-thousand dollars of emergency cash before placing a copy of the manual inside.

Next, they made a quick stop at a drugstore for the pain medi- cation Russell Keller had prescribed as well as for a pair of sunglasses and a Marlin's baseball cap: Hunter's disguise. Speeding to the airport on State Road 836, they flew past a highway patrol car parked in the median. Hunter cringed. "Please, don't follow," he said aloud as he watched in the rearview mirror. The flashing lights came on. "Damn! Here he comes. Now we're screwed!"

"Maybe he's after someone else," Morgan said hopefully.

"Yeah, right," Hunter scoffed.

"Well, maybe he'll let us off with just a warning."

"He might—if everything else checks out OK. But I don't have my driver's license or any other identification, except for one credit card. And I can't let him see that anyway. There's an APB out on me, remember? Besides, I rented this car under an alias."

"Crap! What're we going to do?"

"Switch places." He set the cruise control, pushed the seat back as far as it would go, then glanced in the mirror again. "Shit, he's coming up fast! Come on, Morgan. Slide over here on top of me and take control."

"I bet you say that to all the girls," she said wiggling onto his lap. "I think maybe you planned this."

"I did. I love having beautiful women lap dance on me. Hurry up! I'm getting excited."

She grasped the wheel. "OK. I've got it."

By the time he'd struggled into the passenger seat, grunting, groaning, and moaning as he did so, the highway patrolman had closed most of the gap.

Morgan pulled well over on the shoulder and stopped with the state patrol car glued to her bumper. She lowered the window as the trooper approached. "Hello, Officer," she said with a smile. "There a problem?"

He ducked and peered over his sunglasses at Hunter. "Yes, ma'am, there certainly is, and breaking the speed limit is only part of it. When I clocked this vehicle doing seventy in a fifty-five zone, it had a male driver."

Hunter hung his head sheepishly. "OK, Officer, I can explain. You're right, I was driving. You're very observant." He climbed out of the car and spoke to the trooper across the car's roof. "We're running late for a really important meeting way north of here." That much was true. "I forgot my wallet this morning, so I don't have any identification on me. I was trying to prevent a longer delay than necessary."

The officer walked around to the passenger side and looked Hunter square in the eyes. "I see," he said. "What's your name, sir?"

"Harry Johnson," Hunter replied, maintaining eye contact.

"Is this your Cadillac?" He nodded toward it.

"Yes—well, technically no. It's a rental, sir. I got it yesterday at the Landmark Hotel in Coral Gables. The manager, Lisset Vizcaino, can verify that."

Morgan got out of the car and joined them.

"Do you have any identification, ma'am?"

"Yes, sir." She reached through the passenger window, grabbed her wallet, and fished out her driver's license.

The officer examined it. "You live in Alexandria, Virginia, Ms. Lindsey?"

"Yes, that's correct." He gave her back the license.

"And where do you live, sir?"

Hunter's mind whirled. He couldn't give his real address—or any address in Miami for that matter. The lawman could check it out pronto on his radio. The Harry Johnson alias wouldn't match up. "I live with her." He pointed at Morgan. "She's my girlfriend."

"Let me see your license again, ma'am."

She handed it over.

Looking at it, the officer said, "Sir, what's your address?"

Hunter laughed nervously. "Ah, you're not going to believe this officer, but I don't know. I only just moved in with Morgan four days ago. She came to Miami to help me pack my things. I haven't memorized the new address yet."

The trooper stared at him. "Wait here where I can see you. I'm going to try to verify your story about the rental."

While the officer sat in his patrol car talking on the radio, Hunter said to Morgan, "The rental info will check out, but I don't know what this guy thinks about the rest of my story."

The patrolman stepped from his car a minute later, yanked his pistol, and drew down on them. "Put your hands on top of your head—both of you," he shouted. "And don't move a muscle." He walked forward slowly, keeping the weapon trained on them.

"Shit!" Hunter said under his breath. "They must've discovered the shot-up hotel room. Morgan, when this guy gets to us, distract him somehow."

The trooper moved closer, adjusting his two-handed grip on the Glock 9 mm pistol out in front of him.

"Listen, Officer, there's been a mistake," Morgan said, lowering her hands. "If we could…"

The officer immediately shifted his weapon and attention toward her and shouted, "Put your hands on—"

Hunter broadsided the trooper with a powerful right cross. The pistol dropped to the ground at Hunter's feet and discharged as the officer staggered backward and fell to his knees. The bullet ripped through the right rear tire of their Cadillac, causing the tire to go flat.

"Figures," Hunter mumbled as he snatched up the gun. "I'm truly sorry, Officer. I didn't want to do that. Now take out your handcuffs and cuff yourself to the passenger-door handle of my rental car."

"Mister, you're just getting yourself in deeper," the trooper said, rubbing his chin. "Why don't you give me the gun."

"Officer, I don't have time to explain, and even if I did, you wouldn't believe a word I said. When this is over, I'll look you up and personally apologize. I'll even let you get square with me for that sucker punch. But if you don't cuff yourself to that car this instant, I'll have to shoot you."

The trooper obliged.

"Morgan, put our stuff in the police car. We're taking it."

While Hunter recovered her license from the officer, he made sure that the lawman couldn't see their suitcase being transferred. They didn't need him knowing that they were heading for the airport. Hunter apologized once more, left the pistol and the keys to the handcuffs on the hood of the rental, then slipped behind the wheel of the patrol car.

As they raced away, he glanced in the rearview mirror. "He's right, you know? I am getting in deeper. Now they can add assault and battery on a police officer to the charges when they lock me up.

They'll probably also get me for grand theft auto, discharging a firearm in a populated area, and theft of police property." He looked at her. "I've made you a fugitive too. Isn't that just dandy? I sure hope we make it to the airport before that trooper's backup arrives on the scene."

Hunter turned up the volume on the police radio and checked the mirror again. He quickly exited the state road, made an immediate U-turn, ran one block, hung a right onto Perimeter road, then stomped on the gas.

"Listen, if we get out of town without being arrested, we'll try to contact President Weber this afternoon in Washington. We won't have but a couple of hours. If we fail there, and it's likely we will, we'll have to follow him to every city he visits until we're successful. If we wait for him to return to the States, that would cut things too close before his trip to Cuba. Can you get the president's itinerary from the *Washington Herald*?"

She nodded. "I should be able to. I'll call my coworker Ellen Connelly to see if she can fax a copy to my house."

Hunter dropped Morgan and her suitcase at the terminal then ditched the patrol car in one of the main parking garages. By the time he met her at the counter, she'd already purchased tickets for Mr. and Mrs. Stephen Garrett. While she called her coworker, he went into the gift shop and bought two cheap gold-tone rings, for himself and the missus, and a soft leather briefcase into which he placed the second copy of the operations manual.

As Hunter left the shop, a man in a beige trench coat approached rapidly from across the corridor. Hunter frowned. *A little warm for a coat,* he thought, *especially inside.* The man wore thick-lensed tortoise-shell glasses and looked European, maybe German or Scandinavian. "Excuse me, sir," he said, opening his coat just enough for Hunter to see the long-barreled pistol with a silencer trained on him. "You need to come with me." Grasping Hunter's arm, he directed his movement.

Forced to walk in Morgan's direction, Hunter purposely stared past her at first. When he did look at her, he flashed a warning with his eyes then shook the briefcase discreetly to draw her attention to it.

STEPHEN YOHAM

She nodded. As he and the man passed, Hunter dropped one of the gold bands. It pinged and bounced, then rolled across the tiled floor, distracting the man. Pumped with adrenaline, Hunter dropped the briefcase, elbowed the man in the ribcage, and ran like hell.

Though winded, the man immediately gave chase. He caught up with Hunter at the end of a corridor where a janitor was mopping a restroom floor, the door propped open. Hunter rushed inside and hurried to close the door. The man was too quick. He forced it open, cornering Hunter at the back of the room. The janitor dropped his mop and fled like a scared jackrabbit.

"Who are you? What do you want?" Hunter demanded.

The man pulled out the gun. "Mr. Mahoy. Missed you at the hotel last night." Hunter lunged at the man, shoving him forcefully as the gun discharged. The man tumbled backward over the janitor's mop bucket, landing flat on his back and cracking his head hard on the unforgiving tile. He lay motionless in the spilled soapy water, the gun beside him, blood pooling beneath his head.

Hunter grimaced in pain. "Son of a bitch!" he said through clenched teeth. He clutched his left arm with his right hand. Warm liquid seeped between his fingers. The bullet had penetrated his left arm a few inches above the elbow. It had passed clean through, leaving a relatively small entry and exit wound, but it hurt like the devil. He wiggled his fingers. They worked. Apparently the single-round hadn't struck anything vital; the bleeding was minimal, and he had dexterity in his hand. His heart stopped when he suddenly heard the unmistakable sound of the gun clattering against the tile floor. He spun on his heels. The would-be assassin, still prone on the floor, now had the gun in his grasp and was taking aim. Hunter dived for the janitor's mop. Grabbing it by the head, he swung it like a baseball bat with all his might. He hit the man square in the face just as the gun fired. The bullet barely missed Hunter, lodging in the wall behind him. The man lay motionless once again, his bloodied face distorted by pain.

Hunter reeled. Yet another close call. Too close! How many times could he cheat death? He struggled to his feet. Security would be there any time now, alerted by the janitor. After stepping around the killer, he kicked the gun across the room then checked the man's pockets for a wallet or identification. Nothing but a fold of cash bound with a money clip. That and a slightly enlarged copy of Hunter's passport photograph. He shoved the cash and the picture into his own pocket. Then he rinsed his arm at the sink before wrapping the wound tightly with a small cleaning cloth left by the janitor. He stuffed a second cloth in his pocket and left the bathroom.

He returned to the shop where he'd purchased the briefcase and found what he'd hoped for: A leather jacket. He donned it instantly, concealing his makeshift bandage that already sported a bloodstain. He paid for the jacket while wearing it.

Hunter sailed through the metal detectors at the entrance to the concourse then tacked his way through the crowd to the appropriate gate.

"My wife's already on board," he said, handing his ticket to the attendant.

"Oh, yes, Mr. Garrett. Your wife said you were coming. You're in seat 16-A."

He'd barely made it on board. The flight crew not only sealed the door right behind him but also escorted him to his seat. His arm throbbed wildly.

Morgan's expression transformed from one of worry to one of relief. "I was so scared for you, Hunter!" she whispered. "What happened? And where'd you get that jacket?"

"I'll tell you later. Everything's fine now. You get the briefcase?"

"Yes." She gestured at the floor where the case sat between her feet.

"Good." The plane began taxiing for the runway.

"How far do you live from the airport?" he asked, discreetly elevating his arm to reduce the blood flow and the throbbing.

"Several miles, but we can take the Metro. There's a station a few blocks from my house." Now that he was safe, Hunter's adrenaline crashed, and he soon drifted off to sleep. He woke up about halfway through the flight to find Morgan using the on-board telephone system to call Ellen again. While she did so, he went to the lavatory to redress his wound with the spare cloth in his pocket.

How would anyone have known to look for him at the airport?
he wondered. Then it hit him. The five-thousand-dollar cash with-drawal he'd made at his regular bank the previous day. They'd tapped into his account information. The large withdrawal must have clued them in to his leaving town. The APB out on him would have been another big hint. Didn't take a rocket scientist to figure it out from there, especially since he hadn't surfaced at his home or office. He fin-ished the new dressing and donned the jacket again. Then he flushed the bloodied cloth and cleaned the sink before exiting the lavatory.

Returning to his seat, he smiled reassuringly at Morgan, who whispered, "President Weber leaves at five-forty-five. But that's prob-ably the time he departs Andrews Air Force Base. He'd leave the White House about thirty minutes earlier for his flight to Andrews aboard Marine One."

"Any way we can pass a note to him before he boards that heli-copter?" Hunter asked. "Don't reporters have access to the South Lawn when he departs from the White House by air?"

"Usually they do," she said, nodding. "Let me think about that for a while."

Their flight landed on time at Reagan National, where they caught the Metro to Alexandria, Virginia, then walked the last few blocks to Morgan's house. Colorful fallen leaves crunched beneath their feet as they made their way past the cobblestone driveways of elegant houses.

"Here we are," she announced as they approached the serpen-tine walk of a redbrick federal-style structure with a white door, white shutters, and a gray-slate roof. The grounds were well landscaped and meticulously cared for, like all the others in the neighborhood.

He whistled. A soft, flattering whistle that tapered off slowly and seemed to hang in the air even after he'd stopped. "Very nice. Exactly how much are they paying you at that newspaper?"

She smiled. "Thanks, but actually the bank owns more of it than I do."

"What will your neighbors think of you bringing a stray man home like this?"

"There's no one around this time of the day to see," she said, pressing the key into the lock. "And they'd probably think it's a good thing. They all say I work too much."

She led him across the oak plank floor and down a long mauve-painted hallway trimmed with white baseboards, chair rails, and crown moldings. Gold-framed oil paintings with individual spot-lights lined the plaster walls. Three small chandeliers hung from the nine-foot ceiling, and an ornate silver candelabrum sat on a Victorian sideboard at the far end of the hall. She opened the door to her study and strolled directly to the handcrafted chestnut desk.

Hunter ran his hand along its surface. "I remember this piece," he said, easing into the chair behind it. "It's hard to believe that it's over two-hundred years old. Where was that estate sale that we found it? Asheville, North Carolina?" He smiled. "This was a rare find. I'm glad you still have it."

"I could never part with it, Hunter. It's my prized possession. And yes, it was Asheville." She found the fax Ellen had sent and handed it to him, then pushed the message button on her answering machine.

Hunter's arm was throbbing again, so he elevated it as he studied the president's travel schedule. He also listened in on Morgan's messages. A few came from her newspaper, including one from her boss congratulating her on the article she'd just completed, followed immediately by a demand that she update him on her next project. The last message was from Vice President Al Buchanan, saying he was back in town and wanted to meet with her. He'd left his unlisted number.

"Wow! Personal greetings from the vice president. Just whose side are you on?" he teased. "Looks like I've teamed up with the enemy. A spy in my old flame's clothing."

She propped her hands on her hips, smirking at his remarks. "It's about the article I wrote on his son's death. He spoke with me yesterday morning, but he had to cut the call short."

Pleased that none of her messages sounded romantically connected, Hunter returned to Weber's itinerary. The first stop placed the president in Geneva but for just one day, making it impossible to make the connections to arrive in time to contact him there. "We'll go to London, the second city on the president's itinerary if we miss him today," Hunter said.

"Hey!" She faced him. "What about this idea? If I can meet Al Buchanan at the White House today, I might be able to contact the president. Maybe I could pass him a note."

Hunter snapped his fingers. "That's a fantastic idea. We might not get a better chance."

She reached for the phone and punched in Buchanan's unlisted number. "Hello. This is Morgan Lindsey from the *Washington Herald*. I'm returning the vice president's call." She held up her crossed fingers while waiting. Then she smiled. "Hello, Mr. Vice President. Yes, I just returned to DC and found your message. I may have to leave town again soon, but I could meet you this afternoon if you can fit me into your busy schedule. Four-thirty?" She nodded at Hunter. "That'd be perfect." After a lengthy pause, she said, "Yes, I look forward to it too, sir. I'll see you at the White House at four-thirty." She hung up.

Hunter smiled. "That was smooth, darlin'. Now what should we write in the note? We can't say anything revealing in case the wrong person reads it. Yet we have to say something that'll make Weber want to talk to us."

She sighed. "You know, even if I can pass the note, he may not read it until after he's airborne. That means he won't be able to speak with us until the next time we contact him."

"Which at the very earliest will be a couple of days from now in London," he added. "Morgan, you should wear that stunning red dress you wore last night. Once you're inside, I would think your increased visibility will bolster your chances. The president couldn't help but notice you and maybe accept your approach. But what do we say in the note?"

She shrugged. "I don't know. But I don't have much time, so I'm going to shower and get ready."

"Before you do, I need your assistance, Morgan." He stood and removed the leather jacket, revealing the blood-soaked towel, then sat down again.

"Good lord, Hunter! What happened?"

"Don't get excited. It's just a scratch."

He described the incident as she removed his handiwork and exposed the wound. He stiffened.

"Yeah, I can see it's just a scratch," she said sarcastically. "You need a doctor to look at this."

"Russell's the only one we could call, and he certainly won't do us any good up here in Virginia."

"But, Hunter—"

"No buts, Morgan. And no doctor! They're required by law to report gunshot wounds. It's not that bad, really. The bullet was small, a .22 caliber, I believe. Anyway, it passed clean through the muscle. I don't think it did any real damage. I'm sore as hell, though."

"Hunter, a gunshot wound isn't something to mess around with. What if it gets infected?"

"It won't. Let's just wash it and apply an antiseptic. We have more important things to take care of right now."

She glared at him. "I know what that *H* stands for now, *Hardheaded.* Why didn't you tell me sooner?"

"You would've worried. And we couldn't have done anything about it on the plane anyway." He dug his photo out of his pocket and handed it to her. "This is all the man carried besides the gun and some cash."

"How'd they know you'd be at the airport?" she asked, studying the photo.

He told her what he'd determined.

"That still doesn't explain why they're trying to kill you."

"Not in itself," he said, "but the first time I exited the underground complex, I made a call from a pay phone on the base using my calling card number. So they must know I was there that night. Then last night, base security shot at two intruders—us! These people have obviously decided not to take any chances, Morgan. We'll have to be extremely careful from now on. We've already stretched our luck pretty thin." He grimaced. "And the *H* stands for *Hurting,* definitely *Hurting.*"

CHAPTER

13

It took Morgan about twenty minutes to get ready for her late-afternoon appointment with the vice president. For that whole time, Hunter sat with a pen poised in his hand and stared at a blank sheet of paper. She finally jogged him by reminding him he was running out of time, and he quickly jotted something in small print. He tore the paper along the edge of his message and folded it a couple of times before handing it to her.

"You're staying here, right?"

"Yep. I wish I could come with you, but it's far too risky for me to be seen anywhere near the White House. Besides, the rest will do me good."

Morgan gave him a quick kiss on the cheek and hurried out to her car. She buzzed up Jeff Davis Highway then crossed Memorial Bridge onto Constitution Avenue. Luckily she found a parking space just a short stroll from the East Gate. Marine One was approaching from the south. The noisy green-and-white helicopter transitioned to a hover, scattering autumn leaves in every direction. Half a minute later, it landed on the South Lawn, consuming its shadow at the moment of contact.

A brief walk brought her to the security kiosk.

"Good afternoon, I'm Morgan Lindsey," she said to the guard. "I'm here to see the vice president."

"Oh, yes, Ms. Lindsey. I was notified to expect you. I'll need some identification."

She handed over her driver's license and press badge.

"Here you are, Ms. Lindsey. An aide will meet you just inside the entrance. Enjoy your visit."

She'd toured the White House once before, the tour for the general public. This visit would be different. She tried to contain her excitement. *Look professional,* she told herself, *and act normal.*

At the door she was met by a petite young woman decked out in a crisp white blouse and a conservative navy-blue suit. "Morgan Lindsey?"

"Yes, that's right."

The young woman offered a handshake. "Hello. I'm Jamie Harte. I'll be your escort to the vice president's office. Would you please follow me?"

Moments later she was face-to-face with the vice president of the United States.

"Ms. Lindsey." Al Buchanan rose and crossed to greet her. "How nice to meet you."

"Hello, Mr. Vice President. Thank you for accommodating me on such short notice. I hope I haven't cramped your Friday afternoon."

"Not at all. I'm delighted you could come." They shook hands. "Please, make yourself comfortable. Can I get you anything?"

"No, thank you."

As he rounded his hand-carved mahogany desk, she settled into one of two tapestry chairs that faced him and crossed her legs.

Morgan's emotions—elation, fear, sorrow—all battled for control. Here before her sat the second most powerful man in the free world, exuding confidence and charm. Yet since the previous evening, she knew about his darker side. *He doesn't look like a murderer,* she thought.

Buchanan looked younger than his fifty-four years, and he emanated importance in his obviously expensive double-breasted olive-green suit. It was flawlessly tailored to his tall, slim frame. His richly appointed office furthered the impression of stature. The deeply polished hardwood floor reflected the light spilling in from two tall windows. A gleaming mahogany wainscot lined the fourteen-foot-high walls that automatically carried her focus to the ornate plaster ceiling. Two-hundred-year-old oils hung strategically at eye level. An antique grandfather clock stood in the far corner, the silent sentinel's pendulum slicing away at an invisible enemy, time.

"Did you bring the letter, Ms. Lindsey?"

"Yes, sir. I have it right here." She plucked it from her purse and handed it to him.

She knew exactly which part caused him to raise his eyebrows. As three words—"the Gomez brothers"—slipped from his mouth, she realized that he didn't mean to say them aloud. When he looked up, a glint of anger flashed in his eyes, then it was gone. "You have no idea who sent you this, Ms. Lindsey?"

"None whatsoever," she lied, hoping to sound convincing. "As you can see, it's postmarked Houston, Texas, and has a question mark for a return address."

He studied the envelope. "Do you believe the information in this letter is true?"

"Yes, sir, I do. Last night I met with a young man who was a friend of Juan Carlos Gomez. He told me that one night last week, when Juan Carlos had had too much to drink, he bragged about the Gomez brothers causing your son's death. Juan Carlos's admission and the information in the letter meshed perfectly."

"Perhaps the young man sent the letter," the vice president said, his brown eyes boring into her own.

She shifted in her seat. "My gut feeling is that he did not. And he never mentioned it during our conversation."

"Do you think he'd testify in court?"

"That would be impossible, Mr. Vice President. He was shot to death while he was still talking to me." She flinched.

He sat facing straight ahead with his hands clasped together in front of him on the desktop. He waited until she made eye contact with him again. "I'm sorry to hear that; it must have been awful for you, Ms. Lindsey. Did the gunman get caught? Was it Juan Carlos? He seemed capable of something like that."

"The gunman got away, sir. But it couldn't have been Juan Carlos. He was killed the night before."

"What!" His eyes widened. "How?"

"According to the article in the *Miami Herald*, he was shot in a gun battle at a private home, Mr. Vice President."

She wished she could read his mind. Now that he knew the Gomez brothers were responsible for his son's horrific death, what would he do? She recalled Trooper Pete Mitchell's description of Sean's accident. Did Buchanan want them dead? If so, would he have the surviving brothers killed, or simply let the law do its job? Was he unhappy that he couldn't confront Juan Carlos personally?

"The letter mentions an accomplice in the CIA, Ms. Lindsey. Do you know that person's identity?"

Be careful here, she thought. *Don't screw up.* "I'm still working on that, sir." Second lie in less than a minute.

"I see. Since we obviously won't have the testimony from the young man you spoke of a few moments ago, what do we have? Can anything be proven?"

"One item can, Mr. Vice President. The Scotch bottle the FBI currently holds in its evidence room isn't the one found in the wreck. The state trooper who first arrived on the scene can attest to that."

Except for the grandfather clock ticking away in the corner, the regal office fell silent. Buchanan stared at the letter. Morgan smoothed her dress, drying her sweaty palms at the same time. The grandfather clock clanged out the five o'clock hour, startling her at first.

Finally, she asked, "Mr. Vice President, was Sean's body cremated?"

Buchanan focused on her. He suddenly looked older. "No, it wasn't. Why?"

"There's a course of action that could be taken, sir, but it would involve your consent."

"And what would that be?"

"Sean's body could be exhumed for testing of the poison the Gomez brothers used. You'd have no guarantee of conclusive results, but the pathologist I spoke with said there'd be a good chance of finding it—if he knew what poison to look for."

"Do you know what poison was used, Ms. Lindsey?"

"According to my source, cyanide."

Buchanan stood and drifted over to the window. Shoving his hands into his pockets, he stared out in silence at Marine One. Sadness appeared to consume him, his age increasingly more apparent. *He suddenly seems so human*, she thought. *How could this same man be planning to assassinate the president? Maybe he'll call it off now.*

He faced her. "Thank you for all you've done to find the truth about my son's death, Ms. Lindsey. You've given me much to think about." He gave a quick glance over his shoulder out the window. "President Weber is about to depart for economic summits overseas. I should see him off. Would you care to accompany me to the South Lawn?"

She'd been waiting for the right time to ask if she could meet President Weber. Buchanan's timing was perfect. "I'd like that very much, sir. Thank you for asking."

Morgan followed the vice president out to the South Lawn, where she waited eagerly for President Weber to come into view. Finally he appeared and started across the lawn toward the helicopter, smoothing back his dark windblown hair. He shook hands and chatted briefly with several people and nodded or waved to others. Morgan's pulse raced with the suspense. The president of the United States was only a few feet away from her. Would she get to speak with him? Should she move toward him or stand there like a block of cement? She squeezed the tiny folded note so tightly that her fingers ached. Soon President Weber greeted the person next to her then turned in her direction. Crunch time.

Smiling, she stepped forward, offering a handshake. "Hello, Mr. President. Morgan Lindsey, *Washington Herald*." Even up close, his unlined face and sharp blue eyes didn't betray his sixty-one years.

He shook her hand. "It's a pleasure to meet you, Ms. Lindsey. You've been busy of late. Am I to be the subject of your next story?"

She smiled, leaned forward, and whispered, "An assassination attempt is planned in Cuba on November first. Trust no one. See you in Europe."

When she withdrew, he had a strange expression on his face. As their hands parted, she pressed the note into his palm.

"Thank you for coming today, Ms. Lindsey," he said, discreetly sliding his hand into his pocket.

"My pleasure, Mr. President. I hope to see you again soon."

"And I you," he replied. He moved along the line of reporters, greeting several others before boarding the helicopter. The engine immediately started, and the giant four-bladed rotor came alive, increasing in speed until the blades were only a blur. Within a few minutes Marine One had departed and faded from view.

Morgan hummed her way into the kitchen laden with a gourmet takeout dinner from her favorite Thai restaurant and a bottle of wine.

Hunter looked up from the newspaper he was reading.

"Hi, honey, I'm home. Did you miss me?" she crowed, gliding across the room and setting down her burden in front of him.

He hid his smile. "This smells wonderful. I gather things did not go well out on Pennsylvania Avenue today."

"Au contraire, mon amour." She yanked two plates from the cupboard and tossed them his way.

He scrambled to catch them. "Have you been drinking?" He teased. "You seem a little…happy."

"Not yet. But I will as soon as you open that bottle. There's a corkscrew in the top drawer over there." She pointed with the silverware in her hand. "You're going to be so pleased with me, Hunter. I warned President Weber about the assassination in Cuba on November first and passed him the note too."

"That's great! Were you alone with him?" He searched for wineglasses.

She gestured toward the china cabinet. "No. But I was very discreet. He knows to watch for us in Europe."

"That's fantastic, Morgan! You did a terrific job."

"Yes, I thought so too," she said smugly, clinking her glass against his. "Umm, that's good. I'm curious: what'd you say in that note?"

"Actually, what I wrote still applies even after what you told him. I wrote: *Speak with the person who flashes the mirror—it's vital to your health.*"

They sat down to eat.

"Mirror? What are you talking about?"

"Well, it came to me that I'd use a mirror to flash the sun at him and his bodyguards wherever we try to contact him. Now because of the note, the president will surely direct the Secret Service to apprehend us and take us to him."

She looked up, her fork poised halfway to her mouth. "You know, Hunter, that's absolutely brilliant!"

He shrugged. "What can I say? It's all that came to mind. Listen, after dinner, we need to make reservations for London. And somehow we have to get phony passports. I know a shady character in Miami who could do it, but returning to Miami would be inconvenient and dangerous right now."

She tipped the wine bottle again. "I have a contact who can help us. I've used him several times before. His name's Seymour Banks. He's a retired detective turned private eye, and he's motivated by money. He helped me get the goods on a few local politicians recently. I'll bet he can get us an appointment tonight—if we're willing to pay his price. We'd better get matching fake driver's licenses too, if we can."

*   *   *

The amber streetlights of Bird Road raced across the shiny hood of Enrique Gomez's silver Mercedes as he and Pedro headed home from the funeral parlor where they'd made arrangements for Juan Carlos's burial. Darkened strip malls flashed by, all dead for the night. Only the fluorescent calling cards of fast-food joints and gas stations beckoned passing motorists.

As successful and prominent members of the Cuban exile community in Miami, Enrique and Pedro felt it necessary to have their cousin's funeral open to anyone who wished to attend. A public mass would be held Monday morning; then the procession would travel to the cemetery, where a eulogy would be given.

Pedro lit a fresh cigar and gestured angrily with it. "I am telling you, Enrique, we should forget about the tape or waiting for the police to find Mahoy. Let us just kill him before this becomes a bigger mess, like what is happening with his secretary."

Enrique turned north onto the Palmetto Expressway and accelerated the E-class sedan to seventy. "Pedro, do you not like the report Mahoy's secretary gave to your detective brother-in-law? The report that we paid a small fortune to keep out of the paper? The one where she said Juan broke into her house to find that tape recording about us killing the senator, and then Juan beat her and tried to rape her?" He glanced at his brother. "No? Well, I do not like it either, Pedro. She probably does not even know where Mahoy put the tape, but she does know what is on it. Now we will have to spend a little more money to get rid of her."

Enrique veered east onto 836. "Juan was stupid, Pedro. Really stupid. And you're probably right about killing Mahoy, even though he did us a favor when he shot Juan. A big favor."

"I agree. The trouble is, Mahoy has talked on the phone to that woman reporter in Washington. Then she comes down here and we had that mess at the nightclub. What did she learn there? Damn her! And Mahoy too." Pedro pounded his fist on the dash.

"Relax, Pedro. She will not be a problem much longer. Neither will Mahoy if he is with her." He chuckled. "Bass said he would take care of the reporter, but I took matters into my own hands."

Puffing on their stogies, they rode in silence for a few minutes past a colossal cruise ship docked along Government Cut. Their side-by-side waterfront mansions on Star Island reflected in the bay off to the left.

"Hey, Pedro, I almost forgot to tell you. I received word from Buchanan's office that he will be attending the funeral for Juan Carlos. He is going to say a few words. Isn't that the most ironic thing you have ever heard?"

They both laughed heartily.

*   *   *

Hunter woke Saturday morning to the mouth-watering aroma of bacon. It drew him to the kitchen like a moth to a light.

"Good morning, sleepyhead. Sit down," Morgan said. "Everything's ready. Hope you're hungry." She poured him a cup of freshly brewed coffee.

He was more than hungry. He polished off first one and then a second helping. Leaning back in his chair, he said, "I could really get used to this."

She smiled. "Could you, now?"

"Yep, and just to show what a good sport I am, I'll do the dishes."

He carried the dirty dishes to the sink then filled the bowl with suds. As he scrubbed the frying pan, he gazed through the mullioned window to the sky: clear with a few developing clouds. It reminded him of exactly one week earlier when he'd checked the weather from his bedroom window on the Saturday morning of his fateful flight. He thought about his sailplane and sighed. This would have been another perfect flying day, but he'd be grounded for a while.

As his focus fell back to earth, it landed on a car facing his direction parked two houses away on the far side of the road. Two men occupied the front seat. "What're you guys up to?" he mumbled. "You watching us?"

He finished his mundane but satisfying chore then went in search of Morgan. He found her in her bedroom packing. He led her to the nearest window where he separated the blinds slightly.

"Look at the blue four-door Chrysler sedan just down the street. Is that a neighbor's car?"

She squinted. "I've never seen it before. Why?"

"It might be my imagination, but I think they're watching us."

"Really?" She peered at the vehicle again.

He closed the blind. "Do you have a safe, Morgan?"

"Yes, there's a floor safe in the closet. It came with the house."

"Good. Let's stow the operations manual in there. If we're detained, we certainly don't want it in our possession."

She tossed aside a couple of empty cardboard boxes that had been covering the safe then opened it. Hunter put the manual inside, closed the lid, and spun the dial before replacing the two boxes. Suddenly sizing up the empty boxes and Morgan's luggage, he grabbed the larger box and ducked back out of the closet.

"Morgan, I know you've already packed two suitcases, but forget the smaller case. Everything will have to fit inside the large one."

"Why?" She tossed a hair dryer next to her cosmetics bag.

"If these guys are following us, I have an idea how we might lose them. Let me see your camera for a minute—with the telephoto lens."

He returned to the window and pushed the blind aside enough to allow the powerful lens a clear view. As Morgan repacked, Hunter studied the pair in the car. After a few moments the driver reached for a thermos and filled a cup for his passenger, then filled one for himself.

Hunter turned from the window. "Now I'm sure these guys are watching us. They're drinking coffee!" He slipped the packed suitcase inside the box. "It's a good thing we got these false passports and driver's licenses last night." He handed them to her. "You'd better carry them in your purse. Let's go. And don't pay any attention to the blue sedan when we leave. Don't even look at it. Just drive normally."

"Where are we going?" she asked on the way to the garage.

"To a large shopping mall, one with department stores that would sell just about everything."

"I know a good place. It's not far from here. What do you have in mind?"

"We'll park near one of the department stores, and I'll unload the box from the trunk. You stand next to me and fumble in your purse, pretending to look for the receipt. After a moment, pull out a piece of paper and wave it victoriously. We'll go into the department store, and if we're convincing, they'll believe we're returning a purchase. Once we're inside, we'll move as fast as we can through the store and into the mall itself. At least one of our shadows will follow, but he'll probably lag behind a bit so he won't be spotted. The other will most likely stay with the car in case we double back. In the meantime, we'll crush the box and dump it in a trash can, then call a taxi to meet us at the opposite end of the mall. With any luck, we should be long gone before the men realize we gave them the slip. Of course, your car will have to remain in the parking lot until we return from overseas." Feeling the pull of her stare, he faced her. "What?"

"Your plan is faulty, Hunter. For one thing, the shadow will quickly know that we didn't actually return anything. Besides, my suitcase isn't exactly light. You'll be laboring under the weight of the darn thing in that box, so you won't be able to elude the guy very easily, especially with your injuries."

"I know it's not a perfect plan, but I can't think of anything else off the top of my head. Can you?"

"No, I can't," she admitted. "I guess we'll just have to give it a try."

He carried the box to the garage and pressed the wall button to open the garage door, then made a big show of loading the box into the trunk of her car. They had backed out to the end of her driveway when Morgan flipped down her visor and pressed the remote to close the garage door. Instantly, a deafening boom rattled the car, spinning it halfway around as flaming projectiles rocketed past them. Hunter yanked Morgan down onto the seat and covered her with his body. His heart pounded with hers. They yelped simultaneously when a burning piece of the door slammed noisily onto the hood of her car. Plumes of flame leaped skyward from the remnants of her two-car garage. A fiery ember hissed menacingly against the windshield.

"Son of a bitch!" Hunter said incredulously, then fell back into silence.

Morgan just stared.

"The bastards rigged an explosive to blow when you pressed the remote!" he said. "They must have figured we'd be in the car when we opened the garage door. *Shit!* Get out of here, Morgan! Step on it!"

She just sat there, mouth agape, eyes huge. *"Come on, Morgan, let's go!"* Hunter stomped the gas pedal from the passenger side. The tires squealed, and the car swerved all over the road as he steered with his left hand around the burning obstacles in the street.

The flaming door remnant flew off the hood, banging the roof once during its departure. The blue Chrysler fishtailed wildly through the debris right behind them.

Forced into action, Morgan grabbed the steering wheel. She blew a four-way stop then careened left into an alley behind a block of strip stores. Her Pontiac flew through the narrow run, sending empty cardboard boxes and other trash into the path of the pursuing vehicle.

Hunter turned and watched out the rear window. Boxes bounced off and smashed under the Chrysler. As Morgan skidded hard into a left turn, he said, "Shit, I don't believe this! We have two cars following us! A silver Chevy Malibu is closing the gap on the Chrysler."

"*What!*" She whipped around another corner then glanced in the rearview mirror. "What should I do?"

"I don't know. They're too close for us to abandon the car and run. Just keep going. Get on the beltway if you can. We're gonna kill someone on these surface streets."

Morgan swerved wildly, barely missing a Toyota as she ran a red light. The Chrysler clipped the Toyota's front end and spun around as the Malibu raced past. Then the Chrysler straightened and accelerated again.

"Who in hell are these guys?" he asked, reflexively checking that his seat belt was fastened. Clutching his seat, he turned and looked out the back again. "The Chevy also has two men in it. Oh, shit!"

"*What!*"

"The passenger's got a gun, and it doesn't look like a pistol."

Morgan swallowed hard. "What's it look like?"

"I'm still trying to—oh, my god, it's an Uzi! Turn, Morgan! Turn now!"

"Where?" she shouted. "We're in the middle of the block!"

The rear window shattered and collapsed as five bullet holes instantly appeared in the windshield. Morgan screamed and swerved into oncoming traffic, narrowly missing two cars before sideswiping a parked BMW and a Buick. One of the cars she'd missed, a green Honda, crossed in front of the Chevy, which slid sideways into it. Then the blue Chrysler skidded head-on into the Chevy.

"That was perfect, Morgan! They both wrecked." The smile quickly drained from his face. "Shit! Here they come again! They're damaged, but it doesn't look like that's slowing them down any."

Morgan wheeled onto the freeway ramp, stomped the pedal to the floor, and held it there. The wind whistled eerily through the drafty holes in the windshield, the shrill tune growing louder and louder as the car accelerated. In no time, the speedometer hit ninety. Thankfully traffic was lighter than usual on the beltway because it was Saturday morning.

"Where are they, Hunter?" she asked.

"We've gained some distance. They're coming up the ramp now."

They clipped along at her car's top speed: close to 110 miles per hour. The blurred center dividing wall streamed by like a continuous smoke trail. The aluminum light poles flickered like a gray picket fence.

"Morgan, be careful with your steering. It's incredibly easy to lose control at this speed. The car will drift with the slightest course change."

"It is drifting!" she shrieked, her knuckles white from gripping the steering wheel so hard. "We're going to—*oh, crap!*" The driver's side raked against the dividing wall. The horrible screeching and grinding of metal belched a fireworks of sparks that obscured everything behind them until they'd cleared the wall. "Where are they now?" she shouted, her voice almost hoarse.

"They're still gaining on us—they must be doing a hundred and twenty! I wish we had my Ferrari!"

"I have an idea!" Morgan yelled, eyes glued to the road. "Brace yourself! When they get close, I'll hit the brakes."

"Yeah, that might work. But don't skid or we'll lose control. Let up on the gas so they come up on us faster. OK. Here they come. Get ready!"

She mashed the brake pedal, and the silver Chevy swerved to the right, then lifted completely off the roadway, sailing into the air like a child's toy. Landing, it tumbled over and over, disintegrating more and more with each revolution. The blue Chrysler bounced hard against the concrete dividing wall then spun violently all the way across the freeway until it dropped out of sight down an embankment. A cloud of dirt and grass shot up from where it had disappeared.

Morgan pulled over and stopped, her hands shaking. She rested her forehead on the steering wheel. "You think any of those guys could've survived?"

Hunter raked his fingers through his hair and exhaled a huge a sigh of relief. "I suppose it's possible, but if they did, you can be sure they're not in good shape."

"Maybe we should call fire rescue."

"Forget it, Morgan. Those bastards were trying to kill us. They got what they deserved. We're just lucky we didn't end up that way ourselves. Let's get away from here before the police arrive. Hit the gas!"

CHAPTER

14

"Hello, Stan. Thanks for coming."

"Good morning, Mr. Vice President," Stanley Bass replied. "An invitation to speak with you in your fine office here in the White House is always a pleasure, even on a Saturday."

What a slimy bastard, Buchanan thought. *He kisses ass even when he knows he doesn't have to.*

"What can I do for you?" Bass asked.

They shook hands.

Buchanan made a conscious effort not to wipe his hand on his pants. He hated dealing with this bloated little…what? Toad? No, more like a leech sucking on the system all these years, growing fat on secret funds and lavish meals in five-star restaurants. Throwing his money around and sucking up to people like him, when he had to, and then laughing behind their back because he had the dope on everyone.

But Buchanan needed the director of the CIA in his pocket right now. He sat on the corner of his mahogany desk and said, "Stan, I've just got some alarming news about the Gomez brothers."

The fat bastard sank into a chair, which squeaked in protest. *He'll probably need help getting out of it,* Buchanan thought. "A reliable source tells me that the Gomez brothers could be responsible for my son's death. If it's true, I want them to pay."

Bass gave him a smug little smile. "Would your source be Morgan Lindsey, the *Herald* reporter?"

Buchanan's eyes widened then narrowed suspiciously. "How'd you know?"

"I got a call from the FBI a few days ago. My contact overheard that Ms. Lindsey was investigating Sean's accident. I decided to listen in on her calls."

"A legal phone tap?"

"Good heavens, no!" Bass laughed sharply. "No use wasting time with all that red tape. Not if you want to learn anything worthwhile anyway. More often than you might think, an anonymous tipster will call with information. I can trace such a call and learn a great deal by investigating further. The CIA regularly taps phone lines—for law-enforcement purposes, of course." Bass pasted a smile on his face.

"Then you already know I had a meeting with Ms. Lindsey yesterday afternoon?" the vice president said.

"That's right." The director popped his knuckles loudly. "Scary, isn't it? But phone taps really do help bring information to light. That's what I'd hoped would happen in the course of her investigation."

"Did she receive any mysterious calls?"

Bass smiled. A genuine smile. A smile that showed he was pleased with the question. "Yes. Two, in fact. One from a man with information about Sean's accident and another from Hunter Mahoy, who would not tell her over the phone why he wanted her to meet him in Miami."

"Mahoy? The missing sailplane pilot?"

"Yes, sir."

"Did she meet with him?"

"I can't say for sure, Mr. Vice President, but the conversation indicated that she would. And just last night I traced a call from her house to a Seymour Banks. Ms. Lindsey's trying to get two fake passports—one for a man and one for a woman. I'm checking into that right now. I learned something else that you should know. I spoke with the Miami-Dade police chief, Douglas Sweeney, an old friend of mine." Bass shifted in his seat.

Who does he think he's kidding? Buchanan thought during Bass's silence. *He doesn't have any friends. He barely has acquaintances.*

Bass continued. "Sweeney told me that the Miami–Dade County Police Department has an APB out on Mahoy. He's the prime suspect in the shooting death of Juan Carlos Gomez. Apparently Mahoy was at his secretary Amanda Tayor's house when the shooting occurred. Mahoy's prints were found on the gun that sent Juan to his Maker. Taylor ended up in the hospital."

Buchanan rose to mull over the information. "So Mahoy's the one who popped Juan Carlos?"

"Yes. And I'm sure you realize that we have to find him before the Miami–Dade Police Department does. I've already assigned an operative to watch over the situation—maybe even make something happen down there."

Buchanan leaned against a window frame and stared through the glass, ignoring the vibrant orange and yellow foliage decorating the White House lawn. *Mahoy's becoming quite an adversary, and now he may have tied in with Morgan Lindsey. If he has, she probably knows whatever he knows. Should I have Bass take her out along with Mahoy or wait? She might yet learn the identity of the Gomez brothers' accomplice in the CIA.*

He returned to his desk. "Good work, Stan. I'll speak with Hager and get back to you. But for now, I'd greatly appreciate if you'd look into this allegation about the Gomez brothers. I'll be attending Juan Carlos's funeral on Monday, and I'd like to know more by then, if possible. I realize that doesn't give you much time."

"I'll do what I can, Mr. Vice President. I'll let you know what I find out about Lindsey and those fake passports as well."

* * *

Ellen Connelly looked up when Jack Burton stormed into her office for the fourth time that morning. "Have you heard from Morgan yet?" he asked.

Ellen sighed. "No, Jack, not in the last five minutes. And I probably won't hear from her in the next five minutes, either."

She knew that he was thrilled with the response to Morgan's articles on the mayoral corruption and on Sean Buchanan. Now he wanted Morgan to work on a follow-up series.

"She's a damn good writer, and I really like her, but she's making me crazy." He paced in front of Ellen's desk. "My phone hasn't stopped ringing since those stories hit the street. Morgan's hot right now. Everyone wants to meet with her: senators, congressmen, even the FBI!" He stopped pacing and leaned over the desk, veins popping out on his neck. "Are you sure you don't know where she is?"

Ellen merely studied the nails on her left hand and reached for an emery board in her pencil holder. For a long moment, the tiny buzzing of the emery board seemed to resonate throughout the room.

He reached over her desk and clutched her hand to stop it. "What am I paying you for?" he barked. "Don't you have something useful to do?"

"I am doing something useful, Jack. I'm listening to you rant and rave like a total maniac."

He glared at her but said nothing.

"Look, Jack, I've already told you. Morgan said she's working on a really big story and would call in periodically."

He released her hand. "What story? What's it related to?"

The buzzing started up again. "I don't know. You'll have to take that up with her."

"If I could find her, I would," he griped. "I've left messages at her home number and on her cell voice mail. She hasn't returned any of my calls."

Ellen tossed the emery board onto the desktop and leaned back in her chair. "I promise, Jack, the moment I hear anything, I'll let you know. You need to calm down before you have a heart attack. Why don't you get out of here for a while? Go get a haircut or something."

"Maybe I should, but if Morgan calls—"

"I'll contact you immediately," Ellen said. "Go!"

*   *   *

The flight attendant left Hunter's and Morgan's drinks. He lifted his glass, only to put it back on his tray and gingerly rub his left arm.

"That wound bothering you?" she whispered.

"Yeah. It's throbbing again. So's the leg and the back. From hurrying through the terminal, I guess." He elevated his arm. "I wonder if the Gomez brothers hired those guys to watch your house." He looked out from his first-class window seat, admiring the cloudscape he so loved. "It's the explosion that bothers me most, Morgan."

"Me too," she said, her eyes watering. "They destroyed my beautiful house."

He took her by the hand. "I'm really sorry about that. And actually, only the garage was totaled. It can be rebuilt. But we're alive, thanks to you. Where'd you learn to drive like that? The Daytona 500?"

She managed a smile.

Hunter continued, "Anyway, that explosion, the device that was used, seemed very sophisticated—maybe too sophisticated to be the work of the Gomez brothers, what with the remote triggering the detonation and all." He rubbed his chin. "I wonder why it didn't explode when you left for the White House yesterday?"

"Because I opened the garage door the same way you did today: I used the wall switch. I was in such a hurry that I forgot to close the door. It stayed open the whole time I was gone. When I returned, I closed it with the wall switch again on my way into the house. I didn't use the remote until today. What a fluke!"

Hunter whistled softly. "I'll say." He looked out the window again for a moment then turned back to Morgan. "The other thing that seemed strange was the two different chase vehicles. It was almost as if one didn't know about the other. The guys in the Chrysler were definitely pros."

"Why do you say that?" She squinted against the sunlight tracking across her face as the plane banked into a turn.

He pulled down the shade. "The coffee. Those guys have been on stakeouts before. They were prepared and patient." He lowered his voice. "And even though they had the opportunity, they didn't shoot at us in that busy area. The guys in the other car seemed more reckless, more desperate. They shot up the whole street with that damned Uzi. Innocent bystanders could've been killed. May have been, for all we know. *That* was more like the Gomez brothers."

"Yeah, like the Miami Beach nightclub."

"Right. And because of *that* incident, we know someone tapped your work phone—my guess would be Stanley Bass at the CIA because he's tied in with the Gomez brothers. Bass must have tapped your home phone as well. How else could anyone have known so quickly that you were back in town? I'm glad Seymour Banks suggested that we make our flight reservations at his contact's house last night while we waited on the fake documents. The problem is, we called Seymour from your house."

She wrapped a blanket around her legs. "So you're saying someone probably knows we're leaving the country with false passports, but they don't know where to or when."

"Yes, and whoever was listening also knows you had a meeting with Al Buchanan about his son's death. The real question is, do the wiretappers know anything about the missing sailplane pilot, or does that remain a separate issue with a separate group of players?" He sighed. "Regardless of the consequences, we can't be caught before we contact the president, and we must tell him everything the next time we meet."

Morgan took a sip of her drink then asked, "Do you think President Weber has enough information right now to protect himself if we're intercepted?"

"I've thought about that, and I don't believe so. He'd probably still visit Cuba but with heavily increased security. And, of course, we know that won't be adequate. He needs to cancel the trip."

Morgan yawned while nodding. She lay back and was soon asleep, fueled by a combination of exhaustion and alcohol.

Hunter leaned back and thought about the base under Homestead, and the tunnels under the Everglades, that were a military secret. The US Government had gone to incredible effort and expense to build the complex and keep it concealed. Undoubtedly it would be advantageous to have it remain so. He reflected on his decision not to go to the newspapers, and also what a story like this could do for Morgan's career.

Sighing, he watched her sleeping peacefully. He worried for her safety and wished he hadn't involved her, yet he'd really had no choice. If they both survived this ordeal, it'd be a miracle. And if they did, what would be the outcome of their fateful reunion?

A few hours later, the pilot announced the plane's initial descent into Gatwick Airport. After clearing British customs, they hailed a taxi to the Savoy Hotel. There they found that their spacious suite—tastefully decorated with Victorian wallpaper, carpets, woodwork, and furniture—adjoined a large bathroom with a thoroughly modern whirlpool tub. Both Hunter and Morgan preferred to stay in the more elegant and expensive hotels, enjoying the amenities and services such lodgings provided.

Hunter lived by two maxims. First, if he received what he paid for, it was worth it. And second, never volunteer for anything. He'd broken that second rule occasionally and always seemed to regret it, the events of the past couple of weeks being prime examples of the misfortunes that befall one who volunteers to do the right thing.

Within moments of their arrival, he heard water sloshing into the tub. The whirlpool motor came to life. He smiled to himself. Morgan would be in there for hours soaking up the romance novel she'd bought at the airport. He put off any thoughts of joining her—assuming she'd be willing to have him, of course—and concentrated on the president's itinerary.

According to the printout, President Weber would attend a brunch before a meeting in the afternoon with the prime minister at 10 Downing Street. Weber's day seemed less demanding after the visit to the prime minister's residence. Perhaps they could attract his attention at that location.

He stuck the itinerary in Morgan's purse and tapped on the bathroom door.

"You can come in, Hunter. I'm buried up to my neck in soap bubbles."

Too bad, he thought. He stuck his head in the doorway. "How is it?"

"The book or the bath?"

"The bath."

"Wonderful. I could stay in here all night."

"When you're done with your soak, could you phone Ellen and ask her to check whether anyone's still watching, ah…what's left of your house?"

She stuck out her bottom lip. "I'll take care of it."

"Good. The sooner the better. I'm going downstairs for a while."

With that, Hunter closed the bathroom door then left the room. He rode the elevator down to the lobby where he purchased a newspaper then checked out some of the shops and the in-house car rental agency. When he returned to their suite, he found Morgan on the balcony, looking out at the city.

Without turning, she said, "I spoke with Ellen. She'll call us back in the morning with an answer. I suggested that she act as if she's looking for an address."

Hunter rubbed her shoulders. A light breeze occasionally sent a lock of her hair against his face. He closed his eyes and focused on its scent. A scent that launched him into time travel as fond memories came flooding back. He forced himself back to the present.

"What you wear tomorrow depends on what she tells us. I'm hoping you can wear the red outfit again."

Morgan slowly rotated her head from side to side. "Why would Ellen's information have anything to do with what I wear?"

"Because if someone's still watching your house, they probably have no idea where we are. So we'd be safe using the high-visibility method to attract the president's attention. But if Ellen says no one's watching your house, you'd better wear something more subdued so we can blend into a crowd easier."

She turned her back on the city and gazed into his eyes. "As usual, you're planning ahead. I like that," she said, smiling.

He brushed a strand of her hair aside, keeping his hand on her face. "Do you want something? Are you…hungry?"

She moved away, going back inside. "No, not right now. After that long flight, I'm just tired."

"I wasn't referring to food," he said softly, following her.

She climbed into bed. "I know. Would you turn off the light, please?"

He obliged then crossed the darkened room back to the balcony door. The city lights, pleasant and soothing, almost spellbinding, temporarily eased his fear of whoever might be out there.

CHAPTER

15

General Lamar Hager's phone rang, and he grabbed it on the first ring.

"Lamar? Al Buchanan. I'm on a secure line, so we can talk freely."

Hearing the curtness in Buchanan's voice, Hager braced himself.

"What in hell's going on, Lamar? I just got off the phone with Stan, and he said Mahoy and Lindsey have fake passports, and may have already left the country. I fully expected you to have this situation well in hand by now."

Hager crumpled an old memo and tried for the trash can. *Missed.* "We're doing everything we can, Al. A whole network of people are waiting for them to surface again. It's a real disappointment that Stan's operatives missed them at Lindsey's house yesterday."

"I agree. That would've been perfect. Given all the enemies Lindsey's made with her recent articles, there's no telling who'll ultimately be blamed for that explosion. But the high-speed chase was a fiasco, to say the least."

"That wasn't entirely our doing. We're still trying to determine who the guys in that second car were and who they worked for. They're both dead."

"I don't give a shit about that! I just want you to find Mahoy and Lindsey fast." With that, Buchanan clicked off.

Hager slammed down the phone. *What in hell does he think I'm doing, sitting on my damn laurels?*

He drummed his fingers impatiently on the desktop. What were those idiot operatives up to anyway? It'd been nearly twenty-four hours since the explosion at Lindsey's house and still nothing. Did he have to do everything himself?

He dialed a familiar number then breathed deeply to calm his annoyance while waiting for an answer. "Come on. Be there," he said aloud. Finally the ringing stopped.

"Bass," the director answered curtly.

"Stan, it's Lamar. Have you learned what names Mahoy and Lindsey used on the false passports?"

"Yes, just a few minutes ago. They're going by Arthur Crowfield and Ashley Wells. Since my database is tied in just about everywhere, airline reservations and customs records are being checked right now. It'll take some time, though."

Hager shot another crumpled memo and missed again. "Call me as soon as you have something. Oh, and Stan, do me a favor. Check with British customs right away."

*   *   *

The telephone rattled Hunter awake Sunday morning. He struggled to locate it and to recall where he was. *Oh, yeah,* he thought. *London. The Savoy.* "Hello?"

"Oh, I'm sorry. Maybe I've called the wrong number," a female voice said. "I'm trying to reach Morgan Lindsey."

"Hold on a second." Passing the telephone to Morgan, he whispered, "Must be Ellen."

Morgan grabbed the receiver. "Hello? Hi, Ellen. It's a long story. I'll tell you about it when I return."

Hunter affectionately ran his fingers down Morgan's arm and onto her belly. Studying her shapely body through the silky nightgown, he slid his hand up onto her breast as he leaned over and kissed her neck. She shoved him away abruptly, knocking him off the bed. He hit the floor with a thud and groaned. Painfully, he struggled to his feet clutching his left arm, which was bleeding again, then headed for the bathroom.

"Oh, my gosh! Hunter, I'm sorry. I didn't—"

He waved her off with his good arm without saying a word or even looking at her. The bathroom door stayed open, so he could hear her side of the conversation.

"Oh, yes, Ellen. I'm here. Nothing. I dropped the phone. Uh-huh…yes…OK…no, don't worry, everything's fine…a friend… I can't tell you over the phone. Oh, what'd he have to say? OK, OK. I'll give him a call today. Don't tell him where I am. Listen, I may need the *Herald* to wire some money, but I'm not sure yet. Keep in touch with your answering machine. I'll call again as soon as I know our plans. Thanks, Ellen. Bye."

Morgan hung up and rushed to the bathroom. "I'm so sorry, Hunter. I didn't mean to—"

"Forget it," he said as he rewrapped the wound. "It was my fault."

"I'll do that," she said, taking the gauze away from him. "Hunter, our past is in the past. You can't just—"

"Drop it, Morgan!" he said sharply. After an awkward moment of silence, he asked, "What did Ellen have to say?"

She looked hard into his eyes then frowned and shrugged. "Apparently my house is still being watched. Ellen strolled the sidewalk carrying a bag of groceries so she'd have more time to check it out. A white car with two men in it was sitting nearby. The driver was using a pair of binoculars."

"Good! That means they're clueless. Otherwise they wouldn't have renewed the surveillance. Who do you need to call today?"

"My boss, Jack. He's driving Ellen crazy with questions about me. Apparently he wants to speak with me in the worst way. But I'll deal with that later."

He grimaced as she tied off the gauze.

"There. That should do it," she said, backing up a step.

He studied it. "Thanks. Maybe you should be a nurse. You'd have to work on that bedside manner, though."

He smiled.

She smiled back.

"We have hours to kill before Weber's conference. What would you like to do this morning?" he asked.

"I don't know. Might be nice to see some sights."

"Sightseeing it is," he said. "First stop, Buckingham Palace?"

"I'm for that. I'll get dressed."

A short time later they were downstairs, walking toward their rental car.

"I want to drive," Morgan announced. "You're in no shape."

"Gee, I don't know. I have enough injuries already. A head-on collision might not be the way I want to go."

She slapped him playfully on his good arm.

"Seriously, Morgan, driving on the left side of the road requires real concentration when you're used to the opposite. You sure you want to try it?"

"You praised my driving in DC."

"Yeah, but you did hit that wall. Scared the hell out of me too."

She propped her hands on her hips and glared.

"Fine. It's all yours," he said, holding the door and sweeping his hand toward the wheel.

She settled onto the driver's seat, immediately having trouble adapting to a steering wheel on the right side of the car and having to shift gears with her left hand. "This is so bizarre! So foreign," she said, "pardon my pun. Couldn't you have gotten a car with an automatic transmission?"

"Hey! You wanted to drive." He looked down at the map in his lap. "Let's see now. Turn right at the next intersection." He looked up and yelped, "*Left side, Morgan!*"

"Oh, yeah!" she said, swerving quickly.

After this occurred twice more, Hunter groaned. "Maybe we should've taken the bus."

When they finally arrived in the vicinity of Buckingham Palace and parked, he got out and kissed the ground, then held on to the gold-tipped iron fence and wouldn't let go. Laughing with embarrassment, Morgan left him there.

She snapped several photographs of the palace. Then for fun, she did as countless thousands of tourists have done over the years: attempt to make the English Royal Guards move or flinch or show any kind of emotion. But as always, they remained motionless human statues.

It was nearing lunchtime, so she suggested, "Let's drive around until we find a restaurant."

From a previous visit, he already knew of a popular place just down the street. "Why don't we walk? That way we'll both live longer."

"Very funny," she said.

They had an enjoyable lunch and a spot of tea, then returned to their car and drove toward the prime minister's residence. They parked a few blocks away and walked the remaining distance. For security reasons, the entrance to Downing Street was closed to the public. Hunter, with camera in hand, told the constable in charge that he was a photographer, and Morgan a reporter working for the *Washington Herald*. She rifled through her purse and pulled out the copy of President Weber's itinerary and her press ID. The guard contacted his superior, who verified that Morgan Lindsey, accompanied by one assistant, could enter and join the other media personnel.

"This is encouraging," Hunter said as they hurried up the street. "President Weber must've added your name to the list of authorized press. He's expecting us."

From the outside, the prime minister's redbrick residence with its black wrought-iron fence along the sidewalk appeared almost modest. Looking around, Hunter singled out a spot across the street where they could clearly watch President Weber's arrival yet stay safely away from the small army of reporters and television cameras. Any videotape shot could be broadcast on news stations all over the world. Staying behind camera range reduced advertising their whereabouts to anyone other than the president.

The position would also make it easy to flash the mirror, if the sun cooperated, that is. All morning the sky had been overcast. The local paper forecast the possibility of afternoon sunshine, and the sun had peeked through now and again but not often. Hunter wished he'd brought a flashlight as a backup. Cloudy skies would make the mirror idea useless.

Finally the president's limousine appeared, along with two black Chevrolet Suburbans carrying Secret Service personnel. The sun burst through a break in the cloud, and Hunter eased the mirror out of his pocket.

The Secret Service agents took up their positions, then President Weber emerged from the limousine. Reporters shouted questions, and photographers jockeyed for position. The president smiled and nodded, and occasionally responded to a query as he strolled toward the residence. Flanked by security, he casually approached the entrance to number 10.

Hunter hurriedly captured the sun and flashed it across the shiny brass numbers on the door. Weber immediately turned around, answering someone's question while looking for the light source. Hunter flashed the mirror again just as the sun faded. Weber spotted them. He smiled and waved to the crowd, then turned and entered the residence.

Hunter slipped the mirror back into his pocket. "So far, so good."

"That was brilliant," Morgan said.

"No pun intended?" he asked.

She smirked. "No, no pun intended. So now what?"

"I don't know. I guess we'll just wait."

The reporters disappeared almost immediately, as did most of the security agents. Hunter and Morgan were still trying to determine their best course of action when a man in his late thirties wearing a light-brown suit approached. Hunter studied him closely. A six-footer, the man had short brown hair, a clean-shaven face, and a gait that betrayed a slight limp favoring the right leg.

"Are you Morgan Lindsey?"

"Who wants to know?" she asked.

"I'm Secret Service agent Charles Minsk. President Weber asked me to contact you."

"May I see some identification, please?"

The man produced his badge. The fold-over leather wallet had a shiny silver shield on the outside that had "Secret Service" embossed on it. The inside flap carried a picture ID, along with a signature. Morgan studied it with Hunter looking over her shoulder. The photograph matched the man before them and the signature read "Charles Minsk." Hunter had seen a Secret Service badge at the White House once before and nodded his approval.

She faced the man. "Yes, I'm Morgan Lindsey."

"May I now see your identification?" the agent asked.

She offered her press credentials.

Apparently satisfied, the agent removed a small envelope from his pocket and handed it to her.

Hunter wondered if they should trust this guy. President Weber apparently did. The agent couldn't have known about them otherwise. But what if he was the enemy? What if he was an eye and an ear for Al Buchanan? What then?

"Do you know the contents of the envelope, Mr. Minsk?" Hunter asked.

The agent's focus shifted. "Who are you, sir?"

"I'm sorry," Morgan said. "This is H. Hunter Mahoy. He's here to—"

"Protect her," Hunter blurted. "I'm her bodyguard, Agent Minsk. Where she goes, I go." Hunter locked eyes with him in a silent battle of take-it-or-leave–it.

Finally Minsk said, "I understand. And yes, I do know what the envelope contains. President Weber asked me to relay to you the importance of trusting no one except him or me." The agent spoke to both of them, shifting his focus from one to the other. "If you need to contact the president, it must be through me. And if anyone else approaches you and says they're from the Secret Service, the CIA, the FBI, or any other agency, don't divulge anything. You must deal only with me or the president himself. Do you understand?"

"Yes," Morgan said.

Though still wary, Hunter nodded.

"Good. Where are you staying in case I need to contact you?"

"At the—"

"We'll find you," Hunter said crisply, leaving Morgan obviously puzzled, her mouth hanging open.

The agent seemed surprised as well. He locked eyes with Hunter once again but only for a moment. "As you wish. Until tonight then."

Continuing on in his original direction, Minsk rounded the corner and disappeared.

Morgan started to open the envelope, but Hunter put a hand on it. "Wait until we're in the car."

Nodding, she shoved it into her purse.

They strode for their rental, reaching it in no time. Morgan practically jumped into the driver's seat, slammed the door, then dug in her purse for the envelope.

"Start the car, Morgan, and put it in gear, please."

She gaped at him.

"Just in case we need to depart in a hurry," he said.

"I think you're becoming paranoid, Hunter."

"It's not paranoia if someone's really after you. Humor me."

She did as he asked then opened the envelope. While she read, he focused his attention outside the vehicle. She touched his arm, and he turned toward her. When she opened her mouth to speak, he said, "Don't talk, Morgan, just drive. Start moving!"

She surprised him when she popped the clutch, squealing the car's tires as she merged into traffic.

Realizing he'd scared her, he said, "Don't worry. Just go wherever you want. I need a few minutes to mull something over. Remember, stay on the left side."

Erring on the side of caution, he didn't want her to divulge the contents of the letter out loud. A directional microphone could listen in from a long way off. He read the handwritten letter himself, which made him smile. The invitation for Morgan to join President Weber for an eleven-thirty late dinner at his hotel would do nicely. *That'd be after his evening engagement at Buckingham Palace,* Hunter thought. He stuck the letter back into the envelope then watched in the outside mirror on the passenger's side.

"Make a few turns," he said.

"Why?"

"I think we're being followed."

After a couple of minutes and another turn she asked, "Well, are we?"

"Yes. I'm certain of it. Find a shopping mall where we can park and go inside. We'll try the procedure we'd planned to use in DC."

Morgan nodded. "We just passed one." She doubled back and parked at the center. They hurried inside.

The mall directory showed another exit near a major store on the opposite end. Stopping at a phone kiosk, they called a cab then rushed through the mall.

In a few minutes their taxi arrived. Hunter watched discreetly during the early part of the ride to see if they'd lost their shadow. They had.

When they arrived at their hotel, he gave the cabbie an extra fifteen pounds. "This is for a favor."

"Name it, guv'nor" the driver said.

"We came to London with a few friends, but we've grown tired of their company. We want to spend some time alone. If anyone asks about us, would you mind misdirecting them?"

"Not at all, mate. I understand perfectly," the man said, eyeing Morgan and grinning. "I'd be happy to oblige."

Hunter stopped at the reservation desk in the lobby and asked for an envelope and proper postage to mail a letter to the United States.

"What do you want to mail?" Morgan asked on the way up to their suite.

"The invitation you received today. But I haven't decided where to send it."

"You've lost me. Why do you want to mail it?"

He sat at the Victorian writing desk in the corner of their suite. "Because we don't want anyone to know we've been contacted by the president or that we've met with him. I could easily destroy it, but I thought you might like to keep it. A handwritten letter drafted and signed by the president of the United States might be quite valuable someday. Make a helluva souvenir too, don't you think?"

"Yes, I do. And I would like to keep it. Thanks."

"You're welcome." He thought for a second. "I know! I'll send it to my sister, Ashley. By the way, that's where I came up with the name for your fake passport. Ashley's married name is Wellington, so I just shortened it to Wells. Ashley Wells. Has a nice ring to it, don't you think? Anyway, Ashley will hold it for me until I come for it."

He addressed the envelope accordingly, slipped the invitation inside along with a note, then sealed it. "I'm going to the lobby to mail this right now. I want it out of here."

He hurried down to the lobby and posted the letter, then returned to the room, all in the space of five minutes.

"Why do suppose President Weber's trusting us?" Morgan asked. "Even after my first contact at the White House, I felt that he knew I was sincere. What do you think convinced him?"

"You did, when you mentioned his visit to Cuba on November first."

"I don't see your point."

"That visit hasn't been announced yet. My guess is that the vice president, Castro, and maybe the president's top aides are the only people in the world who are supposed to know. When you divulged that, you authenticated your position, especially since you knew about the change to November first, which had only just occurred."

Her eyes widened. "I hadn't considered that. You're right."

"Of course I'm right. I'm Mister Right."

She rolled her eyes. "You wish!"

Chuckling, he doffed his shoes, lay back on the bed, tucked his hands behind his head, and thought about the conversation he'd have with the president later that evening. He wanted to be certain that what he said would be clear, concise, and convincing. He also contemplated their plans for after the meeting.

It wasn't long before he became groggy and fell asleep.

A vigorous shaking caused him to stir. "Come on, Hunter, wake up. You've got to get ready."

"What time is it?" he mumbled.

"Ten-fifteen. You slept for hours."

Groaning, he rose then showered and shaved. As he dressed, Morgan knotted her hair into a French twist. The black gown that elegantly draped her shapely body was every bit as eye-catching as her red one, and the absence of a bra simply couldn't be ignored. A string of pearls and matching earrings completed his vision of a goddess.

After she applied a touch of perfume and checked her appearance one more time, she said, "I'm ready."

"Morgan, you're absolutely ravishing. You look so elegant I'd think you were going to meet the president."

Giggling, she took his arm and propelled him out of the room.

*   *   *

Colonel Raifer had to get in place Sunday evening. Come morning, the office building would be bustling with people. He paused a few steps from the top of the stairs to catch his breath and massage his aching knee.

The kneecap hadn't been the same since being shattered by a bullet in Africa during his mercenary years nearly two decades ago. The freelance work he was now doing made far fewer physical demands on his weary forty-nine-year-old body, and paid considerably better than that of a soldier of fortune.

Stanley Bass must really want this one badly, he thought as he started up the stairs again. *A couple more jobs with a price tag like this little endeavor's, and I'll be able to retire. I'm getting too old for this shit anyway.*

He reached the landing, shoved against the door's panic bar, then stepped out onto the rooftop of the six-story building. The decorative aluminum framework that disguised the massive air-conditioning system sat just a few yards ahead. *Perfect*, he thought. Hiding within that structure, he'd be almost impossible to spot in daylight, even by helicopter. And because the building had a low parapet, he could stay concealed within the enclosure the whole time. He smiled to himself. This was going to be a walk in the park.

Aided by the moonlight, he maneuvered around puddles left from the previous day's rain, secure in the knowledge that the darkness would hide both him and the case he was carrying.

Bass had updated him on who would be in attendance. Standard procedures would require a check of all rooftops within a given distance, but not this far away. He'd be safe enough. By the time they'd figured out what had happened, he'd be long gone.

He climbed inside the protective framework, opened the case, and began to assemble the nontraceable Israeli-made Galil sniper rifle. The coolness of the smooth steel penetrated his gloves as he carefully handled the pieces. After attaching the high-powered scope, he trained its crosshairs on his target area. He smiled. Where tomorrow there'd be a large crowd of innocent people, tonight he envisioned his mortgage-free secluded beachfront mansion and a fat bank account.

CHAPTER

16

Nurse Emily Thacker started her Sunday graveyard shift at Baptist Hospital in Miami with Amanda Taylor's private room. She pushed the door open, then gasped.

"Oh, my god! Help! Somebody, help!" she screamed at the top of her lungs.

Tearing across the room, she launched herself at the stranger hunched over Amanda. The man was holding a pillow over Amanda's face as he forcibly restrained her. Emily punched and kicked and screamed and dug her fingernails into his neck, but the murderer kept the pillow in place despite her efforts. Finally she yanked his hair with one hand and poked him in the eyes with the fingers of the other. Crying out, the man flung her across the room and into the wall by the door.

"You sorry bastard!" she hollered as he bolted into the hallway. She struggled to her feet in time to see the hefty intruder knock down an orderly who tried to stop him. The orderly gave chase, but the man got away.

Amanda wasn't breathing.

Emily called a *code blue* for room 487, and Dr. Russell Keller scrambled to his patient's side. Keller took over CPR while Emily administered oxygen and another nurse checked Amanda's pulse.

The crash team moved swiftly and efficiently, hooking up monitors and sensors from the crash cart.

"I'm not getting a pulse, Doctor," the other nurse said.

Keller continued CPR. "Prepare to defibrillate."

Grabbing an electrode in each hand, he hurriedly rubbed the gel between them as the nurse bared Amanda's chest.

"Clear!" he shouted then hit Amanda with a charge. Her body jolted from the shock but still no pulse. "Come on, Amanda!" he coaxed as he prepared to hit her again. A second jolt likewise did nothing. "Respond, damn it!" he shouted. "Don't you die on me, Amanda!"

*   *   *

Hunter and Morgan arrived at the Ritz Hotel ten minutes early and went straight to the reservation desk. They waited while the manager called to verify their appointment.

Hanging up the phone a moment later, the manager smiled and said, "An escort will meet you here momentarily."

No sooner were the words out of his mouth when Secret Service Agent Charles Minsk appeared. Minsk's focus shifted from the reservation desk to the front entrance to the main elevators to Morgan. He was discreet—though he did get hung up briefly on the creamy swells rising above the low-cut neckline of Morgan's gown. Hunter smiled inwardly. Maybe this guy was all right, after all.

"Good evening, Ms. Lindsey, Mr. Mahoy," Minsk said politely. "You're right on time. I've explained your presence, Mr. Mahoy. President Weber is expecting both of you. Please follow me."

He led them through a corridor to a private unmarked elevator where he used a special key to open the door. After stepping inside, he said, "You'll have to submit to a search before I can take you to the president. I hope you understand."

They left the elevator and followed him across the hall to a small room where Minsk asked Hunter to empty his pockets, then scanned him with a handheld metal detector. It triggered at the waist, so Hunter removed his belt. The device seemed satisfied with that, but Minsk patted Hunter from his shoulders to his ankles anyway. Hunter wondered if Morgan would get the same treatment. He was sure that Minsk had already decided that the only danger that lurked in that dress had something to do with those creamy swells and the cool temperature of the room. Minsk checked her beaded handbag then waved his magic metal detector—that was it.

The search completed, he led them to the presidential suite and knocked on the door. He escorted Hunter and Morgan past two more Secret Service agents then into an elegant dining room. The table, covered with an exquisite damask cloth, could easily accommodate a dozen guests. It currently had place settings of fine china, silver, and crystal for only four.

Naturally, President Weber would head the table. Of the remaining three settings, two flanked one side. Agent Minsk seated Morgan then invited Hunter to join her.

"President Weber will arrive momentarily."

When Agent Minsk left the room, Morgan whispered excitedly, "I can't believe we're actually about to dine with the president!"

"And you thought I didn't know how to show a girl a good time," Hunter said dryly.

Though thrilled to be there, his thoughts were more focused on the upcoming conversation. How would the president react? Would he believe the tale—a tale so fantastic that Hunter wasn't even sure he believed it himself at times?

President Weber entered, followed by Agent Minsk. Hunter and Morgan rose immediately.

"Good evening. I'm glad you could join me," the president said. "You look lovely, Ms. Lindsey." He wore a black suit with a red tie. An American flag was pinned to his lapel.

"Thank you," she said, shaking his hand. "And thank you for inviting us. Mr. President, this is H. Hunter Mahoy. He's the reason I contacted you. He has quite a story to tell."

Shaking hands, Hunter said, "Good evening, Mr. President."

"Hello, Mr. Mahoy." President Weber narrowed his eyes. "Have we met before?"

"As a matter of fact, we have, sir. At Christie's in Coral Gables, Florida. About a year ago."

"Oh, yes. I remember now. I'd asked you what the *H* stood for, and you replied *Hobnobber*." He laughed heartily.

"Yes, sir. You have an excellent memory, Mr. President."

They smiled at each other, and President Weber patted him on the back. Morgan stared as if in disbelief.

Hunter winked at her.

"Won't you please sit down?" the president said. "I'm most curious to hear what you have to say."

Minsk claimed the fourth place setting opposite Hunter and Morgan.

The president gestured at the Secret Service man. "I'd like to reassure you that you can speak freely in front of Agent Minsk," the president said. "Other than my wife and daughter, he's the one person I trust with my life. I have no secrets from him. You should also know that I've had this room checked for electronic devices, and it's clean, though it would be wise to break off conversation whenever my serving staff enters the room. Any questions?"

Hunter spoke. "Part of what I have to tell you is top secret and could affect the future security of the United States." He looked across the table. "I mean no offense, sir, but are you certain you want Agent Minsk to hear everything?"

"I'm certain, Mr. Mahoy. You may have noticed that Agent Minsk walks with a limp. He'll limp for the rest of his life. He not only dived off a platform to subdue a gunman but also he caught the bullet that was meant for me. Yes, he must be aware of everything you have to tell me, but thank you for asking. Now I'm afraid I must pose a similar question to you about your lovely companion. Is everything you're about to say known by Ms. Lindsey?"

"Yes. She even helped me obtain part of the information at great personal risk."

"That settles it, then," Weber said. "Before you begin, Mr. Mahoy, I'll have the staff bring in drinks and appetizers."

Minsk spoke softly into the tiny microphone hidden in the cuff of his jacket. Almost instantly the dinner staff appeared and began serving.

Turning to Morgan, the president said, "Ms. Lindsey, I apologize for my wife and daughter not being here to join us. Unfortunately they couldn't accompany me on this trip."

"I understand. Perhaps I'll meet them in the future. And please, sir, call me Morgan."

"Morgan it is." Directing his attention to Hunter, he asked, "May I call you Hunter?"

"By all means, sir. Anything but *Hobnobber*."

Everyone laughed.

"While we're on the subject," Agent Minsk said, "I'm Charles."

After the staff left the room, President Weber asked Hunter to begin.

"Portions of this story may be tedious," he said, "so please bear with me." He drew a deep breath and began.

Hunter had reached the point in his story where he'd overheard the conversation between the vice president and Lamar Hager in the office of the underground complex. The staff entered to freshen drinks and serve the salad, and he stopped abruptly.

When the servers had left the room, the president, a stunned expression on his face, asked, "Are you certain it was the vice president and the chairman of the Joint Chiefs?"

"Absolutely, sir."

The president's disbelief was no surprise. Hunter had expected as much.

He resumed his story but paused again at the point where he and Morgan had returned to the hotel after copying about half of the operations manual. The serving personnel had reentered with the entrée and removed the salad dishes.

When they were alone again, Hunter asked, "Mr. President, have you or Charles ever heard of *Operation Ghost Flight*?"

Charles shrugged and shook his head.

President Weber said, "No."

"The remainder of this story is the actual plan as designed in the operations manual. We have two copies of the portion we obtained, which are in secure locations back in the States. Morgan has also read the manual and can verify what I will now tell you."

He described the plan without further interruption. When he had finished, President Weber leaned back in his chair, studied both their faces, then said, "If they catch you, they'll kill you for what you know."

"We realize that," Hunter said, rubbing his left arm. He paused for several seconds. "When I overheard the conversation in the underground complex, the vice president told Lamar Hager that he'd already spoken with 'Stan' about the change to November first. He also said this Stan would document whatever story they claimed. I'm quite certain he was referring to Stanley Bass, your director of the CIA."

President Weber remained silent for a long time. He focused on each of them, ending with Hunter. Finally he said, "Your story is, by far, the most incredible I've ever heard, but I believe you. A great deal of friction has existed between Al Buchanan and me, and at last I know why. I had no idea he blamed me for his son's death. It's absurd, of course, but grief can do strange things to a person. To lose a son or daughter must be the hardest test of a parent's sanity. I can't even imagine how I'd react." He paused then said, "It's difficult for me to accept that these men are planning to kill me for their own gains. But in light of what you've said, there can be no denying it. I'd be foolish if I did."

"Mr. President," Morgan said, "I realize you haven't had time to digest this information, but you should know that Sean Buchanan was actually murdered—by the Gomez brothers. They poisoned him. And Stanley Bass willingly became their accomplice. I've been told that he personally supplied the cyanide. I'm not positive that Bass is involved in *this* scenario, but my gut instinct tells me he is. How and why I can't say. It seems to me, sir, that you must cancel your trip to Cuba." She glanced at Charles. "No security force, no matter how capable and efficient, could guarantee your safety against the detonation of a laser-guided weapon dropped from a stealth aircraft. Since your trip has not yet been publicly announced, you could easily cancel it."

After a moment of reflection, the president said, "You've taken great risks to warn me. I can see that now, and I'm deeply grateful. I hope you know that." He paused then said, "It's still not safe for you. What are your plans?"

Hunter shrugged. "We're going to disappear for a while. We can't go anywhere we normally would until this is over. It's too dangerous. Whatever happens, I want you to know how to get your hands on a copy of the operations manual."

"Good idea," the president said.

"One is in a safe deposit box at Savers Bank in Miami," Hunter said. "Box 2017. Just ask for Maria Sanchez."

Charles made a quick note.

"And the other copy?" the president asked.

Hunter considered his answer carefully. "For now, I'm going to keep that to myself, sir."

Though she didn't say anything, Morgan's face betrayed her surprise.

"May I ask why?" the president queried.

"Yes, sir. Even though this room has been checked, it still may be bugged. I don't know. Call me paranoid. But if I don't disclose that location now, we have a better chance of guarding the proof we'll need in the future."

Smiling, President Weber eased back in his chair again. "I like the way you think, Hunter. Erring on the side of caution is always a good policy."

The staff entered the room to clear the dishes and serve dessert and coffee, after which they were dismissed for the night. Alone again, the president said to his guests, "Since you've known about this for a while, have you thought of any avenues I could pursue, other than canceling my trip to Cuba?"

"I have one," Morgan said. "Publish the story in the *Washington Herald* to immediately expose the traitors. It'd be hard to convince my editors to print it without using the operations manual as proof, though, unless you're the source of the information, sir. If you were, certain aspects, such as the secret underground base, could be left out of the story."

Hunter added, "I considered that option, sir, before I involved Morgan. And we've discussed it since. If we hadn't succeeded in contacting you in time, we would've been forced to go to the press. That would have prevented the disaster—this time. But the way I see it, Buchanan and Hager will simply portray themselves as innocent victims. The press will buy it and sell it to the public because the only way we can tie them to the plot is with the conversation I overheard. A conversation they'd deny and we couldn't prove.

"And I believe we can all agree that if it went into a courtroom, it would be the word of the vice president of the United States and the head of the Joint Chiefs of Staff against that of a lowly tax consultant. I'd be crucified, and you'd have to deal with the political ramifications. Your administration would receive incredibly bad press to say the least. Think about it: your top subordinates planned and initiated an operation to overthrow Cuba for their own gain, utilizing the power of the US military, and it occurred without your knowledge. I'm afraid it would be political suicide for you, sir, at least with regard to your reelection."

President Weber stroked his chin. "I see you've analyzed this thoroughly. And you'd be correct about the political suicide. I've no doubt of that."

"Mr. President, why don't we just shoot down the aircraft delivering the device to the island?" Charles asked.

"We'd be taking too great a chance," the president said, shaking his head. "The pilot might be successful in dropping the bomb, in which case the entire plan would go into effect as designed, and you and I would be history."

"The plane that'll deliver the bomb is a stealth fighter," Hunter said. "It's impossible for radar to detect that aircraft, so there'd be no way to track or target it."

"Hunter's right," the president agreed. "Military people have told me that unless the pilots choose to be identified, no one can locate them. The stealths actually have special panels that the pilots raise when they want to show up on radar. Otherwise they remain invisible."

"And since the attack would take place after dark," Hunter added, "the stealth would be impossible to spot visually as well. Besides, Mr. President, to whom would you give the order to send out a strike aircraft? The chairman of the Joint Chiefs?"

"Good point," the president said, his expression rueful. "Hunter, I may need to contact you during the next several days for more information or your services since the only people I can trust with this matter are in this room."

Hunter nodded. "Morgan and I will have to hide out for a while, so our safe house, if you will, may as well be someplace glorious." He turned to her. "What do you say to Hawaii—specifically, the Big Island? We'll stay at the Protea, one of the major resorts on the Kona side, registered as Mr. and Mrs. Charles Weber."

The president and Charles both were smiling when Hunter looked back at them.

"We'll stay there until this is over, or until you contact us."

"When will you leave?" the president asked.

"Tomorrow morning. Someone knows we're here. We were followed earlier today."

"They were my people," Charles said. "You wouldn't tell me where you were staying, so I had you shadowed. I needed to know where to find you in the event this meeting had to be canceled. By the way, I hate to admit this in front of the president, but you did an excellent job of losing my surveillance team."

The president burst into laughter. "Just a lowly tax consultant and his wonderful assistant!"

"Were your people watching Morgan's house and tailing us in Washington?" Hunter asked.

Charles's brow furrowed. "No. I don't know anything about that."

Hunter sighed. "Just as I figured," he said to no one in particular.

Rising, President Weber said, "If you'll excuse me now, I'd like to contemplate this matter. It's been an enlightening visit, and despite the circumstances, I've enjoyed your company. When this is resolved,

I'd like to invite you both to dinner at the White House, strictly on a social basis."

"We'd like that very much," Morgan replied.

"Good night, sir. We'll await your contact," Hunter said, shaking his hand.

President Weber nodded then headed out of the room.

When the president was gone, Charles said, "I'm worried about the people who were following you in DC. Please be careful, especially at the airport."

Hunter rubbed his left arm again. "We're well aware that our greatest danger is at the airport. But thanks for your concern."

Charles escorted them back to the private elevator. As they rode down to the ground floor, Hunter said to the agent, "When you contact us, make sure your message includes the word Geronimo. That way we'll be absolutely certain we're dealing with you. You might want to give that code word to the president too."

"I will," Charles said. He grinned. "Just like in the movies, eh? Geronimo."

The next morning, Morgan checked around their Savoy suite one last time then closed and latched her suitcase. As she set it by the door, she said, "I still can't believe the president remembered you, Hunter. And I really can't believe you didn't tell him your first name when he asked. *Hobnobber* indeed! How'd you come up with that?"

He shrugged. "I was just trying to be funny—and memorable. It worked, didn't it? Besides, how do you know that isn't my real first name?"

"Yeah, right!" she said, closing one eye and forming the OK sign with her fingers. "I'm sure it is."

Because they were worried about their phony passports, they agreed to split up while in the terminal at Gatwick Airport. As they had done on the trip to London, they altered their appearance somewhat to match their passport photos. Morgan wore her hair pulled up in a bun and donned her dowdiest outfit, while Hunter donned a pair of clear glasses and slicked back his hair. After leaving the Savoy, they stopped just once on the way to the airport to pick up a wire transfer.

The cab dropped them at the terminal at nine-fifteen. Morgan checked her suitcase with a porter then strolled for the ticket counter. From where he stood across the corridor, Hunter followed her progress. Even in her prim outfit, she still turned the heads of several male travelers. Hunter sighed and meandered in the opposite direction, carrying the briefcase he'd purchased and stocked back at the hotel. He visited a shop where he loitered a while. Finally, he bought the morning paper then drifted through the busy terminal in no apparent hurry.

Clearing customs was a major concern. Hunter was more amused than anything else to think that despite having dined with the president of the United States the night before, not to mention being instrumental in saving the life of the most powerful man in the world, they still had to rely on their own devices and not get any help from either the president or the Secret Service so as not to provoke any questions that might get back to Stanley Bass.

Standing sixth in line to see the next agent, Hunter studied the area. Morgan was nowhere in sight. *Good,* he thought. *She should be waiting for me at the gate by now.*

As he inched closer, a commotion two counters over caught his and everyone else's attention. A French traveler was being irate with the agent about something that wasn't allowed through customs. The dispute grew louder as Hunter stepped up for his turn. He hoped the diversion would help him get through without a snag.

"Good morning," he said, making eye contact with the agent as he placed his briefcase on the counter and handed over his passport. "Looks like a problem over there."

"Yes," the agent said, not paying the argument much attention. "Happens quite often, but it's not usually this disturbing."

Hunter cleaned his glasses. "Some people are their own worst enemies. Behaving like that won't get him anywhere."

"No, it won't," the agent agreed, comparing the passport to something inside a drawer that he'd opened. "People need to understand that we're simply doing our jobs. For everyone's safety, regulations must be followed. I'll need to see your airline ticket, sir."

"Oh, yes. Of course." Mystified, Hunter pulled it from his jacket pocket. What was this? The guy hadn't asked to see the tickets of the five previous travelers. Willing himself to breathe calmly, he watched the agent copy down the flight information.

"You were here on business, Mr.…Crowfield?" the agent asked, reading the name from the passport.

Hunter used a handkerchief to blow his nose before answering. "Yes, that's correct."

"Where did you stay?"

He made eye contact again. "At the Savoy."

"Did you have a good trip?"

Why was the guy being so damned thorough all of a sudden? "I did, indeed. It was most successful."

The agent handed him his passport and ticket. "Everything's in order, Mr. Crowfield. Have a pleasant journey back to the Big Apple."

"Thank you," he said, being careful not to leave in too big a hurry. He stowed the documents in his jacket pocket, folded the newspaper under his arm, then picked up his briefcase. As he casually strolled away, he glanced back to see the agent leave the counter and enter a door marked SUPERVISOR.

American Airlines flight 337 to New York was about to board when Hunter reached the gate. Morgan waited near a picture window with a view of the distant runway. Two adorable small children, a boy and a girl maybe six or seven years old, had their hands cupped to the glass. They watched excitedly as a British Airways 747 lumbered along then majestically transitioned into flight. For a moment, Hunter pictured the children as his own, with Morgan as his wife, the whole family going on holiday. *Was it a daydream,* he wondered, *or a glimpse into the future?* He shook off the vision. At an adjacent gate, passengers were preparing to board another American Airlines flight, a nonstop to Chicago.

"I see you made it," Morgan said as he sat beside her.

"For a while there, I wondered if I would. That customs agent asked a bunch of questions and spent a lot of time on me. He didn't do that with anyone else."

She spun in her seat and faced him. "The same thing happened to me. Everyone in front of me passed through with ease, but they grilled me and wrote down my flight information."

"Shit! They're on to us, Morgan. When we step off the flight in New York, they'll be waiting for us."

"What are we going to do?"

He studied the gate attendant for the Chicago flight that had just started to board. Most of the time she checked boarding passes, but because of the long line, she occasionally accepted one or two without question. "Let's try to get on that flight with the boarding passes for this one. If we succeed, we'll hide in the lavatories until the plane starts moving. By then the vacant seats will be obvious."

"What if the flight is fully booked?"

Hunter shrugged. "We'll cross that bridge when we come to it—*if* we come to it."

They eased into the line for the Chicago flight. When they reached the attendant, Hunter winked at her and handed her both boarding passes. "Has anyone ever told you that you have gorgeous eyes and a really beautiful smile?"

She looked at Morgan then back at him. Grinning, she said, "I don't usually receive such flattering compliments from a man who's traveling with a very attractive woman."

"That's true enough, I suppose," he said through his laughter. "This is my sister, Ashley."

"Hello, Ashley. Welcome aboard. I hope you both enjoy the flight."

"I'm sure we will," Morgan said as they stepped past.

She punched him on the shoulder as they hustled through the jetway. "You opportunistic flirt!"

He smirked. "Now don't pout for the whole flight."

They ducked into the lavatories for several minutes until the plane started moving. As it was backed away by the ground crew, they claimed two seats in first class. Hunter sat by the window and watched the plane bound for New York leave its gate at the same time. It ended up in front of them as both aircraft taxied away from the terminal.

When the New York plane began its takeoff roll, he had a good view of it and the runway. He followed its progress as it increased speed and became airborne. Hunter smiled to himself as he wondered who would be waiting for them to get off that plane at JFK in New York—and how long it would take them to figure out that an airline version of a shell game had taken place.

As the plane continued its steep climb straight out off the end of the runway, it suddenly exploded. Hunter's jaw dropped. A collective gasp of horror rose up from his fellow passengers who'd been watching out their own windows. The huge fireball plummeted to the earth, an elongated tail of flames and smoke trailing behind it. A fiery rain traced its path as the smaller burning pieces took longer to reach the ground.

Hunter felt Morgan grab his arm, clinging to it tightly.

"Hunter, is that…?"

"The New York flight," he whispered.

She unbuckled her seat belt, leaned over him, and pressed her face against the Plexiglas. "You're sure?"

He nodded.

"Oh, my god!"

"Bastards!" he muttered. "Those friggin' bastards. They blew up an airliner full of innocent people."

Morgan wiped at the tears flowing down her cheeks. "I—I can't believe it! Why?"

"To get us," he whispered. "They murdered all those harmless souls just to get us." He pictured the two children that he'd imagined as his own. "Whoever did this will pay for it, Morgan. I promise, if it's the last thing I do, I'm going to personally make sure they pay!"

* * *

General Lamar Hager entered his office early on Monday hoping for some good news. He set his briefcase on the desktop, doffed his coat, and went right to work. Searching in a file cabinet when the phone rang, he eagerly reached over his desk and snatched the phone from its cradle.

"Yes?" he asked crisply.

"Hello, Lamar. Stan here. I have some information for you."

"Did you locate Mahoy and Lindsey?"

"Yes and no. You guessed correctly about British customs. They flew from Washington to London, stayed two nights, then purchased tickets on a flight to New York this morning."

"New York?"

"Yes," Stan said. "Because we've learned the names they're using on their fake passports, I picked up on their reservations late last night. I immediately contacted an operative whose cover is security at Heathrow International and told him that no matter what it took, Mahoy and Lindsey were not to make it back to the States. I told him I didn't care how he did it, or when, just that he was successful. Then I gave him their flight information and fake names. I didn't really expect him to take the assignment to the extreme that he did, because I could've posted a team at Kennedy to intercept Mahoy and Lindsey upon their arrival. But what the hell? What's done is done."

"What do you mean 'what's done is done?' Stan, what happened?"

"Then I guess you haven't heard. As luck would have it," he said with a smirk, "that New York flight exploded and crashed just after takeoff."

"Oh, my god! Please tell me there were survivors, Stan, lots of survivors."

"Nope. Not a one."

Hager felt weak at the knees. After a long pause, he said, "So Mahoy and Lindsey are history?"

"Ah, not exactly, Lamar. I checked with the airline just to be sure. Their boarding passes were not used to get on that plane. Apparently they boarded a flight to Chicago instead. Whether it was by mistake or on purpose, I don't know."

Hager sat down heavily, not really wanting an answer to his next question. "Stan, are you saying you blew up an airliner full of people, and Mahoy and Lindsey weren't even on board?" He held his breath.

Dead silence.

Hager hung his head. This was way more than he'd bargained for. But he was in too deep now. He had to stay the course. "Shit! This is bad, Stan. Really bad. Buchanan's going to go ballistic over this. How many people were on that flight?"

"It doesn't really matter, Lamar. And we don't need to tell, Al. Everyone thinks it was an act of terrorism because I had someone call and claim responsibility for it. We can just leave it at that. Besides, Buchanan's on his way to Miami for that funeral this morning. That buys us a little more time."

Hager rubbed his temples. "Mahoy and Lindsey went to *Chicago*? What in hell would they be doing in Chicago?"

"I suspect it's a jumping-off point. Just before they left London, Lindsey received a wire transfer of five-thousand dollars from the *Washington Herald*."

"Have you tracked them from Chicago?"

"I'm working on that now, but I have a feeling the trail's going to run cold."

"Why's that, Stan?"

"Because here in the States they can use any transportation method they choose: planes, car agencies, passenger trains, buses. They could even buy a car with that five grand. Finding them is going to take some time."

"Do us both a favor, Stan. Work fast."

*   *   *

Colonel Raifer remained hidden within the enclosure atop the six-story office building in Miami. The time drew near. Occasionally he checked the developments in his target area through the high-powered scope on his rifle. News and police helicopters had buzzed back and forth since dawn, like worker bees coming and going from the hive. Streets were closed off for blocks around the site. The crowd had doubled in size in the past half hour. Television crews had as well, their live-broadcast satellite masts extended to full height above their equipment vans.

Finally, Vice President Al Buchanan's motorcade arrived.

"About time," Raifer said aloud. The stage was almost set.

He carefully studied the face of every person who occupied a seat near Juan Carlos Gomez's coffin on the raised platform. Behind the flower-draped casket at center stage stood a podium displaying the presidential seal of the United States. To the right of the reserved chair for the vice president sat Enrique and Pedro Gomez and their wives. To the left was the mayor of Miami–Dade County, Julio Fuentes, and some of his cronies.

Won't be long now, he thought. *Come on, Mr. Vice President. Quit stalling. Let's get on with it.*

A police helicopter with a sharpshooter sitting in the open door zoomed toward Raifer's position. To play it safe, he took cover until the craft had passed overhead. Then he quickly retrained his weapon, making minor adjustments to allow for the rising heat waves and the slight breeze blowing across his field of fire.

At last Vice President Al Buchanan approached the stage, flanked by four Secret Service agents. Raifer grinned. *Which one of you guys wants to take it in the leg? Oh, don't worry. It'll be a clean shot. No permanent damage. You'll be a hero, maybe even get a medal.* Raifer waited for just the right moment. After shaking hands and greeting nearly everyone on the platform, the vice president stepped up to the podium. The guests all took their seats. Buchanan began to speak. Everyone sat still and attentive.

Raifer centered the crosshairs and slid his index finger onto the sensitive trigger. He drew a breath, held it, then touched-off the weapon. Enrique Gomez slumped over into eternity. Before anyone had time to react, Raifer squeezed the trigger again. Pedro Gomez instantly joined his brother in the afterlife. Each man received his sentence in the middle of the forehead, the projectile ripping through the brain and blowing out the back of the head.

Chaos broke out. Weapons drawn, the Secret Service agents shoved the vice president to the ground. Two of them blanketed his body with their own. To make it look good, Raifer popped one of them in the leg and the other in the arm. *Who's the Latin man crouched with a pistol in his hand?* Oh, what the hell. Raifer aimed one last time. A fraction of a second later, blood splattered from the man's right shoulder; his pistol discharged recklessly into the sky before falling from his hand.

Raifer smiled. *I'd love to stick around and have some more fun, but it's time to go.* He shoved the rifle and case under the huge air-conditioning unit then sprinted to the roof's access door. He escaped down the interior stairway, doffing his gloves and stuffing them into his pocket as he went. At the ground floor, he wiped his brow with a handkerchief, exited the stairwell into the lobby, then strolled casually out the front door.

* * *

"Kona at last," Morgan said, stretching. "London, Chicago, Dallas, San Francisco, and finally Hawaii. I'm not sure what day it is, what with all the time zones, but I am sure I've been on enough airplanes for a while."

"Me too. And today is Tuesday. You slept through most of yesterday. I tell you what, though, I thought they'd never let the Chicago flight take off from London after that New York flight crashed. I sweated bullets the entire five hours we had to wait in the terminal. They sure took a long time checking our plane. I fully expected us to get caught when we reboarded with the wrong passes. If that male gate attendant hadn't been eyeballing your breasts at the time, we probably would've. Undoing a couple of buttons on your blouse before we got up to him was a smart move."

Morgan smiled. "That little trick's worked for me several times, even gotten me out of a couple of speeding tickets. Men just can't help themselves. They get…distracted. And I agree that we really were lucky to get out of there." She looked around. "This open-air terminal is a refreshing change. What a pleasant breeze."

Hunter hailed a taxi.

"Aloha. Where's your luggage?" the cabbie asked as he reached over the seat to open the back door for them.

"It didn't arrive with us," Hunter said, which was true. "We'll worry about that later. We're staying at the Protea, and right now we just want to hang loose."

The cabbie smiled and put the car in gear. "You've been here before."

Hunter nodded at him in the rearview mirror. "Several times. Someday we may even get married here."

Morgan rolled her eyes and looked out the window, saying nothing more for the rest of the ride to the resort.

They checked in as Mr. and Mrs. Charles Weber. En route to their room, which opened directly onto the beach, they meandered along covered walkways past manicured lawns and flowering tropical gardens prolific with orchids as well as ponds, streams, and even man-made waterfalls.

"This place is gorgeous, Hunter!" Morgan breathed. "It's so peaceful and relaxing. I could stay here forever."

"So could I. We're in for a wonderful time, darlin', starting with an early dinner at the restaurant of your choice."

"That sounds nice. I'm getting hungry."

Inside their room, Hunter sprawled across the king-sized bed where housekeeping had left orchids and chocolates. Morgan freshened up in the bathroom.

"Since our luggage went down with that airplane, we'll have to buy some clothes tomorrow," she said through the door.

He grinned. "Nothing makes a woman's heart beat a bit faster than the idea of a shopping trip."

The twosome shopped Wednesday morning then sunbathed on the beach and sipped Mai Tais all afternoon. On their way through the lobby back to their room, Hunter bought a newspaper. He scanned the headlines as they walked.

"Wow, listen to this, Morgan. There was an assassination attempt on the vice president at Juan Carlos's funeral in Miami."

"You're kidding, right!"

"No, I'm not." He held the paper in her direction.

"Was he wounded?"

"Ahhh…let me see." Hunter stopped in his tracks. "Holy shit! Enrique and Pedro Gomez were both killed! Shot in the head!" He read on voraciously as she opened the door to their room. Following her inside, he sat at the table and continued the article, never taking his eyes off the paper. "Damn! The vice president was missed completely. That's too bad. Two Secret Service agents were hit, but their wounds weren't life threatening." He turned to an inside page. "Well, what do you know…the Miami bureau chief of the FBI, the guy I spoke with about the Gomez tape, Jose Espinosa, was shot in the shoulder. Serves him right after the mess he got me into. Here's some poetic justice: he announced his retirement just last week. Now he'll begin that retirement recovering from a gunshot wound. Apparently he lost a lot of blood but will make a full recovery." Hunter looked up from the paper. "I don't know, Morgan. There's something screwy about the whole thing. Only the Gomez brothers were killed. Buchanan wasn't even touched. Seems strange that the intended target was unscathed while two supposedly innocent bystanders were assassinated."

Morgan looked thoughtfully at Hunter. "Yeah, I think you may be right. Maybe Stanley Bass didn't want the brothers to squeal on him. As director of the CIA, he could arrange a hit like that. But look on the bright side. The Gomez brothers won't be after us anymore. Good riddance to bad rubbish." She kicked off her sandals and flopped facedown on the bed. With a pillow propped under her chest, feet sticking up in the air, she studied the resort literature. "What cuisine would you like tonight?"

No response.

"Hel-lo! Hunter?" She looked up from the brochure. "You still reading the same article?"

"No. I'm reading about the plane crash. Two-hundred-and-eighty-eight people died, Morgan. Damn. Saving the president's life has become *very* expensive." He leaned back and rubbed his eyes. "I don't know. Maybe I shouldn't have done anything after I overheard that conversation in the underground hangar. If I had kept my mouth shut, all these people would still be alive." He brushed the newspaper with the back of his hand.

"Hunter, you're not to blame for any of this. The conspirators are. You've done the right thing."

He looked up at her. "Speaking of blame, the authorities are accusing a terrorist group for the bombing. They don't even have a clue." Seeing her watery eyes, he turned the page and moved on to something else. "Hey, listen to this. President Weber has changed his travel plans because of the assassination attempt on the vice president. Following his meeting in Japan, he is now scheduled to stop in the Hawaiian Islands tomorrow afternoon on his return to Washington DC."

Morgan rolled over and sat on the edge of the bed. "So soon? We just got here ourselves. What time will he arrive?"

"Five-thirty."

"What do you suppose he wants with us?" she asked. "We told him everything."

Hunter held up his hands. "Beats me. But he must have something important in mind to change his plans so drastically."

Morgan stood. "I'm starving. Let's get dressed and go have dinner."

They dined at a nearby steak house where they savored their meal then lingered over dessert and coffee. Afterwards, they strolled the beach, discussing how destiny had taken a hand in drawing them together again. A salty-sweet tropical breeze rustled the coconut palms. Almost as if on cue, a brilliant, fiery shooting star flared overhead, burning across three quarters of the sky.

"Did you make a wish?" he asked softly.

"Yes, I did."

"Well, what was it?"

"I can't tell you until after it comes true."

"I hope it doesn't take too long. I'm not getting any younger you know."

She faced him, her hands propped on her hips. "What's *that* supposed to mean?" she asked in an aggrieved tone, eyes boring into him.

He'd done it again. He had correctly guessed her thoughts, and it made her angry. He had neither expected nor intended that. "It means…never mind. Just forget it."

"Let's head back," she said crisply. "I'm tired.

The return was a silent one. Back inside their room, Hunter switched on the television, hoping to catch something on CNN about the president's trip. After barely mentioning the jetliner bombing and the Miami shooting, the telecast focused heavily on an earthquake that had just occurred in Mexico—a magnitude 7.2 on the Richter scale. The epicenter was on the south side of Mexico City.

Describing the reports as sketchy at best, the announcer stated that the damage appeared substantial not only throughout the city but also up in the nearby mountains. The death toll was expected to run high.

All the news stations were broadcasting the same limited information over and over. He pressed the power button, and the screen turned black. Morgan was already asleep. He said a silent prayer for the victims then took the phone out on the terrace, closed the door, and called Baptist Hospital in Miami. "Hello, Amanda Taylor's room, please."

The operator paused. "Just a moment, sir."

Hunter waited a long time before someone came on the line again.

"Hello. Are you the person inquiring about Amanda Taylor?"

"Yes, I am. Has she already been released?"

"Are you a family member, sir?"

He swallowed hard. "I'm her boss. I brought her to the hospital. I've been out of the country, out of touch for a while."

"I see. Sir, I'm very sorry to inform you that Amanda Taylor died…three days ago."

Hunter dropped the phone and collapsed to his knees. He began crying softly. "Why Amanda? Why not me instead?"

Tears tracked down each cheek. "I'm so sorry, Amanda," he murmured. "I should've thrown away that damn tape—and the recorder. It's all my fault." He stared at the ocean through watery eyes and cursed his own existence. Life was so unfair.

He struggled to get to his feet then walked woodenly far out onto the sand. Feeling almost physical pain, he lay down on his side, curled into a ball, and cried uncontrollably. Finally, emotionally spent, he drifted off to sleep.

Amanda appeared and smiled at him. Her face was more beautiful than ever: flawless, angelic even. He brushed a strand of golden hair from her cheek and peered into her exquisite blue eyes, sapphires of the soul. He loved her, and he told her so as a hundred images of her flashed by, one after another—his personal slide show. The images slowed then stopped on the one it started with. She reached out to him.

"Hunter. Wake up, Hunter."

"I love you, Amanda," he muttered as he was jostled awake.

"Come on, Hunter. Wake up."

Opening his eyes, he squinted at the morning sun rising over Mauna Kea. "Huh—? Morgan?" He put his hand up to block the light. "What time is it?"

"Six-fifteen." She sat beside him. "What're you doing out here, Hunter? I awoke in the middle of the night and couldn't find you. I've been worried for hours."

"I'm sorry," he said, rubbing his eyes. He explained about Amanda, choking up twice before finishing.

Morgan embraced him, crying as well.

Pulling himself together, Hunter offered to take her to the other side of the island for the day. He figured the distraction would do him some good. They returned to their room where he showered and changed.

An hour later they were on their way to Hilo, the side of the island that received most of the rainfall, producing lush and green tropical plants and foliage. Compared to the Kona side, the difference in the landscapes was like the earth and the moon. They spent the day traversing the coast, enjoying the abundant natural beauty. Finally in midafternoon they started back to their hotel, taking Saddle Road, a little-used cross-island route that considerably shortened the driving time back to Kona.

Completing the day's journey near sundown, they entered the resort lobby and found a one-word message awaiting them at the desk: Geronimo.

As they turned away from the front desk, Morgan yelped and jumped back, then put her hand over her heart. "Charles! You scared the life out of me, sneaking up on us like that!"

"I'm sorry," the Secret Service agent said, clearly doing his best to suppress a smile. "I didn't mean to startle you."

They stepped across the lobby to continue their conversation.

"We read that you'd stop in the Hawaiian Islands on your return," Morgan said. "We didn't expect to hear from you until tomorrow because we thought you'd be in Honolulu overnight."

Minsk discreetly glanced around to see if anyone was within earshot. "Actually, we stopped right here at Kona Airport. We need to talk. Let's go to your room."

CHAPTER

Charles Minsk circled the suite, taking in the trappings. Big-screen TV. DVD. Plush leather sofa. Kitchenette with a minibar and a microwave. "Nice accommodations." He stopped near the terrace. "And a gorgeous view of the beach. You two hide out in style. I'm sorry for interfering with your plans," he said, still looking through the sliding-glass door, "but President Weber has requested your company aboard Air Force One on his return to Washington DC. He's waiting for us even as we speak."

"Do you know what he wants from us?" Hunter asked.

Charles turned and faced them. "No. He didn't say. Would it be possible for you to pack now? I have a car waiting."

By the time they reached the airport, twilight ruled. Hunter cupped his hands against the tinted glass and squinted at the tarmac. Air Force One, its sheer size lost in the shadows, sat well away from the terminal, no doubt to keep the prying lenses of photographers out of range. He'd never in his wildest dreams imagined that he'd get to ride with the president aboard Air Force One.

The driver killed the engine, and the car rolled to a stop at the base of the front airstairs. He hopped out then opened the back door for his passengers to exit. A dozen or so security personnel stood guard around the perimeter of the aircraft, including two at the base of the steps.

Charles escorted Hunter and Morgan past security and up the airstairs. "With the exception of my fellow agents, we fly empty tonight. President Weber made other arrangements for the rest of the support personnel. He wants to discuss matters with you privately and without interruption, so we'll have this magnificent craft all to ourselves." They reached the top landing then stepped through the open door. "Grab a seat and buckle in. We'll leave immediately."

The 747 began moving. Instead of taxiing to the beginning of the runway, the pilot initiated the takeoff roll with one-third of the runway already behind the aircraft. This standard procedure for Air Force One kept plenty of distance between the 747 and the perimeter of the airport so that the plane wouldn't become an easy rifle target.

When the jumbo jet leveled out at its cruising altitude, Charles escorted Hunter and Morgan to an eight-person conference room. President Weber entered just after they were seated, and they rose to greet him. "Hello, Mr. President," they chorused.

"Thank you for accommodating me on such short notice," Weber said to his guests, claiming the seat at the head of the table. "To update you both, my visit to Cuba on November first will be announced in Miami by the vice president Saturday evening, the twenty-ninth, just forty-eight hours from now. I have a plan that I believe will bring this matter to the best possible conclusion. What I need from you is more information." He looked at Hunter. "You mentioned that Al Buchanan told Lamar Hager they'd meet again in the underground complex two days prior to my arrival in Cuba."

"Correct, sir."

Weber nodded. "Then I will alter my itinerary to ensure that that meeting takes place. By changing my arrival time at Guantanamo, the two men will be forced to adjust their plans. That means they'll need to communicate with each other. I need a recording of their conversation. That kind of proof will protect me in the event my plan unfolds differently than I foresee."

Hunter studied Weber, thinking that the man looked as tired as he himself felt. He wondered why anyone would want the job of president. It didn't pay that well, considering the responsibility, it aged a man quickly, and sound sleep was likely as hard to come by as real privacy. "Is there another reason why you want that recording, sir?" Hunter asked.

Weber smiled. "You're most perceptive," he said. "And since you obviously know what that reason is, we needn't discuss it any further."

"Yes, sir."

The plane banked into a shallow turn, and the full moon appeared in one of the windows. It was brighter and larger than Hunter had ever seen.

"I have a dilemma on my hands," the president continued. "Normally I'd send Charles with a hand-picked team to get the recording, but if they were caught, Buchanan and Hager would immediately know that I'm aware of their plans. I can't risk that. I need you to do it, Hunter—and you alone." He glanced at Morgan. "I have other plans for Morgan. I know I'm asking a great deal, and sending a civilian with no real experience goes against my better judgment. But it makes sense. You know where the men will meet. You know the complex. You know what's at stake. And most importantly, I can trust you."

"And if I get caught," Hunter said, "I can lie through my teeth until they kill me."

The drone of the jet engines overpowered the silence.

Finally Hunter spoke again. "Of course I'll do it, Mr. President, and gladly. Besides, as long as those two are running around free, I'd be forever looking over my shoulder, expecting them to blow my head off. After the bombing of that American Airlines jetliner, even you couldn't keep me from it. I owe the two-hundred-and-eighty-eight innocent victims who died on that flight."

President Weber wrinkled his brow. "What does that terrorist bombing have to do with this?"

"That wasn't a terrorist's bomb, Mr. President," Morgan said. "Hunter and I were supposed to be on that flight. We purposely boarded the wrong plane at the last minute because we suspected that someone would be waiting for us in New York."

"Are you sure the bomb was meant for you?" Charles asked. "That seems quite extreme."

"They tried to kill us back in DC by blowing up Morgan's garage," Hunter said. "That's quite extreme."

"And they shot my car to pieces while we were in it," Morgan added.

"My god! I had no idea," the president said. He leaned back and rubbed his eyes. "You two have done well to stay alive. I can never repay such a debt."

Hunter cleared his throat. "Yes, you can, sir. Stop those bastards before they kill someone else."

"Believe me, I intend to," President Weber said, locking eyes with him. "What I'm asking you to do now seems tame by comparison to what you've already been through. To get the recording, all you'll have to do is plant a tiny microphone. The signal will be picked up by a remote unit manned by Charles outside the base. Can you return to the underground complex undetected?"

Morgan looked at Hunter. "We allowed the doors to lock, remember?"

Nodding, he thought for a moment as he rubbed the five o'clock shadow on his chin. "Yes, Mr. President. I can return undetected."

"Good! There's another matter you can attend to while you're in the complex if you have time, and if you feel safe enough. I'd like a basic inventory of the aircraft and any armament you find. That might mean exploring the underground complex more diligently. But no matter what, you must exit by eleven o'clock Sunday night, October thirtieth. I'll have Charles make the arrangements now for your flight to Miami."

"I have one question," Hunter said. "If I do get caught, can I expect any assistance?"

President Weber looked him square in the eye. "No. You'll be entirely on your own. I'm sorry. If your mission is successful, however, any information you gather must be delivered to me in person. You should have enough time to meet with me in Washington before I depart."

"Mr. President, you're not still planning to visit Cuba, are you?" Morgan asked. "What if the bomb's dropped?"

"It's best I don't disclose my plans at this time, in case something unfortunate happens and Hunter is caught in the complex. But the result will become apparent soon enough. Rest assured, I'll be safe."

Charles rose. "I'll go make the arrangements for the Miami flight."

Morgan stood as well. "Will you show me to a restroom?"

"Certainly."

President Weber and Hunter watched silently until the door was closed, then faced each other.

"Hunter, I believe you have a fairly good idea of my intentions. I hope you understand that before I can go through with my plan with a clear conscience, I must have the proof that the tape recording will provide. It's imperative."

"I understand, sir."

"The complex may be more active this time. Are you sure you don't want to reconsider your decision to do this for me?"

"I'm sure, Mr. President. Have you thought about how you'll handle the press?"

Weber nodded. "I intend to have Morgan polish the story I dictate, then get it printed in the *Washington Herald* before the rest of the world and the media have time to react. Because she wouldn't be safe in DC, I'll stash her at Camp David."

"Speaking of stories, Mr. President, you didn't believe the farce that someone actually tried to assassinate Al Buchanan, did you?"

"What do you mean?"

"The whole thing was a scam, sir. It was designed to make the vice president look like the target. The Gomez brothers were the real prize. Morgan and I believe Stanley Bass ordered that hit."

"Why would you suspect that?"

"Because Bass was involved with the Gomez brothers in Sean Buchanan's murder. As a result of Morgan's recent article, the true story is starting to unravel. We think Stanley Bass bought some insurance. Now he can't possibly be fingered by the Gomez brothers as their accomplice."

Weber pondered Hunter's words. "That's a good theory, and you may be right. Nonetheless, that incident gave me the excuse I needed to cut my overseas trip short and make a stop in Hawaii."

Morgan reappeared.

Charles followed a moment later. "You're all set, Hunter. You'll fly out of Dulles International on Delta under the name of Mr. Charles Weber. I'll drive you to the airport myself."

President Weber held up a hand. "If my plan is successful, the world can never know what actually happened. The only people who will know are the four of us in this room. It must remain that way forever. It's never to be mentioned again—to anyone."

Hunter spoke first. "I have no problem with that, sir."

"Neither do I," Charles said.

"I'm not certain I know as much as the rest of you," Morgan said, "but I believe you to be a true and sincere man, Mr. President, and I trust your judgment completely. In all honesty, I'm most concerned with your safety."

"I appreciate that, and thank you." President Weber patted her hand. "Morgan, you and I need to outline the story that'll be printed when this awful business is finished."

That signaled that the meeting was over. Charles rose and turned to Hunter. "Why don't we go get some coffee and iron out a few details about your visit to the underground complex?"

Hunter nodded. "Good idea."

Closing the door behind them, they left President Weber and Morgan in the conference room and strode to the galley. After searching through a few cabinets, Charles said, "I usually just go for the instant."

"Anything will do. I'm easy to please."

Charles made a couple of mugs of instant coffee then handed one to Hunter. "We'll arrive at Andrews Air Force Base around ten a.m. Your flight leaves two-and-a-half hours later, so you'll be in Miami by midafternoon."

"That should work well," Hunter said. "It'll give me the rest of the afternoon and evening to assemble the items I'll need to reenter the complex the following morning."

Charles stuffed his free hand in his pocket. "You're planning to enter the complex in the morning? In daylight?"

"Yes. I believe reentry will be easiest and safest by descending the shaft I found at the cabin. No one would expect me to return to that complex, especially through the tunnel. A good friend of mine owns an airboat and knows that area of the Everglades quite well. I'm sure he'll accommodate me. It may be wiser to enter the complex in daylight anyway. The stealth flights occur at night, which suggests less activity underground during the day."

Charles nodded thoughtfully. "I hadn't considered that."

Hunter sipped his coffee. "If I have the freedom of movement that I expect, I should be able to explore the entire complex, inventory the aircraft, and still be in position well in advance of the meeting between Buchanan and Hager. I'm assuming they'll meet in the early evening as they did before."

"You're probably right," Charles said. "Buchanan is scheduled to fly to Miami late that afternoon. I'll get a copy of his itinerary for that trip. Will you leave the complex immediately after planting the microphone?"

Hunter shrugged. "I don't know. The only quick exit would place me aboveground inside Homestead Air Force Base. That may work, but it depends on how active the installation is at that time. In any event, if all goes well, I'll be back in DC by noon on the thirtieth."

"Excellent. That'd give the president a day and a half to analyze your information and finalize his plans. When we arrive at Andrews, Morgan will board Marine One with the president. You'll remain on this aircraft for about a half hour. Radio transmitter microphones will be delivered to me during that time. The president considered wiring you so that I could hear everything you're doing but decided against it. If you were caught, you'd be history, and the cat would be out of the bag."

Hunter chuckled. "I'd rather make history than be history." Raising his cup, he said, "Here's to bagging a slick cat."

"Stanley Bass is certainly a big one, literally and figuratively," Charles said, clinking his mug with Hunter's. "I sure hope we get something on that recording to implicate him as well. Bass spends a lot more time at his thirty-acre compound out on Maryland's eastern shore than he does in Langley or DC. He comes and goes like the wind, rarely answers to anyone, and has more power than any one man should ever have. Seems that no one has any idea what the man really does or when he does it or even why."

It was clear that Charles badly wanted to catch Bass. Hunter smiled to himself over the pun. At the moment Charles was fishing in Hunter's backyard, trying to find out if he would throw in with him. To what depth would Charles go? Hunter envisioned two guys in a rowboat out to catch a whale. Two guys with only their wits to use for bait.

"I hope we get something on Bass too, Charles. If we don't, he's going to be a problem. Will you be manning the remote vehicle by yourself?"

"Yes. The president feels the fewer people involved in this the better. I'll fly down that afternoon and be in place before sunset." Charles set the mugs in the sink. "I'll go make that call for the vice president's itinerary now. You look beat. Let me show you to a private room in case you or Morgan would like to rest."

"That'd be great. I didn't get much sleep last night."

When Hunter returned to the conference room, President Weber and Morgan awaited him.

"Do you and Charles have everything squared away?" the president asked.

"Yes, we have, sir."

"Fine. If you'll excuse me then, I'm going to rest for a while." He rose. "Feel free to move about this aircraft as you wish."

They bade him good night, and after he left, Morgan turned to Hunter with a gleam in her eye. "President Weber wants me to be his personal reporter. Can you believe that? I'll have the advantage on everything that happens—for this incident anyway."

"Congratulations, Morgan. Scooping this story will catapult you so high in the journalistic world they'll have to give you your own orbit."

They left the conference room and strolled toward the quarters Charles had shown him.

"This'll be a first for me," Hunter said as they entered. "Sleeping aboard a plane on an actual bed."

She kicked off her shoes and sat on the bed, pressing her palms into the mattress. "It's nice and firm."

A grin stole across his weary features. "Why does the phrase 'mile-high club' suddenly come to mind?"

Morgan propped her hands on her hips. "Why does the word *horny* suddenly come to mind?" She giggled. "That's what the *H* stands for. And you can just wipe that ridiculous expression off your face. You've been up all night. What you need is sleep, not sex."

CHAPTER

19

"Good morning. Sorry I'm late," Lamar Hager said as he sauntered across General Tom Kelly's office in the Pentagon then eased into a plush armchair. "I always have a hard time getting started on Fridays. Looking forward to the weekend, I guess."

Kelly studied his old friend's face. He'd aged noticeably in the past couple of years. It seemed especially evident this morning. "No problem. In fact, your timing is excellent, Lamar. I just this second finished a lengthy call with President Weber aboard Air Force One. He's sharpening his ax again, itching for something else to chop."

Hager slammed his fist on the arm of the chair. "Damn! Not again! He's already cut everything to the bone."

Kelly slid some paperwork to one side of his desk. "I guess Weber thinks the skeleton needs trimming now.

Hager shook his head. "Speaking of skeletons, Tom, I have something to discuss with you. I see no way to be subtle about this, so I'm just going to blurt it out." He lowered his voice. "We could alter *Operation Ghost Flight* so that Weber becomes a ghost too."

The statement pulled absolute silence into the room, yet it seemed to echo forever.

Finally Kelly cleared his throat. "You realize what you're suggesting, Lamar?"

"It's an idea, Tom. You have a better one?"

"Granted it would certainly solve our problem, but—"

"It's quite basic when you think about it, Tom. A soldier attacks his enemy using whatever means is necessary, or available, to remove the enemy's threat. We've killed before. We had to, we were at war. Taking away the tools necessary for the military to survive, Weber has become the enemy. I'll tell you something else too." He leaned forward. "Weber doesn't know about your extra fleet of stealth fighters, your ghost fleet, because their existence was schemed during the former administration. What do you think he'll do when he finds out they were secretly built without his knowledge? Your head will be on the chopping block. And you just finished saying that Weber's sharpening his ax again."

Kelly swallowed hard against the lump in his throat. The stakes had escalated to a level he'd never imagined. "I don't know, Lamar. I'll have to think about this."

Hager rose and walked to the door. "Don't take too long. The opportunity will be lost soon." He opened the door then closed it softly behind him.

Kelly sighed heavily and reached for the phone.

*   *   *

Hunter waited aboard Air Force One at Andrews Air Force Base. Nearly an hour had elapsed, and Charles hadn't returned. Hunter's suspicious nature started to get the best of him. *Was Charles completely on the level? Could he be involved in the assassination plot? His inside information could easily be used to his advantage.*

Get a grip, Hunter chided himself. *Charles has only the best intentions regarding the president. He even stopped a bullet with Nelson Weber's name on it. But then again, he may not have meant to. Maybe he'd like compensation for that limp he'll have for the rest of his life.* Hunter stared out the window again. *No. No friggin' way. My imagination's working overtime.*

Just then, a vehicle wheeled in and stopped crisply. Moments later Charles appeared in the open door of the aircraft carrying a burgundy briefcase. "Sorry about the delay," he said. "I had…difficulties to overcome." He set the case on a seat and popped the latches. "I'll be brief. You've a flight to catch. These wireless microphones, better known as electronic bugs, have a tiny battery built into them. They're activated by pushing a sharp, pointed object—like a straight pin or the end of a paper clip—into the hole on this end." He held it up for Hunter to see. "These bugs are easy to conceal, but the quality of the sound depends on where they're located. A file cabinet drawer, for instance, would not be as desirable as, say, the underside of a desktop. You have six bugs here. If you plant them all, we're bound to pick up a good signal from at least a couple."

"How long will the batteries last?" Hunter asked, scrutinizing one of the tiny devices.

"Long enough for our purposes. We do have a concern, however, about the location being several stories underground in what's essentially a concrete bunker. The signal may be weak or distressed. As a backup, I brought this digital recorder."

Hunter handled the palm-sized unit. "I have a similar one in my office." That made him think of Amanda. He quickly stifled the thought and handed back the device.

"Then you know it's voice activated and silent because there's no tape. It'll be risky to carry, though. If you're caught, you'll have no way to explain why you have it."

Hunter snorted. "I won't have any way to explain why I'm there, either."

Charles raised an eyebrow. "Good point. Anyway, another drawback is that it'll have to be inside the room where the conversation takes place. In any event, you'll have to be constantly ready to ditch it somewhere if things get hairy, especially if you have recorded evidence by then." Charles hurriedly placed the items back into the briefcase. "Needless to say, use cash to purchase the ticket I reserved for you, and for anything else you might need." He handed over a wad of greenbacks. "We'd better get moving, or you'll miss your plane."

Hunter's flight from Washington was uneventful. After arriving at Miami International Airport, he called his friend Joe Hawkins to set up the airboat ride then caught a shuttle bus to a nearby Ramada Inn.

He registered and bought a newspaper before going up to his room, where he promptly checked the obituaries. Amanda's was there, along with her picture. His eyes watered as she smiled at him. The funeral had already taken place the previous day. *Oh, God. I missed the services.* He sat on the bed and stared at the wall, tears streaming down his face. He couldn't bear that he'd never see her again. She'd stolen his heart, and now she was gone. He wiped his eyes. *The cemetery office would still be open,* he thought, grabbing the phone. Directory Assistance gave him the number and, for a small fee, connected him. He learned that Amanda was buried in the northwest corner near a tall Australian pine tree. Her grave site would carry a temporary marker until the permanent one was ready. The cemetery closed at dusk.

He hung up and called Russell Keller's office. The doctor had left for the day and would not be back for a couple of weeks. He tried Russell's home number. No answer.

Sighing, he stood and stretched, then headed out to get his supplies for the next day.

He caught a cab to the nearest Sports Authority store, where he purchased a pair of in-line skates, a backpack, a flashlight, two water bottles, and a pack of Juicy Fruit gum. He made two more stops before returning to the hotel to drop off the purchases, change clothes, and get a bite to eat.

It was dark by the time he headed out again—by design. He caught a cab to the cemetery, and the driver turned in at the main entrance, stopping abruptly in front of the locked gate.

"Looks like you're too late, mister. Sorry."

"That's OK," Hunter said. "I knew it would be closed by now." He grinned. "I don't think that four-foot-high wall was seriously designed to keep anyone out. What do I owe you?"

"Fourteen eighty-five. Want me to wait?"

Hunter tossed the hack a twenty. "No. I may be a while. But thanks. Keep the change." He grabbed the bouquet of red roses off the seat and climbed out.

By the time the taxi had backed around, Hunter was inside, strolling for the northwest corner. It didn't take him long to find the fresh grave site with the temporary marker reading: AMANDA LYNN TAYLOR. He scanned the cemetery in the moonlight then knelt beside her and gingerly placed the roses atop all the other flowers. His hand shook.

"I'm so sorry, Amanda," he said aloud, his voice quivering. "I was a fool—"

"That's really touching," the husky voice behind him said. "Talking to someone who can't hear you anymore. And in the dark so no one will see you."

Hunter momentarily froze then stood and turned around. He had to squint to make out the man standing not six feet away. A full-length dark overcoat obscured the man's body, and shaded from the moonlight by the tall pine, the man's face was also obscured. But the shiny pistol held in his outstretched arm was easy enough to see.

"Who are you, and what do you want?" Hunter asked. "I don't have much money."

The man's sinister laugh chilled Hunter to the core. "Stanley Bass didn't send me here to rob you, Mr. Mahoy. He sent me here to kill you."

The gun flashed twice, and the air instantly rushed out of Hunter's lungs. He lurched backward. Excruciating pain electrified his whole body as he fell in slow motion to the unyielding ground. He slammed down flat on his back, staring up at the heavens, clutching his chest with both hands. He couldn't breathe. He wasn't sure if his screams were audible or not—it didn't matter. The gravediggers could just make another hole right where he lay, and he'd be with Amanda throughout eternity. So be it.

From somewhere far away he heard, "Adios, sucker."

Then from somewhere still farther away: "Police! Stop or I'll shoot!"

The trench coat fled. Popping sounds everywhere—close, then far, then close again.

Now a loud voice. "Hang in there, buddy. I'll call an ambulance." Something shiny—a badge. A cop. Gone again. Silence.

I'm not dead. It worked. Oh, the pain, though! Gotta get up. Uh! Can't. Too much…pain. Shit. Get your ass up, he told himself. *Get away. Hurry!* Sirens wailed in the distance. *Ignore the pain. Not much time.*

He rolled onto his side, moaning or screaming—he wasn't sure which. Drawing his knees up underneath him, he struggled to his feet. The agony was worse than death. *Focus! Focus and move!* "I'll be back, Amanda," he said aloud. "Have to go now." Hunched over, he staggered to the cemetery's perimeter wall, clutching his chest with both arms. It took all of his willpower to breach the four-foot barrier. The sirens were close now.

He half ran, half stumbled into the surrounding neighborhood, then rested against a huge fichus tree in someone's front yard. He turned toward the commotion at the cemetery in the distance. Enough flashing lights to blind him, enough sirens to make him deaf. They'd surround him soon if he didn't get away from there somehow. A car approached, slowed, then whipped into the driveway. A lighted Domino's Pizza delivery sign glowed on the roof. The driver hopped out, box in hand, and hustled for the house. He'd left the door open and the engine running. Hunter couldn't believe his luck, or his ears. A Beatles song, "Baby, You Can Drive My Car" was playing on the radio. He smiled. He felt half dead, but he smiled.

He struggled to the car, climbed in and backed out, squealing the tires as he left the driveway, the pizza guy screaming obscenities and running after him. He abandoned the car at a nearby shopping mall and caught a cab. Because the taxi ride would be traced, he went to the airport. When the Ramada Inn shuttle bus rolled around, he stepped on as nonchalantly as possible despite the throbbing in his chest.

Safely back in his hotel room, he painfully stripped off his shirt and then the bulletproof vest. His chest was already one huge bruise, the cost of cheating two bullets from very close range.

Early the next morning, the taxi whipped into the driveway of Joe Hawkins's house, setting off a motion-sensor spotlight. Hunter paid the fare then eased ever so gently from the vehicle with the newly purchased backpack in hand.

Joe—a mountain of a man, with a burly beard, fiery-red hair, and freckles—had already hitched the airboat to his truck and stood poised to load a cooler. "A little windy, but it looks like it's going to be a gorgeous day," he said cheerfully. "I love it when the weekend starts out like this."

Hunter stepped delicately. His chest, black and blue from neck to navel, was incredibly sensitive to any movement, including breathing.

"How long's it been since we've gone out together in the airboat, Hunter? Almost a year now, I guess." He slapped Hunter on the back. Hunter screamed inwardly at the pain.

"Good to see you, Joe. And you're right, it was just after Thanksgiving—remember?"

"Oh, yeah. I remember now." Joe laughed. "It was really cold that day, and you jumped over the side when that water moccasin came into the boat. I almost fell out of the boat myself, I was laughing so hard!"

Hunter smiled and painfully stowed his backpack. "I wish you had. That water was freezing."

Still grinning, Joe opened a map and spread it out on the hood of his truck. "Where exactly is this cabin you're wanting to get to?"

Drawing a line with his finger from Homestead to the northwest, Hunter said, "I'd place it about here."

While pointing to the spot, he noticed an airfield northwest of that position. Now he remembered the Dade-Collier Training Facility on the border between Dade and Collier Counties. *So that's what "DCTF" stands for in the underground complex.* Rarely used anymore, the fifteen-thousand-foot lighted runway had been built for jetliners to practice touch-and-gos day or night. But sophisticated flight simulators had just about rendered it useless.

"I know where that cabin is," Joe said in his booming voice. "I've often wondered who owns that."

"It belongs to an uncle of mine," Hunter said. *Not exactly a lie. Uncle Sam is everybody's uncle.* "Some of his friends may meet up with me out there." Another half truth. For Joe's own safety, the less he knew, the better. "Hey, Joe. Can I borrow a pistol in case I see a snake or something? I forgot mine."

"Sure. I'll be right back." He returned a few minutes later with a holstered gun in each hand. "Do you want the .38 caliber Smith and Wesson revolver or the Browning 9 mm semiautomatic?"

"Let me try the semiautomatic."

"It's loaded," Joe said, handing it over. "A full clip, fifteen rounds. The chamber's empty, and the safety's on." He folded the map. "We're wasting time. Let's roll. The best place to launch is way out west on the Tamiami Trail."

Predawn had succumbed to full daylight by the time Hunter and Joe reached the boat ramp. After launching the craft and parking the truck, Joe climbed up to the airboat's control seat and turned the key. The unmuffled engine roared to life; the propeller whirled into a blur. In no time they'd left the canal area and were skimming across the swampy landscape.

Hunter couldn't help but contrast the ride with his trek through the saw grass just two weeks earlier. Then, he had struggled to cover one mile an hour. Now they zipped along the surface effortlessly at well over thirty miles an hour.

After about forty minutes, Joe slowed the craft then stopped. Over the idling engine, he hollered, "We're in the area! Look around to see if you can spot the cabin!"

Hunter did just that. Moments later he pointed to the right, though the movement cost him in pain. "There it is!" he shouted.

Joe throttled up again. With the boat's increased speed narrowing the distance, the cabin grew rapidly in size. It seemed uncanny to Hunter to approach the cabin this way, especially in daylight. He smiled. Old Surprise was already sunning on the dock, early though it was. The huge reptile splashed into the swamp as they eased up to it.

Joe killed the engine, reintroducing the wonderful silence of the Everglades. "Man! Did you see the size of that gator?" he asked as he hopped down from his pilot's seat.

"Yeah. It was a beaut. Too bad we had to disturb it." Hunter climbed onto the dock. "You'd better wait a minute while I make sure the key is where it's supposed to be."

He labored upstairs carrying the backpack, found the key and unlocked the door, then returned to the dock. "I'm all set." They shook hands. "Thanks, Joe. I really appreciate this. And thanks for the gun. I'll return it as soon as I can."

Joe climbed back up to his seat. "Don't mention it. When you get some more free time, Hunter, give me a call. We'll do something fun together. Maybe we can go catch a couple of water moccasins." He laughed.

"Oh, yeah. Great idea. I can hardly wait."

CHAPTER

20

Morgan Lindsey jogged around the grounds of Camp David early Saturday morning, where the president had stashed her for a couple of days. She'd never been to the retreat before, but as she plowed through the cool, misty fog, she wasn't thinking about the camp or the pristine forest surrounding her. Her thoughts were on Hunter. By now he was heading for the underground complex. Heading for danger.

She slowed to a walk, laboring to catch her breath. What if Hunter got caught? She shivered. Maybe he was right not to have told her about the sorties he flew in Desert Storm, especially the one that Russell Keller had described. She'd have worried the whole time. Apparently Hunter and danger were anything but strangers.

That reminded her of the medal she had wondered about.

She jogged back to her quarters and dug in her purse until she found the phone number Russell Keller had given her for his son, Jonathan. Jonathan might not know anything more about the incident, but he'd certainly know the name of his former commanding officer.

A phone call later, she had it—Major Richard Hightower from Annapolis, Maryland. Jonathan armed her with one other piece of information: the nickname that Hunter had affectionately used for his commander.

Morgan called long-distance information for Annapolis and held her breath. Hightower could've moved ten times by now. He could've bought a house in Podunk, Iowa; or Backwater, Louisiana; or even Whiskey Gulch, Alaska, for all her luck.

"I'm sorry, ma'am. I have no listing for a Richard Hightower," the operator said.

She frowned. "Do you have any Hightower listings?"

"I'll check for you, ma'am…yes, I have three—A Sally, a Donald P., and a Jarvis R."

Morgan picked up on the *R*. "Let me try Jarvis."

The operator gave her the number. Redialing, Morgan punched in the eleven digits and waited. It rang four times.

"Hello?"

"Mr. Hightower?"

"Yes."

"Hi. My name's Morgan Lindsey. I'm trying to locate a Richard Hightower and thought maybe you'd know him."

"What do you want with him?"

"Then you know him?"

Pause. "I might."

Morgan was pretty sure she was talking to Richard right then. "It's my understanding that Richard was an officer in the air force and served in Operation Desert Storm. I'd like to ask him some questions about one of the pilots under his command."

"Who are you? Who do you work for?"

She didn't want this guy to hang up on her, but she decided to play it straight. "My name's Morgan Lindsey, as I said. I'm a reporter for the *Washington Herald*, sir. But I'm not writing a story about this. My questions are for my own personal knowledge. I was the fiancé of this particular pilot."

"I'm sorry, Ms. Lindsey. I can't help you with—"

"Please don't hang up, Richard. I know you don't want to talk to a reporter. No one does. But I didn't want to lie to you about what I do. Maybe this will help. The pilot I'm curious about nicknamed you *the Bell Ringer*. I was told you knocked him out during a friendly boxing match."

"*The Bell Ringer*. Holy smokes, I haven't heard that in a while. You're talking about the best damn pilot I ever saw, Hunter Mahoy."

"Yes, sir. That's correct. And I really was his fiancé. I may even be again." Hightower was silent, so she continued. "I know about the mission that Hunter flew when his wingman Jonathan Keller was shot down. Hunter called him *Stick*." She threw that in. "I know about the rescue too. What I don't know, but would really like to, is if Hunter received a medal as a result of that mission."

"He sure as hell did, Ms. Lindsey—the Congressional Medal of Honor."

She dropped the phone and had to scramble to pick it up. "Are…are you sure about that, sir?"

"I'm positive. I was at the ceremony when the president decorated him with it."

"The pres…*president* awarded it?"

"Yup. Right there in the Oval Office. I'd just retired from the service, but I was invited at Hunter's request. I was thrilled to be there too. I can tell you that. No reporters, though, and no fanfare—also at Hunter's request. It was just President Conner, Hunter, and me."

"When…when was that?"

"Let me see. A couple of months before Nelson Weber took office, so that'd be, ah…not quite three years ago."

She and Hunter had split up by then, she realized. "Why did it take so long after the incident for the medal to be awarded?"

He laughed shortly. "The Congressional Medal of Honor is not handed out lightly, Ms. Lindsey. Facts are checked and double-checked. Besides, it's usually awarded posthumously, so in most cases they don't have to hurry. I'll tell you something else. It would've had more impact on Hunter if it hadn't been for that other mission."

"Which mission are you referring to?"

"The one where all those civilians were killed in that bunker."

"Oh, yes, I remember that," she said. "Over a hundred, wasn't it? Mostly women and children. The US thought the Iraqi leader was in there. That's why they bombed it." She paused. "What did that have to do with Hunter?"

"He flew that mission, Ms. Lindsey. He's the one who hit that bunker."

She dropped the phone again.

"Ms. Lindsey? Hello, Ms. Lindsey?"

"Yes, I'm here."

"Please tell Hunter I said hello. And give him my number. I'm here most of the time. Tell him the *Bell Ringer* wants to pull his chain again."

"I'll do that, Mr. Hightower. Thank you for talking with me."

*　　*　　*

Hunter waited about fifteen minutes before opening the hatch and descending into the tunnel. He wanted to make sure that Joe didn't return for some reason and not be able to find him. He set up the stove and put on water for coffee. While the water heated, he thought about what he needed to do.

To inventory the aircraft and armament, he'd travel the northwest tunnel first. After looking at Joe's map that morning, it dawned on him that the tunnel must lead to the training airstrip out in the middle of the Everglades. Aircraft may be stored underground there.

He fixed his mug of coffee and carried it out to the porch. The placidness of the great wetland consumed him. *The end of autumn, he thought. Hard to tell out here, except for the temperature.* Change came slowly to the Everglades. Time was irrelevant. Suddenly his chest ached. "Bastards," he mumbled. He couldn't even visit Amanda's grave to say good-bye. One way or another Bass would get his; it was just a question of when.

Satisfied that Joe wouldn't be returning, he placed the key in the chair on the porch, then locked the door from inside. After releasing the latch under the hatch, he tilted back the table, screaming with pain as he did so. He then opened the second hatch and rested it against the first.

Hunter descended several rungs on the ladder and stopped. For the first time he noticed magnetic alarm contacts on the inner hatch. The magnet that'd been placed on the hatch door with double-stick tape had come loose, probably due to the humidity. As a result, it remained in contact with the other magnet, keeping the circuit from triggering an alarm. *How'd I miss seeing this before?* he wondered. He was amazed he hadn't bumped it by accident and set it off. He left it alone and carefully closed the hatches.

He descended the ladder slowly, his badly bruised chest testing his tolerance for pain at a level he'd never known before. The backpack was cumbersome in the tight space; it constantly scraped the wall of the shaft, making the journey twice as bad. It fought him all the way to the bottom.

"Finally!" he said out loud, dropping his burden on the tunnel floor.

He sat on the cold concrete while he switched his sneakers for the in-line skates, then stood, and strapped on the holstered pistol before donning the backpack again.

Moments later he tenuously rolled northwest. He'd last worn in-line skates a few years earlier on South Beach and hoped he'd quickly get reacclimated to them again. He had plenty of miles to cover.

Encouraged by the tunnel walls racing past, he gritted his teeth against the pain and increased his pace. He had to be doing close to fifteen miles per hour. The cool breeze caressing his face invigorated him and spurred him onward. Skating the tunnel was like skating under a strobe. The overhead lights flashed by in a constant rhythm: light, dark, light, dark. Minutes passed, then quarter hours, half hours, even hours. Time blurred like the concrete at his feet. He'd reached perfect speed; he'd hit his zone. In that near-hypnotic trance, he felt no pain, no effort, no fatigue.

About three hours later, Hunter stopped to rest. He drank from a water bottle. *Can't have too much farther to go,* he thought, wiping his chin, *unless I'm wrong about this tunnel's destination.*

With the lights mounted in the center of the ceiling, the paint stripes on the floor spaced an equal distance no matter which way he faced, and the drainage grates down the center, the tunnel looked identical in each direction. Only one way existed to differentiate one direction from the other: the electrical conduits and the fuel pipeline on the far wall.

Rest time's over, he told himself, starting off again.

After skating for another forty-five minutes, he finally reached his objective. The tunnel ended at another hangar, a hangar larger than, but otherwise similar to, the one under Homestead Air Force Base. He listened for a while to be certain he was alone. Satisfied, he started counting the stealth aircraft stored there.

Behind a door labeled HIGH VOLTAGE, he found four large electrical panels with words stenciled in black paint on their front covers. The one closest to the door read "NORMAL EMERGENCY LIGHTING"; the next, "MAIN LIGHTING"; the third, "EXHAUST FANS, NIGHT VISION, AND DOOR." The last panel was labeled "MISCELLANEOUS." Only the first one had the main switch in the on position.

He flipped the switch, and everything went pitch black. He couldn't see a light anywhere. He turned it back on. Moving to the main lighting panel, he flipped that switch. Now every light in the entire hangar shone brightly. The eerie sight of the many stealth fighters, each tucked into its own bay, reminded him of bats in a cave suddenly made visible by illumination. Uncertain what the other breakers operated, he decided against turning them on and flipped the main lighting switch off again.

Soon he came upon an area where the construction of the hangar changed. The rows of support columns ceased, and the ceiling in this area, dome-shaped like in the tunnels, reached a height of perhaps fifty or sixty feet. About forty feet apart, two rows of recessed lighting in the floor ran in straight, parallel lines extending toward the far end of the hangar. Hunter followed the floor lights until they reached a point where the floor and ceiling inclined about thirty degrees.

What in the world is this? He removed the backpack and his skates, then slipped into his sneakers and grabbed the flashlight. Struggling up the incline, he shone the flashlight along one wall at the ceiling, crossed slowly to the other wall, and then back again. Returning to where he had left the backpack, he looked down the hangar. He turned and looked up the incline again and shook his head.

He followed one row of the recessed floor lights back into the hangar about a hundred feet. Then standing between the two rows of lights, he faced the incline again and stopped.

It suddenly hit him. He was standing on a runway! The aircraft accelerated through the hangar, then shot up the slope and out into the night sky. A huge door that opened on tracks at the top of the incline had to be at ground level because it was way the hell up there.

He remembered the panel in the electrical room marked EXHAUST FANS, NIGHT VISION, AND DOOR. The exhaust fans would vent the fumes from the jet engines back to the surface, especially during takeoff. Since the facility was obviously built some time ago, the underground runway was probably originally designed as a backup for the surface strip, which was cleverly touted as a practice runway for airliners. The surface strip would be vulnerable in an attack. Now they had a completely different advantage with the use of the stealth fighters.

A takeoff aboveground would be extremely noisy and difficult to conceal. With this setup, the fighters built their speed while still underground, and the moment they reached the surface, they were airborne and invisible to radar. The stealths had to land on the conventional runway when they returned, but they could do that quietly and under the cover of darkness. *Damn, I'll bet it looks like they're going to slam into a wall when they rip through here and approach that incline!*

Hunter strode to the backpack and swapped his shoes for the skates again. Skating slowly back to the tunnel, he finished his count of twenty-two stealth fighters. He wondered if these aircraft had been moved from the hangar under Homestead. Originally the air force was to have received fifty-nine of these black beauties, he recalled, but then the number was reduced to forty. *Why were most of them here?*

He took a break and downed a couple of sandwiches and a Milky Way bar, then started skating back through the tunnel again. Soon the strobe-like effect flashed much faster than before. If he could maintain that speed, he'd reach Homestead in four hours. But he couldn't maintain it. It was a ridiculous pace, and the painful body bruise was killing him. Each breath felt as though it would be his last; his chest had him convinced it would. The strobe quickly burned out, replaced with conventional bulbs that took their good old time to pass by.

He stopped to rest again when he reached the ladder he'd descended earlier. Encouraged and familiar with the remaining distance left to cover, Hunter felt that he'd complete the journey in ample time to place the microphones—even if he skated at a much slower place. He'd consumed the last of the water and entertained the idea of climbing the ladder to refill the bottles. But after considering the pain he'd have to endure, he decided against it. He'd hold out until he reached his destination in about two hours.

He hadn't counted on becoming so fatigued. It took him nearly three hours to reach the hangar under Homestead Air Force Base where another sixteen stealth aircraft lurked in the shadows.

Exhausted, he removed the six electronic bugs and the palm-sized digital recorder from the pack. He popped a piece of Juicy Fruit into his mouth, donned his sneakers again, then stashed the pack and the in-line skates behind an aircraft before heading for the stair-well. After all the fast skating, walking seemed foreign and incredibly slow—but far less painful to be sure. Still, it hurt to climb the stairs. He was glad he only had to battle one flight. He glanced through the vision panel in the stairwell door. All quiet. Half a minute later, he slipped into Hager's office, closing the door behind him before turning on the light.

He used a paperclip from the middle desk drawer to activate the six bugs. Standing on the desktop, he carefully placed two micro-phones into different ceiling tiles several feet apart. He had to hurry, but he also had to be careful. He couldn't risk any of the bugs being spotted. He eased down then wedged two others into the framework of the desk. Another went behind the huge map on the back wall, and the last he stuck with the chewing gum to the back of a pho-tograph near the door. With little choice about where to place the digital recorder, he clambered onto the desktop again. He clicked on the device as he set it above the dropped ceiling, then climbed down and hurriedly dusted off the desktop before checking his watch.

Buchanan would arrive anytime now if he was going to make his engagement later that evening. Hager had probably gone out to get him, which would explain why his office was vacant.

Hunter killed the light and left in a hurry. He'd barely started down the hall when he heard the ding of the elevator.

CHAPTER

21

President Nelson Weber sat in the Oval Office Saturday evening, rubbing his temples against a throbbing headache. Would Hunter's mission be fruitful? Time was growing short, and he still had a great deal to accomplish before his plan could work. If all went well in the underground complex, he'd have more information to act upon. If something went terribly wrong—well, he'd just have to continue on his present course. Changing now would be disastrous.

He rose and stared out the window. Night was creeping into the city. The streetlights had come on, and traffic was thinning. The lighted Washington Monument stood out alabaster white against the darkening sky. When that sky brightened Monday morning, Charles Minsk would be dispatched to Guantanamo Bay to speak with the base commander. Immediately upon his return, he and General Thomas Kelly would tend to the required software navigation package.

A humanitarian visit to earthquake-ravaged Mexico City meshed well with the president's plan. He'd use that trip to keep Buchanan and Hager occupied and off balance while other matters were finalized. An airline pilot who'd flown Air Force One in the past would arrive in Washington on Monday afternoon. His knowledge and expertise had been utilized before. Weber sighed heavily then returned to his desk. He picked up the phone and called Andrews Air Force Base to verify the status of the presidential aircrafts.

*   *   *

The elevator door was opening and Hunter had nowhere else to go, so he darted into the office next to Hager's. The seconds ground like hours as he listened to the sound in the hallway. Hard-sole footfalls amplified until they boomed just outside the door his ear was glued to. He didn't relax his grip on the pistol until the footfalls continued on to the next office. *Only one person*, he thought. *Could be Hager.*

The person left again a couple of minutes later. Hunter had planned to return to the hangar, but now he'd have to stay put.

Another fifteen minutes passed uneventfully. *Where the hell are they?* he wondered. *Shit! Maybe they're meeting somewhere else.* Sitting on the floor just behind the door, his back against the wall, Hunter was so exhausted that he had to fight to stay awake. A slight push on his bruised chest solved that problem. Finally he heard the elevator bell again. The door opened, and muffled voices soon transformed into understandable conversation.

He had a momentary flash of panic as the men drew close to the room that he occupied. *What if they come to this office?* He hadn't thought to lock the door! Too late to do anything about it now. His heart pounded wildly as the men stopped just outside. Their voices echoed in his head.

Then the knob started to turn. The door opened a crack, and a menacing blast of light bore into his eyes. He shoved his feet against the back of the door.

"This door's stuck," the vice president said.

"That's the wrong office, Al. We want the next one."

They moved on and entered Hager's office.

Hunter breathed again. His pulse began its descent. For a while, he thought it would never return to normal. He held the door slightly ajar so that he could listen in on their conversation. They talked at length about what would happen on the island of Cuba after the explosion. Hunter grinned. It was precisely the evidence President Weber needed on tape.

"Lamar, when do you plan to make the transfer to the ship?"

"Two weeks after Weber's demise in Cuba. As the new president, Al, you can keep a watchful eye on the necessary agencies. We don't need anyone too interested in our loading activities during that time."

"Are the ship modifications complete?"

"Almost. They'll require a few more days, then she'll set sail for Guantanamo."

"Will all the aircraft be loaded in one night?"

"Should be. But everything has to get below decks before daylight. If we encounter any delay, we'll be forced to wait for darkness again."

"Are all the stealths here in the hangars?" Buchanan asked.

"No. The last two are flying in from New Mexico tonight. Colonel Blake will be here to meet them. He's done a fine job handling this operation."

"Does he know anything about Weber being a target?"

"No. Blake's a soldier following orders, nothing more. Like everyone else in the world, he'll believe that Castro blew up Air Force One. Only Cunningham, the pilot making the drop, will know it was our bomb. He doesn't know about Weber either. He thinks Castro's the only target. By the time he learns otherwise, it won't matter. Because that stealth will have to take off during daylight, we can't risk it leaving from this complex. It will launch from a remote location several hundred miles from here. The plane's already fueled and armed, and the pilot is in transit even as we speak. His flight path will keep him out over open water, so there'll be no chance of anyone in South Florida spotting him."

"I certainly hope not, Lamar. I presume the armament has arrived."

"Yes. It's all downstairs. We'll ship the remainder after we finish the bombing in Cuba."

"How's Tom handling his end? Any trouble?"

"He's been jittery, especially since I mentioned taking Weber out with this operation. I wish we could've kept him in the dark about that. But if he wasn't made aware in advance, he might've backed away at the most critical time. If the orders don't come from him about moving all these aircraft and continuing raids on Cuba after Weber's death, we're sunk. Right now he's afraid someone will notice the increased activity with the stealths. He's been keeping up with the schedule, though."

"I'm glad to hear that," Buchanan said. "How'd you convince him to go along with this anyway?"

"I told him if he didn't, I'd reveal the lie he's been living since the fifties."

"What lie is that?"

"Tom isn't using his real name. He was part of a raid during the Korean War in which scores of children were brutally killed. He switched dog tags with a dead soldier who was not part of that. I've known about the deception for years. It was just the persuasion I needed: threatening to make it public and ruin his career. That means everything to him, you know—his career. For him, to be shamed that way would be worse than death itself." He paused. "You're sure Weber's flight will touch down at seven o'clock?"

"I'm positive. Weber changed the time himself, and he changed it to our advantage."

"Perfect! It'll be dark by then. Our pilot can target Air Force One right there on the airfield. You'll be in the White House, correct?" Hager asked.

"I thought I would be, but since the Cuba trip hasn't been announced yet, Weber considered canceling it completely and going to Mexico instead. As you know, he promised support from the United States to the earthquake victims in Mexico City." Buchanan chuckled. "After I volunteered to go to Mexico City to handle that situation, he agreed to meet with Castro as planned."

"When do you leave?"

"Tuesday afternoon."

"So you'll be in Mexico City when the bomb detonates?"

"Correct. And you'll be with me," the vice president said.

"What do you mean?"

"Weber wants you to go with me. In his mind, our visit will be more effective if we show that the US military is being activated to move in supplies and equipment. He's already prepared a statement for you to read when we arrive."

"But what about this operation?"

"It's no problem, Lamar. Just tell our pilot to hit McCalla Airfield at seven p.m. sharp. The rest of the plan we set into motion ourselves anyway."

"I guess that would work."

"It'll have to because you'll be with me in Mexico."

"So when should I join you in DC?"

"I won't arrive there myself until Tuesday at noon. I'll be attending Senator Greenley's funeral in California on Monday," Buchanan said. "Ironic, isn't it? It's fortunate I met with him when I did. He not only had suspicions about the actual number of stealths the air force has but also where those aircraft were stationed. He threatened to go to the *Washington Herald*, like he did on that mayoral election. It was the damnedest thing too. He got himself all worked up and had a heart attack. Imagine that!"

"Is that what really happened, Al?"

"Does it matter? The main thing is he can't interfere with our plans. Anyway, you might as well meet me at Andrews Air Force Base just prior to our departure."

"All right. I'll stay here through Monday night, and head for Andrews first thing Tuesday morning."

"Fine. Remember, we won't be in Mexico City long. After we're informed of the explosion in Cuba, we'll make a hasty return to Washington. As acting president, I'll give you the order to dispatch the military to Cuba and to personally oversee the operations down there."

"Actually, even with these recent changes, *Ghost Flight* is culminating nicely," Hager said.

"Yes, it is."

Another pause.

"Listen, Al. Something's happened, and I was going to wait until I knew more to tell you, but…Hunter Mahoy finally turned up last night at a cemetery in Miami."

"Well, it's about time. So is he dead?"

"We don't know. Bass posted an operative near the grave site of Mahoy's secretary. She was buried a couple of days ago. Bass said his operative shot Mahoy in the chest twice at point-blank range, but then the cops showed up. Or maybe they were watching the cemetery too. Anyway, in all the confusion, Mahoy disappeared. He hasn't been found on the street, in any hospital, or even at the county morgue."

"Shit, Lamar! The guy's like a fucking ghost! If he's been shot twice, why can't anyone find him?"

From his hiding place in the office next door, Hunter grinned at the sound of Al Buchanan slamming his fist into the side of the file cabinet.

"You haven't found Morgan Lindsey either, have you?" Buchanan snarled.

"No, we haven't. But we did some checking: Turns out that a couple of years ago she was engaged to Mahoy."

"Lamar, we already know that the reporter is in bed with the missing sailplane pilot!" Buchanan said impatiently. "And I still can't believe you botched the opportunity to get them after that explosion Stan had set up at her house. I could've done better with my eyes closed."

Hunter could practically see the steam coming out of Hager's ears when he said icily, "You mean like that bungled mess you set up at Miami International Airport?"

"It's not my fault that failed," Buchanan griped. "Stan assured me it would be handled professionally."

"Like the airliner in London?" *Just as I suspected,* Hunter thought. *Stanley Bass was behind the destruction of that jetliner!*

"What are you talking about, Lamar?"

"Never mind. All we had to do was question Mahoy to find out what he knew, not try to kill him. That incident at Miami International complicated everything."

"Mahoy's a threat to our plans, Lamar. We know he was on this base because of the calling-card record Stan pulled. Maybe Mahoy poked around here just to satisfy his curiosity about what collided with his sailplane. Or maybe he knows more. Either way, we can't take the risk, especially since he's tied in with Lindsey. I'm telling you, Lamar, she's a sharp cookie. Three years after all the evidence was destroyed, she learned that the Gomez brothers murdered my son. And all the while, those fucking bastards pretended to be my friends. Three years! That's a long time. They damned near got away with it."

"Yeah, but they finally got what they deserved," Hager said. "And you were really lucky you didn't join them that day. You had a close one, Al."

"It wasn't close at all, Lamar, for crying out loud! I had Stan set that up for me. I just wish I could have pulled the trigger myself."

Hunter's jaw dropped. *Buchanan* had ordered that hit!

"Anyway," the vice president continued, "Mahoy and Lindsey have to be dealt with. Either she's dangerous and he's a loose end or vice versa. It doesn't really matter."

Hagar cleared his throat. "Maybe Mahoy just had the scare of his life with that midair collision and decided to become reacquainted with his old flame. And now they're hiding who knows where because a man tried to kill him at the airport in Miami. And a couple of days later, two cars chased them away from her burning house in DC."

"Then what was he doing on the base?" Buchanan asked.

"I don't know. Maybe it wasn't him. Maybe someone stole his phone card."

"I'm not buying it, Lamar. And Lindsey personally knowing Mahoy is too much of a coincidence. I don't like it. Find them and kill them. I don't care how you do it, but do it soon."

"They'll be harder than ever to locate after that cemetery shooting."

"Then put more people on it. Do whatever you have to, but find them. Now, is there anything else we need to discuss?"

"I don't think so," Hager replied meekly.

"Good, then let's get out of here. We'll have plenty of time to talk on the flight to Mexico City. Just make sure our pilot knows what time to hit that airfield."

"Don't worry, I will. He's been paid in advance for this mission, and he'll be well informed."

Hunter heard the closing of a drawer and the jingle of keys, so he eased his door shut. Hager's office door slammed, and the men's voices grew louder then faded as they passed farther down the hall. Hunter waited for quite some time before venturing into Hager's office. He flipped on the light, climbed atop the desk, and recovered the digital recorder above the ceiling. Leaving all the bugs in place, he retreated to the relative safety of the stairwell. Now Hunter understood why President Weber wanted an inventory of the aircraft and armament. Apparently he had suspicions about someone else being involved, probably the guy named Tom. Whoever he was, he had to be some high muckety-muck within the air force because he'd ordered the transfer of stealth fighters.

Hunter recovered his backpack and donned the skates again. Then he hurriedly searched for the armament, eager to get aboveground and off the base as quickly as possible. If he didn't find it right away, he was out of there. He spotted a passageway on the left and skated there in a heartbeat. The small tunnel, just large enough for a truck to drive through, led to a huge storeroom. Hunter's eyes bugged out. *Holy shit! I've hit the mother lode.* Stacked in endless rows were pallets and pallets of various types of weaponry packed in wooden crates, their identification letters and numbers stenciled on the sides.

Moving down each aisle as fast as he could, he dictated the numbers into the digital recorder and estimated the quantities of each. When he had a good sampling of what was there, he noted that the items he'd logged amounted to less than one-third of the total inventory. He also noted that he'd counted twenty-two aircraft in the northwest hangar, with an additional sixteen in the hangar under Homestead. He further stated that he didn't have time to investigate the tunnel to the northeast, which he assumed led to Miami International Airport.

Shoving the recorder into his pocket, he started to leave the munitions store. Suddenly the corner of the nearest crate shredded right before his eyes, scattering splinters like fireworks as a deafening noise erupted from behind him. He dived for the cover of a munitions pallet, hitting the floor with a thud and a scream. His eyes watered instantly as he lay doubled over from the pain in his chest. But he didn't stay there long. Pistol in hand, he crouched next to the pallet and returned fire. After wasting three bullets by sticking the gun around the corner and shooting blindly, he poked his head out to see his adversary. The guard was blocking the exit. Another volley of projectiles rained in at him. His heart pounded like a jackhammer with a stuck trigger. He glued himself to the pallet, his back pressed against the crates.

Shit! I've got to get out of here before a dozen more guys show up!

Skating hunched over, he used the stacks of crates for cover and worked his way around the room. The guard spotted him crossing an aisle and blasted again, striking the backpack at least twice. Hunter fired several rounds, forcing the guard to take cover then raced to the end of the aisle. He slowed his pace way down. Rolling slowly and quietly now, he stole up against the pallet that the guard was hiding behind. When the guard stuck his head out, Hunter pressed the barrel of the 9mm pistol into the man's cheek. "Don't move!" he hissed. "Don't even flinch! Now, drop your weapon!" It clattered when it hit the concrete. "Very good." Beads of sweat tracked down Hunter's face. He wiped them away with his free hand. "Turn around slowly and put your hands on that crate." He gestured with his chin. The man obliged. "I'm really sorry about this," Hunter said, just before he whacked the guard over the head with the butt of his gun. The man collapsed to the floor, unconscious. Hunter took the guard's handcuffs and cuffed him to one of the heavy metal straps that bound the pallet together.

He holstered the pistol as he rose then sped from the munitions store just in time to hear voices coming from the stairwell. *Damn! Now I'll have to find another way out.* He reversed directions and tore through the hangar like a man possessed. Before entering the tunnel, he looked back, amazed that no one yet followed.

*   *   *

As Al Buchanan traveled from Homestead to Miami on Saturday evening to announce President Weber's visit to Cuba, he thought about the sale of the already-obsolete surplus stealth fighters. Normally he never would have been able to coerce Hager into participating in the sale of the aircraft to another country, but a new and vastly improved stealth prototype, with advanced avionics and weaponry, had already begun testing. Because of its expensive price tag, Weber had recently canceled the project, but Buchanan liked it and promised Hager its renewal after he took occupancy of the Oval Office.

Even so, Hager had remained reluctant to sell half of the existing stealths to foreign countries until he came up with the ingenious idea of installing a concealed explosive charge wired to an electronic descrambler in each aircraft. A different identification code assigned to each descrambler could be electronically hit by bouncing a signal off a military satellite. The descramblers were capable of both, signaling the exact locations of the aircraft, and detonating the explosives. That meant that they could use the stealths for their own purposes in Cuba then sell them for an incredible amount of money, and later track or destroy them at any time and anywhere in the world, even years from now. And since the air force had secretly built twice as many stealths as it claimed, which Al knew nothing about until Hager had told him, this presented a perfect way to dispose of the ghost squadron.

*   *   *

Fueled by adrenaline, Hunter skated as fast as he possibly could, singing the Eagles tune that was stuck in his head: "Somebody's gonna hurt someone before the night is through." Amanda came to mind. She'd loved that group. Now that it was too late, he wished that he had told her his real first name. She'd asked about it countless times. He wiped at his eyes and switched over to Beatles songs.

Two and a half hours later, Hunter heard something echoing through the chamber and nervously stopped to listen. "Now what?" he said half aloud. At first he thought it might be a truck but soon recognized the whine of a jet engine. The sound rapidly intensified from the direction he was headed. He didn't have much time and he'd never be able to out-skate its advance. The only place he could possibly hide was in the center drainage ditch. He tried lifting a grate, but it was too heavy. He strained one last time, cried out in pain, then gave up.

With the aircraft almost upon him, its piercing sound resonating everywhere, he lay motionless facedown on the floor next to the wall and covered his ears. Moments later, a stealth fighter appeared, its landing lights burning into his very existence. Somehow the pilot didn't see him, though, and the craft passed uneventfully. He started to get up when the lights of a second aircraft reflected on the tunnel walls. He hugged the cold concrete floor once again, cursing his predicament. This time he wasn't so lucky. The second fighter stopped abreast of him, and the engines slowed to idle.

"Hey, you there! Can you hear me?" the pilot shouted.

Hunter played dead, fearing he soon would be.

"Hey, fella! Can you hear me?"

Finally the engines spooled up again and the fighter continued on down the tunnel. Hunter calculated that it would take the pilot over an hour to reach the hangar, then another fifteen minutes or so to park his aircraft before reporting what he'd seen. Hunter figured he'd be safe until then—unless, of course, the handcuffed guard had been discovered.

Skating for his life, he pumped against time and distance for the northwest hangar. The cabin was out of question now. He had nowhere to hide there. His only hope rested with the distant hangar.

Nearly two hours later, completely exhausted, and thirsty as hell, Hunter finally reached his destination. *Thank God! I couldn't have gone much farther.* He raced to the electrical room, doffed the pack and the skates, then hurriedly put on his sneakers; both had bullet holes in them. He threw the switch on the panel marked EXHAUST

Fans, Night Vision, and Door. The hangar instantly glowed red under the special night-vision lighting. The huge door tracked open, allowing a wonderful rush of fresh air into the complex. He wiped the sweat from his forehead and bolted for the incline at the end of the hangar where he could get aboveground and escape into the brush. He wasn't fast enough. Several Jeeps raced from the tunnel into the hangar, screeching to a stop.

Hunter ran to the closest stealth, figuring the cockpit would make a good place to hide. Then another idea took over. He removed the wheel chocks before he popped the canopy. The noisy exhaust fans had become his allies. Grunting, he struggled up into the cockpit. As the canopy closed, he focused first on the men in the Jeeps, then on the stealth's instrument panel. He'd always wanted to fly one of these babies, but this wasn't exactly what he'd had in mind. He strapped himself in, recalling the cockpit lessons he'd received from an air force buddy. He flipped a couple of switches, adjusted the altimeter, and started the engines. The displays came to life. With just a slight touch of the throttles, the stealth lurched forward eagerly. *This isn't much different than the F-16,* he told himself. *It has the same fly-by-wire flight-control system.* He pointed the jet toward the incline and swallowed hard. Perspiration broke out on his forehead again. He wiped it away nervously.

The drivers of the Jeeps squealed the tires and laid rubber as they gave chase. Intense gunfire added to the noise of the jet's engines as bullets flew in his direction. Some embedded into the fighter. Others ricocheted off the many concrete surfaces, sparking everywhere like fireflies run amok.

Hunter was jammed back into the seat as he shoved the throttles to full power. He held the stick slightly forward of neutral to keep the wheels glued to the concrete. *I sure don't want this thing to get airborne while I'm still in this hangar!*

He fixated on the incline. Seemingly determined to collide with the little stealth jet, the steep concrete slope raced toward him with exponentially increasing speed and size. *Oh, shit! Maybe I'm going too fast!* The airspeed indicator teetered on 120 miles per hour when he hit the ramp; the G forces tried to suck his body through the bottom of the craft. He almost blacked out.

An instant later, the graceful, batlike fighter streaked into the moonless night sky like a crazed meteor defying gravity. Hunter retracted the landing gear, banked hard to the left, and climbed out on a northeast heading.

The title of an old war movie popped into his head, *God Is My Copilot.*

CHAPTER

22

"Son of a bitch! How in hell am I going to explain the theft of a stealth fighter from this complex?" Colonel Randolph Blake screamed as he dented the hood of a Jeep with his bare fist. "Shit! We can't even go after it—there's no way to track the damn thing. Major Kruzinski?"

"Yes, sir."

"Do you know if that aircraft was refueled after its last mission?"

"It wasn't, sir. None of the stealths on this end of the hangar were."

"How much range will that rogue pilot have with the fuel on board?"

"A couple hundred miles or so, Colonel. Three-hundred max."

Blake scratched his chin. "That'd cover half of the state of Florida, all of the Bahamas, the Dominican Republic, Cuba, the Caymans, and the Yucatan Peninsula in Mexico. Damn!" He dented the hood again. "Major, would you happen to know if that particular aircraft retained any armament?"

"I believe two remain on board, sir."

"Oh, great! More good news," Blake snarled. *I'm not gonna report this incident to Hager just yet,* he thought. *I'm tired of getting my ass chewed. Who knows? Maybe I'll get lucky tomorrow and find that stealth abandoned wherever it exhausts its fuel.* He eyed the men around him. "The damage is done. Close the hangar door, and shut down those noisy fans. Major Kruzinski, come daylight I want you and three of your best pilots to take F-15s from Homestead and search a 250-mile radius from this spot. The rest of you search this complex from one end to the other. Find out how our uninvited guest got in here. And mention this incident to no one. Do you understand? No one."

*   *   *

Well aware of the commercial airline flight path into Miami International Airport, Hunter buzzed the stealth fighter over the Everglades at just seven-hundred feet. He verified that the special panels that render the aircraft visible to radar were not deployed then familiarized himself with the cockpit. *I wonder what's in the internal weapons compartment?* He punched up the stores monitor. *How nice. Two two-thousand-pound laser-guided bombs. I should plant one on Buchanan and Hager then vaporize Stanley Bass with the other.* The thought made him smile. *This baby's a dream to fly.* But where would he go? Maybe he'd cruise up to DC and land right at Edwards Air Force Base. He glanced at the fuel display and frowned. Nope. Couldn't do that. Not enough go-juice. He tapped on the glass with his index finger. Damn! Why hadn't they refueled this thing? *Wait a minute! I know where I can go.* His old skydiving stomping grounds in Deland was the perfect place. That sleepy town had a good-sized uncontrolled airport with concrete runways plus hangars large enough to conceal his stolen black beauty. And Deland was only twenty miles from Daytona. He could catch a commercial flight back to DC from there.

Hunter banked the nimble F-117 Nighthawk more toward the east and climbed to three-thousand feet. Just for the fun of it, he made a couple of lazy-S turns then executed a crisp eight-point roll. He sure missed flying jets. He might still be in the air force if he hadn't been ordered to hit that damn bunker in Iraq during Desert Storm. Intelligence had sure screwed up on that one. But he was the one who had to live with the knowledge that he'd killed over a hundred innocent civilians, mostly women and children. No one was ever going to order him to do something like that again.

He pitched the nose up toward the heavens and studied the stars for solace. *What a beautiful night! This is what flying's all about. Too bad I don't have someone up here to share it with.*

The moon rose straight out ahead of him, quickly growing from a tiny sliver to a full pumpkin-colored orb, a fitting color for late October; Halloween was just two days away. The glowing heavenly body hovered in the windshield, casting its mystique on him and the ocean's surface, which lay just ahead.

He crossed over the East Coast slightly north of West Palm Beach. A couple of miles offshore, he made a gradual turn to the left. The pumpkin swung around to his right. He'd remain out over the Atlantic, following the coastline until he reached Daytona Beach. From there he'd have a short hop due west to Deland.

The black ghost cruised along at over four-hundred miles per hour, and the flight was so smooth it seemed as though he wasn't even airborne. Out of habit, he checked the instrument panel in a clockwise manner. *Wow! I'm really going to be close on fuel.* He rocked the wings then tapped on the display again. *Damn! I only have about a half hour to go, but I might not make it to Deland. I'd better climb while I can.*

Twenty minutes later, at an altitude of fifteen-thousand feet, Hunter turned due west for the final leg of his flight. The enchanting lights of the fairyland far below tantalized him. But to land in Daytona would be a mistake—it'd draw way too much attention. He lined up with the four-lane highway jutting from the west side of the city then throttled back to conserve whatever fuel he had left. With just seventeen miles to go, it was going to be close.

The Deland Airport had no landing lights, which made the large darkened area within the city's ring of illumination hard to miss. The airport beacon soon became apparent. Hunter recalled that the runways were laid out in a triangular pattern, with one leg parallel to the highway. Maintaining fifteen-thousand feet, he'd closed the distance to about six miles. Just as he banked the Nighthawk to line up with where he knew the runway would be, the engines sputtered and died.

*　*　*

Lamar Hager dialed the familiar number and waited through three rings before hearing the gruff hello on the other end.

"Stan...Lamar here. I'm calling from Homestead. With all that's been going on, I forgot to ask you the other day, did you complete the relocation of your spy satellite?"

"You bet. It's been sitting directly over Cuba for the past seventy-two hours jamming communications. No one can connect to the island unless we let them do so. I've got everything covered: television and radio, military frequencies, satellite transmissions, landline and cell telephones. Hell, I even have ham radio operators blocked out."

Hager grinned. "Good work. Al will be most pleased. It looks like we're all set."

"Yep. By the way, Lamar. I have some news on the Mahoy/Lindsey front. Mahoy rented a car under his alias, Crowfield, three days ago in Hawaii, on the big island."

"Did you say three days ago?"

"Yes, that's right. I'm trying to find out where they stayed, but so far nothing's surfaced. I'll keep on it."

"Thanks, Stan."

Hager hung up then drummed his fingers on his desktop. *Mahoy and Lindsey were in London when Weber was in London. Then they were in Hawaii when Weber stopped in Hawaii. It appears they've been trying to contact him, but they must not have succeeded. Weber hasn't canceled his trip to Cuba. No use aggravating Al over nothing.* Still. He grabbed the phone and hit the redial button. "Stan, Lamar again. Forget Hawaii. Start checking the DC area for Mahoy and Lindsey."

*   *   *

Hunter pointed the nose of the stealth below the horizon and concentrated on his flying. He had to hit his target with the silent black dart, but it wasn't designed to be much of a glider, and without a chute, he couldn't bail out. As the altimeter began to unwind, the expression "Do or die" came to mind. He hated that expression. He maintained two-hundred miles per hour, knowing full well that the speed would diminish rapidly when he extended the landing gear.

"Looking good," he said aloud, keeping the airport centered in the windshield. Balancing the angle of his controlled dive with the airspeed, he allowed the craft to get sucked into the black hole. Eyes wide, he shifted in the seat and drew a deep breath. He prayed it wouldn't be his last. When the altimeter hit four-hundred feet, he eased back on the stick and flipped on the landing lights. *OK, runway, I'm committed. Where the hell are you?*

Instantly illuminated, a hungry forest of towering pines reached up to swallow him. Oh, shit!

His stomach lurched into his throat as he hauled back on the stick. The craft just barely clipped the last tree before skimming over the freshly cut grass apron that led to the runway. He dropped the landing gear and dumped full flaps as the concrete raced toward him. It grabbed the wheels at 150 miles per hour and didn't let go. He stood on the brakes. As the aircraft slowed, he steered it to the grassy edge and stopped. He killed the landing lights along with the rest of the systems on board and popped the canopy. *Thank you, Lord! I owe you for this one!* He wiped the perspiration from his brow and sat quietly. The crisp night air cooled his lungs. After his eyes had adjusted to the darkness, he struggled down from the cockpit. His knees didn't want to support his weight, and his legs moved woodenly. He lumbered stiffly toward the hangar where he'd learned to skydive many years earlier. The place looked much the same, from what he could see. A silhouette moved past a lit window at the rear of the hangar. He hoofed it over there and rapped on the glass.

"Who is it?" a raspy male voice hollered.

I don't believe it! After all this time. "Leroy Rinehart, is that you?"

"Yeah, it's me. Who in hell are you?"

"A wayward pilot who's lost his way. You know me as Turkey Bird." Hunter counted six seconds before the response.

"Holy shit! Turkey Bird Mahoy! Meet me at the door."

Cigarette in hand, Leroy hadn't changed a bit. His dirty-blonde hair, caught in a ponytail, hung to the middle of his back. The full beard and mustache joined at the corners of his mouth, which currently displayed a genuine smile and gold-capped front teeth. "Come on in! Man, I never thought I'd see you again."

"It's a small world, Leroy. I sure as hell didn't expect to find you here either, especially at night."

"Normally you wouldn't have, but the old lady and I broke up again. I'm crashing in this hangar for a while."

"You talking about Karen? She was quite a looker."

"Still is. Prettier than ever, in fact." He shrugged. "We'll get back together. It's just a matter of time. So what brings Turkey Bird Mahoy back to the quiet burg of Deadland?"

Hunter chuckled at the analogy. "I landed a bird out there." He thumbed over his shoulder. "It's a special bird for a special purpose, Leroy, and I need to hide it before daylight."

"Why didn't you taxi it over here?"

"I couldn't. It's out of fuel. Had to make a dead-stick landing. You have something I could tow it with? It's sitting on the edge of the runway right now."

"Sure. My pickup's out back. Let me grab a rope, and we'll go get it."

As they rolled up on the stealth, Leroy leaned closer to the windshield and stared. "Damn, Hunter! You made a dead-stick landing in that thing? I'll bet that's a first."

"You're probably right. But I need to keep it a secret. It's really important." He could trust Leroy—no doubt about it.

Within a few minutes, they'd towed the plane to the hangar and backed it inside an oversized spray booth that Leroy used for painting light aircraft. The stealth just barely fit. Its twin vertical stabilizers cleared the ceiling by no more than an inch. Leroy tugged at a piece of pine branch caught in the seam of the bomb-bay doors. He wrenched it free and tossed it at Hunter. "Looks like you cut it a little close out there, Turkey Bird."

Hunter caught it. It had a small pinecone and a few needles on it. He grinned. "Yeah, maybe, but those trees needed trimming anyway."

"I see you got your tail feathers shot up too. Where have you been with this thing?"

"Don't ask. Hey, can I use your phone?"

"Course you can."

Eager to get to Washington, Hunter called the airlines and made a reservation on the first flight out, which wasn't until nine-thirty the next morning.

"Why don't you crash with me tonight, Turkey Bird? I have a spare bed. We can catch up on old times, and I'll drive you to Daytona for your morning flight."

"If you'll let me spring for dinner, you've got yourself a deal."

"You're on, man. Hey, if you want to, we can refuel that bird right now while no one's around."

"You can do that?"

"Sure, man. I have keys to the fuel trucks that belong to the Fixed Base Operator at the west end of the field. I work for him during the summer months because the college kids he usually employs head home for the summer."

"The stealth may have to stay hidden here for quite some time, Leroy. It'd be nice to have it fully fueled, though. But we need jet fuel. Does the FBO have that?"

"Yeah. We get some chartered jets in here once in a while." He snorted. "Some of the college kids have rich daddies."

*　　*　　*

Hunter arrived at Reagan National just before noon on Sunday, carrying an olive-colored duffel bag and wearing torn blue jeans, a beat-up jacket, a frayed baseball cap, and a pair of dark sunglasses— all loaners from Leroy. Inside the duffel bag was a change of clothes more appropriate for meeting with the president. Despite the disguise, Charles Minsk had little trouble picking him out in the crowd. But then again, Charles knew exactly when to look for him.

They shook hands.

"Nice rags," Charles said. "You look like you just stepped out of the sixties."

Hunter tilted the cap to better hide his face. "I'm lucky I can step at all."

"We sure were glad to hear from you when you called. President Weber and Morgan are at the 'cottage.'"

Hunter smiled at the Secret Service's term for the White House. "How'd the recording turn out? The electronic bugs work OK?"

Charles frowned. "No. Apparently the many levels of concrete and steel caused too much interference. We didn't receive anything intelligible. Did you get anything on the recorder?"

"I hope so. Haven't actually listened to it yet."

"Any problems in the complex?"

"Nothing I couldn't handle," Hunter said, being vague on purpose as they walked toward the agent's car.

They headed out of the airport and soon arrived at 1600 Pennsylvania Avenue. Charles whipped into a parking space assigned to the Secret Service. "I went to Morgan's house this morning for her laptop computer and the copy of the operations manual that you'd stashed in her floor safe. Her garage is toast. You two were really lucky."

Hunter gave him a half smile that disappeared quickly. So Morgan had disclosed the location of the second copy. *It's just as well,* he thought. He wondered what else she'd told them.

"You OK, Hunter? You're moving like a snail."

"Yeah. Sore is all. I must've skated eighty or ninety miles yesterday. I need to change, Charles. Can't go see 'the man' looking like this."

Charles grinned. "Don't worry. We'll hit a bathroom on the way."

When they entered the library, the president and Morgan were sitting side by side at a table, looking over the manual. Morgan leaped up and embraced Hunter enthusiastically. He stifled a scream, moaning softly instead.

"What's wrong, Hunter?"

"Too much adventure, I guess. Nothing a little rest and relaxation won't cure."

The president stood as well, offering his hand and smiling warmly. "Good to see you again, *Hobnobber.* Morgan has filled me in on what you've been through the past couple of weeks. You've really put it all on the line to save my old hide. Good lord, man, why didn't you tell me you'd been shot?"

Hunter looked away for a moment, feeling an odd mixture of embarrassment and pride. "The wounds weren't serious, sir, and they're healing nicely."

"Nonetheless, I'm in your debt."

"Glad to be of service, sir." He fished the digital recorder from his pocket and handed it over. "I hope what you need is on there."

"So do I," Nelson Weber said. "Please sit down. As you can probably imagine, I'm amazed at how detailed and well thought out the operations manual is. And how they've been able to conceal it from me. Normally a covert operation like this would be approved by me before it went anywhere."

Hunter cleared his throat. "I've been wondering, Mr. President. Who's the secretary of the air force?"

"General Thomas Kelly. Why?"

Hunter's worst suspicion had been confirmed. "I believe the recording will explain it best, sir."

Hunter studied President Weber's face as the device played. He appeared dismayed when Tom Kelly's involvement was made evident. Then came the conversation about Hunter in the cemetery. Hunter had forgotten that was on there. He wished he'd erased that part. Everyone's gaze went from the recorder on the table straight to Hunter's eyes. Morgan's expression was one of complete shock.

He hit the stop button. "What're you all staring at? Haven't any of you seen a dead man before?"

"How? What? I mean, explain!" Morgan stammered.

"Bulletproof vest," he said. "Don't leave home without one."

"But two shots—at point-blank range," Charles said. "You wouldn't have been able to just get up and walk away. You had to be badly bruised at the very least."

"You're right, Charles. I didn't just walk away. It was more like a stumble and crawl. But I had to get out of there, so I did."

Morgan propped her hands on her hips. "Show us the bruise."

He shook his head. "I don't think that's necessary."

"I'd like to see it too," President Weber said.

Hunter shrugged then struggled to unbutton his shirt before spreading it apart. His entire chest was a hideous black and blue, even more colorful than it'd been the previous day.

"Oh, my god!" Morgan muttered. The expression of shock returned.

"It looks worse than it is. Really," he said, gingerly rebuttoning his shirt.

"I hope so," Charles said. "Because it looks like you should be in a hospital. Have you seen a doctor?"

"Not yet. Haven't had time."

"I'll call my personal physician to come take a look at that," the president said.

"I appreciate that, sir, and I'm sure it's a good idea. But it can wait until later. The pain's nothing today compared to what it was yesterday." He reached over and started the recorder again.

Dismay registered on the president's face one more time at the vice president's command to find and kill Hunter and Morgan.

When the conversation portion had finished, Hunter switched off the device.

"That's a remarkable recording," President Weber said, "and it's precisely what I needed to corroborate what I must now do." He paused then asked, "Is there more?"

"Yes, sir. The remainder describes the armament. It involves mostly numbers and might require someone knowledgeable in weaponry to decipher them."

Charles hit Play. After a few minutes, President Weber nodded, and the agent stopped it again.

"I recognize a few of those numbers," the president said. "That armament was earmarked for Operation Desert Storm and supposedly no longer exists. I'm sure you can imagine that with a military operation the size and scope of Desert Storm, the logistics would be a nightmare. It would be difficult to keep track of every piece of weaponry—where it went, whether or not it was used, and if not, when it was returned."

Everyone sat quietly until Nelson Weber spoke again.

"I'm scheduled to depart for Cuba tomorrow afternoon at three-thirty. Hunter, Morgan, I'd like you to accompany me. The media won't be invited. Morgan, you'll be the only person on the flight qualified to write the story, and I'll work closely with you to make sure it says exactly what we need it to say. Naturally, we won't disclose anything that might be damaging to the security of the United States. Hunter, I understand you're quite a photographer. I'd like you to take pictures of whatever seems appropriate."

"Sir, are you sure that this flight should take place?" Morgan asked. "What if you can't stop the bombing?"

He smiled. "I have every confidence in the world that we'll all be safe. May I assume you'll join me?"

"I wouldn't miss it," Hunter replied.

"Count me in too," Morgan said.

"Good! Since Buchanan and Hager are out of town, I suggest you two stay here in the White House tonight. That way I know you'll be safe."

Hunter tried to hide a yawn behind his hand.

President Weber laughed. "Most of our guests show a little more enthusiasm when they're invited to stay overnight. Maybe that *H* should stand for *Humdrum*."

"Staying here would be wonderful, sir," Morgan said excitedly. "As for Hunter's safety, when I finish with him for his boorish behavior, the *H* will stand for *Handicapped*."

"I think he's already achieved that designation," the president said, chuckling. He turned to the agent. "Charles, will you show them to our guest quarters?"

"Certainly, sir."

As they stood to leave, President Weber added, "Oh, I almost forgot. Mrs. Weber and I would like you to join us for dinner."

Glancing at Hunter, Morgan said, "We'd love to, sir. We've been looking forward to meeting Mrs. Weber."

"Excellent. We'll see you at dinner then."

CHAPTER

23

Captain David Cunningham had spent the past two weeks confined to his concrete walled, ceilinged, and floored underground quarters at Homestead Air Force Base. He wasn't really in jail, but he might as well have been. He had no television or radio reception, and no communication with the outside world. He hadn't seen the sun or the sky, breathed fresh air, or had any company. Since his midair collision with that damned sailplane, he'd watched videos, listened to music, exercised, played solitaire, read books, and slept until bored out of his mind.

Finally, three days before his special mission, the brass had him flown to a remote ranch in southern Texas with its own private airstrip and hangar. He enthusiastically welcomed the change. He jogged great distances to vent his frustration and reveled in the warm sunshine and sweet Texas air. The stealth that he would be using to bomb Castro at McCalla Airfield in Guantanamo sat hidden from prying eyes inside the small hangar.

Eager to launch his Nighthawk, he flew the mission over and over in his mind, committing every detail to memory until he could do it in his sleep. He was as ready and as willing as he would ever be, but still he had to wait.

*   *   *

Morgan finished dressing for dinner and joined Hunter in the White House guest room designated the Queen's Room. Wallpapered with a mauve print of tiny roses, the room had white baseboards and trim, including a chair rail about three feet above the polished hardwood floor. Two canvasses of flowers, mounted in ornate gilded frames, hung on adjacent walls. An area rug separated the antique Jenny Lind bed from a quaint writing desk and chair.

She twirled with excitement. "Dinner at the White House! I can't believe it! And with the first lady. I'm so eager to meet her."

Hunter smiled. "I can tell. It's a fitting way to wrap up a truly exciting weekend, don't you think?"

"You've had way too much excitement to suit me," she said. "How does your chest feel? Does it hurt?"

"Only when I breathe."

She frowned, brows knitting with concern. "Hunter, do you think we'll be safe when we make the trip to Cuba with President Weber?"

"Of course. He wouldn't ask us along unless he had the situation well under control. My guess is he wants us close at hand so we'll all have the same facts. He probably wants to keep tabs on us as well. Given what we know, I can't say I blame him."

She began to pace. "I suppose you're right. But what if something goes wrong? What if he can't prevent the bomb from being dropped?"

"Then the press will make martyrs of us, and we'll be written about in history books." He grinned to ease her fears.

She stopped pacing, crossed her arms, and stuck out her bottom lip. "That's not funny, Hunter."

"No, I suppose not." Pulling her to him, he wrapped his arms around her. "I'm sure there's more to Weber's plan than we know. I have a pretty good idea of what he has in mind, but that doesn't matter right now. What does matter is that he knows what he's doing and has the resources at hand to deal with the situation how he sees best. We have to trust him the same way he's trusted us."

At seven-thirty Charles Minsk appeared and escorted them to the family dining room.

"Will you be dining with us tonight?" Morgan asked the Secret Service agent.

"No. I have some work to do for the president, but I may join you after dinner. Enjoy yourselves."

Charles had scarcely left when the president and Mrs. Weber entered the room.

"Good evening," President Weber said as they approached. "Hunter and Morgan, I'd like you to meet my wife, Victoria. Victoria, this is H. Hunter Mahoy and Morgan Lindsey."

"Hello, Mrs. Weber. We've looked forward to meeting you," Morgan gushed.

"It's a pleasure, ma'am," Hunter put in. "And may I say, you look lovely this evening."

"Thank you, Mr. Mahoy. Tell me. What does the *H* stand for?"

He placed his hand over his heart and bowed slightly. "*Honored*, ma'am. Truly honored. And please call me Hunter."

She smiled as they shook hands. "Nelson put me up to asking you that. And I'd appreciate you calling me Victoria. I'm indebted to you both. Nelson has told me of the plot you've discovered and of your valiant efforts to help."

Hunter had seen pictures of the first lady in magazines and on television and had always thought her attractive, but the images didn't do her justice. She was a truly beautiful woman. She reminded him of Jacqueline Kennedy.

President Weber led everyone to the table, and they all sat down. Victoria immediately commented on Morgan's elegant frock, and the ladies were quickly lost in the world of women's fashions. Hunter and the president launched into a subject they both found fascinating, flying. Hunter recounted many of his airborne adventures, purposely omitting the last. President Weber described the thrills and dangers he'd experienced flying Sabre jets during the latter part of the Korean War.

Hunter really liked Nelson Weber. The most powerful man in the free world was as down to earth and cordial as one person could be to another. That night they were just two buddies swapping war stories with zeal and one-upmanship. President Weber quietly confided to Hunter that he couldn't possibly top the story Morgan had told him about Hunter's rescue of his wingman in Desert Storm.

"She told you about that, sir?"

"Did she ever! Had me on the edge of my seat. You deserved that medal, son, don't ever forget that. I'm impressed. And here I thought I was sending in an inexperienced civilian on that Homestead mission."

Hunter smiled sheepishly then glanced over at Morgan, who was obviously enjoying her visit with the first lady. He'd fully expected Morgan to check into the medal he'd been awarded, but hadn't anticipated her telling the president. He wasn't sure if he was glad of that or not. He'd never told anyone about it because he didn't see how he could without looking as though he was bragging. The whole thing had been dumb luck anyway. He should've been killed ten times over on that sortie.

Over dessert and coffee, the conversation shifted from subject to subject, eventually arriving at the White House decor. The ladies soon excused themselves to investigate the furnishings in the other rooms.

The president stood and crossed the room to a sidebar. "Tell me, Hunter: do you imbibe?"

"I've been known to on occasion, sir."

"Excellent. I have an exquisite brandy I've been dying to share with someone." He returned with a crystal decanter and two snifters.

A discreet knock sounded on the door, and Charles entered.

The president smiled. "Ah, Charles. Perfect timing. Grab yourself a snifter."

"Thank you, sir, but I'll have to pass. I'm on duty tonight. I'll take a rain check."

With time growing short before the flight to Cuba, the men discussed alternatives, possible delays, weather, flight paths, and various other details that needed to be well understood.

President Weber swirled the brandy in his glass as he asked, "Charles, when is the vice president scheduled to leave?"

"At two o'clock, sir."

"That's an hour and a half ahead of our departure, right?"

"Right."

"Good! Contact Tom Kelly. Try to reach him personally if possible. Make sure he's aware of the revised departure time for Air Force Two."

"I'll try to reach him immediately, sir," Charles said then excused himself. He held the door for Morgan and Mrs. Weber to enter as he was leaving.

"Did you ladies have a nice evening?" the president asked.

"Yes," Morgan said eagerly. "It was most enjoyable."

"It certainly was," Victoria added. "You know how much I enjoy company that isn't related to politics, Nelson."

"Speaking of politics, Victoria, we have that engagement at the Kennedy Center tonight." He faced Hunter and Morgan. "I'd love to invite you, but I expect heavy press coverage, and you two must keep a low profile for the next couple of days." He smiled paternally at Hunter. "And get some rest. You'll need to be at the top of your game for a little while longer."

*   *   *

Early Monday morning, Charles drove to Andrews Air Force Base just outside of DC. He prepared for his flight with Lieutenant Chad Gibbons, a well-toned young man stepping into a military-issue khaki jumpsuit.

"You ready?" Gibbons asked as he finished suiting up.

"Almost." The agent tugged at the harness of the parachute. "How tight should these straps be?"

Gibbons grabbed his helmet then tossed one to Charles. "It looks like you've got it covered. Let's go."

They strode toward the fully fueled F-14 Tomcat fighter jet waiting on the tarmac. "This your first time in a fighter, Agent Minsk?" the pilot asked as they climbed aboard.

"It is," Charles replied, strapping himself in. "It's my first time to Cuba too. I'm looking forward to both."

"We won't be making too many radical maneuvers on this flight, so I'm sure you'll enjoy the ride." Gibbons donned his sunglasses and glanced skyward. "Cool and clear. Perfect flying weather."

He fired up the engines then taxied for the runway. "Tower, this is Echo 337 requesting a special takeoff."

"Roger, 337. You're cleared for an aerobatic takeoff on nine left. Have a good trip."

Gibbons shoved the throttles to full power, and the F-14 screamed down the runway, its dual plumes of bluish afterburner flame rivaling a comet's tail.

Sucked into the back of his seat, Charles said into his headset, "Damn! I thought this was an airplane, not a rocket."

Gibbons looked over his shoulder and grinned, then hauled back on the stick. The fighter blasted away from the earth, accelerating rapidly while going straight up. "Now it's a rocket," he said.

Terra firma shrank behind them at a dizzying speed.

Less than a minute later, leveling out at ten-thousand feet and approaching five-hundred miles per hour, Gibbons directed the craft due east toward the Atlantic Ocean. "We'll fly well offshore so we can cruise at mach 1.5. Cuba should appear in our windshield in an hour and forty minutes."

Right on schedule, the island of Cuba loomed on the horizon. It jutted from the breathtaking sapphire Caribbean Sea like a diamond-encrusted emerald resting on blue velvet.

"It's more beautiful than I could've possibly imagined," Charles said with awe.

"It certainly is," Lieutenant Gibbons agreed. "Guantanamo Bay's on the southeastern tip. Won't be long now." When the base came into view, he said, "Show time." He punched in the correct radio frequency. "McCalla Tower, this is Echo 337 requesting an emergency landing. Do you read? McCalla Tower, 337. Do you read?"

No response.

"Their communications must still be out, Charles. McCalla Tower. Do you read?"

Still nothing.

"It's no use, Lieutenant. Let's go ahead and land."

As planned, Gibbons shut down the number two engine then banked the Tomcat to line up with the runway. They touched down a couple of minutes later and taxied to a nearby hangar where they climbed down from the cockpit.

The base commander came roaring up in his Jeep with nearly a dozen men in support, including two military police officers.

"Lieutenant, what's your point of origin?" the commander asked, leaping from his vehicle before it came to a complete stop.

Gibbons snapped to attention and saluted. "Sir, Washington DC, sir!"

"What are you doing here?"

"We were en route to the USS *Nimitz* in the Caribbean Sea, sir. We experienced a problem with the exhaust temperature in our number two engine and had to shut it down."

Charles read the officer's name tag then stepped forward. "May I have a word with you, Commander Spector? Privately?"

Spector eyed him momentarily then nodded.

As they strolled away from the hangar and the others, Charles presented his Secret Service credentials. Commander Spector's eyebrows shot up, but he said nothing.

"President Weber sent me here to speak with you personally, Commander," Charles said. "The story Lieutenant Gibbons just gave you about our aircraft was for the benefit of your men. Our aircraft is fine. I know you're aware that President Weber is to meet Fidel Castro here on this airfield on November first. We've recently learned of an assassination plot to coincide with that meeting. President Weber has dispatched our ambassador to Cuba to warn President Castro, but Castro's jittery because of the unexplained communications jamming all over the island. Apparently he's refusing visitors of any kind right now. The ambassador is still trying, but…"

Charles stopped walking and faced the commander. "It's entirely possible that a powerful bomb may detonate on this field at the designated time of the meeting. With any luck, we'll be able to prevent the explosion. But there's no guarantee. As a last-ditch effort, President Weber wants you to greet Castro upon his arrival and warn him to leave immediately. You won't have much time—if any. If Castro cuts his arrival time too close, and you can't warn him off, he may be history." He paused. "I have a few other matters to discuss with you, Commander, but first I need for you to direct your maintenance personnel to take a look at the F-14 so that our cover story holds water."

CHAPTER

Tuesday, November 1, dawned as a thick, gray blanket of mist and fog. The dreary pall lingered on well into the afternoon, an appropriate shroud for the mood of President Nelson Weber and everyone in his party as they headed out to Andrews Air Force Base aboard Marine One. There, the dismal group transferred to Air Force One, which sat expectantly on the rain-soaked tarmac.

The jumbo jet soon taxied out onto the runway. Its engines spooled up to maximum power, and the 747 surged forward with ever-increasing speed.

In no time at all, the magnificent bird lifted the spirits of every soul on board when it punched out of the gloom into radiant sunshine. Charles Minsk and President Weber conversed quietly. Hunter, sitting just two rows in front of them, inadvertently overheard.

"Were the modifications to Air Force Two completed in time, Charles?" the president asked.

"Yes. Only one call will now connect."

"Any problems installing the software?"

"Installing it? No. But getting it proved difficult, sir. It had to be tailor-made in a hurry, and in secrecy. General Kelly barely had time to load it into the system before the ground crew started prepping the aircraft."

"Did the pilot arrive on schedule?"

"He arrived early," Charles said. "We devised a plan for his safety, and he's fully aware of the risk, as are Kelly and the steward."

"Good. Any change in the communications problems down in Cuba?"

"Not yet, sir. If the problem clears, we'll be notified immediately, and you can contact Castro directly. If not, what can I say? You've done everything you possibly could to try to warn him. Even if you called this thing off, sir, that bomb is going to hit McCalla Field, because we still don't know where the stealth is flying from. And, of course, even if we did, we wouldn't be able to see it on radar. Our only other hope is for the Guantanamo base commander to warn Castro in time."

"You've done an outstanding job arranging all of this so quickly, Charles."

"Thank you, sir. It certainly has kept me hopping."

"I can imagine. Were you able to confirm whether Tom Kelly boarded Air Force Two with the vice president?"

"Yes. The pilot called me personally on his cellular to say Kelly did make the flight. He also said it was spooky not having a copilot on board. I sure hope you're right about Kelly. If he has a change of heart—"

"I'm concerned about that too, Charles. He's the real unknown in this whole equation. All we can do now is hold our breath."

Eavesdropping on their conversation, Hunter heard enough to verify that he'd correctly guessed President Weber's plan. He didn't understand every detail, but most of it made sense.

He shifted his focus to Morgan. "What're you doing?"

"Working on an outline."

"How can you do that without having all the facts?"

"It's only a rough guideline."

"May I see it?"

She shrugged. "Sure, but there's really not much to it." She handed it over. "What do you think?" She cocked her head slightly.

He read it and gave it back. "You'll have to make some changes. You're assuming too much."

"Well, of course I am at this point. Changes are inevitable. I'm just trying to get a head start, that's all. What time do you have?"

He stared at her. "You know, I'm completely baffled at how a big-time reporter like you can operate without a watch."

Morgan grinned. "I used to wear one, but it constantly reminded me of how late I was for everything. Now I have a good excuse for my tardiness."

He shook his head. "I'm not even going to try to argue with that logic. It's four-forty."

"Not even halfway yet," she said.

"No, not yet." He stifled a yawn. "Damn, I can hardly keep my eyes open. Think I'll stretch out for a while." He played with the control of the arm of his roomy seat so that the back reclined and the footrest came up.

Morgan adjusted her own seat. "I think I'll join you. All the excitement is finally catching up with me."

But sleep eluded Hunter for the longest time. Over and over his mind wrestled with the question, would Castro survive or perish?

*　　*　　*

"What a fool Nelson Weber is," the vice president scoffed, looking from Lamar Hager to Tom Kelly. "Having me traveling to Mexico City aboard Air Force Two is bad enough, but having you both accompany me is real idiocy. Plus, the whole damn thing is a waste of my time."

"I'm surprised you even made the trip, Al," Kelly said.

Buchanan looked him in the eye. "I had to. Weber was going to cancel his visit to Cuba today unless I went to Mexico. Sometimes I think he's more concerned with appearances than running the damned government. I'm sure that's why he had you and Lamar join me. He figured it would bolster his image to send the chairman of the Joint Chiefs and the secretary of the air force down here to organize and plan how we'll help the Mexican people with their earthquake disaster." He shook his head angrily. "It galls me that I have to follow his policy on this."

"Look, Al," Hager said, shifting in his seat, "you have no other option. Press conferences have already been held, so the whole world expects the United States to help immensely. And as president, you won't be able to back out because you wouldn't be able to save face."

"Ironic, isn't it?" Buchanan scoffed. "I'll finally be in power, and Weber will still have his way, though posthumously this time."

"When do we arrive in Mexico City?" Kelly asked.

"Around six p.m." Hager glanced at his watch. "Won't be long now."

"Has anyone seen that steward?" Buchanan asked, clearly annoyed. "Weber's ruined these flights with his cost-cutting measures. First, he prohibits the press to travel with us, and now we have minimal or no staff to serve us." He glanced around. "I want another drink, and I can't figure out where that damn steward went."

"I'll find him," Kelly offered, rising quickly. "Be back in a minute."

When the air force man had left, Hager turned to Buchanan. "You know, Al, I've flown from DC to Mexico City before, and it didn't seem like the flight took this long."

"You feel that way too? I thought it was my imagination. Well, at least we won't have to stay long. The moment we receive word that something happened to the president in Cuba, we'll return to DC."

"Oh, great," Hager said, oozing sarcasm. "Another long flight." He leaned over to look out the window.

"Can you see the city yet?"

"No. It's completely dark down there. I don't see lights anywhere."

Kelly reentered, carrying a tray of drinks. "The steward seems to be having a bit of airsickness," he explained, handing Buchanan and Hager their glasses. "I just poured these myself."

Suddenly the intercom crackled to life. "Mr. Vice President and gentlemen," the captain announced, "we've been requested to delay our arrival for a while. Air traffic control in Mexico City reports that they're experiencing a powerful aftershock. They need time to assess the condition of the runways. It'll be twenty to thirty minutes before we're allowed to land."

"Damn! Just my luck!" the vice president grumbled.

"Look on the bright side," Hager said. "We'll spend less time on the ground in Mexico City because now we'll arrive close to seven."

"And we all know the significance of that hour," Kelly added.

"I'll drink to that," the vice president said, raising his glass.

*   *   *

Waking from a brief nap, Hunter returned his seat to the upright position and found the cabin empty except for Morgan. She soon awoke as well. Hunter stared out the window at the silvery-blue moonlit cloud deck. It extended for as far as he could see, completely obliterating the ground. He was lost in thought when President Weber returned a few minutes later.

"We'll be landing shortly," the president said. "But before we do, you should know that what I've done has been done with a heavy heart. It goes completely against my morals, and I took no pleasure in it whatsoever."

The man has aged ten years in the past few days, Hunter thought.

The president leaned closer and continued, "I firmly believe, however, that my actions are appropriate and just, and will produce the best possible solution for the citizens of the United States, Cuba, and the rest of the world, for that matter—"

"Pardon me," Charles Minsk said crisply. "I need to speak with you in private, sir."

Weber excused himself and left the main cabin with the agent.

Morgan wrinkled her brow. "Hunter, have you any idea what the president was about to tell us?"

He nodded. "I have a fairly good idea."

"Well, you want to fill me in on what's happening?"

"I'd rather wait for the president to do that," he said, glancing first at his watch and then out the window.

It was 6:40 p.m. when they descended into the cloud deck.

*   *   *

"What time is it?" the vice president asked. "We've been in the air a long time."

Tom Kelly checked his watch then studied Buchanan's face before answering. "It's six-forty."

"Damn! That's forty minutes beyond our scheduled arrival time," Hager said. "Do we have enough fuel for this?"

Kelly lowered the Bible he'd been reading. "Relax, Lamar. Plenty of extra fuel is loaded for contingencies just like this."

A minute later the captain appeared in the cabin. He made eye contact with each of them in turn. "Gentlemen, I'm sorry for the delay. I've just been informed that we'll be allowed to land in about fifteen minutes. I suggest you remain seated and keep your seat belts fastened until we're on the ground. Now if you'll excuse me, I have to attend to a small matter in the rear of the aircraft."

Kelly locked eyes with the pilot, who nodded discreetly before starting to head aft.

The vice president stopped him by asking, "Is there a problem?"

"Just a minor one, sir," the pilot said, facing him. "I've noticed a slight problem with the plane's pressurization. I want to check the seal on the rear door. You may have noticed we're flying at a much lower altitude than normal, but there's nothing to be alarmed about. If you'll excuse me now."

"Imagine that," Buchanan said snidely. "A brand-new 280-million-dollar aircraft, and they have a problem with the pressurization."

Kelly glared at him. "If you understood just how complex a machine this marvelous aircraft is, you wouldn't be so quick to criticize."

"That's exactly the response I'd expect from an air force man," Buchanan said, directing his comment at Hager.

As planned, the pilot of Air Force Two joined the steward in the escape module compartment.

"I'll seal the hatches," the pilot said. "Go ahead and get into the capsule."

"Where's General Kelly?" the steward asked.

The pilot shrugged. "In the main cabin. He knows it's time, and he's on his own. We can't wait any longer. Let's go while we still can."

The escape compartment contained two capsules. The pilot and steward crammed into one, leaving the other for Kelly. After they strapped into the padded cylinder, the pilot pushed the button marked JETTISON. Nothing happened.

"What's wrong?" the steward asked anxiously, double-checking his safety harness.

"Nothing. It takes a minute for the compartment to equalize with the outside atmosphere."

A few seconds later, the pod plunged from the underbelly of the 747, buffeting violently when it first hit the slipstream. It stabilized quickly and plummeted for two-thousand feet before the parachute automatically deployed, arresting its descent.

Tom Kelly discreetly looked at his watch. Nearly ten minutes had elapsed since the pilot had made his way to the escape pod. *Soon,* he thought to himself as he refocused on the passage in his Bible that he'd been reading.

Suddenly the vice president said, "What happened to that pilot? We're supposed to land anytime now."

Hager yawned and stretched, then said, "That does seem odd."

Kelly closed his Bible and set it aside. He eyed his old friend. "Maybe there was more of a problem than the pilot thought," he suggested.

"I don't like it," Hager said, jumping to his feet. "I'm going aft to find that captain."

He returned a few minutes later, wide-eyed. "I can't find him anywhere. I can't find the steward either. I looked in every compartment, every bathroom. I'm going to the cockpit to speak with the copilot."

Tom Kelly stood, acting concerned. "I'll go with you."

They strode to the cockpit door and knocked loudly.

No response.

"What do you think?" Hager asked, perspiration now dotting his brow.

"Perhaps without the captain in the cockpit, the copilot doesn't dare leave his seat," Kelly said. "Let's just open the door."

They tried the knob, but it was locked. Again they knocked, to no avail.

Kelly went to a window and looked out. "I don't remember a large body of water near Mexico City," hoping he sounded convincing.

"What are you talking about?" Hager pushed him aside and looked for himself. "That is water," he said to the Plexiglas. "We must still be over the Gulf of Mexico." He faced Kelly. "Our flight path would have taken us across the panhandle of Florida and over the Gulf, so we wouldn't see land until shortly before our arrival."

"You're wrong," Kelly said, eager to see Hager sweat. "We'd be over land for a full hour before reaching Mexico City, and we should be seeing the city lights right now."

They pounded on the cockpit door again, with no response, then rejoined the vice president and told him what was going on.

"What you're saying doesn't make any sense," Buchanan said, clearly alarmed.

"I know," Hager replied, "and it's nearly seven o'clock."

*   *   *

Morgan turned Hunter's wrist toward her. "Six-fifty-five. We should be landing soon. Wonder what's taking President Weber and Charles so long."

At that moment Air Force One descended through the cloud base, and suddenly city lights glowed for as far as they could see. Morgan pressed her face to the window. "Wow! Look at the size of this place. I can't see the coast, though. It must be on the other side of the aircraft."

"The coast isn't on either side of the aircraft, Morgan."

"What do you mean it's not on either side? Havana's on the coast."

"It is, but we're not over Havana."

"If that's not Havana down there, what city is it?"

"Mexico City."

"*Mexico City?*" she asked, puzzled. "I thought we were going to Cuba."

"Well, we're not. We're going to Mexico City. *The vice president is* going to Cuba."

"You mean…" Her voice trailed off as she realized what was happening.

"That's right. The vice president is about to be the victim of his own plot. That's what President Weber was alluding to earlier."

"Good heavens! What a brilliant solution."

"You realize that this part of the story must be kept secret forever, don't you? And I'm not talking about a little secret, like the one Russell Keller told you about my exploits in Desert Storm, or my Congressional Medal of Honor that you've been looking into."

She blushed. "How do you know about that?"

"It doesn't matter. The point is, I found out. That can never, ever happen with this."

*　　*　　*

Vice President Buchanan stood with Generals Kelly and Hager before a console in the communications room aboard Air Force Two. They attempted to contact Stanley Bass at the CIA, but failed to make a connection. "Shit! He's probably out stuffing his face at some five-star restaurant," Buchanan said, then tried the Pentagon and the FBI, to no avail.

Finally, he tried Air Force One, which he said might still be airborne. The call connected, and he placed it on speaker when President Weber came on that line.

Buchanan cleared his throat. "Nelson, it's good to hear your voice. We have a situation here. We're still in the air over Mexico, and we can't locate our pilot. I know that sounds crazy, but the pilot went to check on a pressurization problem a while ago, and we haven't seen him since. We can't locate the steward or any of the Secret Service personnel either."

"What time do you have, Al?" Nelson Weber asked.

Puzzled by the question, Buchanan glanced at his watch. "It's, ah…three minutes to seven. Have you heard of any problems with aftershocks in Mexico City, Nelson?"

"No, I haven't," President Weber said. "In fact, I'm staring at Mexico City right now. It's a beautiful sight. The lights run for miles."

"*Mexico City!*" The vice president was dumbfounded.

After several silent seconds, the president asked, "What's the matter, Al?"

Al Buchanan slumped against the console.

"Al, are you there? Hello?"

"This is General Hager, Mr. President. We can hear you."

"Good. I have a question I want to ask you both before I land in Mexico City."

Hager stared at Buchanan.

"How does it feel to assassinate yourself? I have to tell you, that was one hell of a plan you had in *Operation Ghost Flight*. And if not for the fluke of one your pilots colliding with Hunter Mahoy in his sailplane, it would have worked. By the way, Hunter and Morgan Lindsey are alive and well. They're right beside me, listening in on our conversation. We know all about Stanley Bass too. He'll be dealt with accordingly. By the way, Al, Stan was the Gomez brothers' accomplice in Sean's death, and you blamed me all this time. Oh, and don't worry about losing your pilot, Air Force Two can land itself. The software program Tom Kelly installed for me will give you a super-smooth landing at McCalla Field in Guantanamo. I guarantee it."

Kelly spoke up. "It's worked perfectly, Mr. President. No problems whatsoever."

Buchanan pivoted and glared at Kelly, who wore a smug expression.

"Tom! What are you doing still on board?" Weber asked. "Why didn't you leave with the pilot and steward as we planned?"

"It's better this way, Mr. President. Treason should always be punishable by death. I'm simply carrying out my own sentence. I've made my peace. I wish my coconspirators had more time to dwell on their impending demise, though."

Buchanan suddenly came to life. "Mahoy and Lindsey," he spat, "you've ruined everything! I hope you burn in hell!"

Hunter's voice filled the speaker. "Well, sir, that's precisely where you're about to go. And you richly deserve it for the murder of so many innocent people, not to mention trying to kill us." He paused. "What's most satisfying for me is knowing that you'll spend eternity without ever again meeting up with your son. He won't be in hell. He had a good, moral soul. Think about that while you still can."

*   *   *

Cloaked in darkness high over Guantanamo Bay, Lieutenant Chad Gibbons circled in his F-14 Tomcat and monitored the infrared night screen. Finally, Castro's helicopter appeared, approaching McCalla Field from the northwest at 6:57 p.m. One lone vehicle sat waiting on the edge of the runway. *That must be Base Commander Spector. Sure hope he's watching the time.*

Gibbons also paid close attention to his onboard targeting radar. In the unlikely event that the invisible stealth showed itself, Gibbons sat poised with armed air-to-air laser-guided missiles to shoot it down.

Castro's helicopter landed at 6:58 p.m., and the rotor blades slowed. The ground vehicle raced to the craft and stopped quickly.

*   *   *

Hurry up, Commander! Tell Castro to fly the hell out of there, then get out of there yourself!

Captain David Cunningham swooped down on Guantanamo in his stealthy Nighthawk at precisely that same moment. From Texas he'd flown his craft east-southeast over the entire length of the Gulf of Mexico, eastward over the Florida Straits between the US mainland and Cuba, and then due south. Now he had McCalla Air Field, and more importantly Castro's helicopter, in his targeting radar screen. He zoomed in the display to maximize the size of his objective then armed both two-thousand-pound laser-guided bombs on board. As he'd done countless times before, he centered the crosshairs on his objective. The chopper had just landed, and a ground vehicle pulled up alongside.

"I don't know who you are, pal," he said out loud, "but you're in the wrong place at the wrong time!"

Cunningham pressed the release button and started counting. He figured about twenty seconds to impact. At five seconds, the helicopter's rotor blades started to increase speed rapidly. He kept the crosshairs centered. At eleven seconds the chopper lifted off.

"Now, where do you think you're going?" He kept the crosshairs centered.

At seventeen seconds the whirlybird transitioned into forward flight.

"You're not going to make it."

At twenty seconds the chopper was picking up speed.

All of a sudden a giant aircraft appeared on the runway from the right side of the targeting screen, not a military aircraft but a passenger one. A Boeing 747.

"*Oh My God! No!*" Frozen in horror, Cunningham watched helplessly as the jumbo jet rolled toward the departing helicopter. The crosshairs were still centered.

*   *   *

Air Force Two appeared on Lieutenant Chad Gibbons's monitor aboard the F-14 Tomcat at 6:59 p.m. There was still nothing on his targeting radar, though that was no surprise. The 747 landed and tooled down the runway toward Castro's helicopter, which had lifted off in a hurry.

*   *   *

"We just touched down, Mr. President," Kelly said anxiously, "and the aircraft is slowing rapidly. Good-bye, sir."

"Good-bye, Tom. God bless you."

"*Weber, you fucking bastard! You can't do this!*" Buchanan screamed. "*You'll have to answer to—*"

*   *   *

At the flash, Lieutenant Gibbons jumped in his seat. He stared blankly at the display. The bomb had scored a direct hit on Castro's helicopter the instant the chopper crossed over the top of Air Force Two. Both craft exploded into a single tremendous fireball. It appeared as if Castro's helicopter had collided with Air Force Two, but Gibbons knew that that wasn't the case. Though his targeting radar still remained clear, he looked up through his canopy, searching the night sky for the elusive stealth. Farther off to the south, he saw another explosion. This second fireball occurred in the air at an altitude slightly below his own fifteen-thousand feet.

*   *   *

When the line went dead, Charles Minsk checked his watch but said nothing. President Weber stared straight ahead. Morgan began to sob. Hunter wrestled with multiple emotions: sadness for Tom Kelly, relief that it was over, elation that justice had been done, and remorse that he'd a hand in the deaths of the three men.

After a while President Weber faced them and said sullenly, "When we land in Mexico City, I won't yet know anything about what has transpired. I will meet with the Mexican officials as scheduled and prepare to depart with them for the earthquake-damaged areas. At that point Charles will hurriedly inform me of the tragic incident in Cuba. I'll make apologies and a hurried retreat, explaining that I'll have to return at a later date. You two will remain on board throughout all of this since I'd have no way to explain your presence, but I'll ask Charles to pipe the live broadcast over the onboard audio system so you can hear what's going on. I'm sure he can catch the media's signal off a satellite."

Weber looked at Morgan. "My dear, you and I will have plenty of work to do on the return flight, but right at the moment I just want to clarify what we'll say to the press, and the world, about why the vice president and I switched destinations. We'll start by saying that in a surprise move, Fidel Castro had agreed to give up his rule as dictator in Cuba and allow free, democratic elections in exchange for immediate economic and medical aid from the United States, as well as the elimination of the US Naval Base at Guantanamo Bay.

"We'll further state that Castro personally requested Vice President Buchanan make the trip in my place because Buchanan spoke fluent Spanish and had already been somewhat involved with the problems in Cuba. We'll say that Castro asked us to send top military officials to discuss the logistics of removing all US military personnel and equipment from Guantanamo, hence the presence of Generals Kelly and Hager. We'll claim that the decision to switch destinations was made only recently and kept quiet for security purposes." Weber paused. "Do you agree with the tone of this press release?"

Hunter looked the president in the eye. "I have no problem with it, sir."

"Nor do I," Morgan said.

"So be it," the president replied somberly.

CHAPTER

Hunter took a seat beside the open door, slipped on a pair of head-phones, then watched through his camera lens as, flanked by security, President Nelson Weber descended from Air Force One to the tarmac. After the president greeted the waiting Mexican diplomats, the media hit him with a barrage of questions. He declined to answer them individually, reciting his prearranged statement instead.

As planned, Secret Service agent Charles Minsk soon hurried from the aircraft to the president's side and spoke with him privately. Doing an excellent imitation of shock and sadness, President Weber lowered his head and appeared to grow weak at the knees, leaning on Charles briefly for support before regaining his composure. He whispered something to Charles, who nodded and then returned to Air Force One. The army of media personnel waited to be clued in as the president of the United States spoke briefly with his Mexican counterpart. The two men embraced and shook hands before Nelson Weber returned to the press area.

"Ladies and gentlemen, I regret to inform you that a crisis has arisen that requires my immediate return to Washington."

The reporters became a frenzied mob, launching another barrage of questions as cameras flashed from everywhere. Weber held up both hands in a gesture of surrender. When the media settled down, he continued, "I realize you have many questions. I'm sorry, but I have no answers at this time. The report I just received is sketchy at best, and I cannot comment further. I can only say that the United States is fully committed to helping the Mexican government and its people recover from this devastating earthquake. United States military aircraft will begin transporting emergency equipment and supplies starting tomorrow. Temporary shelters and heavy machinery will be among the first items to arrive. I have also promised materials and skilled personnel for the rebuilding of the infrastructure, in due course. The United States and Mexico will work together diligently to expedite the recovery process."

Behind him, the engines of Air Force One, which had just been shut down, were restarted. Charles descended from the aircraft again then walked to President Weber's side and waited for him to finish.

"I will return personally as soon as is possible. If you'll excuse me now, I must depart immediately."

After a final handshake with the president of Mexico, Weber labored toward Air Force One flanked by Charles and several other Secret Service agents. Once again the reporters launched into a shouting match of questions while shutters clicked endlessly, including Hunter's. At the top of the airstairs, President Weber paused then slipped inside. A moment after the airstairs were retracted and the door closed, Air Force One departed. The plane hadn't been on the ground twenty minutes.

President Weber and Charles excused themselves to finalize some details, leaving Hunter and Morgan in the lounge.

"I wish you hadn't tossed my cell phone," Morgan said. "I need to call Ellen. If she and I hustle, we can finish the article in time for the morning edition and beat every other newspaper into print. It'll be tight, though."

"They'll hold the presses for a while, won't they?" Hunter asked.

"Yes, for a story like this they will."

"Why don't you give me Ellen's number? While you're working with the president, I'll ask Charles to place the call."

"That's a great idea."

"Where do you want her to meet you?"

"At the *Washington Herald*."

Air Force One soon leveled out at cruising altitude, and Charles appeared, requesting that Morgan join President Weber in the presidential office. He escorted her with Hunter in tow then led Hunter upstairs to the communications room. They placed the call but got a busy signal.

Since they needed to wait a few minutes before trying again, Hunter used the opportunity to ask some questions.

"I confess that I overheard part of your conversation with President Weber. Was Castro warned?"

"Yes, but unfortunately, not in time. President Weber had a trusted fighter pilot he'd engaged in the past fly reconnaissance over Guantanamo."

"Did that pilot witness the explosion?"

Charles stuck his hands in his pockets and leaned against a console. "Yes. He confirmed that Castro's helicopter arrived on the base just three minutes before Air Force Two. The helicopter had barely become airborne to depart when the bomb struck. That information will help us with our press release."

"Did the pilot of Air Force Two get out safely?" Hunter probed.

"We believe so. He and the steward were to jettison together in one of the escape capsules. And one was utilized. We haven't yet received confirmation of their rescue. The second capsule was for Tom Kelly."

"Where were the men when they jettisoned?"

"If all went as planned," Charles said, "they bailed out near the Cayman Islands after nightfall. Though it's highly unlikely that anyone would spot the capsule in the dark, we disabled its strobe light anyway. The capsule's emergency transponder will aid a small navy vessel dispatched to rescue them. When the rescue boat is in sight, Air Force Two's pilot will scuttle the capsule so that it will sink to the bottom of the Caribbean. It will never be found."

"What story will the pilot and steward give to explain why they're floating around in the Caribbean?" Hunter asked.

"They'll claim to have been flying to Grand Cayman in a private plane that developed engine trouble, so they had to ditch in the sea, and their plane sank. We filed a flight plan for a light aircraft leaving from a private airstrip in Central Florida to back up that story. The pilot and steward carried a change of civilian clothes. Their flight uniforms will go down with the capsule."

"What happened to the security personnel aboard Air Force Two?"

Charles smiled. "They exited the aircraft by way of the rear airstairs just prior to its departure from Washington."

"Clever," Hunter said, rubbing his chin. "I know Air Force Two was on autopilot when the crew bailed out, but I didn't realize the plane had the capability to land itself. The autopilot is that sophisticated?"

"Sure. In fact, it actually would have been possible for the plane to take off, fly the entire route, and land itself without a pilot. With the proper software, the computerized navigation system can monitor the systems on board and instruct the multifaceted autopilot to correct for air speed, wind drift, altitude, and head winds. It can even control fuel flow to the engines to maximize their efficiency and consumption. We did, however, need a pilot to taxi the aircraft to the beginning of the runway. Since Tom Kelly had the software custom made in a hurry and installed at the last minute, we deemed it necessary to keep the pilot onboard for most of the flight to handle any contingency. McCalla Air Field in Guantanamo is the smaller, less active of the two runways on the base. And it's farther to the east, away from the reception area and most of the facilities. Kelly's software instructed the autopilot to land the plane there."

Hunter thought for a moment then swallowed hard. "Listen, Charles. I was wondering, can you get me the telephone number and the GPS coordinates to Stanley Bass's compound on the Maryland shore?"

Charles stared stone-faced at him in lengthy silence as the plane's engines droned steadily. Then the corners of his mouth curled upward. "I don't know what you have in mind, Hunter, but I think I like it. I'll get that information before we land."

"Is Bass married, Charles? Does he have children?"

"I doubt if he asked those questions about you or Morgan," Charles said. "Nor did he concern himself with all those people on that airliner. But no, Bass has no children, and he divorced years ago. Rigors of the job, I guess. He lives alone."

After a brief, weighty silence, Hunter asked, "What became of the stealth pilot who dropped the bomb?"

"We don't know yet. A team of Army Rangers is in position at the Dade-Collier Training Field in case he returns there, but we haven't heard from them. Our reconnaissance pilot, however, reported seeing a brief but brilliant fireball just south of Guantanamo Bay. Though he couldn't comment on its source, he said it occurred in the air over ocean waters soon after the bomb detonated."

"Whew. That sounds like a double-cross to me," Hunter said. "And it makes sense. The vice president wouldn't have wanted that pilot around to blackmail him later."

"I agree," Charles mused. He picked up the phone. "Let's try that call again?"

The second attempt to reach Ellen was successful. She immediately agreed to meet Morgan at the *Washington Herald* later that night, dying of curiosity as she was to find out what the reporter had been up to for the past two weeks. The suggestion that she have her boss hold the presses for Morgan's story furthered that curiosity. Hunter then returned to the main lounge, leaving Charles to contact the Ranger team.

As he stared out the window, Hunter rehashed his conversation with Charles. Someone could have easily placed a timed explosive on the stealth and connected it to the release of the precision-guided weapon that hit the airfield. The fighter's debris would sink into the ocean waters below, leaving no wreckage, or pilot, to be found.

Hunter wondered if others were involved in the vice president's plan. The only person still alive whom he knew about was Stanley Bass. As director of the CIA, Bass wielded great power and resources, and would have been privy to any covert or black operations sanctioned by the current administration. *By threatening to use this information to tarnish President Weber's shining armor, he could easily avoid exposure of his involvement in this plot,* Hunter thought. Bass would also continue with his plans to have him and Morgan killed to keep them from talking. No doubt about it, Bass was a loose end who could easily become a loose cannon. He had to be dealt with, and quickly. Their very lives depended on it.

For the first time since this adventure had begun, Hunter realized it would soon be over. He contemplated the transition back to his boring job, with his boring clients, and the never-ending boring paperwork. Without Amanda, it would be completely intolerable. He would not return to it. He'd place his house up for sale, quit his job, and move—perhaps to DC. Little else needed to be considered. One thing was for sure. Morgan's career would skyrocket.

A couple of hours elapsed before Morgan rejoined Hunter. She looked exhausted.

"Are you finished with the story?" he asked. "We'll be landing soon." He started massaging her shoulders.

She groaned with pleasure. "For the most part. Man, that feels good." Rolling her shoulders, she added, "We have the story fully outlined with specific notes about the most important details. Certain statements will be direct quotes. I'll fine-tune the article with Ellen, editing and rewriting until I feel it's ready for print. We'll probably use a couple of the photos you took as well—if they turn out OK." She smirked. "At that point, we'll hand it over to our boss, Jack, for his final approval." Morgan chuckled. "Jack's going to be so thrilled, he'll be beside himself. Naturally, the White House press corps will get the same basic information because there's no explainable way that President Weber can give it to me exclusively. But at least I'll have a head start. And, of course, I'll have insight into this story that the other reporters couldn't possibly have. Nobody's going to believe how fast the *Washington Herald* gets this one into print."

Soon after Air Force One landed, Marine One departed for the White House, and the press dispersed. Now it was safe for Hunter and Morgan to exit the empty 747. Hunter called for a taxi, which took them to the *Washington Herald* building.

"I can't be of any help to you here," he said, "so I'll see you back at your house."

"That's fine," Morgan replied, exiting the cab. "If I'm lucky, I'll get there before dawn." She closed the car door then trotted toward the building.

The cabbie faced Hunter. "Where to, bud?"

"Reagan National. And step on it."

At the airport, Hunter called Russell Keller again. He got the answering machine this time and left a message with Morgan's home number. He then boarded the next flight to Daytona, which arrived at 2:00 a.m. He rented a car and drove to the airport in Deland. Leroy was nowhere to be found, so he broke a window to get into the old hangar.

Minutes later, the stealth fighter sat in the darkness at the end of the nearest runway. Hunter eased the engines to full power, rumbled down the aging concrete, and lifted off. As he climbed steeply into the night sky, he turned north and accelerated the craft to its top speed of 650 miles per hour.

*　*　*

Muttering angrily to himself, Colonel Raifer rang the doorbell, his breath visible in the cold night air.

"Ah, Colonel. Come in," Stanley Bass said, opening the door wide.

Colonel Raifer nodded briskly, then stepped inside. "I don't mind meeting here at your home, Mr. Bass—in truth, I prefer it to your office in Langley—but why in God's name does it always have to be at four in the morning?" He removed his overcoat and hung it on the rack by the door.

"I'm an early riser, Colonel. You know that. Come sit by the fire and take the chill out of your bones."

You're an insomniac and a workaholic, Raifer thought. *Just pay me my friggin' money, and I'll be on my way.*

Raifer leaned close to the gas fireplace and warmed his hands, turning them over to heat both sides evenly like a slice of bread in an old-fashioned toaster. "This thing does a great job, doesn't it? Maybe I'll install one in my place in North Florida."

"Speaking of great jobs, Colonel, that last one you did was primo. I mean, really nice shooting. And hitting that FBI bureau chief was a convincing touch." Bass left the room and returned a minute later with a briefcase, which he handed over. "It's all there, Colonel, plus an advance on your next assignment."

Raifer popped the latches and fanned through a few of the many packs of twenties, fifties, and hundreds. He smiled. "And what would that entail?"

*   *   *

Hunter had cruised along invisibly in his black ghost, following the coastline for nearly two hours. He'd already entered into the targeting computer the GPS coordinates that Charles had given him. A cell phone rested in his lap—a loaner from Charles. He checked his current position then armed one of the precision-guided weapons on board. His destination lay just ahead. He closed his eyes and visualized all that had occurred in the past two weeks. The image of the New York–bound jetliner exploding in midair remained the most vivid by far. He could still see the faces of some of the passengers boarding that aircraft, including the young brother and sister. Steeling himself, he checked his position again then picked up the cell phone.

*   *   *

Bass fixed his hired assassin and himself a drink before easing into a chair in front of the fire. Handing Raifer two photographs, he said, "H. Hunter Mahoy is a tax consultant from Miami, and Morgan Lindsey is a reporter for the *Washington Herald*. They've been together of late, and both may be in the DC area even as we speak."

"What does the *H* stand for?" Raifer asked, studying the prints.

"*History*," Bass replied. "Because that's what I want Mahoy and Lindsey to be. I've called off all other efforts on this, so you won't have any interference. Naturally, I'd like it done as quickly as possible, but no matter how long it takes, I want you to get them, both of them. If you have to—"

The phone rang, interrupting him. He set his tumbler on the coffee table and reached for the receiver.

*　　*　　*

Hunter shallow-banked the stealth fighter and lined up for an initial pass.

After just two rings, a man answered.

"Stanley Bass?"

"Yes, that's correct. To whom am I speaking?"

Hunter shifted in the seat. "A vigilante."

"Who is this?" Bass growled. "What do you want?"

"Justice. Two-hundred-and-eighty-eight innocent people died in a plane crash because of you."

"I don't know what you're talking about."

"Like hell you don't. Sean Buchanan was another one of your victims. And then there are incidents like the European hit man at Miami International, the bombing of a garage in Virginia, the phony assassination attempt on the vice president as a ploy to kill the Gomez brothers…I can go on."

"Hunter Mahoy!"

"That's *H.* Hunter Mahoy. And the *H* stands for *Harbinger.* The Grim Reaper is at your doorstep, Bass, or to be more accurate, directly above it."

"How did you get this number?"

"That's not important. What is important is that you know what's coming, and that there's nothing you can do to stop it." He banked the F-117 again and lined up for his bomb run. "You want to hear a funny story about the stealth aircraft you guys have been using down in Cuba, Bass?" Hunter hovered his index finger over the release button. "I borrowed one. Weapons and all."

"You're bluffing!" Bass said defiantly.

"Am I now?" With the crosshairs centered, Hunter mashed the button. "I think it's fitting that you should perish in exactly the same manner as Al Buchanan, Lamar Hager, and Tom Kelly, don't you, Bass? Yep, my Grim Reaper cloak is none other than a matte-black stealth fighter, and my sickle is the laser-guided bomb that's just about to slice into your house."

"You crazy bastard, Mahoy! I'll get you if it's the—"

Circling high overhead, Hunter watched the tremendous fiery explosion through the gold-coated cockpit windows and muttered, "Last thing you ever do."

He pointed the aircraft due south and punched in another number on the cell phone. "Charles, sorry to disturb you, but I thought you might like to know that I just heard about an explosion at Stanley Bass's residence. It must've been a gas leak, or something like that."

*   *   *

"You have a lot of explaining to do, young lady!" Jack Burton snapped. "And this had better be damn good to have dragged me out of bed at this ridiculous hour."

Exhausted, Morgan handed him her completed story and waited quietly while he read.

His eyes opened wide, his chin succumbed to gravity, and he almost missed the chair he sat in as he turned to the final page. He studied her weary face for a moment then called the press room. "This is Jack Burton. I have that story we've been waiting for, and I'm bringing it down personally. Make sure everything's ready. I want this printed in record time."

EPILOGUE

Hunter returned to Washington DC, via commercial airliner, and arrived at Morgan's house just before noon. On the way in, he picked up her morning paper. Filling half the front page in large, bold print, the headline read "US Vice President and Top Military Officials Killed in Cuba. Fidel Castro Assassinated."

Hunter settled at the kitchen table just as Morgan dragged herself in from her bedroom, her eyes still half closed. Groping her way to the counter, she started the coffeemaker.

"How'd you sleep, darlin'?" he asked, looking up from the newspaper.

"Like a log, but I still feel beat."

"I can relate to that," he said, rubbing his eyes. "I guess we'll both feel better after a few days of rest. Hey, listen to this:

> The vice president of the United States, Albert James Buchanan, along with the chairman of the Joint Chiefs of Staff, General Lamar Jefferson Hager, and the secretary of the air force, General Thomas Allen Kelly, were killed at the US Naval Base in Guantanamo Bay, Cuba, on November 1 at seven-oh–two p.m., eastern daylight time."

Her eyes widened in mock surprise. "I'm so shocked!" she said archly. "How did that happen?"

"Well, I'll just read on and we'll see:

> Preliminary information indicates that Air Force Two was disintegrated immediately upon its arrival at McCalla Air Field by a powerful explosion that originated from Fidel Castro's helicopter. It has been confirmed that Castro was also killed, along with his brother, Raul, and three other top officials of the Cuban government."

Hunter looked up from the paper and laughed shortly. "You can bet they're dancing in the streets down in Miami. The celebration will probably continue for months. Let's see now. Where was I? Oh, yeah,

> A navy pilot, who happened to be making an emergency approach to another airfield on the base, was eyewitness to the explosion. Lieutenant Chad Gibbons watched from aloft as Air Force Two landed near the Cuban helicopter that had brought President Castro to the base just minutes earlier. Lieutenant Gibbons stated that he looked away from the two craft to concentrate on his approach but looked back in time to see the initial flash of the explosion. He is positive that it originated from Castro's helicopter."

"Wow! An eyewitness to an event of such importance. Can you imagine that?" Morgan said, bringing cream and sugar to the table.
He moved the paper out of her way. "Imagine this,

> All evidence at this time indicates that Castro unknowingly transported the bomb to the base aboard his helicopter. Air Force Two and its occupants suffered the incredible misfortune of being caught in an assassination plot against Castro,

apparently planned by some of his top aides. It is believed that the conspirators intended for the bomb to detonate on the US Navy base and also kill the president of the United States. However, at Castro's request, the vice president made the trip instead of President Weber."

Hunter put down the newspaper and leaned back in his chair. "I'm sure there'll be plenty of speculation about that. I mean, really! Why would Castro's aides want to kill the US president?"

Morgan shrugged. "Maybe they don't like his policies. He's done a lot of things the Cuban government didn't expect."

Hunter grinned. "That may be true, but you're speculating. Let's see what else this article has to say:

> The officer in charge of the base, Commander Steven Spector, reportedly met with President Castro immediately after the Cuban helicopter landed, then excused himself to check on the arrival time of Air Force Two. Having witnessed the explosion from a mile away, Spector realized that virtually nothing would remain of either aircraft or their occupants. He reported that some nearby structures suffered blown-out windows and other minor damage but had no information that would allow him to comment on further loss of life. Commander Spector did confirm that the personnel on duty, in the sentry boxes and control towers, were well away from the blast area."

Hunter set the paper aside when Morgan brought him a steaming cup of coffee. He took a sip. "Charles said the commander was incredibly lucky. Apparently the force of the explosion overturned the commander's vehicle as he raced away from Castro's helicopter."

Morgan picked up the paper, read a moment, then shook her head. "You're not going to like this next part, Hunter:

> Visibly shaken by the news, President Weber made this statement before requesting privacy for personal mourning: 'I am deeply saddened and cannot express the loss I feel. Albert Buchanan, Lamar Hager, and Thomas Kelly made the ultimate sacrifice while in service to their country. They will be sorely missed. My sorrow extends to their families and friends in this time of grief.'"

"Damn!" Hunter slammed his fist on the table, spilling his coffee in the process. "That really pisses me off! Instead of being exposed as filthy traitors, their names will be preserved in history as peacemakers. Shit! They'll become American heroes."

She threw him a dish towel. "I told you that you weren't going to like it. I had a hard time with that, too, but I really believe President Weber has chosen the best solution to the problem." She grabbed the newspaper. "Listen to what else he had to say:

> While still aboard Air Force One, I received information from Stanley Bass, director of the CIA, that one of his operatives, who had secretly infiltrated the Cuban government, had uncovered the assassination plot against Castro. My staff made an immediate but futile attempt to contact Air Force Two. Unfortunately they did not receive our transmission."

Hunter snorted. "Well, what do you know? President Weber used Stanley Bass and the CIA to validate the incident. What a stroke of genius! Bass certainly won't be able to refute that claim—or any others, for that matter."

Morgan looked puzzled. "I don't understand. The president called me at the last minute and had me add that paragraph. Why can't Bass refute it?"

Hunter looked her hard in the eye. "I guess you haven't heard. Stanley Bass was killed last night when his home exploded. The police think a natural gas leak caused it, but I know for a fact it was an unnatural occurrence. A promise, after all, is a promise. And I keep mine."

Stunned, Morgan dropped into the closest chair, a genuine look of surprise now on her face.

"One thing's for sure, Stanley Bass won't bother us anymore," he said, slipping the newspaper from her fingers. He finished reading the president's statement.

> "To prevent a bloodbath in the scramble for power left by Castro's death, I have dispatched several thousand US Marines to Cuba to take control of the island. We've received little or no resistance from Cuba's army or populace at this time. It is much too early to determine how Cuba will be governed, but I believe a transitional government should be established until free and democratic elections can take place, possibly within a year. I will personally introduce legislation to remove the present embargo and all restrictions related to trade with Cuba. In light of recent events, Guantanamo will remain a US Navy base indefinitely, and regularly scheduled airline travel to and from the island will be established in the near future."

Hunter tossed the paper aside and sipped his coffee for a while. Finally he said, "To coin a phrase, 'All's well that ends well,' I guess."

Morgan sighed. "I suppose so, though it bothers me that we printed a lie."

He shrugged. "I prefer to call it a half truth. Life is full of them." He took another sip of coffee. "So what will you write about next now that you have the scoop of the century behind you?"

"I'm planning a follow-up piece on Sean Buchanan's murder, starting with the letter you sent me."

"*Really?* You mean I'm actually going to get some credit this time? Oh, by the way, President Weber offered me a job, and I accepted."

"What kind of job?"

"As a Secret Service agent, with assignments similar to Charles's. I'll have to endure a couple of months of intense training, of course, but I don't expect any difficulty with that. The president said he liked the way Charles and I worked together and couldn't think of anyone who would be better for the job. If the truth be known, it's probably also so that he can keep tabs on me."

Morgan grinned broadly. "A Secret Service agent! I'm so happy for you, Hunter." She wrapped her arms around him. "I'm happy for us," she added.

"I'll have to look for a place to live."

"No, you won't. You can live right here with me. I've no intention of allowing you to escape me again."

"Is that so?"

"Yes, it is!" She kissed him, long and sweet.

"That was nice. Wait a minute!" He leaned back to study her face. "Are you playing me for a sucker? You don't need help with the monthly payments again, do you?"

"Come on, Hunter; I'm serious. We belong together. Stay with me."

He moved away from her. "I don't know, Morgan. I'm used to parking my car in a garage."

She threw another dishtowel at him. Hard this time.

He laughed as he caught it. "Incidentally, President Weber has already given me my first assignment."

"Can you discuss it with me?"

"Sure. I'm to return to the underground complex for the original operations manual. He's afraid to trust it to anyone else at this point."

"You have to go back into that complex again?" she asked incredulously.

"Yes, but it'll be easy this time. Everyone at that facility has been debriefed and reassigned. Apparently they were all just following orders. They had no real knowledge of *Operation Ghost Flight*. The complex will remain dormant for a while. Besides, I have to travel to Miami anyway. I need to personally apologize to a certain state trooper—after I finish clearing my name with the police department, that is. President Weber's going to have the attorney general intervene on my behalf. Get this, it turns out that I was working undercover with the government, exposing the unlawful business practices and investments made by the Gomez Brothers Corporation, along with some of its politically connected partners, a statement that's basically true. Oh, yeah, and I also have to quit my other job, call a real estate agent to list my house, and get my cat."

"You have a cat?"

"No," he said crisply, "we have a cat. His name is Mistletoes."

Morgan smiled. "Only an ex-air force pilot would give a cat a name like that. Is he affectionate?"

"Very much so. And he's really good about coming when you call."

"Oh, speaking of calls, you had a message from Russell Keller. I found it on my machine when I got home in the wee hours. Apparently he's out of town. He said he's been trying to reach you for days about a really important matter. He seemed eager to get in touch with you."

"Yeah, I've been trying to get a hold of him too," Hunter said. "He probably thinks I don't know about Amanda's death."

"Maybe so. Here." She reached for a piece of paper. "This is the number he left for you. It has an overseas area code of 61. Maybe Russell finally took that extended vacation he always talked a about."

"Sixty-one? That's Australia. I was there on business a while back," Hunter explained. "No wonder I couldn't get in touch with him."

"When do you leave for Miami? Not tonight, I hope."

"No. I'll fly down this weekend." He grabbed the cordless phone and punched in the number. "I just realized, Morgan. Saturday marks exactly three weeks since I became embroiled in this bizarre odyssey. I've been undercover, under wraps, under gunned, and underground. Yet at the moment I have only two questions: should I return the stealth fighter that I currently have stashed away or keep it to operate my own ghost flights? And could anything else possibly happen that would require me to once again go down under?"

The call was picked up on the other end. "Hello. This is H. Hunter Mah—ohmigod! *Amanda?*"

ABOUT THE AUTHOR

The eldest son of eleven children, Stephen Yoham was born and raised in Miami, Florida. While in college he worked for a construction company, and eventually became their vice president.

After that, he worked for his family's business for a few years, before starting his own business.

Travel has become a passion of his, and has rewarded him with a wealth of wonderful experiences, including backpacking, hang gliding, skydiving, scuba diving, water and snow skiing, flying, soaring, sailing, and long-distance bicycling. At the age of twenty-four, he bicycled with a friend from Miami to Washington D.C., and then on to Jackson, Michigan, finishing the last few days in ten- to fifteen- degree temperatures. In addition, his interests include writing, reading, woodworking, and photography.

The day before his thirtieth birthday, Stephen married Judith Marie; this year they celebrated their thirtieth anniversary. They both love animals, and for over two decades have had purebred shelties, and several cats as part of the family.

The craft of writing has long intrigued Stephen, and he has discovered that between the challenge, hard work, and experience gained lies the true reward of satisfaction. His first novel, Operation Ghost Flight, is currently under literary contract. His second novel, Project Firefly, is under consideration, and he has begun work on a third, tentatively titled, Half the Nines. In addition, he has written a poem, "These Fresh Tears," which was published in the National Library of Poetry's anthology, Beneath the Harvest Moon.

CPSIA information can be obtained
at www.ICGtesting.com
Printed in the USA
FFOW03n0411080417
34274FF

9 781684 097135